WALKABOUT WOMAN

Michaela Roessner

BANTAM BOOKS
TORONTO • NEW YORK • LONDON • SYDNEY • AUCKLAND

Although I did intensive research for this book, hoping that the detailing would give the tale a sense of believability and accuracy, the individual characters and their lives, especially the religious experiences, are solely a product of my imagination. In no way should they be regarded as a real description of the way the Aboriginal people experience their lives.

WALKABOUT WOMAN
A Bantam Spectra Book / September 1988

ISBN 0-553-27545-3

Published simultaneously in the United States and Canada

Bantam Books are published by Bantam Books, a division of Bantam Doubleday Dell Publishing Group, Inc. Its trademark, consisting of the words "Bantam Books" and the portrayal of a rooster, is Registered in U.S. Patent and Trademark Office and in other countries. Marca Registrada. Bantam Books, 666 Fifth Avenue, New York, New York 10103.

PRINTED IN THE UNITED STATES OF AMERICA

KR   0 9 8 7 6 5 4 3 2 1

Acknowledgments

Many thanks to Elizabeth Lynn, who was midwife to this book, and all the members of her writing workshop, particularly Reba Leon, Jim Van Scyoc, and last but not least, Gerald Perkins, who loaned me books and freely shared all sorts of knowledge from his stay in Australia. Thanks also to Marc Laidluw for steering me to reference material for the second half of the book.

I owe a debt of gratitude to my editor, Shawna McCarthy, for her helpful suggestions and for sticking by me through the whole looong process. Thanks also to David Hartwell, whose perceptive comments some years ago helped me make a crucial turning point in my writing.

And last, a tip of the hat to my husband, Richard, for his good-humored patience throughout the whole thing.

PART I

Almost Beginnings
1949

"*Raba, Raba, time to warm my hands to lay the words upon you, time to wake you up to life,*" Auntie Djilbara sang, waving her hands palm-down over the cook-fire. Raba shivered a little in the morning coolness, enjoying the sensation of goose bumps on her small, spindly body, clad only in a loosely wrapped dusty blanket. Soon the sun would be up to begin its slow bake across the ochre desert. Raba was already quite awake, rising early so she could breakfast with Djilbara. Father was gone up north, so her mother was busy caring for her two little brothers, and had been happy to let her spend time with her clan aunt.

Djilbara turned to her. Raba dropped her makeshift cape, screwing her eyes shut tight in anticipatory pleasure.

Djilbara touched her with dry, gentle fingers: forehead, eyes, nose, mouth.

> *From the fire I give you*
> *Grow strong here*
> *Do not turn*
> *The words go into you*
> *Do not take*
> *Do not take*
> *Share your hunt with all*
> *You were born for all of us*
> *The whole camp rejoiced*
> *When you were born*
> *Do not see evil*
> *Do not speak bad words*

3

Raba felt her aunt's touch pull away as a pleasant tugging sensation on her skin as the woman turned momentarily to add more warmth to her hands over the fire. Then she touched Raba's chest, pubic area, thighs, knees, and feet.

> *Don't neglect your mother*
> *Don't neglect your brothers*
> *Don't neglect your neighbors*
> *Put your feet on the*
> *Ancestor's path*
> *Grow tall*
> *Don't sway and draw men's gazes*
> *Grow strong*
> *Dream strongly*
> *Until the words have lived*

The morning ritual over, Djilbara set Raba to helping her cook seedcakes. This was Raba's favorite time: she could ask Djilbara anything she wished, before the men came to eat with them. Her aunt said that this was their very own mystery, that Raba shouldn't spoil it by being careless in the questions she asked other people the rest of the day.

Raba poured some batter onto green leaves placed on the coals, watching it spread and curl a little at the edges as it cooked. With her other hand she waved away the ever-present bot flies. As the paste cooked into bread, it released an aroma of warm comfort.

"Why does Huroo say he's a Goanna when he's an Emu?" she asked. Huroo was her favorite friend.

Her aunt glanced at her sharply. "Why do you say that? What makes you think he's an Emu?"

"All you have to do is look at his shadow as he walks along. His shadow strides like an Emu, it looks Emu, you can see Emu spirit coming out from all inside of it."

Djilbara turned away from the little girl to tend the tea billy, buying time for herself before replying. Camp children were used to answers that came slowly from their elders.

How to keep Raba safe? The child saw clearly and shone clearly. She was a *badundjari*—a dream spirit. Someday the old men would notice her, and what then? When she was grown would they send the *djinagarbil*—featherfeet killers—after her? That must not happen. Djilbara must keep the little girl safe. She had been protecting the child since before her birth, when Raba still lay in her mother Kultuwa's womb. That early, Djilbara had recognized the miracle of Raba. The child was a living dream of the Land. Raba could grow up to lead her people back to the Dreamtime. But for now, she was just a little one, and very vulnerable.

The question about Huroo was a perfect example of how Raba could get into trouble. Even Huroo's mother didn't know he was Emu. Her husband was of the Wallaby clan, which according to the tradition of the tribe meant that all his sons would be part of the Goanna lizard clan. But Hurro's mother had also had a lover, Numada, who was a powerful and headstrong man. All of Numada's children would have been Emus. Although the affair had been secret, he loved Huroo's mother possessively and decided that though he couldn't have her as his wife, she would bear his child.

Djilbara remembered clearly the time of Huroo's conception seven years before. It was the same year that Raba was born.

Numada had been away in the hills. Djilbara knew now that he had been making a strong magic. He returned in the grip of a powerful dreaming. At the time she'd marked the change in him and wondered, but put it down to men's magic and paid no more attention. But he had been dreaming the child he would send into his lover.

Huroo's mother later told her in confidence that Numada met her when she went alone to get water each day, and made love to her as one possessed; bending her back against the boulders surrounding the well, the feeling and sounds of his skin against hers blending with the smell and coolness of the water below them. Before they'd been tender and close with each other. Now he was strange and intense, leaving her abruptly each time. She came to fear and also crave those meetings by the well. On the fifth day he turned on her, telling her he was done with her and she must go back to her husband. In a fury she left him. A child was born to her to the exact day count from when she'd next made love to her husband, but Djilbara knew the delay to be part of Numada's sorcery. To this day Huroo's mother thought of the boy as her reward for returning to her husband.

Huroo had inherited his mother's beauty and so far looked like neither man. But what about when he grew up? This was

Numada's evil, because the boy would marry into the wrong clan, innocently speak to those he should ritually avoid, and not speak to those he should. And because he came from powerful magic and was a strong spirit, who could tell what trouble this would cause both here and in the Dreamtime?

The only people who knew so far were Numada, herself, and sharp-eyed little Raba, who could see the truth in shadows. Raba was still too young to know when and why to keep quiet, and how dangerous those who broke clan taboos could be. Djilbara prayed the girl's vision would grow soon to show her the openedness and closedness, the good and evil in others, so she would know when and when not to speak. In the meantime the two of them had these morning talks, which she hoped would keep Raba safe for a while.

The tea still steeped when she turned back to Raba, who was wriggling and making faces, impatient at what was a long delay, even for her.

"Huroo doesn't know he's an Emu, nor does anyone else. The spirits have given you a special gift in letting you see his Emu spirit. No one else can see it. They trust you to keep that secret, even from him. This is a great sharing on their part."

Raba looked crestfallen. "Did I do bad? Are the spirits angry because I told you?"

Chuckling, Djilbara picked her up and hugged her tight. "You must like Huroo a lot. No, you didn't do bad to tell me. Aren't I the *Wuradilagu* of this camp, who all the women come to for advice? The spirits sent you to me so I could tell you that it was a secret to be kept. You really must never tell anyone else. It could be dangerous for you, and for Huroo."

"I promise. I promise."

"Promises, promises," a deep voice mimicked. "And what are all these promises, Little Kangaroo Ears?"

"Greetings, husband. And give my greetings to my brother there with you." Djilbara set Raba down as two tall men strode up to her campfire. "Raba thought she did something wrong, and being a good girl she felt badly about it." This was addressed to the man she called husband. Raba and she shared a private grin.

This husband and brother were neither, by marriage or blood, but by tribal designation. Talbiri belonged to the pool of men from which Djilbara could marry, and Migay to the group she could not, so he was considered an official sibling. Both were unmarried at present, and brought her game in exchange for her cooking.

Talbiri picked up Raba under her arms and swung her up into the air, letting go and then catching her. She shrieked with laughter and excitement. "My, my," he said. "You are beginning to look just like your name. You really are growing kangaroo ears."

"I am not, I would have felt them growing," she protested, but she touched her ears to make sure just the same. Finding them girl-size, she grinned at him. "I like you, Talbiri. Why don't you really be Auntie Djilbara's husband?"

He shot Djilbara a sidelong glance. "Well, I wouldn't mind that at all, at least a little."

Djilbara snorted. He'd been hinting he'd like to spend some time in her tent at night. She didn't intend to marry him, but she'd heard he was a good lover, and was almost decided to give in to his flirting.

Raba helped her serve up breakfast: Iltjota grass seed-cake, tea and sugar from the mission store, baked Goanna lizard left from the night before. Migay sat down near Raba. As "siblings" it was forbidden that he and Djilbara converse, so he talked to Raba as a way of communicating with her. Raba found the whole situation fascinating. She knew that one day she wouldn't be allowed to talk directly to her little brothers either.

"So, Miss Ears," Migay continued the teasing. "What are you going to do today?"

"Auntie Djilbara is going to send me to look for the bee's house for honey and eggs."

"Sugar bag and bee eggs?" Migay smacked his lips. "We're going to have to hunt up a 'roo if your Auntie is going to feed us so well."

"She *and* my mama are going to dig into the bee house when I find it," Raba said pointedly.

"Oh, I see. And do you think your mama would like a nice big 'roo haunch, too?"

Raba smiled condescendingly, letting him know that for an adult he was clever to pick up her hint so quickly. She'd like to be able, for once, to remind a grown-up of Sharing. It was usually the other way around.

"Well, I have something important to tell you, so you'd better stretch those big furry ears towards me and listen strong. Hunt all you want anywhere that's normally safe today, except to the northwest of the mission school. The old men are making big magic out there, and it attracts demons that devour small children. You remember Djurban, don't you?"

She nodded, big-eyed. Djurban had been a ten-year-old found dead last spring on a clay-pool several miles away. His neck was broken, with nowhere high to fall from. Some said the demons lifted him up into the sky and dropped him. Some said the featherfeet killers found him spying on sacred ceremonies. The whole camp had mourned for weeks.

"So promise you won't go there."

"I promise."

She liked to watch him eat. She could see the seedcake glow inside his throat, slide down past his ribs. Those glowed some, too, just for a moment, picking up strength from the food. She giggled to herself. She already knew the other children couldn't see things the way she did.

"And be careful in camp."

"In camp? Is there going to be trouble in camp?"

"No, just a little excitement. But don't tell the other children. Do you promise?"

"I promise." Her third promise to grown-ups already this morning! It threatened to be a long day. "I won't see anything anyway. I'm going bee-hunting."

"That's right. How could I forget?"

"Raba, you're all done eating. Why don't you begin your hunt before it's too hot?" Djilbara interjected. She wanted to ask the men what was going on without the child there. "The sun is alive now. The bees will be waking up."

"All right, I'm going." Raba started to romp off, then stopped and pointed ahead. "I'm going east," she said seriously.

"That's what you want to do," Talbiri agreed. But after she was gone, he turned to Djilbara. "Actually, do you think that's a good idea? It's all gully-land to the east. Can she find her way? Will she be safe?"

"She has good path-sense." These men would never know what good path-sense Raba had. Many times Djilbara had taken Raba into the desert, letting the little girl find the way. And always, no matter what the child's mood—silly, empty-headed, serious, or dreaming—her feet instinctively found the little paths that traced the Ancestors' Great Wanderings, the small models that only the women knew of, one of the few magic ways left to them. The Ancestors' Great Wanderings had created the whole of the Land. With those patterns embedded in miniature within her, Raba could never be lost.

The only harm Raba could come to was from the old men and their sorcery. Or stray white-fellas, who, being empty inside, could be filled by any passing bad spirits.

"So, husband, tell me of the imminent commotion in camp."

Migay and Talbiri looked at each other. Migay nodded, then Talbiri spoke. "First, we have something else to tell you. One of the women who clean at the mission came back to camp with news. While she was clearing away the Christian white-fellas' dinner, they were talking that it's time to take the next mob of little ones into their school. Raba was one of those named, and we know you're teaching her the Law and the Way. We wanted to warn you. Maybe you can take her away on a trek, and save at least a few months."

He watched for her reaction with worry. Raba was not the first girl she'd taught and helped raise, but he'd never heard of Djilbara being so attached before to one of her charges.

"Tell my sister, too," Migay said, looking past the woman, "that Christian white-fella Mrs. Thompson is coming into camp today to look for the children and their parents."

Djilbara groaned. So soon! Too soon! School meant the Christian white-fellas locked the children up all night in the dormitories and all morning in the school. They could only come back to the camp and their families in the afternoon and on the weekends. The missionaries with their "Don't do this" and "Don't do that" came at the only time in the children's lives they should be able to do everything. Before they were old enough for the taboos to apply.

Yet at the same time she felt a slight relief. She had been sensing a mysterious pressure from an unknown source, an interior unease that frightened her since she could not "see" its direction; where it came from, where it was going. Yet that sort of "sight" was the heart of her function within the camp. For the first time in her life she'd had an inkling of what blindness was truly like. Raba's being taken away from her by the missionaries would explain what she'd been experiencing, for she could not "see" into the thin, opaque existence of the white-fellas. And Raba's entering their school was not, after all, unexpected. Nor would it stop her education with Djilbara—just slow it down.

Migay scowled. "Them damn Christian white-fellas. They hit the children. Then they complain when we *men* have fights. But they hit our children!" He stared at the ground. At the age of nineteen he was not yet a fully initiated man, and his own years in the mission school were not far behind him. He'd been beaten frequently there.

Auntie's campsite lay at the south end of camp, so Raba cut up the center before heading out towards gully-land. She skirted camp dogs, played balance games on an old truck chassis.

"Raba, Raba," a mob of older children came up around her and gave chase, trying to tickle her. As they closed in, drew away, closed in again, she felt their presence on her skin as pressure, vacuum, then pressure again, like the blacksmith's bellows. "Where you going, little Raba?" She finally stood her ground and imperiously pointed a finger at them.

"I'm being sent to do food work. I'm going to find a bee's house."

"We're going hunting. We'll get some nice fat lizards. Come join us."

Raba shook her head.

The oldest boys leading the mob, Wooleroo and Djura, were almost old enough for initiation and took great pride in leading the ragtag pack of boys and girls. "My Daddy's coming home from the stockman's soon," said Wooleroo. "My Ma says he'll be sick of white-fella food, and want a feast of real grub." Wooleroo was filled with self-importance and also an eagerness to please. He'd heard he'd be initiated by the Wallaby clan, which meant rites of great pomp and dignity. He announced to the other children that they'd escort the "little one" a little ways into the Outback.

"You noisy mob," said Raba crossly. "Don't you come with me. You'll scare the bee-people away."

"What's that?" They all heard a humming in the air.

"It's the bee-people, telling you they're angry." But as she spoke she knew that wasn't true. The humming surrounded them, growing louder, more ominous. The children stopped moving as the humming grew to such a point of intensity that Raba's teeth hurt. Then it stopped abruptly. She felt a release of tension from the others, but for her the sense grew stronger, like a blow. All of a sudden, into the silence, leapt seven fearsome creatures, gaudy in ochre, red, black; mouths filled with sharp, filed teeth. As their feet hit the ground they screamed, filling the camp with thunder cries. *Wadjura!* Demons! The children scattered like a flock of birds. Raba made a long dive along the ground, hit rolling, kept tumbling till she hit the side of a tent, and tried to burrow into the sand there. Wooleroo was right behind her, running up the taut side of the tent. Two of the *Wadjura* came up and yanked him down by his ankles, almost trampling Raba as they did. Each grabbed him by an arm and dragged him away shrieking, back across camp. As they retreated Raba felt rather than saw their personas peeling away in layers, translucent skins of magic and terror; down to the dusty brown solid cores of the camp hunters, decked out with power to appear as demons.

"I have never heard of such a thing." Djilbara was outraged. "Sending the Dog Clan with their abduction rites to gather the initiates for the Wallaby ceremony."

The two men looked sheepish. "We've never heard of such a thing either," Talbiri admitted, tugging at his beard. "But you know how this place is. There are ever more powerful old men here, more and more sacred objects. More tribes. More ways of seeing and understanding the Way and the Law."

Djilbara was afraid. Why hadn't she felt this? She generally ignored the initiation rites. Without ever having seen one, she knew what took place in them. Her senses monitored the old men's doings for her: she always knew the cadence and pulse of the camp's life. Why hadn't she sensed this aberration?

Raba laughed, running through the desert. This was the best of days. Now she knew the commotion Migay had warned her of, and why the northwest of camp had been forbidden. She'd really thought the initiation men were *Wadjura*. Djilbara was right when she said the old men's magic was strong. Her best friends, Marindi and Huroo, would be sorry that they'd missed the event.

So the day had started off with excitement. Now she was off on her own in her beloved Land. She sang very high. The glinting sands in the red dunes sang back. Everything was full. When she came to an acacia or gum tree she could feel the eyes of the animal spirits within them, pressing right up to the woody pores.

Eating breakfast with her aunt and the two men she'd smelled the flux of another time in their sweat, heard the rich tonality of the many lives they'd lived in the timbre of their voices. Their skin exuded the warmth of all the animal spirits they'd ever been or would be. Their shadows swelled with magic.

And out here, so did the shadows of the mulga, the nervous thin shadows of the spinifex grass, the sand dunes themselves. Especially the sand dunes.

The only flat shadows she'd ever seen belonged to the white-fellas. Which didn't surprise her at all, because the white-fellas themselves were flat, like paper, and only belonged to one time and one place.

She sang to the dunes and they bounced her song back, telling her of what lay on the Land in between. She caught a fine trace of sound—a few lines in a pattern, like a bark-painting—and traced the thin sound back to its source, a spiderweb. Doing as her mother had once shown her, she plucked two strands from the outer circles, thanking the spider for its sharing and promising it a gift of bee eggs. She carefully tapped the two threads together between thumb and forefinger, the spider glue on them forming a single, thicker string. She wandered among the desert bush looking for flowering plants, humming.

When she found a bee working away in a blossom, she matched the cadence of its hum with her own. It marched slowly within the perimeters of the blossom, caught in the circle of sound, drowsy with its task. Still humming, Raba carefully draped the end of the spider strand around its abdomen once, the stickiness holding it in place. Her song slowly trailed away. Untranced, the bee lifted off. Even when it could no longer be seen against the sky, its spider banner glinted silver. Raba leapt to her feet, ready to follow it from flower to flower until it returned to its home.

Djilbara was furious with herself. She'd attributed all the strange feelings she'd had to the unusual beginnings of the initiation rites. She was wrong. They had another source.

After the tumult in the camp, she eventually made her way to the tent of Raba's family. Mrs. Thompson had already been there. Raba's mother, Kultuwa, had told the white-fella woman that the child was with Djilbara, being purposely vague as to where they could be found. But Mrs. Thompson hadn't found her in the camp. Was she still searching for Djilbara and Raba, or had she returned to the mission?

Entering a cooking space between tents, Djilbara encountered a group of youngsters moping around.

"You're a sorry-looking mob," she greeted them.

"Good morning, Auntie Djilbara," the oldest and most dejected-looking replied. Djilbara smiled to herself. Djura was undoubtedly disappointed that his friend Wooleroo had been taken for initiation before him.

"Have you seen Raba?"

"Yes, ma'am. Just before the *Wadjura* men came for Wooleroo. She said she was going bee-hunting."

"Good, so I'll still be able to find her out there."

"I don't know, Auntie. Depends on if white-fella Mrs. Thompson finds her first. She asked us where Raba had gone. Didn't seem happy—said Raba was too little to be messing with bees. I bet she makes her stop."

"Mrs. Thompson knows where she is?" Djilbara asked sharply.

"We didn't do wrong, did we? We showed her where Raba tracked off from the camp. We'll show you, too."

Hurrying off after the double line of footprints, Djilbara cursed herself. If she could find Raba first, they would cut back along the rock bed and decamp immediately. They could trek for at least a couple of months before returning to the inevitability of the mission school.

Raba laid three stones together to mark the way to the stump she'd found the bees nesting in. From there it would be easy, for it lay not far from points connecting to the path of the Rainbow Serpent's Wandering. Her chore for the morning done, she had a few more hours to herself to wander.

Small animals scampered everywhere, as if they knew there would be no children hunting them today; the Zebra finch, her mother's clan animal, lizards, a carpet snake, rabbits. They were in the scrub to Raba's right. To her left were the ridges of gully-land. She sang. The animals sang back as many small voices, but the sands in the dunes glittered and shone and sang to her in a unified chorus. *Raba, Raba, come play.*

She turned to her left, scrambled up the nearest rise, and slid down into the gully-maze.

As she walked along the ground, the bank glittered and pulsed with its own light. *Raba, Raba, why do you walk so funny? Why are you walking up in the sky?*

She giggled. "I'm not walking funny. I'm walking on the ground."

No, you're walking in the sky. Come down and walk with me.

Feeling a sudden sense of vertigo she looked up, and saw she *was* walking with her head way up in the sky. Her feet were on the ground, but it seemed so only because the ground was trying very hard to keep up with her. Otherwise she'd float away. She felt a twinge of fear. She remembered that at one time in the Dreamtime the kangaroos drifted along like clouds, their feet never touching the ground.

It's all right. I'll help you. The ground grabbed her ankles. *Turn your feet down.* Sand shifted around them, deeper around her legs, with a firmer hold. She kept walking, although she was now face down on the ground. She didn't remember falling. *When did I fall?* she thought. *How can I do this? I'm walking into the sand.*

Now all of her was in the sand; she was face down in the sand, but her footing was sound and as she took each step the sand slid away from her. It sang as she walked. The grains coming towards her had a different sound than those going past her or those already behind her. But now it was beginning to work into her skin in little cutting bits. She whimpered. The sand "sky" should have been red. Instead it was a whirlwind of sparkling lights. The bright grains were digging their way through her skin, stinging. *It's all right, Raba. It will just hurt a little. We're going to eat away your body and give you a new one.* She was pushing into the sand as she walked and it was pushing through her. It ground into her eyes, eating through her now-closed eyelids. It ate into the delicate labyrinths of her ears. Even its song hurt. She still kept walking, slowly, crying, but all her tears were blood, and as soon as they pooled on her etched cheeks the sand ate that away, too. She kept walking for there was nothing else to do. If she turned to go back, she knew she would still be struggling through the sand land. *Just a little more. It will be better soon.* She could tell when it ate clear through her eyes because she could feel it grinding into the sockets. *Open your eyes now, Raba, and see*. She opened her mouth instead to cry "I can't, you've eaten my eyes all up," but the sand rushed in and started abrading against her teeth and down her throat. *Open your eyes now*.

She opened what would have been her eyes and looked down at her palms. A light played over them and everywhere on her body that she turned and looked at. Whether she had eyes anymore or not, she could see again. She saw that where the little glinting grains had eaten into her, tearing away her flesh, it had left itself behind in replacement. Her new "skin" glowed with rainbow lights, and she suddenly realized that the spotlight that accompanied her gaze was the reflection from her new, crystalline eyes. It still hurt. In fact, it hurt even more, for the sand was attacking the toughest part of her, her bones. *This is the worst, Raba, then it will be easy. You must walk even more strongly*. Raba pitched into the sandstorm in agony, but willingly now, distracted from the pain somewhat by her new sight. With each step she could see more clearly.

The sand thinned, and she could see hazily to a new Land, wetter and greener than the bush she was used to. Raba sensed powerful entities moving about. She remembered the feeling of another time and place lurking just behind the faces of her kin. She felt as though she had broken past their flesh and was sinking into that other time. "Which spirit are you? Are you the Emu? The Wallaby?"

The glinting light laughed and sang: *I am their mother. I am their father. I've brought you from my bones-time to my flesh-time. This land is too empty without the songs of your people for so long, and the animal spirits are incomplete without their human souls*. "Can I stay here?" *Not yet. You must not go all the way yet. Turn, turn, turn around*. She did, and felt herself spin free of the sand. She felt her new bones clearly within her. *You must go back and learn more. With your new body, with me a part of you, you will be able to see as you learn. You are a good pathfinder, are you not?* Raba nodded, light glinting from her tangled new hair. *You must learn a new way to walk. You must walk backward along the path you came, without looking back. Look just once and see the trail you've made*. Raba looked into a whirlwind tunnel, and sensed that somewhere above them in this other, wet Land, a new green ridge had just been formed.

She turned again and walked, feeling for each step

carefully, her feet pulled backwards by the yearning of each earlier footprint. She walked slowly, each step taking her a little farther from the hazy green vision she still saw in front of her. Then she could see only sand again. She passed, backwards, little glowing splashes, where her blood had dripped when her skin was being flayed. The crystals of sand had eaten it where it had fallen. She remembered Djilbara saying once that the Dreamtime was not-time, so maybe she had been here forever. She was tired. She was sleepy. Walking, she kept walking, feeling the sand pressed against her back as she slid through it.

All at once there was a new feeling of emptiness on just a small spot on her back. She almost turned her head, but remembered that the spirit of the Land had told her not to look back. She wiggled a little and felt more of that lack of pressure. It was the sky against her back now! Carefully she eased the backs of her thighs, her arms free. Then her head, and she smiled down into the sand. Now there was just her chest and belly.

A terrible scream filled the sky, and Raba felt a pounding, pounding, pounding down the gully-face behind her. She matched it with a hideous, pain-filled cry of her own as hands pulled her out and around, ripping her too soon from her new parent, the Land. She caught a glimpse of blood welling and smearing from her stomach, then she was looking up at whiteness that dazzled like the glow of the sands: clouds, and framed against them a flat, white face.

Hidden

Djilbara made no sound when she saw Mrs. Thompson staggering down the bank carrying Raba in her arms: she was running too hard, little enough air for just breathing. Raba was dying—she could see it. The child's life was pouring out in great gouts of light. Her bones were completely luminescent, shining against the blue sky like long, white-hot jewels. All of her glowed, except for an ugly opaque hole in her middle.

I must keep running, Djilbara thought. *I must keep
running, for when I stop the first breath I take in will come
back out with all my soul and all my magic in it in a wail that
will crack this world.*

She scrambled up the slope. As she reached to grab Raba's
dangling leg she felt a living, pulsing warmth in it.

Mrs. Thompson was even paler than usual, as if the blood
splashed on her pastel dress had drained from herself, rather
than Raba. Djilbara snatched the child away from the missionary. There was a nonsensical, liquid sound; Mrs. Thompson
was speaking to her.

"Oh my Lord, I'm so glad you came. That someone came.
Letting such a little one out in this wilderness alone. She was
suffocating in the sand—I found her just in time. I think she'd
taken a fall from the ridge above. I thought I'd faint when I saw
her stomach. At first I thought she'd impaled herself on a rock.
But really, really, it's just superficial—abrasions from the
sand—just skinned herself."

The watching part of Djilbara's mind let Mrs. Thompson's
words drone past her like water and evaporate. Looking at
Raba, she let her gaze sink past the first shining layer of dark
skin, and found more shining underneath it. And more—layer
after layer of fine-grained kaleidoscopic light, right down to
those glowing bones.

There are times on the desert when one can see what lies
beyond the horizon reflected as an image in the sky. Looking
into Raba's bones was like that. Djilbara should have been able
to see through them. Instead, mirrored shimmering and
upside down within them was another country. She was drawn
to it, like a thirsty animal to water, and with a start she knew
she was looking directly into the Dreamtime. She wondered if
she could reach it this way, if she could sink right into Raba and
step beyond and away. Frightened, she withdrew.

Closing her eyes, she began to listen instead to Raba's
pulse. The pattern of its beat traced the Ancestors' trails. Her
veins, arteries, and capillaries emcompassed the whole country within them; everything the Land had been, was, and
would be. As Raba breathed Djilbara could feel the Land
breathe. And in another time that was also now, the Dreamtime breathed in cadence.

Raba had been completely transformed, by the Land
itself, except where the shallow blood slicked on the girl's

stomach and chest. There the Land-pulse fluttered in sucking breaths, like an old man's sloppy, failing heart. There was a sound of pain and confusion—not from Raba, who felt nothing right now—but from the Land itself, caught in transition in its exchange with the girl. It was left reaching out with the last of its gift for her. If that transition had been complete, Raba would have been completely transformed. What then? From the vision she'd seen in Raba's bones, Djilbara guessed that Raba would have bridged the gap right now between waking life and the Dreamtime. Soon . . . they could have all left soon.

"You fool. What have you done? You bloody, stupid fool!!" Djilbara screamed at the missionary. She stood, clutching Raba. If her hands weren't full with the child, she would have picked up a rock and hit Mrs. Thompson in the face with it, again and again, till the white-fella woman was dead and her skull crushed in, blood running down to soak the basin floor.

Djilbara started trudging back to the camp, her shoulder sockets and arms aching. Raba had grown impossibly heavy for such a small child.

Mrs. Thompson stood for a moment in shock, then came running after. "Oh. My. No, you don't see. I know, you're hysterical. Believe me, I was too at first. But she was already unconscious there in the sand. I got there in just the nick of . . ." She stopped as Djilbara turned and glared at her.

Step after step across the slow, muddy-minded Land. What would she do with Raba? Who could know what the Land had meant to happen? If the process had been completed, then there would have been nothing to do but watch and see its impulse unfold. Now the girl was a target for anyone who had the least bit of true sight. Men, jealous of the petty power they held, would not tolerate her potential threat. While she was weak they'd come after her like a pack of hunting dingos. Somehow Raba must be hidden and healed before the elders saw her, and the Land soothed. Djilbara turned on the meekly trailing missionary. She knew she could tell the fool anything.

"This is your fault. Bad white-fella magic. You broke taboo, but the spirits can't hurt you, so they hurt Raba instead. For a white-fella hurt, we can do nothing: so white-fella hurt, white-fella must heal. Raba must go to the infirmary."

Mrs. Thompson stood blinking in confusion. This fierce

Abo woman was obviously crazy, but in her weird logic she had finally arrived at a sensible solution. "Yes, of course. We'll go straight to the infirmary. Dr. Blackston will look at her and she'll be just fine, you'll see." She cautiously dropped behind.

Djilbara started up again wearily, snorting to herself.

The infirmary was past the school and the children's dorms, on the northeast side of the settlement, so they didn't need to pass through any of the camp to get there. Djilbara was relieved that they didn't risk running into any of the old men.

She guessed that Mrs. Thompson would be happy not to have any run-ins with the Abos with the child's blood all over her.

They called for Dr. Blackston and Raba's mother, Kultuwa. Djilbara insisted that Kultuwa be informed that a taboo had been broken, that she not bring her sons with her. Seeing the glance the white-fellas exchanged, she added sharply, "What do you think the old men will do when they hear Raba was found hurt with her blood all over Mrs. Thompson's dress? When they heard a taboo was broken, they'll be angry but maybe not rush down here. Maybe wait to find out what taboo is, wait to hear what Dr. Blackston say."

The missionaries looked uneasy. Their worst run-ins with the settlement were usually over broken taboos. Experience had taught them that the powerful elder men loved to diagnose and prescribe in these cases, but they moved cautiously at first to be sure that they didn't unknowingly break any sacred laws themselves.

Djilbara waited. She and Raba were alone in a little examination room. Lying dark but glowing on a white cot, Raba looked lost in the bandages wrapped around her middle.

"My girl in there?" Kultuwa's anxious voice came from the hallway. Djilbara beckoned her in and watched as she went straight to her daughter and touched her forehead, closed eyes, and the pulse at her throat with soft fingers. Raba's mother was a strong, broadly built woman, usually with a quiet air about her, but she was visibly shaken now. Her hands brushed the tops of the bandages and she looked inquiringly at Djilbara, who nodded. Gently she peeled them back, looked for a long moment, then carefully patted them into place. She sat on the floor by the cot.

"What does the white-fella doctor say?"

"He hasn't been here yet. They're bringing him from a stockman's where there was an accident."

"They told me there was a taboo and not to bring my boys. Djilbara, what happened? She doesn't look too badly hurt, but she's lying so still, and something feels very wrong."

Djilbara described the events as far as she understood them. ". . . the white-fellas are blinder than witchety grubs. The missionary woman walked directly against the Land," she ended in a fury. "They are like paper. They should be torn into little bits and thrown into their own fires. I myself will point the bone at Mrs. Thompson."

Kultuwa sat for a while. She said nothing in the attitude of one open and blank, not thinking, waiting to absorb answers from her surroundings. Djilbara was not surprised at her seeming lack of reaction. She was a good, solid woman; loving and intelligent. But she was not gifted in the way that Djilbara and Raba were. She could only sense the slow, deep shiftings of life; the intimations of wrongness and rightness in events.

Finally she spoke. "You are too harsh, Djilbara. What the missionary woman did was wrong, but it was because she was blind. In their own way the white-fellas try to care. They just do it wrong. They won't listen to us, so we have to try to listen to them and understand them. That way we can think around them and not have to hate them."

Djilbara looked at Kultuwa with disbelief and impatience. "You really don't understand, do you? If Raba's transformation hadn't been interrupted, we might not have had to worry about living with the white-fellas at all. The Land had its reasons to change her. We're coming to the time to go Home."

Kultuwa shook her head. "You can't know that. Not now. Don't put all that on my Raba. She's too little, and she's hurt."

Djilbara wanted to point out to the woman that Raba was not hers, that children were the greatest part of the Sharing that they all survived by, especially Raba, who would change them all. But she saw how she must look to Kultuwa's eyes: a possessed woman who was willing to trample a small child to achieve her goal.

"Kultuwa, I didn't arrange for this to happen to Raba. She was called. And yes, she is hurt. You sensed the wrongness. Try to imagine what the old men will see, and what they will do. Don't waste your pity on the white-fellas. Save it for your daughter."

Kultuwa's face contracted with fear. "Do the old men know anything yet?"

Djilbara shrugged. "I'll find out. Listen for anyone coming and I'll go *badundjari*."

Djilbara's eyes didn't close, but Kultuwa could feel her slipping away. The empty infirmary room slowly filled with, not the sounds, but the sense of the sounds of the desert. Through Djilbara, Kultuwa felt the ever-present buzzing of the flies, the shifting of hot air across the baked red clay, the scratching of claws as lizards scurried to shade under the mulga trees. She forced herself back to the quietude of the stuffy room. She had to stand guard. But the struggle to keep the two impinging worlds separate was hard. How could Djilbara and Raba stand this sort of constant conflict? She dozed off.

Guiltily, she started awake at the sound of a hand on the door handle. Djilbara was sitting erect in the chair, serenely alert.

"G'day, ladies. Do you want to tell me what happened here?" the doctor asked. Kultuwa could tell from the doctor's voice that he'd already talked to Mrs. Thompson. She waited to hear what Djilbara had to say. It might tell her some of what the *Wuradilagu* had seen while she was dream-walking.

"Mrs. Thompson has broken taboo here," said Djilbara.

The Aborigines were used to looks of skepticism from white-fellas at the word *taboo*, especially Christians and doctors. She gave an empty, cackling laugh, then her face transformed into a mask of grimness.

"You think I be just a crazy black-fella woman? You look at girl and say to me if you think her hurts count for how sick she be."

"Of course, I'll look," the doctor soothed. No matter what he thought of the situation, Djilbara was a sharp woman of considerable power in the camp, and needed to be treated with respect.

He looked Raba over conscientiously. "You're right. Her injuries aren't that serious, which jibes with what Mrs. Thompson had to say. Sometimes people go into shock at the sight of their own blood. I've seen it happen with superficial facial injuries, where there's profuse bleeding but little real harm done. Of course, skin damage, even when shallow, can be serious. I've never come across anything quite like this kind of epidermal trauma. Still, the worst she's likely to come out of the experience with is some scarring. I can treat her for shock and potential infection, but that's about all. Do you want to bring in your medicine men?"

Djilbara shook her head. "No, the old men be initiating the boys. Must stay clean, away from broken taboos. Christian white-fellas break taboo, then white-fella medicine must heal. I'll bring good herbs, and Kultuwa and I do a purification. Raba must not go back to camp till then."

"How long do you think all that will take?"

"Two weeks, maybe."

"That's rather a long time. That will take her right up to the start of the school year."

Djilbara said nothing in reply.

"Well, then, the infirmary's pretty empty right now. I don't suppose it will hurt. We'll put her in the women's ward in a day or two. Until then, she can stay in one of the 'fever rooms.'"

"Kultuwa and I take turns watching over her."

"That really isn't necessary." He caught a look from Kultuwa. "But do as you wish."

"What about the old men?" Kultuwa asked as the doctor's footsteps faded down the hallway. She spoke in a low tone even though none of the white-fellas could understand Aboriginal language.

"They sense a big change, a major break with the Dreamtime. But so far they're so caught up in themselves that they aren't looking any farther than their own transgressions for the source. At least for now."

"But just keeping Raba here won't change anything. Her wounds might heal, but as soon as she gets out they'll know."

"That's why I must go out tonight," Djilbara said.

At sunset Raba became restless. Muted light from the one small window threw overlapping washes of lavender, mauve, and rose across her, so as she turned feebly against the bandages she looked like a Barramundi fish trying to swim against the current of a light-dappled river.

Djilbara had left several hours before. First she'd had to arrange for Kultuwa's sons to be taken care of for the night.

Next she'd wanted to track down Talbiri. As one of the hunters he could be trusted to get word to the old men out at their magic sites of the events concerning Raba. It would be a muted, distorted version, conveyed in such a way that they would come to the conclusion that their errors in the initiation procedures were ricocheting as malevolent energy across the landscape, causing ignorant white-fella women and innocent children to stumble into taboos.

The light through the window dimmed and the room gradually became as dark as its own shadows. Kultuwa left her chair and eased herself onto the bed so that she could hold Raba in her lap and quiet her. The Christian white-fellas would not come back and disturb them for the rest of the night. Cradling Raba, she was startled. Along the path of her daughter's pulse she could feel footfalls. Alone with her, Kultuwa had been able to forget that Raba was part of the Land. But touching her now, she could feel steps in the girl's heartbeat. She recognized the footsteps as Djilbara's, and knew the *Wuradilagu* had started her journey into the Outback.

Around and about within Raba's body, Kultuwa felt Djilbara walking. First she walked the little trails of Raba's birth pattern, walking them over and over, strengthening them. She was singing, too; the blood in Raba's veins hummed like a bullroarer. Later Kultuwa felt Djilbara encircling the old men's ritual camp in large irregular loops, crooning a wall around them, so that the magic they were dreaming there would bend back in towards them.

From there Djilbara headed out across the Land, walking weavings of footsteps across the intersection of Great Ancestor paths. Every once in a while she stopped, or so Kultuwa thought, because although Raba's pulse still beat, it seemed heavy, anchored in one place. Was Djilbara stopping to greet spirits, or to build some magic?

Finally, in the last, longest hours of the night, the footsteps became lighter and lighter, and faded off into the distance. Raba began to breathe like a normal child in sleep, as if she and the Land had at last undreamed each other. Reassured, Kultuwa allowed herself to nod off, too.

Djilbara arrived back at the camp and infirmary to relieve Kultuwa of her post at midmorning. Kultuwa hesitated to give it up to the *Wuradilagu*; Djilbara looked more in need of rest than either herself or Raba. She had an acrid, sweated-out smell that stung in Kultuwa's sinuses. Her eyes were red and strained. But she insisted, and Kultuwa left to return to her boys. Djilbara sat motionless in the chair by Raba's bed for hours, listening to her breathe. In the small, close room, in the stifling heat of midafternoon, she finally curled up on the floor and slept.

Mission School

"Guwara, what is this letter?" The teacher pointed to a figure on the blackboard.

The boy stood, trying to puzzle out her question. He looked distracted, as if more interested in exploring the new, strange textures of the crisp white shirt and creased black pants against his skin.

Raba heard someone behind her whisper: "*I* know, *I* know. It's a kangaroo. Look at the spine and big pocket belly. But teacher drew it wrong. Kangaroo's standing upright—she should be leaning forward more."

Guwara ignored the whispering. Clearing his throat, he said haltingly, in English, "It sounds like this, teacher: *Thnk!*" He made the sound of a launched spear falling straight to thud into flesh. "And then: *buhhh*," a long, soft sound.

"That's almost right, Guwara. The second part is correct. This is the letter *b*, children, and it is pronounced *buh*."

"That's silly. Why don't they call it *buh* then, instead of *bee*?" This time Huroo was the whisperer. His voice trailed away as the teacher looked in his direction.

No sharp words accompanied the glance. Encouraged by the lack of disapproval, other children murmured "buuh" and "buhh," fitting the sound to their mouths and seeing how it was partly the same as the shape they were trying to memorize. Marindi began to giggle and shape a bubble of spittle with each soft pronunciation. There was the "crack" of a hand being slapped and a yelp.

All the newcomers, the first-graders, sat silent in shocked embarrassment for the teacher. No adults they knew acted like that. Sharing the classroom with them, the second-year students kept scribbling away in their form books.

"Take out a piece of paper, students. We're going to practice writing the letter *b*, in both its small and capital forms."

Miss Landell walked between the desks. She stopped to help one little boy who was having trouble keeping the spines of his small *b*'s to a manageable length. She came close to enjoying teaching only at moments like these. She wasn't good at explaining things to groups of people; she wouldn't have been even if these were white Christian children who'd grown up speaking English, so she didn't hold it against these youngsters. It was just that her years of secretarial work hadn't prepared her in so many ways for this task. Untrained as a teacher, she often found herself frantically trying to remember her own years of schooling. But she also praised the Lord for her office experience. Because of it she knew much more about the subjects she was supposed to teach—grammar, spelling, and so on—than many of the other missionary-teachers here.

"Miss Landell?" Mrs. Thompson stood at the door with a sheaf of papers in her hand. She came up to where the teacher was standing. "We need for you to fill in part of these forms. They're for the government subsistence checks—alterations for the parents of new students." Glancing over her shoulder, she caught sight of Raba. Leaning in towards Miss Landell, she whispered, "That's her, the one I told you about. The one that had the fit in the desert. Watch out for her. She's a real troublemaker."

Miss Landell followed the older woman's gaze. Raba had looked up, aware of the attention. Miss Landell thought her an unprepossessing child to look at; thin, with the broad, flat nose common to her people. Her dark unruly hair was bleached russet in places from the desert sun. She had quiet, sad eyes.

"Raba is never unruly in class." Actually, she was the only one of the new crop, or any of the children, for that matter, who didn't rush off like an animal uncaged in the afternoon to the camp. In class she seemed to drink in words as if she really wanted to learn.

"Don't let her fool you," Mrs. Thompson hissed. "The Devil has clever ways. She's possessed by the anti-Christ."

Miss Landell doubted that Raba could understand Mrs.

Thompson's words, but she could see the child flinching away from their vehemence.

"These are young, impressionable children," she told Mrs. Thompson firmly. "If you wish to speak to me about them we should go out in the hallway." She could see the relief on Raba's face as she led Mrs. Thompson away.

"You must be careful. You've only been here for six months and you don't know these people," Mrs. Thompson continued. "They're the progeny of the Devil."

"I can't agree with you. Primitive, ignorant, and ungodly they certainly are. And very much in need of discipline. But evil?"

"I used to be sympathetic, too. But every time I've tried to help them they've turned on me. They don't know the meaning of gratitude. I saved that very little girl's life and I've gotten nothing but criticism for it. No matter how hard we work to save them, the children all grow up to be the same as their slovenly parents. You still have two and a half years to go in your work for the church. They could be heartbreaking for you."

"Then I'll just have to put my trust in the Lord that that won't happen. I can understand your concern, but I intend to follow Christ's dictum. The one that goes 'Suffer the little children to come unto Me.' Now, if you'll excuse me, I have two classes to teach."

Back in the classroom, Miss Landell shook her head. She suspected that Raba was being used as a pawn in the endless conflict between the adult Abos and the missionaries. It saddened her because she felt the little girl might be one of the few children receptive to an education and the acceptance of salvation through Christ's love.

She turned her attention to the class. The first-graders had been at the mission school for only two weeks. The prospect of setting them on the road to literacy seemed endless. "Children, we will now review the vowel letters: a, e, i, o, and u."

Raba liked learning to read. The letters were like little bones to her. Strung together they formed the skeletons of words and sentences. She could see that when she learned to read they would be fleshed with things and actions, muscled with ideas.

The classroom was spare, echoing the lean structure of the words. There were rows of tables and metal stools, their paint scratched and chipped. The pale green plaster walls were undecorated except at the front, where a picture of the Christian white-fella boss, Jesus Christ, hung behind the teacher. Raba liked the picture because it was pretty and because it was strange. Jesus had a soft white face, a beard, and hair longer than any of the missionary men, who were all cleanshaven. His clothes looked like the layering of cast-offs the people in camp wore. There were no other pictures on the walls to distract the children from lessons. When teacher had to show them something, she would hold up a book for them to look at.

The other children fidgeted in the bleak environment. Raba enjoyed its emptiness. It was a space her mind could fill. Whenever she went back to camp now or wandered outward, she would begin to panic. The rocks, people's faces, tools, and game hanging from poles outside tents, the tents—everything—shimmered and bulged at her. It was as if they were trying to speak to her all at once in many voices in words she could not understand, all with a different important thing to tell her that she must understand at once. She would return in relief to the dorms with a crowded and throbbing head.

There the other children became again separate, comprehensible entities. The food the missionaries served was plain and merely filled her, instead of trying to penetrate her from the inside with meaning. She even liked the clothes the missionaries made them wear. The skirt was airy. And although the blouse itched against the peeling scabs on her stomach, it also hid them. When the sores oozed, her skin contracted away from contact with the fabric, but the other children looked more uncomfortable in their new clothes than she did.

"Class is dismissed for today. Line up for chore assignments," said Miss Landell. "When you're done you have permission to go home. But remember not to be late coming back for Chapel this evening."

Raba was told to report to the laundry room. Some older girls were there already, singing and laughing as they beat dorm linens against washboards set aslant in big sinks.

"He-ey, Raba. This your first time at washing?"

Curled about the doorway, Raba nodded shyly.

"These sheets are hard to do. The Christian white-fella women like them very white. Start out with these kid's clothes first till you get used to it. They're smaller, too."

One of the girls, Aylupa, set another washboard beside her in the sink and drew up a crate for Raba to stand on. Raba picked up a white shirt from a pile of school uniforms and copied Aylupa's rhythmic movements, holding her head back from the pungent odor of the soap.

The singing started up again.

Last night I went a-dreaming with you,
We passed the sleeping Wallaby
As we walked to the salt-pan where you made love to me.
The evening star saw us as we walked to the salt-pan
Now when I see the Wallaby I hear your song inside of me
When I see the evening star I feel your hands upon me
When I see the lightning . . .

They all heard shoe-clattering footsteps turn the corner down the hall and come towards them. Without missing a beat, and altering the melody line only slightly, the song switched to English.

> *. . . walk me 'cross the river, Jesus*
> *And set me on your path forever*
> *Save my soul from drowning, Jesus*
> *And guard my each endeavor . . .*

Peering around Aylupa, Raba saw a missionary woman enter, her lips and the muscles around her eyes held tightly.

"If you're going to sing, it might as well be that, but it's still displeasing to the ears of the Lord."

The singing softened but continued, young faces virtuously smooth and devout.

The woman consulted a list. "You're Raba, aren't you? How are you doing?" She held up the shirt Raba had been working on, studying it. "You'll have to scrub harder than this. I know you're small, but God gave you muscle enough. Practice on this first till you get used to it," she said, handing Raba one of the odd cast-offs the children wore back to camp.

Nodding, Raba huddled back up to her place by Aylupa, relieved to see she'd been handed a sleeveless gray sweater. No worry about having to get that white.

They listened to the woman's footsteps recede. The song increased in volume and reverted back to its Aboriginal lyrics.

When I see the lightning I see your face in its flashing
When I see the carpet snake
I feel you coiling around me
Last night I went a-dreaming with you.
Last night I loved you.

Finishing the chorus they burst into laughter. "Too bad they don't know any black-fella talk. They might learn something, have more fun and make better babies."

The big girls started gossiping about their lovers, and Raba concentrated on her chore. There was so much sand in the sweater. Whoever'd worn it must have been rolling around on the ground. Her sight went finer and finer down into it. She could see all the little sand grains way in deep. As she worked them out they took bites of the woolen fibers as they went. The wool kept getting thinner and thinner. Worse, her fingers seemed to be made of hungry sand, too. As they worked the soft strands they fed on it, tasting flavors of lanolin and mutton. She lifted it out of the rinse water and caught a sob in her throat. There were two holes she didn't remember being there before, and several other places where the fabric looked ready to go.

"What's the matter, Raba? You crying?"

"Look at this." She poked a thumb through one of the holes. "That white-fella woman is going to hit me for this."

"No, don't worry. That happens all the time with the camp clothes. The missionaries give them to us all worn out already, and the Outback does the rest. They complain that we don't keep clean in camp, but hell, sometimes it's only the sand that holds these things together. If we washed them all the time, we'd be better off wearing spider webs. Though I got to admit, this one in particular is impressive." Aylupa held up the vest for the others to see.

Raba trembled.

Three sinks down, Mitika snorted. "The white-fellas like to see us wear old clothes back to camp. They're such poor-fellas it makes them feel better about themselves. They can't understand that we don't care."

"Well, I care," said Aylupa. "Not about the clothes, but

with having to put up with how the white-fellas think. I'm tired of it. I'm getting out."

"How're you going to do that?" asked Raba. "You aren't done with school yet. They won't let you go."

"They can't get rid of you fast enough if you're pregnant." Raba eyed Aylupa's stomach dubiously.

"Not yet. We haven't lain together enough for a spirit child to come and get built up."

"You and who? Jana? That's who you're betrothed to, isn't it?"

"No. I like Jana, but I want to be with Wanaluma. My folks want me to get out of here as bad as I do, and they're fixing it up with the elders to change the betrothal. They've been letting me and Wanaluma sleep together in their tent when I can get away, but it hasn't been often enough."

"But Wanaluma's only nineteen. He's still got seven or eight years left before he's done with his full initiation and counted as a full man so he can marry."

Aylupa shrugged. "That's all right. We can move in together before that."

Mitika hissed. "I hear Mrs. Durney coming back."

Raba had finished washing another piece, a knit shirt. She hurriedly held it up to Aylupa to show her more lacey perforations.

Aylupa laughed. "And she said you weren't working strong enough. But she won't notice on those clothes, you'll see."

The missionary sorted through their work. She didn't give Raba's a second glance.

Relieved, Raba turned and bent to put her pieces in carrying baskets to take out to dry.

She heard a sharp, enraged intake of breath. Before she could turn to see what had happened there was a strong whack to her rear and she was sent sprawling into the wet laundry. Entangled, she couldn't get a purchase on anything to right herself. She finally twisted around, her blouse pulled out of her skirt, her skirt riding up on her hips. One of the scabs on her stomach had been abraded off and was beginning to ooze. Hovering over her was the blotched, heaving, bulging-eyed *Wadjura* face of Mrs. Durney.

"Filth! You people are filth! You can't leave your Devil's-spawn ways back in camp, you have to bring them with you here." She picked up Raba and shook her. "Don't you *ever* do that again." She threw her back into the damp clothes and thundered out of the room.

Lying there, shivering, Raba didn't cry. She felt so cold, as if a wind were blowing through her. She lay there, afraid, not knowing what the slightest movement might bring.

The other girls were laughing; laughing so hard Mitika had sat down, holding her sides, and another girl had tears streaming down her face.

Aylupa pulled her out of the basket, picked her up and hugged her. Between the bigger girl's shaking with laughter and her own trembling, Raba felt almost as though she was still being rattled about by Mrs. Durney.

"Oooh, the look on that woman's face. You all right, Raba?" Not receiving a reply, Aylupa pulled her away a little to get a look at her. "You're not all right. Did she hurt you anywhere?" Instantly sobered, the other girls clustered around in concern.

Raba shook her head.

"You're just scared?"

Raba nodded.

"Do you know what happened?"

Another shake of the head.

"Well, when Mrs. Durney turned around and saw your bare ass shining up at her she just went crazy. The look on her face was the funniest thing I've ever seen."

"I don't understand."

"Well, the one thing white-fellas, especially Christian white-fellas, can't abide is the sight of naked lower parts. So when your skirt hiked up and Mrs. Durney got an eyeful . . . whoo-ee!"

"But in camp I don't wear nothing most of the time."

"That's camp, although the white-fellas don't like it there either. But this is here. You've got to understand, Raba, that this is a taboo for them, just like we've got our own taboos. And most of the time theirs don't make any sense to us and ours don't make any sense to them."

"So what am I supposed to do? Never bend over? Never walk in a full wind?"

"No, just open your eyes when you wake up in the morning and see how everyone else is dressing."

Raba looked blank.

"You know—those little white pants they gave you a pile of when you first got here? You put them on under everything, just like everyone else does."

"Who else?"

The older girls looked at each other. Mitika started giggling.

"You mean *none* of the first-graders are wearing their underpants?"

"Nobody told us. We thought they were little pairs of shorts for wearing back to camp. Who'd be dumb enough to wear white shorts?"

"Those stupid white-fellas didn't think to tell you. Used to be the first and second yearers were in the same dorm room together, so you'd find out from the older kids. Then as more people came in from the Outback, they built our dorm; the big girls' house. Then all the other grades got their own rooms separate."

"Why've you got your own house?"

"They think it makes it easier to keep an eye on us, keep us away from the boys."

"Does it?"

"Yeah, some. But we still get to go back to camp anyway, although they keep trying to keep us busy with chores. Hey, Raba, you want to help me?"

"Sure."

"Next weekend there's going to be a big Corroboree. The poor-fellas were going to try to keep us in the dorm, but the elders have invited them to come watch the dancing after the rites, so they're going to let us attend. They figure they can keep an eye on us easy. Wanaluma and me are going to go off together somehow. We're thinking up a plan, and you can help, too, if you want to."

Included in the big girls' plots! Raba grinned, forgetting Mrs. Thompson's twisted white face, Mrs. Durney's red one, and her sore rear end. "Oh, yes, that would be fair dinkum."

After they'd hung the laundry to dry, Raba was told by one of the teachers that she was to be punished for indecency. She was not allowed to return to camp that day and would have to spend the afternoon alone in the first-year dorm room.

She hung her head, having learned since starting school that looking ashamed was a useful tool. She scuffed her feet slowly all the way back to the dorm. By the time she got there everyone else had already left. She was glad, because she wouldn't have liked to have hidden from her friends how relieved she was that she had a day off from the ordeal of returning to camp. Since she'd awakened that morning a month ago in a small, spare infirmary room, she'd felt differently about camp and the desert.

She found the pile of underpants that none of them had been wearing and put on a pair. Lying down on her cot for a while she wriggled around, not sure if she liked them for their smooth texture and roominess or disliked them for binding at the waist.

She got up and went to the window. It faced the boys' dorm. Huroo was out there on his hands and knees, weeding the scruffy flower patches surrounding the building. From the way his shoulders hunched and the stiff way he held his body, Raba guessed that he, too, was being punished. She watched him until he slowly disappeared around the corner of the building.

She wandered between the beds and explored the dresser drawers. Jayulya's mother had given Jayulya a comb of sugar-bag in a jar. Raba helped herself to a chunk of it. She found a picture book of animals Djilbara had given her under Marindi's pillow. She sat for a while looking at it.

She heard the doorknob turn and a single person enter, but she didn't look around. A weight settled beside her on the bed. After a bit a pale arm passed in front of her and turned the page. "These animals here live in a land called Africa. They're called antelope," Miss Landell said quietly. "Antelope," Raba repeated.

They looked at pictures of creatures from Africa, India, Asia, and the Americas. Miss Landell would tell her the names and sometimes she'd repeat them. But when they got to the pages of animals from Australia, Raba fell silent, just touching the pictures with her finger as Miss Landell said their names. Eventually Miss Landell left as quietly as she'd come. Raba browsed through the book for a while longer and then replaced it under the pillow, thinking to herself that Miss Landell seemed nice for a white-fella, even if she was all mixed-up and didn't know the right names for the Willy-wagtail, the carpet snake, the kangaroo, and the others.

She was sitting back on her own bed, humming, trying to

remember the words to the songs the big girls had been singing, when her classmates returned from camp. Marindi was excited.

"You should have seen what we just seen, Raba. Your momma got worried when you didn't come home today. Aylupa told her that Mrs. Durney had hit you and pushed you and shook you. Your momma took a stick and found Mrs. Durney at the mission store. She was yelling at her for a long time, shaking that stick at her. She say she tired of the Christian white-fellas messing with you. She say if Mrs. Durney ever hit you again, she'll find Mrs. Durney and hit her with the stick. Auntie Djilbara and Migay had to drag her off, finally. What's this all about?"

Raba's mouth hung open in surprise for a moment. Then, with a screech, she pounced on Marindi and pulled off her skirt. Looking at her as if she'd gone mad, Marindi tried to fend her off. Whirling around, Raba lifted up her own skirt to show off the underpants. "That's what it's all about. Look at you and look at me. Those Christian white-fellas are crazy. That's what we're here to learn about." And she explained the rest. But as the other girls rifled through the pile of underwear, Raba sat down by herself and tried to picture her soft-spoken, calm, strong mother in the scene at the mission store.

Chapel was in the mission church. The boys sat on one side and the girls on the other. Sometimes Chapel was the white-fellas lecturing them on how to act or not act. Other times it was storytelling from the Christian white-fella book. Today the reverend told them the tale of the miracle of the loaves and the fishes. Raba sat enthralled. What a grand Corroboree!

Walking with Huroo to the dining hall afterwards, she was enthused. "Wasn't that a good story, Huroo? What a great sharing! Their Jesus-fella must be the dinkumest!"

Uncharacteristically, Huroo scowled at her. "That's all lies, Raba. If *they* want something they call it sharing. If *you* need something they call it stealing. I was hungry after class and they'd sent me to the kitchen for chores. I took a bun to eat and big Mr. Thompson came up and said I was a thief. He made me stay and work all the rest of the day without going back to camp so I wouldn't do it again. Our stories are better. The white-fellas should hear about Wata-urdli, who turned the two dead, starved little 'roos his selfish sons gave him as his share into two whole flocks of fat living ones to punish them for not sharing."

Raba studied Huroo covertly. He was so pretty, with thick eyelashes and long legs for a boy his age. He would be tall, as the Emu he was grew up inside of him. And she could see that he would be more than that, too. His spirit would be a deep, cool well in this parched land, the kind of place that the *Wanambis*, the Rainbow Serpents, came to to rest and replenish their wisdom.

She took his hand in hers and wiggled her fingers between his until they were entwined.

"Don't be angry, Huroo."

He looked at her shyly. "I'm not angry at you, Raba."

On a Friday afternoon a week later, Raba trudged back to camp, surrounded and camouflaged by merrier classmates. As she always did when she left the mission, she felt slightly queasy. It came from a muffledness that seemed to have its sources deep within her, but which extended beyond her like the fur of a 'roo. The sensation of her bare feet touching the sand was removed, as if she was still wearing mission shoes. Somewhere inside, though, she clutched a hard, smooth resolve. *I must go home to help Aylupa at the Corroboree*, she thought.

The noisy mob passed a seated clump of elders, who were playing cards and avidly discussing religious points of the ritual tonight. As the children passed, one of them raised his head into the hot, slight breeze, like a dingo who's caught a scent of prey. Raba found herself instinctively hunching down smaller in the middle of the group.

They came upon some older boys already busy painting themselves for the dances they would participate in. The younger boys shed their mission clothes on the spot to be decorated, too. For a few minutes the girls lingered, offering their opinions and artistic advice. As they left Raba caught a glimpse of Huroo with his head in Djura's lap, laughing at the cool sliminess of white pipe-clay being applied to his forehead in a criss-cross design by the older boy.

Only Marindi and Raba were left, arms around each other's waist, by the time they approached their homes at the southern end of camp. Marindi's family lived in an old-style brush shelter.

"Raba, what's wrong? You're never happy anymore."

Raba leaned her head on her friend's shoulder, and struggled to find words. She knew that there had been a time when she hadn't been sad, when the camp and the Outback had been joy and life to her, but she couldn't really remember what that had felt like. She wanted to say that there was a promise; she was caught in this dullness waiting for it to come true. But she couldn't have said what the promise was or who had made it. Something in the warmth and weight of Marindi's encircling arm, the hardness of her shoulder, sank down past Raba's invisible barrier, and an aching soreness came rushing up to meet it. She realized with startled gratitude that she was about to cry, and that that would feel sharp, real, and good.

"You two look like the two sisters pursued by the hero Ngurunderi, turned to stones by him in the Great Water."

Marindi jumped. Djilbara had come up silently behind them.

"Auntie Djilbara, Raba's been . . ." Marindi began.

"Yes, I know," Djilbara said, drawing Raba to her. The child clutched her about the waist, burying her face in the woman's shift. "Raba's been sick." She winked at the other girl. "She might even be sick again tonight. That would be too bad. Someone would have to take her home and miss the fun."

"Oh yes. I forgot." Marindi gave a knowing laugh, and then ran home.

Having diverted Marindi, Djilbara turned her attention to Raba.

"Auntie, it's not supposed to be like this," came the muffled voice at her hip. Raba started to sob.

"I know, little one, I know."

But Djilbara didn't know what to do about it. Should she unsing and unwalk the web, exposing all that shining, unprotected latent talent? Until something changed, Djilbara dared do nothing. Every night she went searching in her dreams for answers, and in all her travels had not met up with a single spirit. It was strange how empty and barren her sleeping landscape had become.

"Come with me, Raba. I'll make you some herb tea and then walk you to your mother's." The herb tea would have seeds that numbed and a good dose of rum to calm the child enough to endure the ceremony that night.

At dusk the camp made its way in twos and threes, family

by family, to the desert at its western edge. There the middle-aged men had been clearing the area for a dance ground and campfire all morning. Designated ritual cooks of both sexes had been baking tubers and batter breads there through the afternoon. The odor had been sweetly tormenting the camp. Mapping out a pattern on the ground with ochre oxide, the elders indicated where the various clans should sit. In the dark and excitement it would be unseemly if a man found himself close enough to one of his "mother-in-laws" to speak to her. With this arrangement the various moeties were ritually safe, and Dreamtime patterns reinforced.

Raba sat with a group of children at the edge of the campfire. In back of them were rows of women. Sleepy and numb from Djilbara's drugs, she felt removed enough to enjoy the proceedings.

Three men, each playing a *didjeridu* longer than themselves, led the singers and drummers with their sonorous cadences. There were some casual, ribald, taunting dances between various "husbands" and "wives" groups. Talbiri and her mother, Kultuwa, mimicked their way through a "scolding set" in one of these that had her actual father, Waku, newly home from stockwork, hugging himself and crying with laughter.

The *didjeridu* picked up a new melody-line; their song became both haunting and heraldic. Some of the women rose to their feet with a formal, ululating cry.

Flanked by their attendant elder tutors, the five new initiates loped into the clearing, back from their month-long trek in the desert. Heads down, bodies painted, they stamped their feet in a sort of shuffling dance. Raba grinned to herself. They all moved rather gingerly, especially Wooleroo. When they pounded their spear butts on the ground, the little boys leapt from their place by the campfire with excited yells. That was the signal for their welcoming dance. Surrounding the initiates they spun and leapt about them. Firelight strobed and licked their brown, black, and white patterned forms. The initiates towered above them, their sojourn away seeming to have spurred their growth.

Their actual and clan mothers stood up together and sang a melody both doleful and joyous, greeting them as new men and bidding farewell to them as children. More than one of the women was weeping when they sat down again.

There was a lull in the ceremonies as the new young men stiffly greeted their families, accustoming themselves to the formal relations they would have with their relatives under the clan taboos. Gone was their casual, childhood freedom. Gifts were given to sponsors and tutors, camp gossip caught up on.

A single drum began a beat, and everyone looked up to see a man standing alone in the middle of the clearing. They gradually quieted. Assured of their attention, he began a chanting songline.

> *I am Kakan*
> *Of the Grass Seed Clan*
> *Born on the Path of the Two Men in the north*
> *Here visiting with you now*
> *At a time when the Grass Seed sprouts*
> *Far from my own land.*
> *I am the keeper of the sacred,*
> *The Grass Seed waits on me*
> *And I must do my duty*
> *Or the Grass Seed will not grow*
> *And will hide itself from my family*
> *And all the other creatures.*

He went on to ask the camp's aid in helping him perform an increase ceremony, so that he would not be remiss in his duties even so far from home.

The old men nodded approval of his rendition. They had spent the last few nights and days with him, dreaming and comparing their dreams to create a proper song for his petition.

They sang a chorus querying if he had attended his home increase site properly in the past year. He chanted that he had, mentioning cleaning it and making appropriate sacrifices, without going into any secret-sacred details.

They sang back welcoming him and pledging the camp's support in this endeavor as part of the maintenance of the Dreamtime. They asked if he'd brought the necessary sacred objects with him. He replied that he had. The old men sang that they would bring forth their own power objects to bind to his for the task.

At that point the songline was interrupted. Makwora, grizzled and lame, faced the contingent of women.

"Sacred objects are going to be brought forth. So as not to offend our ancestors and interrupt the Dreamtime, and to save yourselves from death, all children under the age of initiate, and all women, must hide their sight."

Blankets were brought from waiting piles and stretched tentlike over the clumps of women and children. Edges were tucked tightly under arms and legs.

Through blankets and past the rustling of the other children, Raba could hear the muffled continuation of the songline.

Kakan chanted for a long time the ancestral tale of the Grass Seed; how his family had come to be its ritual caretakers. He sang of its virtues to man and beast, and its place in the Dreamtime.

Feeling a faint chiming in her bones, Raba knew some sacred objects had been brought forth by the man. They felt very far away, echoing the distance they had come.

The elders announced that to do the rite properly it would be necessary to both go to the site and to bring it here. The whole camp would have to be taken dream-walking. They would act as guides and "carry" the camp.

Raba gasped as she felt more sacred objects emerging from their storage places. These were dangerous, glowing, and had been loaded with power. She knew they sensed her, and if they pointed towards her they would . . . but the old men aimed them over the horizon towards the north, and fired them. The power streamed away, gathering up the camp in its momentum and drawing it along its path. All of the children involuntarily shuddered as, without moving from their places under the blankets, they felt themselves walking along that pathway, now traced inside themselves. They stretched out along its arc, slowing as they reached its zenith, then gaining momentum and weight as they crested down the other side. At the same time they felt the other place rising up to meet them. The camp condensed with this place, and a wave of subtly different scents washed over them; the balance of iltjota grass much stronger, more moisture in the air, less of the pungency of gum and acacia. The camp settled in this place, gaining solidity.

Smelling also the sharpness of small, bright lights, Raba knew that more sacred objects had emerged, these drawn forth from small dilly bags. Directed by the men, these scattered over the ground, sinking their energy down into the soil, seeking the dormant grass seeds. Their high-pitched song matched their brightness as they called forth the spirit of the grasses to rise and join them in the sun for yet another year.

Wandering in their task, some of them found Raba.

Raba, why are you hiding from us? We can see you only dimly. Why are you all wrapped up?

Everybody little has to hide under the blankets, she thought back at them.

We can see you there clearly enough. But you're wrapped up in paths as tight as a cocoon. You should be out among us. Brilliance started cutting edges around her. A sensation of fresh clean air flushed against her, and she realized that her skin felt and smelled crusty and stale. A dull pulse started in her midriff and she remembered. *I'm wrapped up to protect me. I was hurt.*

Don't be afraid, the lights soothed. *You've outgrown these bandages, you're swelling against them. You must come out. Everything will heal in time.*

As Raba emerged from a month's isolation she alternately chilled and burned. Sweating, she blindly struggled to find Djilbara under the blankets. She crawled over other children, who protested, and under adult legs.

"What are you doing, little one?" a woman asked.

"Where's Auntie Djilbara?"

"Raba's feeling sick," another voice said. Raba sensed Djilbara moving towards her from the other end of the blankets. "Wait here for her. I didn't think you were supposed to be 'ill' until just before the white-fellas come."

Djilbara reached Raba and held her. The protection she had woven for the child had been cut and was slipping away, strand by strand. In fear she wrapped as much of her own body around Raba as possible, a physical block to the old men's inner sight. But even as she did so she could feel that some of their attention was distracted from the ceremony and turning this way, seeking.

"Raba, what happened?"

"The lights came and took me out."

Djilbara cast herself into the night and found, at last, the spirits she'd been seeking the last month.

She's been chosen. Would you endanger her?

She has indeed been chosen. Woman, are your fears greater than your faith? Do you hold your own powers, or the old men's, to be greater than ours? Raba is part of the Land now, and we and the Land will teach her and protect her.

Djilbara returned to the little girl. "Raba, can you talk to me at all?" she whispered. She was answered with a nod. "Those lights—if you could hold them in your hand, what would they look like, feel like?"

Imagining one in her hand, Raba felt its weight and shape. In her mind's eye she opened her fingers and looked at it closely. She whispered back, "It's a stone, Auntie; smooth and rounded with a pattern on it." Djilbara's grip on her tightened: an ancestor stone, the place where the souls of the powerful sometimes lived after their deaths.

"There's something else, Auntie." She pulled Djilbara's head down even closer to her. Even so, Djilbara could scarcely hear her. "You know how the old men tell us that we have to hide under the blankets because there are things that would hurt or kill us?" She paused. "Well, that's true of some of the things. But there are other things—the stones, the lights, I mean, that *want* to see us. I think . . ." she could hardly make herself say the words, ". . . I think the old men don't want us to see the lights or the lights to see us because we'd recognize each other. And that would be good. So why don't they want us to?"

"I think you're right," Djilbara replied. "I promise that I'll tell you someday." They felt a lurch. The men were beginning to pull them back along the path, arm over arm, with all the strength of their souls.

When the camp had returned to the mission site, the last of the songline was sung, tethering things back in place. Runners were sent to the mission to let the white-fellas know that they could come watch the rest of the dancing and join in the feasting if they wished to (which they wouldn't, of course). The blankets were drawn from the women and children and folded. Raba by now was so chilled her teeth were chattering. One of the women held aside a blanket to wrap her in. Much to-do was made of her being ill.

"She needs to be taken home," said Kultuwa.

Aylupa was instantly there. "I'll take her back and stay

with her." She picked up the child and murmured in her ear, "Raba, you've done such a good job of pretending to be sick."

Djilbara gripped Aylupa's shoulder. "She really is sick. Go on with your plans, but don't stray too far from her tent."

Huroo was tugging at her elbow, his body paint streaked and smudged. "Can I go, too, Mother Djilbara?"

"That's a good idea. That way you can come and get me if I'm needed."

The missionaries were beginning to arrive at the Corroboree. Passing them on the way out, Aylupa explained the situation to them. "Raba took sick, so Huroo and I are going to take her home and watch over her." Knowing of Raba, the white-fellas gave them a wide berth.

The three of them passed through the silent, deserted camp. Halfway to their destination a tall shadow slipped from behind one of the dwellings and joined them, Wanaluma. Taking Raba from Aylupa he carried her the rest of the way. He laid her down in the tent, still wrapped in the blanket. Huroo curled up next to her. Aylupa and Wanaluma left, and the two children dozed off to soft murmurs and moans from behind the tent.

Later, while the rest of the camp still feasted, Djilbara silently followed three old men who had slipped away from the proceedings. As she feared, they made straight for Raba's home.

Makwora pulled aside the tent flap and the other two men entered. One of them gently disengaged the sleeping Huroo's arm from its protective embrace around Raba's neck. Then, drawing away the blanket, he exposed her stomach. Makwora opened the tent flap wide to cast as much light from the night sky as possible onto Raba. He looked at her for a long while, then shook his head.

"I would have sworn on my ancestor's soul that there was a new *maban* in the camp tonight, and that the source was this child." He patted his stomach, where his own *maban*, power object, resided. "But it is plain to the sight I was wrong. Of late there has been so much confusion, as if there were turmoil in the Dreamtime. Perhaps I am getting too old to see the signs anymore. I'm sure there is something, but we will have to look elsewhere."

As they left Djilbara trembled with relief, and wanted to laugh at the irony. Raba's damaged, incompleted midriff had saved her. If the old man had looked at her anywhere else, had really tried to perceive, he would have seen that the entire rest of the child was now *maban*.

She went in and resettled the children.

Red Rocks Trek
1952

Raba perched high on the red stone outcropping. Behind her a cliff tucked inwards, shading her from the sun's scorch, but radiating a slow warmth from its own morning basking. It was striped in ragged mineral banners of ochre, burgundy, and charcoal gray. Raba could feel the sensation of the colors on her back as ripples of light. She gazed over the landscape in front of her: a jumble of boulders etched like lace, leaping stone monoliths, undulating gorges. The ancestors must have been transformed here in the middle of dancing.

If she had been back at the mission camp, from the vantage point of the sand ridges she would have been looking out over a gibber plain, its flat surface dotted with spinifex and round stones. The smell would be of pleasant dustiness even when there was no wind, what with the coming and going of trucks, dogs, and the people in the camp. Here the smell was the clean dryness of dustless stone threaded with a secret wetness of waterholes deep within the rock.

Although she had been here only twice before, this place, this area, felt more like home to her than the camp. She had been conceived and born near here. Who knew how long her spirit had lived here before attaching itself to her parents?

She stretched her legs out over pleasurably rough sandstone, fascinated with their new length. She had grown considerably in the three years since starting mission school, but never so much as the last few months. At night she could hear her bones growing, making soughing sounds as they breathed in, then expanding with each exhalation.

Raba knew that it was her new growth that was responsible for this trek so far from camp. All the families still went out wandering together several times a year, but rarely for longer than the three weeks it took to run out of the staples they had grown so fond of: tea, sugar, tobacco, and flour. So to come so far, to her birthplace, with Djilbara in attendance, had to mean that the journey was for her.

She was a little excited, wondering what was to come, but not nervous. She was surprised at not being nervous; she probed and poked inside of herself trying to find where the nervousness was, waiting to spring out at her. But it wasn't there. Instead she found inside a feeling of traveling, as if her feet were coming down, one foot in front of the other in a natural continuity, each moment growing calmly from the last.

A breath of wind—only felt, not heard—flowed through rock channels and up past her. She was not surprised when it was followed by the lazy voice of its owner.

"Little one, what are you doing away from your guardians?"

"I have permission to go explore, and do chores later. Everyone else wanted to nap after our journey."

She could feel a *Wanambi* uncoil from the gorge below her and rise invisibly up into the air, swimming on its currents. "You dare much to come here. Not so many years from being a woman and so close to my waterhole. You must know that is forbidden."

"I'm nowhere near your waterhole. It's up and around the cliff behind me, beyond the crevasse, and hidden in a deep chamber."

"If you know that much, then you must have been there."

"I took care to know where it was so I wouldn't go there."

Raba tracked its voice. She was beginning to be able to see it. The sun reflected watery glints off its scales. She could make out its full serpentine length, its beard, its mane.

"Don't you have the sense to be afraid of me? I am *Wanambi*."

"I can see that. But I have broken no taboos, and I belong here as much as you do. Besides, you're too thin and transparent to be able to eat me. You look like broken pieces of the white-fellas' windowpanes."

"No. From here you're the one that's transparent—a crystalline child. You couldn't begin to make a meal for me."

Holding out an arm in protest to demonstrate her solidity,

she saw that when the *Wanambi* undulated in a certain way, at a certain angle, that she did catch glimpses of dense, opaque muscle coursing through real water, not air. She lowered her arm, at last a little frightened.

"Where are you?"

It laughed. "Right in front of you, of course. This is my home."

"But it's different there," she insisted.

"Like you, I'm a traveler. But I'm surprised that you can see."

"How can you be traveling? You just said this was your home."

"Yes, and I never leave my home. But there are many ways to travel, not just from place to place in a line. I'm one of those who travel between places and between times. To me, you and your people look like ghosts, although I gather that's not your perception. I must say, though, that the more I look at you the less like a ghost you appear. You remind me a little of the *Inapatua*."

Raba stiffened in indignation. The *Inapatua* were embryonic rocklike creatures that eventually had become men and women in the Dreamtime. "I do not look like an *Inapatua*. I'm becoming very tall, not like a lump at all."

The *Wanambi* laughed again. "Well, maybe not just like the *Inapatua*. But you do have that same look of becoming something. I think, like me, you'll be one of those to travel the in-betweens someday."

"You said there were others. You mean the other *Wanambis*?"

"Yes, of course, all of my kind. But others besides, who travel in even different ways."

"Who are they?"

"Perhaps you will meet them." The *Wanambi* turned, wending away from her down through the rock channels.

"Where are you going?"

"I'm hungry now." It teased her. "And you aren't substantial enough for me to feed upon."

"Don't leave yet. Give me a song to take back."

"Do you have a song for me, little one?"

Raba was ashamed. "No, but I will bring you one someday."

"When you have one for me, I will share one with you.

But do not approach me once you are a woman, not on this side of the Dreamtime."

It faded farther away, then turned to consider her for a moment. "I do have a thought for you. You have the smell of these rocks. I'm sure if I tried long enough I would remember you. You seem to have carried yourself in mostly one piece from life to life." And then it was gone.

Her family had camped at the base of the *Wanambi's* escarpment in a cottonwood surrounded creek soak. Returning, she found her father making a campfire, taking care that no smoke blew back up into the rock formations, a taboo. Kultuwa and Djilbara were cleaning fish and freshwater mussels from the creek to cook over the coals when the fire burnt down. Flicking silvery scales with their fingertips at Dhuma and Balayang, Raba's younger brothers, they laughed as the boys flinched away from them.

The fire started, Waku called his three children to help set up brush shelters. He braced fallen branches into the sandy soil of the banks of the soak, pushing them in hard, pressing them this way and that till he was assured that they were sturdy. He wove lighter branches between them for a roof. Then he instructed the youngsters to pile grasses and shed-debris in a thick mat on top of that. The boys could only reach the lower edges. Raba started where they left off, and her father finished the highest parts. On the inside, though, the structure was so low that he had to stoop to enter it. Dhuma and Balayang scooped up the sand there to soften it, then smoothed it down to a reasonable evenness. "There," Waku said with satisfaction. "No more naps in just rock shade; a softer sleep with some breeze off the water to cool us."

After supper Waku built up the fire again and they all sat around it singing children's songs. It burned cleanly, without smoke, so all that Raba could smell of it was the pure hot scent of the wood.

Winking at her, Waku stirred the fire. A spray of sparks erupted. "So, little miss, you think this journey was made for you, do you? Well, it was time for me to start teaching the boys hunting."

Holding her head towards the fire, she glanced at him out of the corner of her eye, not taking the bait. He'd already begun teaching her brothers how to hunt, and there was no need to go so far away from the mission camp for that reason.

He grinned at her lack of reaction. "Well, the real truth is that your mother's the reason we made this trip. Just like it was because of your mother that we had to return here when you were born, after having spent so much time here just nine months before that. I seem to spend my life pleasing that woman." This time the side-long glance was his, directed at Kultuwa, who acknowledged it with a stifled smile.

"She said when she picked up your spirit that it was very clear that you would be stronger if we returned for your birth to your *djibija* place, so that it would be as if you'd come from here twice. But I think it was really because she has such a fondness for freshwater mussels."

Kultuwa blushed. It was true that she'd eaten more steamed shellfish than any of them.

He picked up a stick and leaned across to tap Raba on the hand with it. "So never think that anything is just for you. There's always more to it."

Later, the rest of the family retired to the shelter to sleep, glad to be settled at the end of the long trekking. Djilbara and Raba went walking, their path echoing the creek's course. The space between them felt as concrete and alive as their own bodies. When they spoke, it was as if it were an attentively listening third person. Noticing this before on occasion, Raba had asked Djilbara about it.

"Of course, it's listening. The air itself is a spirit," was her reply.

Now her aunt said, "Today you saw a Rainbow Serpent." It was a statement of fact.

Raba nodded, trusting Djilbara to feel the affirmation.

"You must have acted properly. You're still alive. Did you ask it for a dance or song?"

"Yes, but it gave me a thought instead." Raba told her the *Wanambi's* words.

"Raba, do you know what that means?"

"No, Auntie. Do you?"

Djilbara started to speak, hesitated, then said, "You know already that you come from here. As for the rest, you will have to learn to see, to understand it."

In the morning Raba woke with a hunger for antbed chunks and *nardoo*, seed damper. She moped about the cottonwood tree the food stores were hung from, waiting to help with breakfast preparation. With the songs and touches she had learned when smaller, she scooped a little of the gruel on her fingers and smeared dabs on first Balayang and then Dhuma's forehead, nose, chest, and stomach. Giving them their bowls, she returned to her mother with her own bowl to be filled.

Kultuwa shook her head. "Only the men will eat today. We must get ready to go."

Raba's eyes widened. Her stomach contracted as she watched her brothers and father eat, the golden food sliding down, glowing and absorbing into their bodies. She felt shrunken and cranky. When Kultuwa turned her back, she moved to plunge her fingers into the pot. Djilbara's hand gripped her wrist.

"No, try to feel light and clean," she advised.

Digging sticks and dilly bags in hand, they left the campsite. Kultuwa led the way, then Raba, and Djilbara brought up the rear. Cutting away to the southwest, away from the creek's meanderings and the base of the stone escarpment, they passed first over a downward-sloping rock plain. Where it began to drop away into a series of more cliffs, they scrambled down a shallow fissure.

This was the beginning of what might have been described as an actual trail, carving its way through uptilted layers of shingled stone; past copses of casuarina trees hidden in secret valleys, their roots searching thirty feet deep to subsurface wells.

Looking at her mother's back in front of her, feeling Djilbara behind her, Raba knew that they were not there yet; they were just approaching their travels. When they at last intersected with the path they were seeking, she felt it as a blow of recognition: her empty stomach thudded with a strong pulse, responding to the familiarity they'd just stepped upon. Both the stomach and the trail echoed each other's emptiness. Ceasing to think, she became walking. Soon she was leading the group, unaware of Djilbara and her mother watching, studying her. At times the path could not be seen to the two grown women's eyes—they seemed to be wandering aimlessly. But Raba could feel it continuing—sometimes up at throat level in the air, other times deep in the earth, through the solid rock, and their feet traced its pattern on the surface of the ground.

At one point she heard her mother make a noise way back in her throat, could feel her trailing behind. She turned to look, and her mother's eyes said urgently, *"Here, it was here."* Kultuwa was standing by a cluster of three boulders that formed a sort of chair. The lowest one was smoothly indented on top. The second curved upwards from it at a comfortable angle, the third provided a backrest and shade. It was a natural place for a woman tired from gathering food to stop and rest. Raba shook her head. "I know, I know," she said impatiently. This was where her infant spirit had come to Kultuwa to be accepted. "But that's not the most important place," and she continued on.

They snaked along a seam up the side of a gorge. Raba only stopped when they reached a ledge that overlooked a flood wash. Although now dried up, there was still enough moisture down there for reeds to survive. "Here." It was too narrow for her to turn and speak to her mother. "This is where I first saw you. This is where *I* knew, and chose. The other place was where you knew and chose, later."

"This ledge disappears. We can't continue," said Djilbara. "Let's go down there and talk." Kultuwa was staring down at the reeds. Raba knew that the path did continue; into the solid rock, then through the air over the gap between the next canyons, and on for a very long way.

Among the reeds they sat for a while, unspeaking. Coolness from the moisture still in the ground rose and washed along the back of their legs.

"I remember," Kultuwa finally spoke. "I was so pleased to find this reed bed. I came another way." She pointed. "From where the boulder seat was. That season there was still water. I filled my seed bag with reeds for weaving . . ."

"And roots for eating," Raba continued for her. "I was watching you."

Her mother shook her head and stared at her. "I've never known anyone to remember so clearly. There should be just bits and dreams. I should have had to show you where it happened."

They sat in silence a while longer.

"The path you chose coming here; how did it feel to you?" Djilbara asked the girl.

"It felt strong, but hollow, empty. Like a mussel shell after its owner is gone." Raba shot her mother a sly glance.

"Raba, do you know what your name means?"

"Of course." Raba smiled, and automatically her hands flew up to waggle by her ears. "Kangaroo ears."

"What else? It means something else."

She thought a while before it came to her. "The thread crosses we use in rituals, the littlest ones."

Djilbara nodded. "The patterns in the crosses, the length and color of the threads used, form maps. Each thread cross shows a way, and is itself a path. When your mother came to me, pregnant, I named you—guessing. I *know* what you are now. Now we can truly start teaching you.

"Your mother and I are going to start a fire and get a billy boiling for tea. I want you to look around until something speaks to you . . . as an old friend. Something that asks you to take it home with you. Something that misses you and that will someday want to work with you."

Kultuwa rubbed sparks from fire sticks while Djilbara gathered kindling and Raba wandered. A small blaze started, and Kultuwa sighed. "I hope for our sakes that a large boulder doesn't turn out to have been her best friend in her last dreaming-life."

But when Raba returned she shyly showed them an age-smoothed knot of mulga wood. "It sang to me," she told them.

Several mornings later, Waku called for a break in the routine their days had taken since arriving at the creek soak. Each day Raba, Djilbara, and Kultuwa disappeared together. Whatever direction they set off in, he took the boys out for hunting lessons in the opposite one.

This morning, though, he and Kultuwa gathered up some food in a dilly bag and made ready to go.

"Where are we going today?" Dhuma asked, gathering up his spear and stone knife.

"You aren't going anywhere," Waku replied.

Dhuma set his things down. "Well, where are you going, then?"

"Hunting," his father said. Dhuma turned to pick up his weapons again. "Without you. Your mother and I are going hunting together . . . to see if we can flush up another Raba-spirit," Waku continued, winking at Kultuwa.

"Oh, that." Dhuma snorted in disgust. And he was tired of all the attention that Raba was getting. After they'd left he said sourly, "It's not as if they don't do it all the time anyway."

Raba and Djilbara looked at each other. "I'm sure you'll find it much more interesting yourself in a number of years," Djilbara told him.

Her father had been half-joking; still, Raba cast her senses out. It would be nice to have a sister, especially from here. It might be another old friend. But though there were spirits enough nearby, none were looking for a new home.

"Any luck?" her aunt asked.

"No." Raba shook her head. "They'll just have to have a good time trying."

Later that afternoon the boys splashed in the pond. Floating on their stomachs on makeshift rafts, they stalked each other in water wars. Djilbara and Raba took to the shallows, out of their way. The older woman lay on her back between Raba's legs with her head in the girl's lap. Combing her fingers through her aunt's hair, Raba worked free strands from the matted clumps. They had all been neglecting their grooming the last few days.

They talked about people in the camp. Djilbara asked her questions about the mission school. They were laughing about some of the schoolboys' pranks and fights when Djilbara turned the questions back onto Raba.

"Do you remember when you blacked Huroo's eye last year?"

Raba hung her head. The original quarrel had been with Guwara, but it was Huroo she had finally been angry with. Guwara was bragging about going on Walkabout in a few more years. The other boys hooted at him, pointing out that they would all be going on Walkabout eventually. When Raba chimed in, he had a diversionary target.

"Not you, Raba. You're a girl."

"You're stupid, Guwara. The whole camp goes on Walkabout together." She wasn't really peeved—she knew he was just making noise, and that he wasn't really even thinking of her.

But then Huroo had cut in, and that was different. He was quiet and serious. "He's right, Raba. You don't get to go on Walkabout—not on the initiation one. That's the important one." He looked at her with a wondering pity, noticing for the first time the gap between them. Knowing for the first time that their experiences would diverge and they would be like separate kinds of animals, foreign to each other.

She saw that look and understood it with a pain that reached right through her. And rejected it.

"You're a liar! You're a liar!" She flung herself on him, punching as hard as she could. Shocked and caught off guard, he'd fallen straight down, with her still on top flailing away. The other boys pulled her off and held her. Blood streaked his face from a shallow cut, his eye was swelling shut, but he still looked at her with pity, really seeing her for the first time. "You know, Raba. You do know." And he had walked away.

"He was right," Djilbara said. "I could understand your anger, but not your surprise. You know of no woman from the camp who's ever gone on that kind of Walkabout."

"I'd never thought of myself before as different. Not in that way. Just different in the way that I'm Raba, you're Auntie Djilbara, Balayang is Balayang. And Huroo is Huroo. It was so unfair. All of them acting as if they knew more than me, and that's not true. I know more of who Huroo is than he does."

Making a hushing motion with her hand, Djilbara frowned. That was a subject not to be spoken of.

She lowered her voice. "There is a difference, but not as great a one as the men think. But it's important to let them think that, or we risk losing the little that we have. You know that the men have all the power and interpret the Law. I've been cautioning you for years to be careful, especially around the old men."

"It's bad for the men to have all that and us to have so little. You never told me why," said Raba.

"That's one of the things you're here to learn. What all girls must learn. It's not all the men's doing.

"A long time ago, in the Dreamtime, women had great power and magic. It was stronger than the men's is now. The men didn't like this. We didn't share enough with them. They plotted and stole it away from us. Now we must not look at sacred objects or most ceremonies because we no longer have the power to deal with them, so the magic could harm or kill us. Or worse, it could unbalance our world or the Dreamtime.

"But what the women say and the men won't talk about is that when the men stole from us, the Dreamtime was lost, so they have been punished, too. They flounder and try so hard to understand and interpret the Law, which we all once knew. We have all been punished."

"But the Dreamtime is also now," Raba protested.

"Yes, but not here. Sometimes we live on its edges. We don't know how to truly return to it."

"Then what is the use of all this?" Raba lashed out, flinging an arm to encompass their surroundings. "Why bother to bring me here? Why teach girls anything?" She was close to tears.

Djilbara patted her thigh. "Because we do have some things left. That's what I've been teaching to you all your life. We have to come back slowly with what we have, learn from the past. Learn to share and be whole. When someday we return to the Dreamtime we will be the stronger for it. All of us, the men and the women.

"That's why the mission camp is both a good and a dangerous place for you. The oldest men came out of the desert to the station because of the easy food, and the tea, the sugar, and the white-fella medicine. Coming from many different places and tribes, they brought their sacred objects with them, so the mission is now a place of concentrated power. You can draw from those spirits, but if you fall across the wrong things . . ." (Raba remembered long ago the power boards sensing her just before being fired) ". . . well, if the magic itself doesn't punish you, the old men will. Let them think what they must. That won't stop you from learning. Camouflage yourself a little."

"Will I never get to go on Walkabout?" Raba still looked unhappy.

Djilbara smiled up at her. "Maybe there's things the boys have to go through that we don't, that we have already. And we have other kinds of Walkabouts." She flung her hand, imitating Raba's earlier gesture. "Like this."

Raba was still unsatisfied.

"Maybe you'll get to go on your own Walkabout someday. But you'll be much older—a woman. Maybe with children of your own."

Sitting up, Djilbara stretched. "That's enough. My hair is at least ten times untangled, and you've learned enough for one day. Slip into the water and sneak up like a crocodile on your brothers. They'll enjoy that, and you still need to play. You're not a woman yet."

The day before they broke camp there was little food left. Waku didn't want to bring down something large and have to leave what remained or to carry it. Early that morning Raba woke before the others and gathered up her spear and spear-thrower. A wallaby would be too big, she decided, and a carpet snake would be too small.

Dhuma crawled out of the brush shelter sleepily. "Are you going hunting? Wait for me!"

She gestured him back. "You're not the only ones father taught to hunt. This is my hunt, alone."

Out on the rock plain she found a large Goanna lizard, warming its night-chilled blood in the morning's first light. She moved slowly, like another lizard, standing still as one of the stones whenever it turned its head, until she was close enough. Steadying her body, she slung, killing quickly, as she had many times before.

This time, though, she watched her prey's dying closely. She could see some of its energy, with its blood, sink away into the rocks. Some of it sizzled for an instant on the surface of its skin and then steamed into the air. The hard core of its individuality stayed for a moment, watching her watching it, then slowly relaxed and faded imperceptibly into its flesh.

For the first time she wept after a hunt. Then she picked the lizard up by its tail and carried it back to the campsite for their breakfast.

Damage and Repair

Several months later Raba woke one night tossed by turbulence. Her eyes snapped open and she expected to see her sheet-wrapped form bouncing around the narrow mission school bed.

But everything was still. So still it was as if there was an absence of air. Moonlight lay in curving strips across the sleeping figures of Marindi, Jayulya, and her other classmates. What it didn't illuminate rested in shades of flannel-soft gray. The roiling inside of Raba abruptly receded. Air emptied out of her lungs in a rush. Then the wrenching waves hit her again and she gripped the sides of the bed, seeking a sense of equilibrium. Something was ripping through the Dreamtime. A few of the other girls moaned or turned fitfully, some residue of the disturbance washing up on the shore of their dreams.

Raba staggered from her bed to the window, legs trembling, mind fragmented with shock. Lanterns were being lit in the camp. Someone was reviving the banked campfire. It was too far for her to hear voices, but she sensed the back-and-forth resonances of the elders calling out questions to each other. She pinpointed the knifelike spark of Djilbara rushing through the settlement, answering a confused cry of pain.

Raba stayed by the window for several hours, waiting for answers to come from the activity in camp, waiting for another attack. But the settlement projected as much uncertainty as she felt, and another assault didn't come. She finally crept back to bed to a night of curdled dreamings.

The next morning in school was an exercise in listlessness. "If I didn't know better I'd swear on the Good Book that all the children, from the littlest ones on up, had hangovers," Raba overheard one of the teachers telling another.

In the afternoon Raba worked in the kitchen cleaning lunch dishes as her chore. Aylupa was there, too, washing and peeling vegetables for dinner. She and Wanaluma had two babies already. She hadn't escaped the missionaries completely after all. She worked for them part-time to pay off medicines her children needed.

"I feel so bad today," she told Raba. "And my littlest one was crying all night. Someone must have been messing about in the Dreamtime last night. The old men are upset. They say somebody or somebodies are sending to them from up north. They can't make out what's being said, but whoever it is has been getting closer and closer all day. So I guess we'll find out what the trouble is soon enough."

Raba's shoulders tightened in anxiety. Her father was working up north at Glaryarrie Station. Had her waking last night been in response to danger to him?

She didn't have much time to worry. A few minutes later a jeep came careening past the kitchen window down the main road to the settlement, crammed full of men still in their jackeroo clothing.

Raba expected it to veer off to the camp, but it curved out of their sight to the front of the mission. She and Aylupa looked at each other. They set down their work and raced out of the kitchen.

The jeep was parked right up to the steps of the mission office building. Men were milling on the porch, shouting angrily at the mission director and the reverend. The white-fellas were waving their hands, ineffectually trying to quiet the men. Elders were running up from the camp. Women, both white and black, and a few schoolchildren, were peering from around the corner of the building.

"I can't understand you when you're all speaking at once," the reverend pleaded. "Pick just one of you to tell us what happened. In English."

The men looked at each other and then cleared a space. A man stepped forward. With relief Raba saw that it was her father.

Waku's manner was always lighthearted, almost clowning. But now anger gave him a hard dignity.

"Yesterday after working Mr. Fordham say we have leave to go into that town up there, Coober Downs. He say we have special permission to go to the cinema. He say there be first regular movie, and then another movie, special one that he think we like. So, we go."

The other men nodded in agreement.

"Many black-fellas there, from town and from the sta-tions. First movie was good—American western. Second movie good, too, at first. White-fella elder from big-town school show peoples from Nullarbor Plain. Show how they make things, what they live like, have them tell ancestor tales. All very good, like big-mob sending. But then . . ." he paused, incoherent with fury. "But then they show sacred things, objects and rituals. There were women and children in the audience, who *saw*!

"Why for those white-fellas do that? Now so maybe the spirits come and kill those children who saw? That what the white-fellas want? This new way for white-fella to kill black-fella?"

"But what happened?" the reverend interjected.

"It be all craziness; the Dreamtime angry, people yelling, running, hiding." Raba could picture men bellowing, women frantically trying to hide their own and the children's heads under jackets and clothing. "All men go as fast as they can back to their homes."

"How did you all get here so quickly?" asked the director.

Waku pointed and the men cleared away so that the jeep was visible. "We jump in station jeep and drive all night to get back here to tell you so you stop these other white-fellas. We're proper buggered out."

"Oh my Lord," the reverend said. "Fordham will think they stole it. Quick, John, get him on the line and explain before he calls out warrants on them, if he hasn't already." He turned to the Aborigines. "You may all be in grave trouble because of this."

"No!" said Waku forcefully. "Station black-fellas go back to him to complain, too, very angry. Why he want us to see that film?"

"You don't understand. You drove the jeep here without his permission. He could call the law out on you."

"No. *You* don't understand. All-a-time we work hard to not lose the Dreamtime, to keep the world together for everyone. How we going to do that if you white-fellas break the Law? You wait. By'n'by we get tired and let the whole thing go to hell. You see someday."

The reverend drew in a breath to reply, but the director interrupted him, standing halfway out of the screen door with the phone stretched as far along its cord as it could go. "Edward, I've got Fordham on the line. He wants to talk to you. His blacks are furious, and so is he. Says he had no idea the Anthropology professor who put that film together could be so stupid as to put their ceremonies in."

The reverend started to turn back to the Aborigines, but they were clustered around their elders, talking excitedly in their own language.

The spectators began to disperse back to their work or lessons.

Raba had listened with growing indignation. There were white-fellas with more access to her people's magic than she had, white-fellas who had been trusted to watch the most sacred of ceremonies. The desire to see that film gnawed at her. Someday she would find a way.

For several days after that Djilbara kept her busy. They walked broad patterns over the gibber plains, sang interwoven chants, knotted special dilly bags, and buried them at specific junctions in their wanderings.

"The nets of the Dreamtime were torn and must be retied," Djilbara told her.

Raba could feel other people in other places throughout the Outback working similar repairs.

But before the damage was reversed, while the Dreamtime was still flapping loose and in danger of flying away, Raba felt a large force launch itself through the gap and disappear, leaving a vacuum in its wake. What had that been? Her senses stretched and searched for something missing. The *Wanambis*! The power of their presence was missing. Dangerous as the Rainbow Serpents were, their absence left the structure of reality weakened and fragile. She searched for where they might have vanished to, or some trace of their destructive power of wind and storm. But they were simply gone. She found herself fretting, frightened by this further disruption to life. Djilbara didn't speak of it, but Raba knew she sensed it, too, for her face was always tense and strained.

Two days after that Raba woke to a feeling of wholeness once again. She laughed aloud, looking up at the ceiling of the dorm room, which glowed softly with reflected morning light. The *Wanambis* were back. She didn't know where they had gone to or what they had done, but the satisfaction of discharged power lingered over their place in the Dreamtime. And the fabric of life was knitted back into place.

Apprenticing
1953

It was two months into the new school year and for several weeks the students had been subjected to Mr. Wickham's highly abridged version of medieval history. His classes tended to be tainted with his religious views. Today he was lecturing about the day-to-day life of the average people: ". . . dwellers on the land, peasants, people like you. They were devout and pious; their entire lives centered around duty to God."

The three rows of ten-year-olds, five to a row, nodded, eyes glazed. Mr. Wickham nodded back, beaming.

His words set Raba daydreaming. Mr. Wickham's own ancestors had been people like them, living interwoven with their land and their gods. She wished she could be back in the camp, like the peasants in their villages and fields.

She could be lolling in the dappled shade of the gum trees, her head full of the day's heat, listening to the men telling tales of the Dreamtime. She could be winnowing grass grains with Kultuwa and her clan mothers, learning the song cycles that let the seeds grow, be gathered, eaten, and grow again. Or she could be playing with the rest of her mob, acting out the old tales, boys and girls taking turns at the roles of chorus and actors. Of late, Marindi got to be the sun-woman more than anyone else.

She risked a glance at Marindi. Her friend was already plumping out a little into curves. The older boys, passed through the first stage of initiation, were beginning to defer to her. Raba looked down at her own thin, gangly form. Marindi would go through her women's rites long before Raba.

She struggled to return to attention as the tone of Mr. Wickham's lecture changed.

"Now, I don't want to paint the picture too rosy, here. There were those who secretly coveted traffic with Satan. The righteous had to be continually on their guard. History records the following witch trials in England in . . ."

Again, many of the children nodded. They knew well what happened to women who infringed on men's magic. Raba, however, felt herself drawn from her reverie like a thread being drawn from a spool and passed through the focus of a needle's eye. These were women who had power! They were punished not because they had mistakenly stumbled onto taboos or were seeking to know magic, but because they already knew it. And there were men witches, too, Mr. Wickham admitted, so they must have helped the women learn, as Djilbara was helping her. Where was the looseness in the stern white-fellas culture that had allowed that? She guessed that for them, too, the women had once held the power. She'd always thought that the story of Eve was the white-fella-men's jealous mistelling of the tale.

How could she find out more about these women? Had any of them survived to teach others? Would she know them if she saw them? Would they be well-fatted with reality, instead of flat and insubstantial like all the white-fellas she knew? Would they have anything to teach her? Would there be songs that she could give to them?

A bashful little first-form student brought Mr. Wickham a note at the end of class. The teacher looked at it a moment and then gave it to Raba. So at the end of the school day she met with Miss Landell in the beginner's classroom instead of returning immediately to camp.

The woman smiled warmly at Raba, who was still her favorite. Raba smiled back. She liked Miss Landell, too, who seemed, of all the white-fellas, to be most like a person.

"Raba, you've been given permission to help Djilbara for several days. We don't want you to fall behind in your studies, so I'll be tutoring you when you return. It means you'll have to give up some of your afternoons for studying for about a week."

Raba nodded. She knew that.

"I'll enjoy teaching you again."

"I'll like that, too, Miss Landell."

Tapping the end of her pencil on the desk, Miss Landell's gaze turned inwards. Raba knew that with the white-fellas that meant that they were thinking of what words they would say next.

"I understand that Djilbara is teaching you to be a native healer and women's counselor, like herself."

Raba nodded again, this time warily. Healing was a touchy area with the white-fellas, especially the Christians.

"Well, I think it's wonderful. I think you'll make a fine healer."

Raba blinked in surprise.

"But I'd like you to think of something . . . not something else, but something to go along with that."

Again Raba felt wary.

Miss Landell looked at her, at a loss for words. How do you tell a ten-year-old, no matter how bright, that you feared to lose all that potential in just a few short years? Lost to an adolescence of carousing promiscuously with the boys, and then swiftly after that being married off, more than likely to some withered old man.

But it *would* be in just a few years; three, no more than four. So although it would be too soon for a white child, the time to start acting in Raba's case was now, to at least plant seeds of thought.

"I've seen that the healing that your people do works very well. And I know that your people sometimes think that our medicine is also effective. Even your elders seek out Doctor Blackston for vaccinations and advice. What I wanted you to think about is that you could be both."

"What do you mean?" said Raba.

"Finish up all the way through school here, studying with Djilbara on the side. Then afterwards, you could go to the university in the city. If you studied very hard you could go on to medical school and become a doctor, or at least go to nursing school. When you were all done, you'd come back here and be the best healer anyone in these parts has ever seen, black or white." And, she thought grimly, the church could foot the bill. Raba would have to be ready to be used as a showcase, but it would be worth it.

"I don't think the old men would like that," Raba said.

"Why not? There can be women doctors."

Raba looked at her in frank amazement. She wasn't arguing against that. Even if men held most of the power, there had always been women healers, since the beginning of the Dreamtime. But it was one thing for the old men to go to Doctor Blackston for help with ills caused by white-fella sicknesses or transgressions. It would be a completely different thing to go to one of their own women for the same thing.

"Promise me that you'll think about it," Miss Landell said.

Raba shifted a little from foot to foot, uneasily. "All right, I'll think about it." She *was* thinking about it. If she went to the university maybe she could find out about those other women, the ones Mr. Wickham had been talking about.

Djilbara and Raba left at sunset. The sky cast saturated light back onto the settlement; brassy orange where the sun still touched, glowing purple shadows where it did not. At the southern end, not far past Raba's parents' tent, they came upon some of the older boys and girls starting a campfire, arranging stones in a circle for sitting; already flirting, gliding against each other in their chores as if by accident. Djilbara clapped her hands and coughed as they approached.

"Hmmph!" Raba was disdainful. "Look at that Koolka, still carrying on with Wawi. Since he started initiation she should barely be talking with him, let alone singing at him. She's in his mother-in-law clan."

Djilbara agreed. "I'm afraid if they keep it up, Koolka's going to find herself married off very soon, whether the missionaries object or not."

Wawi heard Djilbara's approach warning, and with a quick whisper to Koolka, the lovers separated to opposite ends of the campsite, averting their faces from each other and Djilbara and Raba.

After they passed the youngsters, Djilbara laughed. "You can always tell when it's the white-fellas' Saturday day. The rest of the week it's just the older boys not in school hanging around together out here, telling tall tales . . . and trying to tell themselves they're having a good time . . . waiting for the girls to be let out."

She looked at Raba. "In a couple of years you'll be out here, too. It's a good time in life."

"And after that they'll marry me off . . ." Raba thought about Miss Landell and the white-fellas university, ". . . maybe to one of those old men."

Djilbara shook her head. "Not necessarily. I'll have something to say in that matter."

They were out of sight of the settlement now. Djilbara motioned Raba off the trail. They came to a spot unmarked by any landmarks. The *Wuradilagu* knelt, holding her hand palm-down about a foot above the ground, moving it back and forth, feeling for something. Satisfied, she began to jab into the earth with her fire-hardened digging stick.

She picked up the thread of the conversation again. "I don't want you to think that the old men are bad. They work very hard to maintain the Dreamtime and the Law. It's just that they could be dangerous for you. That's why you must be cautious around them. But they can be good men. My first husband was a powerful elder, very strong in magic."

Raba was astonished. "I didn't know you were married."

"Twice. The first time when I was thirteen. It was before I came to the mission camp. I lived with my family. There were about sixteen of us, give or take a few babies, and we traveled on the land, stopping sometimes at settled camps and towns, but mainly living in the old ways. I was trying to learn. We'd come across a few women now and then who had songs to sing me, and sometimes I'd stay behind with them for a while, catching up with my family weeks later down the wanderings. But none of the women were *Wuradilagu*."

She had dug a deep and narrow hole. She began carefully to clear away more of the sandy earth by hand.

"There was this once-yearly grand Corroboree. I was of marriageable age and had been through my women's initiation. Narritjin was there, and I could tell he liked me. He was known throughout the Oenpelli lands for his kindness and wisdom. He'd outlived his two wives. I asked my parents to arrange a marriage with him. They were pleased with me for that."

"You wanted to lie with an old man?" Raba made a face. She bent down to help Djilbara, but the woman waved her away.

"I'd already had other lovers. The way we lived there weren't as many boys around as here, but there were no missionaries to keep us apart. Narritjin was different. He knew a lot; more than just the magic I'd married him for. We had a good time together.

"He knew why I'd married him, and he liked it. He liked being my teacher. He showed me things. The other elders would have banished him if they'd known. I knew years later that I'd been lucky in my choice of him. Perhaps my inner power guided me to him. Or his to me. Most older husbands would have beaten me for the way I was; younger husbands, too." As she said this she withdrew an object wrapped in paperbark from the ground and stared at it thoughtfully.

Raba brought her back to the conversation. "Is that all? What happened? Where is he now? You didn't have any children?"

"We had one child, two years later, a boy. Narritjin died another two years after that. I married again at my clan's choosing. My second husband was a good provider, but we didn't get along and he tried to stop me from healing. I was already coming to be recognized as a *Wuradilagu*. I finally had to make his life so miserable he let me go. I came to the mission camp the next year."

"What about your son? Did he die, too?"

Djilbara laughed. She was carefully unwrapping the package. "Oh no, he is very well. Chivaree is almost twenty now. He lived with me at the camp until his first initiation. You were too little then to remember . . . you were just starting to walk. After that I didn't want the missionaries meddling with him, so I sent him to learn the old ways with his father's people. I see him once or twice a year when I go on Walkabout to the Oenpelli lands."

"Will you ever marry again? I know you like Talbiri a lot."

"I don't think so. Why should I? I have a good life, and I can pick my lovers as I choose, much as I did when I was a girl. And my lovers can't tell me how to live my life the way a husband would."

She tapped the thing she held in her hands to bring Raba's attention to it. It was a coiled root-vine, from a plant that didn't grow in the desert.

"This is a parent-vine, a women's rope, traded long ago from *Wuradilagu* women who live near the Great Sea. This place is empty, and I wove a dreaming around the hole it rests in so men won't sense it. Women use this in magic to flee from men who are wrong-side of the Law towards them. If a man should find it he couldn't use it, but he could destroy it. Even so, it would make him ill, maybe kill him."

"What are we going to use it for?" Raba asked her.

"Do you know Mitika?" Djilbara said in way of reply.

Raba nodded. Mitika was Aylupa's best friend, and one of the older girls Raba most looked up to. Three months ago the whole camp had been festive at the birth of her first child, a son. Even after the travails of birthing Mitika had looked confident and serene.

"Do you know the camp gossip about her?"

"Yes," Raba said. "One day, while I was in school, the whole camp heard her screaming in her tent. Then her husband, Burunu, came out from there and went to the elders saying she'd poisoned him with a taboo. The elders sent them both away."

"Her parents are worried about her and have asked me to go out and see if I can fix the taboo," Djilbara told Raba as she filled the hole back in carefully, whisking the sands to smoothness. "Burunu told the elders the error was in 'womanish ways,' and the old men won't touch that kind of problem. Mitika's people are afraid that any day now Burunu will return to camp with cuttings of her hair, to let them know to go out and fetch her body and make funeral preparations."

Raba pondered the lives of adults as they walked across the gibber plain. The sky faded to the color of smoke, then the darkest of blues, liberally scatter-shot with stars. An hour and a half out of camp they came upon a solitary tent. Sullenly stirring the campfire with a stick was a muscular man in his late twenties. The light from the fire showed no silhouettes in the tent; it was empty.

"Call out 'we have come,'" Djilbara murmured to Raba as they approached.

Raba did so. The man stood up. Facing them he was a featureless cut-out shape of black. But when he turned in the direction of some boulders off to the edge of the camp, the hot light from the fire caught on his features, showing him to be scowling. He threw down the stick and ducked into the tent.

"You can come out now," Djilbara said to the boulders when she and Raba reached the fire.

There was a scuffling noise and Mitika clambered weakly from behind the rocks. She was wrapped in a blanket and clutching her baby.

Raba was shocked at her appearance. During the birth celebrations Mitika had been sleek to the point of plumpness, and glowing. Now her former schoolmate was thin and trembling. There was an angry discoloration along the side of her face and neck. She held the baby stiffly with one arm.

Haltingly she came into the light. Djilbara stood and watched her as the younger woman seated herself before the fire. Then the *Wuradilagu* leaned down to where she'd set her dilly bag on the ground.

"Raba, set the billy to boiling. I need to make compresses and some tea."

"Raba," came a loud voice from within the tent, "tell the *Wuradilagu* that the unclean woman must not use or touch my drinking tin or in any other way further taint my possessions."

Djilbara ground her teeth. She raised her voice to a shout. "Raba, tell the proud father and loving husband that if he wishes himself and his family to be purified, as the elders wish it, he will not say another word but take his bedroll and get out of here. In three days he may return and I will tell him if he is lucky enough to be allowed to remain the husband of this 'tainted' woman."

Several minutes later the man slid from the tent with a bundle in hand. He glided into the dark without a word to any of them.

Djilbara turned to Mitika. "Now tell me exactly what happened."

The baby started crying. Mitika shifted painfully, trying to make him comfortable. Raba reached out and took him from her. He looked thin and ill, too. He was shivering, so she took him into the tent and rummaged around till she found an old shirt to wrap him in. When she came out Mitika was talking in a whispery voice, her gaze fixed on the dust at her feet.

". . . so it was my fault, but I wasn't trying to be wrong-fella. I was trying to do the ceremonies for my son and his father the way I'd been taught. But my body hasn't been the same since the baby. I kept bleeding for longer after the birth than I'd been told I would. When it finally stopped Burunu said not to worry about it. I still didn't feel just right—not bad, not like now—just not quite right. I fixed the special clan foods for Burunu. They were the first he could eat since I became pregnant. Then, just as I was serving them to him, I could feel my thighs becoming wet. I was wearing a white-fella-woman's shift. I went into our tent and pulled that dress up and looked. I'd started bleeding again, way too early, right then when I was serving him. That's the worst taboo I know. Burunu came in the tent to find out what'd happened to me and saw. He'd been smiling and joking up until then. When he saw me bleeding, he threw me into the tent post and hit me for a long while. Then he went off to the elders. When he came back he said they told him not to touch me, as it made the taint worse, otherwise he would have killed me right there. He packed up our tent and we left. He won't have anything to do with me or the baby. I've been trying to find food enough on my own, but it's hard because my arm won't move and I'm afraid to leave the baby alone. And I don't have enough milk."

Djilbara was wrapping an herb compress around the injured arm. "Tonight you'll drink some medicine tea for sleeping and a little seed damper gruel so your stomach won't cramp. The tea will also help your milk flow again, a little." She smiled across the fire at Raba. "Tomorrow my assistant here will catch us a rabbit or lizard. She's a good hunter. Their flesh will make a strong-fella of you."

They bundled the young mother and her child up before the fire. Raba started to scrape out a sleeping depression for herself in the warm sand, but Djilbara stopped her.

"I know you're tired, but it will be a while before we can rest. You're here to watch and learn, and to be my 'tongue,' since clanwise I can't speak directly to Burunu. But I'm also about to start my own cycle. If I tried to purify at the same time it would compound the problem. I need you to be my proxy."

They went out into the desert. The moon was shining three-quarters, on its way to becoming full.

"That's good," said Djilbara. "It's better when the moon is fatting up."

She stood Raba in front of her, both of them facing the moon. "The moon is a man," she explained, "and the sun is a woman. When men do magic at night they face away from the moon in deference, and because, being men, they must face the same way he does. Since we are women we can face him gladly, as lovers, and speak to him directly. Turning our backs to him would be disrespectful. If you were just apprenticing, I would stand before you. But since you will be doing the work this time, our positions are reversed."

Djilbara began to sing a songline. Raba felt Djilbara's power project into her with each phrase and it chimed within her young body, growing larger and larger, filling her until she had to open her mouth to let it out in an enlarged repeating phrase. It echo, echo, echoed away from her up to the listening moon. The tones, coming from Djilbara, were heavy and rich with her impending flow. They were sieved clean through Raba to emerge amplified and crystalline. With the end of each stanza the residue from the *Wuradilagu* abated from Raba like a tide. She stored this sensation of women's maturity that she herself wouldn't experience for several years.

They chanted for hours. The night was chilly on the bare skin of Raba's back. But the moon, singing back, scorched her in front with a sensation of white heat from his light. She wondered if there were other women in other lands, Mr. Wickham's witches maybe, singing the moon man their songs. What would their songs be like? Did the moon like them as well as he liked Djilbara's? She was tempted to find some way to call out that question to him, but Djilbara's power filled her and held her to their task.

She could hear spirits in the desert around them. Their voices were unintelligible, but the tone was of irritable complaint. They were not happy that Mitika had been sent out among them. Djilbara sang to them, too, songs as soothing and kind as lullabies.

The next few days were spent in endless rituals, relieved only when Djilbara sent her out on hunting expeditions. She would return to find the *Wuradilagu* engaged in one form of

herbal work or another on Mitika; compresses, poultices, teas.
The young mother's left arm was now braced in a splint.

Djilbara had Raba scratch diagram after diagram into the
ground with her digging stick. Mitika lay in the center. Raba
circled her with the sacred vine and then embellished her
body, covering it with lines and whorls of red and yellow
oxides. Raba squatted on the outside of the pattern and sang
until she was hoarse, Djilbara whispering the words to her.

On the day that Burunu returned, Mitika was looking less
gaunt and strained. Her milk was flowing again. The baby,
although still thin, was no longer feverish.

Djilbara and Mitika sat with their backs to Burunu as he
approached. He sat down cross-legged at the edge of the
camp. Raba faced him. Djilbara spoke quietly. Raba repeated
her teacher's words in a loud formal voice, almost shouting.

"Mitika broke taboo, which was bad. She is a young wife,
not much more than a girl, with her first child, your son. When
her body was not right, after the birth, it was your responsibility to tell her to come to me or the other women for advice,
instead of telling her to forget about it. This laxness resulted in
the condition that broke the taboo.

"Those who have broken taboos, even when innocently
and by mistake, have been known to die instantly at the hands
of the gods.

"You, an ignorant man, usurped the gods in choosing to
punish Mitika as you did. The gods themselves would have
done so if that was what they wished.

"When you brought her out here you did not provide food
for her and the child, while waiting for the elders to send
someone to you.

"You are very lucky. If Mitika had died from the beating,
or if she and the child had died from starvation, their ghosts
would have followed you until you'd paid retribution with your
own life. Mitika is a young and foolish wife. But she works hard
and means well. You, on the other hand, have shown yourself
to be a poor-fella of a husband and father, with thoughts only of
yourself, and no heart in sharing. You may not return to your
family until you have proved yourself. The old men will decide
what you must do."

Burunu was sitting passively, but Raba could sense his
discomfort and inner turmoil. It would have been bad enough
just being reprimanded by Djilbara. But to have the judgment

coming from the mouth of one of the camp children was humiliating. She guessed that he wished he'd killed Mitika on the spot, back at the mission.

Afterwards they left him behind to break camp. Djilbara and Raba, carrying the baby, were well in the lead. They needed to arrive home first to announce verification of Mitika's purification. Mitika was a small smudge on the horizon behind them. Djilbara turned frequently to make sure she was in sight.

"What are you doing?" Raba asked her.

"With the distance between us it would be easy for Burunu to steal up behind her."

"Why would he do that?"

Djilbara answered indirectly. "She would disappear, and he would say that a *Wadjura* devoured her."

Raba nodded her head. "He was embarrassed and angry when you had me speak to him."

"Yes, he reacted inside like a small child, and as such he is dangerous."

She turned and waved an arm at Mitika to stop where she was. "Watch for her," Djilbara instructed Raba, as she stepped off the path to rebury the vine and other sacred objects they'd used.

When she returned they continued their journey back to the camp. Raba broached the subject that had been worrying her for days.

"Auntie, will they make me marry when I'm old enough?"

Djilbara looked surprised. "You sound as if that would for a certainty be terrible. You might like the idea when you get there."

"But if I didn't. Would they make me, or could I be like you?"

"I don't know yet. But very few husbands are like Burunu, or my second husband. Our men are good men."

"I didn't mean because of that," Raba replied. "I was thinking of what you said when we came out here about being able to choose who you wished, without them being able to run your life. Also . . ." she hesitated. "One of my teachers said I should think about going to the white-fella school. She said I should learn both black-fella and white-fella medicine."

Djilbara looked disturbed. "Raba, you know that wouldn't work. Even if you learned, you wouldn't be accepted."

Raba squirmed. "I know that, but I thought if I went I'd really study something else. Mr. Wickham told us in class about white-fella women who were *Wuradilagu*, whose magic hadn't been stolen by the men. If I went to white-fella school I might be able to find out about them, maybe even find if there are any left. Miss Landell would help me get into white-fella school. She's nice. Not like the other white-fellas. She really likes me. And she must like all of us. She's stayed longer than any of them besides Dr. Blackston, but she doesn't talk about boss-man Jesus-fella all the time."

Djilbara stopped and stared at Raba. She grabbed the girl by the shoulders.

"Listen! This is important. The white-fellas that are most dangerous to us are not the ones that kill or take away our lands, or the stupid ones like most of the missionaries here. The dangerous ones are the nice ones, the smart ones, like your Miss Landell. Because they can make us have doubts about ourselves, taking away our souls, leading us away from the path back to the Dreamtime. In that way they're more to be feared than the old men."

Raba looked shaken.

But not as shaken as Djilbara was. She would have to keep an eye on this danger from a new direction. She fervently hoped that Raba would grow out of these desires, and see the white-fellas for what they were.

Badundjari Spying

The inside of Djilbara's tent was small and close. Piles of cookwear and bundled herbs, clothing, and odds and ends took up half its interior. Several blankets layered to form a bed filled most of the rest of the space. Light filtering through the canvas walls rendered everything in tones of gray and beige. Midday sun entered through the tent flap as a small triangle of white light flung down on the ground. Only a few flies buzzed within the tent, but they were so numerous outside that their relentless drone was the prevalent sound throughout the camp. One side of the tent thumped as a dog tried to avail himself of the narrow blade of shadow there.

Sitting on the blankets Djilbara was carefully pouring herbs into scraps of paper she'd folded into little packets. Every once in a while she'd softly call out instructions on where to find something she needed to Raba, who was clambering among the piles of objects. Talbiri was napping, wrapped long in a crescent around the *Wuradilagu*.

"When will you be back?" Raba whispered, handing over a packet of sugar and a box of tea.

"About two weeks. Used to be six, but the mission truck will give me a ride as far as Kooniba Station."

"Why don't you just go *badundjari*? Then you could leave this afternoon and be there by the end of night."

"Because I'd be too tired when I got there to do anything. Not for healing, not for staying up late catching up with Chivaree. And I don't trust leaving part of myself behind for that long."

"I'd look after that," Raba assured her. "Me and Talbiri could do that."

Djilbara shook her head. "You study with me, you study at the mission school all the time. You need some time to play with the mob."

"Yes'm. That'll be nice," Raba said dutifully. But she had other plans. The only times she could conduct her own personal exploration of magic was when Djilbara wasn't around to sense her.

"Have you decided who you're going to stay with while both me and your folks are away?" Djilbara asked her.

"That's no problem," Raba said. "I'll still have to finish up my tutoring at the mission school. I've got three more days to catch up on. On the weekends I'll stay with Marindi or Huroo's family. I'd like to visit with Mitika and the baby, too. That is, if Burunu isn't still angry."

"You don't have to worry about Burunu anymore," said Djilbara. "He left on a Walkabout yesterday, and it was clear that he doesn't intend to come back. So it's a good idea to go see Mitika. Be very kind to her. And don't forget to check in on your brother Dhuma and see how he's doing." Dhuma was in the second year of school now, and like Raba was left behind when the family went trekking. "You should all have a quiet, safe time of it, with most of the men up north for cattle-branding, and the elders and initiates out in the desert."

"Quiet time of it everywhere but in this tent," Talbiri grumbled, stretching. Scratching his beard, he stood up as tall as he could in the tent into a stoop. He pulled on a pair of shorts and a white-fellas old sports jacket, ducking to clear the tent flap as he left.

"Where are you going?" asked Djilbara.

"Where do you think, after a full billy of tea?"

"Bring me back some water from the well?"

He thrust his head and one long arm back into the tent. He grabbed Djilbara to him and rumpled her up and down in a hug, half in and half out of the tent. Off balance, they toppled over. He nuzzled her throat. "Will you marry me if I do?"

Laughing, Djilbara untangled herself. "I'll seriously consider it."

He grinned back, but the grin wasn't entirely happy. "That's what you always say."

Raba giggled through all of this, but when Talbiri left she frowned. "He'll get tired of waiting and marry someone else. And whoever it is won't like it if he keeps coming around to you. Then you won't see him anymore."

Brows knitted, Djilbara stared down at her herb packets. "You're right, I know. I'll lose him to a wife, or wives, someday. But I'd rather that than change the way we are by marrying him myself."

Raba held on stubbornly. "He's the best for you. He's worth being the one to settle down with. You're being foolish." She weighted her voice with the solemn tone of prophecy pronouncements. "I *know*."

Djilbara's mouth dropped open in amazement, then she whooped with laughter. "Aren't you getting to be a proper cheeky one."

That night, as was often their custom, the fifth-year girls waited. They lay in their beds faking sleep until the last of the missionaries' bedchecks. Then they knew the white-fellas would be safely off making surveillance on the big-girls' dorm until late in the night. When they heard the woman who was this night's dorm mother crossing the compound, they slid from their sheets and huddled together on Jayulya and Ninual's beds. Raba stripped off her nightshirt, freeing herself from at least one layer of the dorm's heat and closeness. She wore only a hair-string belt around her hips.

"Next year those poor-fellas will be making late-night checks on us, too," Jayulya whispered. Their promotion next year to the other dorm, with all its attendant promise of adventure and danger, was one of their favorite night party topics.

Ninual made such an extreme sour face that it could be seen even in the near blackness of the room. She looked at Jayulya and Marindi's already blooming bodies. "Yes, lots of fun for some of us," she said. "We'll get to spend a year playing sentry for you and the older girls while you sneak out to see the boys. It's going to be fair dinkum for us, catching all the blame for you and none of the fun."

Marindi and Jayulya looked at each other and giggled. They leaned against each other in an affectionate contest until they both toppled backwards, almost off the bed. "Don't be cross," Marindi told Ninual. "We'll all pass our women's rites sooner or later. Why don't you have Raba conjure up a song for you to make you grow faster?"

Raba could feel rather than see Ninual's look of hope as the other girl turned towards her. She rubbed her own chest, flat as a claypan on the gibber plain, with one hand. "If I had such a spell don't you think I would have used it on myself already?" she countered.

The conversation switched to the male initiations. The boys now going through the rituals out in the desert, several years their senior, would be among their potential lovers.

As the other girls chattered, Raba lowered her hand from her chest to trail her fingers across her midriff. The flesh there had long ago healed into a granular scarring, not unpleasant to to touch, but surely not desirable in a lover.

Even worse, at times it hindered her in her learning and training. The scarring sunk far below the skin to her center. She'd progress smoothly with her magic and then she'd flounder, skidding across that blank spot in her perceptual abilities. When she was apprenticing with Djilbara that could be worked around. The *Wuradilagu* would carry her over the blind area. Then they'd backtrack together, filling in the gap with knowledge.

But more and more she was going out on her own, unknown to Djilbara, to talk to the spirits, walk her own paths, develop her own songs, spy on the old men when she could. At those times her handicap frustrated and sometimes stymied her. Often the flow of magic could not be maintained with such jarring interruptions to its rhythm. Raba also knew that she was adding an extra element of risk to an already dangerous occupation. But her desire to learn these days was more compelling than thirst or hunger. She told herself that such a drought wouldn't have been visited upon her if it hadn't meant to be quenched. She took her survival for granted. She was obsessed and distraught with the thought that because of her disability she would never learn all she was sure she was meant to know.

"Raba, the *Wuradilagu* tells you stories the rest of us don't get to hear," Yemma, a tiny, plump girl, interrupted her thoughts. "Can you tell us if this is true: My sister told me that the real secret of the men's first initiation is that instead of just cutting the foreskin off like they tell us, the old men really cut their whole penis off and give them a new one taken from an Emu, and that's why they look so different afterwards." All the girls laughed, including Raba.

"I haven't heard that one," Raba said. "I'd be surprised if it was true. What if you put an Emu penis on a boy from an opposing clan, like the Goanna? It would probably fall right off. Do we know any Goanna men like that?"

"My mother's brother-in-law is a Goanna," Jayulya chimed in. "From what his wife has to say about him as a lover, maybe it is true after all." They laughed so hard at that that Marindi finally choked out, hiccuping, "Hush, the white-fellas are going to hear us clear across the mission and come back to quiet us up."

The other girls continued with their tall tales, intensely curious about the rites the boys went through.

Let them wonder, Raba thought. *Tomorrow I will know.* She marveled at her luck; Djilbara and her parents out of the camp at the same time the initiations were being held. *If it happened like that, it was because I was meant to know.*

"We'll never know," Marindi said glumly, as if echoing Raba's thoughts.

"That's all right," said Ninual. "They never get to find out what goes on in our rites either."

"Yeah, but they don't seem to care. As if ours is just child-playing, just because we don't get anything cut off."

"I wouldn't really want to know—to know for certain," said Jayulya. "Women who mess in men's magic meet up with *Wadjuras* and the featherfeet killers soon afterwards."

The girls shivered, a pall cast over the conversation. The topic changed swiftly.

"Raba, you're so busy all the time learning that you never get to play," said Jayulya. "With Djilbara gone you can come out with us. Tomorrow there's no school. A big mob of us, little ones and the boys, too, are going off to the dunes and have a campfire of our own and act out stories. All but Yemma and Tulapa here; they have to stay and do chores for the white-fellas." The two girls mentioned groaned. "We need you to be the *Wuradilagu* in our plays. It will be just like real then."

"Just because Djilbara is gone doesn't mean I get to play," Raba replied. "I've got chores to do, too. I'm supposed to gather some herb seeds for her while she's gone."

"You could be the sun-woman *and* the *Wuradilagu* if you come with us," Marindi said, trying to tempt her. The other girls murmured in approval at Marindi's sharing.

"The herbs are seeding now, so I must gather them tomorrow." Raba grinned. "But I'll hold you to that . . . Djilbara's gone for two weeks, so I'll still have lots of time to play."

The intense heat of the last few days had broken. Great winds flew high. The clouds up there were blown into wispy shapes, and the turmoil above echoed close to the ground: Kicking, erratic breezes skimmed sand from the crest of the dunes and played against Raba's legs as she trudged over them. As she traversed on the windward side, her tracks eroded behind her. Her ankles ached from the climbing. She'd needed to travel a long way from the camp for the secrecy she wanted.

She found a dune undercut by the play of the wind. Its inner curve had already been passed by the sun, so it would lie safely in shadow for the rest of the day. Stretching out there, facing inward to the dune, Raba closed her eyes against the sand. Wriggling and burrowing, she felt the edges of her skin begin to loosen and separate into infinitesimal particles. As the epidermal layer scattered outwards, each succeeding layer also thinned and followed it. Raba almost laughed at the crumbly, ticklish sensation. She knew of no one else who could go *badundjari* in the ways she could. When a gust caught in the tunnel of the dune, she flowed out and away with it, transformed into a sand stream. Her stubbornly unchanged center, watery-black and membrane thin, swept along with it like a cloud's shadow.

Once out and coasting over the gibber plain, the grains of her being resonated in a query song that she cast out from her. Where had the old men gone for the initiation rites? They were too far for her to have walked to, she already knew. Not in the places where she usually spied on them.

Her song echoed back to her from one direction, and she channeled herself along its path. She caught what snatches of breeze she could, leaving them when they diverted or threatened to scatter her. Sometimes she sank to the ground, becalmed, just creeping along, waiting to launch herself onto the next slight wind.

She found the ceremonies taking place on an ancient clay-pan. Settling to the ground near a saltbush, she sifted herself into the sand and dusty red clay. Other entities were gathered about to watch the proceedings. She recognized a *Mimi* spirit, not visible, by the long nervous column that its scent—salty and flower-sweet at once—took up in the air. The *Janga Yonggar*, chief kangaroo spirit, could be felt by the pressure of its bulk. And scattered here and there was the focused sight of the elders' *mabans*, standing guard. Raba lay quietly, shedding all thoughts that might attract their gaze, and became simply watching.

A large elongated brush shelter had been erected. There was an entrance at each end, one of which was encircled outside by a ring of flat stones, set flush to the ground. A short distance away other shelters clustered around a campfire. There the initiates were being painted by their sponsors. They wore hair-string and woolen bands around their foreheads and upper arms. Trade-good pearl shell strands circled their necks and ankles. The boys had not been cut yet.

Some of the old men chanted in a clearing meticulously picked clean of pebbles and plant debris. Bundles of wood shavings were tucked into their headbands, covering their foreheads. Standing in a circle facing outwards, they swayed, eyes closed and sight directed inwards towards their *mabans*. They were singing away the Willy-wagtail bird, a procedure preceding all men's magic. The Willy-wagtails were trouble-makers who loved to spy on men and then gossip to the women. The song was gentle and persuasive, though, rather than threatening. It would be dangerous to chance killing a Willy-wagtail. The death of their spirits brought violent storms.

Then several of the old men entered the long shelter.

Raba could feel them lining up in a gauntlet along its two walls. The rest of the old men and the sponsors herded the initiates into the stone-lined circle. An ancestor soul encased in a pebble was placed on each stone to seal them in.

Two of the sponsors sat with their *didjeridu*. Sonorous droning filled the air, permeating each particle of matter. Raba, already gone *badundjari*, felt the skin of everyday reality melt away from the men as the time and place they existed in leveled to join her and the other watching spirits.

The men inside the hut began to sing a round, a song with no beginning or end, as if it were a snake devouring itself in an infinite circle. The hut changed, rippling with flesh. Entering one by one, the initiates crept inside. Makwora waited at the other end by a small fire. Beside him were several stone knives laid on a strip of gum tree bark.

Lulled and absorbed by the droning song, Raba was drawn along with the consciousness of the initiates: security, warmth, slow seductive movement along the passageway and the channel of the song. Somehow it was familiar. Abruptly she felt a gathering fear from them—impending pain, the unknown waiting on the other side.

Recognition struck Raba. And with it a rage and repulsion so strong that she found herself back out on the plain, vibrating with fury.

What she had remembered, what she recognized, was her own birth. The initiates were literally being reborn in a monstrous parody of the passage through their mothers' wombs. The men had the audacity to take for themselves the one function still sacred to women! This was defiance of the way in which all animals were born. It was an insult to the Land itself. Raba shifted and shimmered, wanting to cohere in her human form and scream out curses on the men. It wasn't enough that they had stolen most of the women's magic. They were so greedy that they had to have it all.

She felt danger closing around her. The *mabans'* sight sensed her, a shrill presence in the tranquility of the proceedings, and were coming to investigate. Raba trembled and lay still, but it was too late. As she tried to creep away, her shadowlike center betrayed her; it was a moving shadow on the surface of the claypan with no apparent owner.

They hadn't encircled her yet. The *mabans* glowed with alarm in the places they were kept, the stomachs of the old

men. All but one of those left at the entrance of the birthing
house leapt up and came running.

Raba managed to flow out and away, but her progress by
herself, grains of sand tumbling over each other, was too slow.
The old men gained on her. She cast herself onto a breeze, and
the men burst into a ululating cry. A *Garhain*! Batlike man-
monsters from Arnhem Land: an evil omen to be found
preying near an initiation. They began to withdraw *mabans*
from their centers and fling them after Raba. The crystal stones
passed through her sand grains harmlessly. But when one
grazed the darkness of her center, it burned. She keened in
pain.

The breeze veered near a clump of stunted desert mulga.
She slipped in amongst them, huddling in the shade of their
roots. Three of the men began to search through the trees
systematically. Raba stiffened with fear as the bottom of a foot
began to descend on her, afraid if she moved to avoid it she'd
be seen. She pulled in her edges tightly and it narrowly missed
her. As the man passed she saw that he was looking up into the
branches. That was where a *Garhain* would drop from,
enfolding and smothering its victim. Unsuccessful in their
search, the men turned to make another pass through the
trees. This time their gaze was directed lower, at the ground
and roots. Raba edged through the shadows to the outskirts of
the trees and leapt onto the next breeze. Three more men
were waiting to see if the quarry would try to escape that way.
Their cries alerted the others in their search. The chase began
anew.

Raba was tiring. Back at the camp she could have outrun
any of these aging men. But here, on the edges of the Dreamtime, their experience and power gave them the stamina of
coursing dingos. Panting, she called out to the watching spirits
of the Outback. They stood where they were, watching
passively, neither helping nor hindering. She sank to the
ground in despair, and tried to prepare herself for death.
Shuddering, she wondered if her fate would be that of the
lizard she'd once killed: dissipation.

As the sense of the men came oppressively near, she
turned her sight up to the sky. There was a half-remembered
resonance of memory, of glaring whiteness and deep blue. But
now the blue was lightened by the foam of windswept clouds.
They were traveling fast, so fast. If she possessed that speed
she could have escaped.

That thought filled her. Before she could identify it as hope, Raba flung herself upwards, leaving her center anchored back on the ground. It lay there, suddenly completely still. The old men closed in, circling cautiously, *mabans* in hand.

Raba stretched thinner and thinner, climbing upwards on a breeze until the men below faded to dots. She couldn't even see the dormant shadow that was part of herself. But she could feel it tugging and straining.

Her foremost grains caught the edge of the river of high winds and she was yanked onto its currents. Fast! Too fast! The rest of her sucked upwards with a snap, and way down below she could feel her center begin to rip, a momentary sensation of fluid seeping at its edges. She was whipping away from it. In the last instant of contact she released its traction to the ground. It came spinning up and along the river after her, black teardrops centrifuging away. It hit her hard when it caught up to her; striking, scattering, and almost blowing her back out of the torrent of wind.

Far below the startled men looked up, trying to see where the *Garhain* had vanished to. But Raba was already swept far beyond them, curled in a black knot of agony, carried away by the racing winds.

Portraits

Raba floated for a long while, conscious of nothing but her pain. Each thudding throb fell through her, like stones being dropped one by one, forever, into a well. The barest touch of cooling that accompanied each pulse was the caress of the winds whisking her along.

Finally the pain lessened. She felt other things. The texture of the air stream bearing her was cold, silky, smooth, with a tang of moisture. At some point there was a slight change to its rhythm; somewhere not too far ahead it became an entirely different song. The resonances of that change echoed back faintly against the tide of its currents.

She opened herself to see what lay around and beneath

her. In its huge humps and spindles of contour-etched stone, the Land below reminded her of her birthland. But instead of rising from the bare flatness of rock plains and desert, they emerged from nests of swamp-groves and forest. Raba's sight ached from the vibrations of the colors—big patches of velvet greenness intertwining with bright red and yellow stone.

Far in the distance the Land changed to a narrow, sandy crispness. After that was blue, where the sky seemed to blend down to the Land, and the Land curved upwards, the edge of a circle, to meet it.

Perfect, thought Raba. *The wind will carry me down along that blend of sky to the ground.*

But the closer she came, the farther the blue extended, splitting into two tones of color. She remembered the stories of her tribe, and the white-fella schooling, and realized that she was looking out on the Great Sea. The wind was flying her swiftly towards it. That was where the change was, where the wind began a different dance with its mate, the ocean.

At first Raba felt drawn to it. She thought of the old men chasing her, the sometimes oppressiveness of camp where she needed to be secretive, of all the hiddenness—herself, Djilbara, and Huroo as Emu, unseen. She thought of the trouble she would be in when she returned to camp, even if the old men didn't recognize her as the *Garhain* they'd driven away on the desert. And if they did recognize her, what then? Her center convulsed.

She could be safely away. Beyond the winds were other lands, places she'd seen in books in the mission school, and the weird world the white-fellas came from. Maybe there were still women witches there she could find and learn from, as she'd been learning with Djilbara.

Djilbara. She remembered Djilbara. How much she'd given Raba, and how little Raba had returned as yet. Raba's heart ached with that debt. She remembered the solidity and love of Kultuwa and Waku. And Marindi. And Huroo, so beautiful and so lost to himself.

The farther she looked across the winds onto the sea, the thinner and more barren the world beyond seemed. She felt a wrenching from below, felt the Land begin a wail at the loss of her. She was leaving the Dreamtime, her home, reality in all its depth and magic. The world beyond was bare, flat, inhabited only by ghosts.

The winds were pulling her along. Soon it would be too late. The wind was rushing to its love, the ocean, and would not flow backwards. Terrified, she let go and sifted downwards, her center drifting after her.

She had the sensation of coming to rest on rock. Her sands settled into the outlines of a human child, coalescing, and she slept.

She awoke to the impression of activity somewhere nearby. People or spirits were traveling with great purpose. She crept from the curve of sandstone she lay on to a bordering wedge of trees. Beyond them was a hill of ochre-colored stone. She waited in the cover of the trees. In a few minutes a spirit walked along the curve of rock on a pathway that led up and out of her line of sight.

She could see the spirit faintly, its form shimmering like heat waves in the air. It was tall and moved with grace, as if slowly dancing in ritual on level land instead of trudging up a hill. Its eyes were larger than owls' eyes, and all black. It had a narrow blade of nose and no mouth at all that Raba could see. Haloing its face was an enormous rounded headdress, perhaps of bound hair, tiny tassels garnishing its contour. It walked upwards over the land's crest. Several minutes later another spirit passed the same way. Then three came together down the path.

Djilbara had described these spirits to her; they were *Wandjina*, the original authors of *Djilbidi*, the Law. Native to Arnhem Land, they were known and held in awe by all the Aboriginal people.

Where were they going? Raba crept parallel to the path under the cover of the trees, but the copse soon ended. To continue to follow the spirits she would have to come out in the open. She did so slowly, as if she were hunting game, freezing in place whenever another *Wandjina* came into view. The spirits ignored her, or did not see her. At last, growing bold, she approached one.

"Great Spirit, where are you going?"

The *Wandjina* said nothing, continuing its journey without slacking its pace.

She stood directly in the path of the next spirit.

"Great Spirit . . ." she began as it loomed upon her. And then it was gone. Whirling in confusion, Raba saw it marching away. The *Wandjina* had passed right through her, leaving no sensation at all. They must be traveling through another place, one that lay over this one. Losing her fear entirely, she scrambled up the hill after it.

It led her to a broad but shallow cave. Inside were dozens of paintings of *Wandjina*, rendered in pigments of clay-white, charcoal black, ochre, and rust. Some were freshly retouched. Others were faded back to original stains that looked as if they'd been born in the rock. In one corner of the cave was a small pile of broken and worn twigs, grinding stones and pigment, and the remains of an old fire for burning charcoal.

The spirit she'd followed approached one of the paintings. Not slowing its pace at all, it walked right into the picture, its form bleeding at the edges to fill the painting's contours. And then the cave was empty, except for Raba and the silent portraits.

She squatted on a boulder to watch, arms wrapped around her knees. Spirits came and went for the few remaining hours of that day, disappearing and emerging at random intervals from the paintings—strange to see an image appear to bulge with life for an instant as a *Wandjina* strode out from it. With dusk the activity ceased.

Raba needed neither food nor water in her *badundjari* form. Back under the dune where she'd flowed into dream-walking was a hollow outline of herself in the sand. It felt hunger, thirst, and the burning sun, and could not be left for too long. But as a dream spirit she still felt exhaustion and the need to heal from the *maban* wound and the injuries from her escape. She curled up by her boulder and slept.

The next morning the spirits only occasionally came and went from the cave. Whatever errand they had been on was complete, or perhaps they were traveling by different routes.

No longer distracted by the study of their activities, Raba had time to think about her predicament. She had been gone for a day. An alarm would be going out in the camp as Huroo and Marindi's families discovered that she'd stayed with neither of them the night before. By this afternoon they'd be searching for her in the Outback.

She doubted that the initiation party would have returned to the mission, since they'd successfully driven off the *Garhain*. But they would have at least dispatched a messenger or attempted a "sending" to warn of the *Garhain's* presence in the area. The camp would be doubly worried about her absence because of that. In spite of the nagging worry she felt, she giggled at the irony of being threatened by a shadow-monster that was actually herself.

Then she was concerned again. She'd never intended to be separated from the rest of her body for so long. If it perished she would live out the rest of this life in *badundjari* form.

What could she do? She stretched upwards, sniffing, testing the local breezes. They were small and flirtatious, in love with the Land that bore them, never straying too far. Her experience the day before told her that the great, high, steady winds blew against her in this region—their hearts ran singlemindedly to the Great Sea.

Although she was swifter as *badundjari* than in her full-body, it would still take her weeks to follow the Great Paths home, and that would be far too late.

She wondered if there was a way home for her along the routes the *Wandjina* traveled. It was a risk, but she knew she'd found those of whom the Rainbow Serpent had spoken, others who could "travel the in-betweens."

She approached the wall cautiously, afraid that one of the spirits might emerge as she was trying to enter. Picking a painting close to her own size, she pressed herself against its cool, rough length. Nothing happened. She stood there, the stone's mild granulation buffing the skin on her arms and chest as she wriggled with the smallest of movements, trying to absorb past its surface.

She walked back to her boulder perch and sat there for a while, staring at the images. What had the *Wandjina* done differently? Perhaps it was that they walked straight into the rock. She leapt down and marched resolutely towards her chosen painting, only to be rewarded with a banged and scraped nose. She tried other images with the same result.

She sat in thought again. She didn't remember any painting being used by more than one *Wandjina*. That must be it. They truly were portrait pictures, and only the individual owners could use them as portals. And there were, of course, no Raba portraits. That could be remedied.

Raba left the cave. It would be sacrilege to include herself among this company of great spirits. She explored the area about and eventually found a shallow depression under a rock outcropping, too insubstantial to be called a cave. But it was just large enough, and its approach was hidden by some bushy casuarinas stubbornly emerging from a rocky seam.

She took care in assembling the tools and materials she needed, raiding the *Wandjina* cave for grinding stones and the few scraps of leftover charcoal that she could find there. She clawed, pried, and jabbed chunks of pigments from the cliff walls. She broke off green twigs and sticks of varying sizes from trees and bushes. When she was done, all her acquisitions were laid neatly in a row in the narrow space before her rock canvas.

Raba contemplated the rock face, unsure of how to begin. An outline! She stood against it, one of the grinding stones in hand. She would scratch into the surface, tracing herself, reaching as best she could around the contours of her body, switching hands when she had to. She poised, the edge of the stone against the wall. She hadn't begun, and it already felt wrong; too cramped and small. It was as if she were building a doorway that she would forever have to stoop to enter. She had a premonition. *I will come here again, when I'm grown.*

She stepped back a couple of feet. Although the depression was in shadow she imagined it as if the sun was lancing long behind her, casting her shadow large against the rock face. Leaning forward, she traced the silhouette thus created by her mind's eye.

She ground down chunks of red iron oxide into rough powder. Spitting again and again into the mound, she formed a spreadable paste. She chewed the end of one of the thicker sticks into a brush. Loading this with the red paint, she filled in the outline of her form. It took her several hours to finish the piece; brushing in large areas, stippling spots of ochre and white with the ends of the smaller twigs, smudging in patches of black. When piles of pigment ran out, she mined for more. She sang incessantly:

> *Stone walls accept my image*
> *Take me where*
> *The* Wandjina *go*
> *Stone walls*
> *Stone walls*
> *Let me pass beyond.*

Great Wandjina *spirits*
Let me follow you
Don't drive me away
Let me walk your paths this day.

Earth, sand, and clay
Be the colors of my flesh
Sink into these walls
Then let me sink into you
Let me travel home
Along your brightness.

Finishing, she stepped back with the eerie feeling she felt when she looked in a mirror or caught a glimpse of herself in passing the white-fellas' glassed windows.

A bigger Raba stood flat in the wall, red-brown skin more garish than her own. It was spotted in delicate patterns of white—the tracing of her bones—and ochre, where the lines of her magic flowed like a sandstorm inside her. Eyes, large and black, touched with white at the corners, stared blankly out at her. The hair was rendered as a wild red and black crown, in contrast to the neatly contained haloes of the *Wandjina*.

She'd expected the thick, awkwardly applied pigment to adhere in crusts, flaking off at the slightest touch. But it had soaked in, the thirsty stone showing through like grainy skin. Djilbara had told her tales that the most sacred of the cave paintings were self-portraits drawn by the ancestor-spirits in the Dreamtime. The Aborigines in their role as caretakers of this world retouched them periodically so that the pictures would retain their power. Her painting had the same born-from-stone quality as the most faded images in the *Wandjina* cave.

She returned the grinding stones to their place near the spirit mural. The twigs she used to sweep away traces of unused pigment before scattering them under the trees.

She took a deep breath and looked around her. Now that she was ready to go, Raba was afraid. Surrounding her was a Land she could understand: trees, rock, caves, sky, birds soaring overhead. What she would be passing into she didn't know. And there were no old men pursuing her with hunting-death in their eyes to make her leap past her fears.

But what if her own painting rejected her as the *Wandjinas'* had? She would be trapped here, and her husk left back in the dune would wither and die. Djilbara might never find her. New panic goaded Raba into action. She plunged towards the portrait.

There was an initial sensation of flesh meeting stone, and then the image reached out to absorb her. She felt her physical boundaries expanding to fill the painting's outlines. She sank into the rock as it reached through her. She could feel it sealing itself into place behind her. She felt as if she was standing with her back to a window; if she turned she would see out onto the floor of the depression and the cluster of sheltering foliage as if she were in a room looking out.

In front of her was pitch-black, sensationless. If there were some sort of window behind her, it was casting no light into this place she found herself. She couldn't tell if there were walls around her or even a floor beneath her feet. She stepped forward awkwardly, with no sense of footing. That one step took her up against an obstacle. She pushed and it gave a little. Pressing her whole body to it she began to sink through, as she had through her portrait, but more slowly. This must be where the *Wandjina* went to. She pushed more and stretched farther into yielding space. The black faded to a soft jumble of dim colors.

Something was holding her back. It was her center, beached in the darkness like a fish. She wiggled and turned, trying to get it at an angle where it could slide on edge through the barrier. But it held fast, stuck. She strained, groaning, the sounds caught and thrown back at her from all angles in gritty tones, as if she were caught in the facets of a honey comb.

Raba gave up the struggle at last, and allowed herself to pull back and cohere around her flat, obstinate center. She stood in the blackness, trembling. She couldn't travel to where the *Wandjina* had gone.

What would she do now? Panicking, she began to flail around wildly, and lost all sense of footing. Was she falling? She tried to back out through her painting, but it was gone. Was she on her back or upright? She could smell nothing, touch nothing. In terror she ran, she thought, unsure whether her feet were really beneath her. She could be racing in place. She stopped in despair, panting. She would be lost forever in this nothingness. She must have been moving, or she wouldn't have lost her place behind the picture. She moved her feet up and down in the motion of walking, though she had no sense of direction. She let her feet carry her, her mind blank, overwhelmed by fear.

When she regained a sense of awareness, it was through the bottom of her feet. There was no feeling of ground beneath them, but they were walking to some sense of pattern. Her first thought was a wondering *this is a new way of walking the paths*. She walked for what seemed like hours with long strides and sensed that she had moved just inches analogous to her own world. And at the same time in some ghostly form she passed through the edges of existences unimaginable. Once she took three tiny steps and with them felt herself cross the entire Outback and then turn halfway back into it. She began to sense a whole new form of patterning, and lost her fear in fascination and absorption.

Finally she realized that for quite some time she had been walking parallel to familiarity. For an instant she was tempted to ignore it and go on, forgetting all else in the desire to explore.

Foolish Raba, she could imagine Djilbara's voice saying. *How many risks are you willing to take at one time? Curiosity must be tempered with judgment before it can be considered wisdom.* Raba burned with embarrassment and a touch of returning fear. The heat of those emotions was answered alongside her. She pressed her hand to that spot. Her hand thrust through to more warmth, to a source of genuine heat. She waved her fingers around and they ran through the dusty grittiness of sand. Reaching farther, up to her elbow, she felt air and sunlight play along her skin. Plunging her other arm and head in, she burrowed up through and then onto the floor of the desert. She was home.

Lying on her back, bathed in late sunlight, Raba let out a warble of joy, and then froze. She recognized where she'd emerged: near the old men's initiation site, not far from the clump of trees she'd hidden in when they chased her.

She lay still, hoping there were no elders nearby who might have heard her.

With her breathing she extended her senses outward in a slow spiral. She was cautious, ready to encounter other consciousnesses. The vicinity was empty, except for one dull glimmer. She raised her head and saw only the flatness of gibber plain. In the distance, silhouetted against the horizon were the brush shelters. They sang flat tones of abandonment. The birthing structure was disassembled. The men had moved to another site after their encounter with her. Somewhere they would be singing songs to repel a *Garhain* from the rituals.

She scrambled to her feet and reconnoitered the area. Here were the clump of trees. Here was where she'd been cornered. Scattered around were teardrop shards of obsidian. They were flecks of herself, bled away when the one *maban* had grazed her center, and more when she had torn herself upwards to flee with the wind. Sobbing, she knelt in the sand and began to pick them up one by one. She pressed them to her stomach, but they fell away through her fingers. She gathered them up again, and then saw that there were more, spread over the desert. She'd never find them all. *Now I will never truly be whole*, she thought.

She turned back to where she'd emerged from the desert floor. There was a Raba-shaped depression that the breezes would soon smooth. Not far beyond, lying among some stones, something shone. It was a *maban*, watching her. The elders must have left it behind to look out for the *Garhain*. Raba clutched the glass fragments as if they could protect her. It was too late. The *maban* would be relaying a message to its owner by now.

She was in her own shape. The men would not mistake her for a *Garhain* this time. If she dove into the sands to the between-passages, they'd see where she went from the imprint in the desert floor. She stood, immobilized by uncertainty. Minutes went by and she sensed no impending threat. The *maban* just lay there, projecting no resonance of who its owner was. Raba approached it. It should embody an unmistakable character. But it was blank. This was the dull glimmer she'd noticed earlier.

She picked it up. Shaded by the rocks, it felt cool in contrast to the desert heat. It was an oblong chunk of crystal.

One of Raba's arms cradled her stomach, holding the black teardrops she'd gathered. She started to place the *maban* there with them. It flashed in a sudden scorching. With a yelp she dropped everything. She picked it up more cautiously and held it two hands-widths away from her belly. She could feel a reaching warmth. She drew it closer and that sensation became a slow but endurable burning. Clenching her hands she brought it in contact with her stomach, grimacing with pain. The skin there flared with the sensation of heat, then seemed to melt. Something in the crystal melted, too. The sensation grew too intense to bear. She pulled the *maban* away, half afraid her skin would come with it.

Raba touched the spot with her fingers. Her stomach retained the mild, pitted scarring she bore there. But where there had been contact with the *maban* she could glide her fingers a little more smoothly, as if it had been slightly polished. She ran her hand along the edge of the crystal. It, too, showed a change to the touch—the beginning of an edge, as if it had been stropped just once on a knife leather. Now she recognized the crystal. This was the *maban* that had grazed her during the chase. In cutting her it had lost the memory of its owner. No wonder it hadn't been gathered up by the old men along with the other thrown *mabans*.

She felt a flash of rage. Here she was, holding a *maban* that now belonged to her that she couldn't absorb, in a Land where the watching spirits had left her to be hunted by old men who subverted nature's way. From every angle she viewed the situation, and it looked wrong. How could the Land have allowed the old men to do those things and not punish them?

Raba is singing anger, the sands called out.

"*Now* you speak to me. You were silent when I lay ready to die in the old men's power."

You knew you were risking danger seeking knowledge that way.

"Are you saying I shouldn't have risked it? That I was wrong, but the old men weren't?"

There is always some danger in learning, even in your training with the Wuradilagu. *And in this you knew you were especially at risk. No one is exempt, even the favored—not you, and not the elders.*

"You didn't help me. That I now understand. But you let the old men go free."

Why should they be punished?

Raba stammered before she could force the words out. "They mocked one of the only magics left sacred to women. They spat on their mother's wombs. Being born once through those wasn't good enough for them."

Raba, think. A snake sheds its skin many times if it is to continue to grow. Think back, very far, about yourself.

Raba thought back. She hazily remembered the sands tearing away at her, being eaten. The terrible agony as cell after cell was devoured, the aching as each was replaced.

Would you begrudge the men their rebirth when you have already had yours?

"But that's different." She shook with remembered pain.

Yes. Although yours was not finished, it is still more complete than theirs will ever be. And they must help each other, while I bore you myself.

Raba was ashamed. "I was wrong to judge them." Another thought occurred to her. "If I hadn't become angry they wouldn't have discovered me, and I could have kept learning."

The sands didn't answer.

The sun was drawing close to the horizon. Shadows of saltbush and stone lengthened in anticipation of dusk. Raba, holding the *maban* in one hand, lay down in her eroding depression in the sand and slipped into the travel passageway.

Her feet danced along the patterns, anxious to join their flesh in the sand dune and become whole again. Tracing the paths-between seemed to take forever. Raba wondered if she should have hiked back to the spot *badundjari*, but she would have risked coming across search parties. Someone might recognize her in this form. Three long steps, two small steps to the right, a step backward that left her feeling upside down. The process went on and on. With one step she felt herself gaining a shadow, black as it was in the darkness. Backing up, she felt herself start to merge with it. She stopped, and bent down to place the *maban* at her feet. She couldn't take it with her—she wouldn't be able to explain it. Then she stood up and backed out into the sand dune, slowly filling in the husk that waited for her.

She became conscious of two things at the same time; voices all around her and the dryness of her lips. She drew out a swollen tongue to lick them, and tasted blood oozing from the chapped cracks.

"Raba, we found you! Are you alive?" Someone was shaking her. She tried to open her eyes, but they were crusted shut. A hand gently rubbed them clear. The first thing she saw was Huroo, felt his hands cupping her face. His eyes looked so dark and moist, while her own burned. His brows were etched with concern. The space behind him was landscaped with the forms of the rest of the children's mob bending over her. There was the scent of Marindi kneeling beside her, one arm under Raba's shoulders, lifting her clear of the sand.

"We found you before the grown-ups did!" one of the little ones yelled in excitement.

Marindi's voice sounded soft in her ear. "We've been so worried about you. A runner came warning of demons. No one could find you in camp. With Mother Djilbara and the old men gone, no one knew what to do. Your tracks were blown away with the winds. We were afraid you'd been killed."

The elders were still gone! Raba rejoiced. She would have time to think up a story to cover her absence.

"Where were you? Where are the herbs you went looking for?" Marindi asked.

Raba mumbled past parched lips.

"No, never mind. Don't try to talk now. Time for that later," Huroo said, dribbling a thin stream into her mouth from a waterbag.

He and Guwara locked arms to make a chair of sorts to carry her. As they stooped to pick her up, she noticed protection amulets dangling from their necks. All the children were wearing them.

When they reached the top of the dune, Huroo looked down at the ground, then back over his shoulder to where she'd lain. He frowned. Raba knew what he was seeing. There were many tracks, from bigger feet than the children's. An adult search party had already been there and hadn't seen her. He looked at her, silently questioning. She dropped her gaze, as if she hadn't seen his look. It was going to be hard enough to think up an alibi to keep the adults at bay without having to argue past Huroo's perceptiveness, too.

Puberty
1955

"I think Ngulwen is selfish. She's in Coober Town as happy as can be, while our lovers are all shut up in the dorms for helping her run away with those two brothers," Marindi complained.

"I don't know. What do you think, Talu?" asked Jayulya. Being twelve, she naturally deferred to a girl three years her senior.

Set apart from the conversation, Raba listened glumly from what she'd come to think of as "her" stone at the adolescents' campfire. She shifted irritably from one haunch to another and back. She kicked a pebble into the coals.

"Ngulwen didn't know the boys were going to whisk her off like that. Even if she did, she couldn't know that the missionaries would ground all the boys that age afterwards," Talu replied.

"A lot you care, with one of your lovers away on second rites and the other off with the men in the south dealing with that sheep fever," another girl chimed in. Talu shrugged.

"Ngulwen could have figured it," Marindi said, keeping the argument alive. "The missionaries are always going to holler kidnapping when a girl goes off like that. Now she's rolling around all day and night with the Loborlilli boys while my sweethearts have been locked up at the mission for four weeks now, with two more to go till the white-fellas let them out."

"Don't complain so much. Think how eager, hard, and big they'll be when they finally get out," Talu teased. "And look how hot you are already. You'll have the best time in your whole life, and you'll have Ngulwen to thank for it."

Marindi snorted, unconvinced.

Raba sighed to herself, isolated by her inexperience. The first weekend out here she'd been nervous about having to

take a lover as the aftermath of her woman's rites, and was
relieved by the dearth of men. By the second weekend she was
anticipatory. She and Djilbara had been together alone in the
Outback several weeks for her initiation. Djilbara had been
anxious to see Talbiri again by the end of that time. The
Wuradilagu was disappointed to find him away working stock
when they returned. Raba tried to imagine that sort of desire
for herself, as if it were a set of white-fella's clothes she could
put on at will.

Raba hunched her shoulders, relaxed them, then drew
them up again. It had been two more weeks and now she was
bored and anxious, feeling trapped in eternal childhood. She
stood up and tossed more kindling on the fire. Some of the
mulga branches were still a little green and threw acrid smoke
back at her.

"Look at it this way," Jayulya said, implementing Talu's
view. "How often do we all get a chance to be together like
this, without our relatives or the white-fellas hanging over us?
And there's lots of things we can't talk about when the men are
here. Things about them." She grinned slyly. "For instance,
because Talu here is shut up in a different dorm room than us
at night, how else would I have found out from her that Mahlji
likes this . . ." she cupped her hand and rotated it sensuous-
ly, ". . . just when he's about to . . . ?"

Raba dropped her eyes. She rubbed her left foot with her
right. She wished she could be back at the children's campfire,
on the other side of the settlement. Guwara and Huroo were
holding forth there. At twelve, they wouldn't be initiated for
another year. Numiel, now the oldest uninitiated girl, would
be playing the role of sun-woman.

But Raba couldn't go back. Since passing her woman's
rites she was a grown-up in their eyes. Huroo even refused to
talk to her, believing her to be from an opposing clan, although
technically he could continue speaking to her until he passed
the second phase of his initiation at eighteen.

Her loneliness here festered into anger at him. Huroo was
jealous because she'd reached adulthood before him and left
him behind. Then her anger turned on herself. She knew they
were not from opposing clans and could always be friends,
even lovers, but she had no way to tell him, or expect him to
know.

She picked up a handful of dusty sand and rubbed it between her palms until it sifted away, leaving a powdery residue on her skin. The other girls' chatter faded to a lusty drone in her mind. Since she seemed doomed by circumstance always to be a child, women's rites or no, she would probably be able to talk to Huroo forever, if he'd only let her.

She felt the approach of a vehicle long before the other girls heard it, but she paid no attention. It was just a heavy, atonal jumbling of metallic parts, foreign as a white-fella, moving sluggishly through the lighter, cleaner fabric of the Dreamtime.

It was Marindi who heard first and understood what it meant. "I hear a truck!" she cried. "Coming from the south. Maybe it's the men coming back from the sheep stations."

Then they all saw its headlights. Instead of continuing up to the settlement, it turned off the road into the Outback towards them. Like a moth it was drawn by the glow of their fire.

The truck stopped well off in the dark. The girls could hear men clambering down and then the traditional polite warning of approach at night: a clapping of hands and high whistling. The girls all burst into laughter. "Why, who can that be?" Talu sang out in an overly sweet voice. "Who could that be, creeping up as silent as a *Wadjura*? Should we be afraid?"

The men strode into the firelight, laughing, too, still dressed in their jackeroo clothes of jeans and denim jackets. They were an older mix than usually visited this gathering site. "We wanted to see the whole camp. You're the first stop on the way," Migay said. "Where are all the younger rakes? What's wrong with them, leaving you women alone out here to concoct mischief?" One of the older girls explained about Ngulwen and the missionaries' punitive action. "Well, some of us will just have to stay and keep you company."

The men caught up on more camp gossip and told the girls some of their adventures on the sheep stations. Talbiri was among them. He looked startled to see Raba. She didn't know why. She'd been gone on her rites when he'd left. He seemed to be avoiding her, although they weren't from contra-indicated clans. She felt ashamed. He must be able to sense she was still a child and out of place in this company. The other girls' eyes and skin glowed in response to the men's presence. She felt shrunken, diminished.

One of the older men drove the truck up to the mission. About half of the rest drifted away on foot to see their young wives or sweethearts, or their parents. Raba watched Talbiri go. He set off at an angle that would not lead him to Djilbara's tent.

"Where is Talbiri going?" she asked Kunja, a short, merry-faced young man sporting an impressive moustache.

"Why, he's going . . ." he began. Out of the corner of her eye Raba saw Migay gesturing him to be quiet. Kunja didn't see him. ". . . to Mitika's, of course," he continued. Raba turned to Migay. He looked embarrassed.

"When did this happen?" she asked him. He shrugged, not meeting her eyes. *It's my fault this happened now*, thought Raba. *Talbiri drifted away when Djilbara took me out to the desert for my rites.*

They all gathered around the campfire, automatically sitting in proper clan alignments. The young women radiated excitement at the unexpected turn their evening had taken. The nervousness Raba experienced her first weekend here returned tenfold. She had spent her life surrounded by these men, but never before had their presence danced jittery on her skin.

Kunja was renowned for his ability to tell a story, and attention gravitated naturally towards him.

"There was this jackeroo," he began, "who was returning a long way to his home from stationmaster Mr. MacKenzie's. This jackeroo's name was Imumunda, after the long-neck turtle, which was his totem.

"It was that time of the year when the geese fly over the land to their lagoon homes to nest. When Imumunda saw a smoke-hawk flying fast across the sky, he knew if he followed that hunting bird he'd find good food to take home with him."

Kunja described Imumunda tracking the hawk over the countryside, further accenting his hero's tale with "finger talk."

"Finally he followed that bird into a box canyon, only to find he'd been tricked. There was nothing there. When he turned to go a big-eye *Wadjura* was blocking the way out." Kunja's audience trembled.

The story of Imumunda continued with great jeopardy as he tried to escape from the *Wadjura* and the malignant spirits of the dead the demon conjured up to capture the young jackeroo. The listeners by the fire found their hearts racing with the story's pace. They held their breath or let it out, gasping, according to Kunja's whim. He orchestrated delicious shivers against roasting flashes.

". . . when he came running over that rise, the cries of the ghosts were cold on the back of his neck. Imumunda could see the campfires of his kin, just like this campfire here, down there below him. He knew that if he could just get in a good leap across that gap he'd be safe. So he gathered up his legs underneath him; he was just about *screaming* the song of the *Janga Yonggar,* the great Kangaroo spirit, to give him strength for that jump. And right then something grabbed him, all freezing and boneylike, 'round the ankle. He looked down, and he saw . . ." A low wail started. The sound seemed to come from out in the desert. ". . . he saw," Kunja leapt and shrieked "*Wadjura!*" The fire exploded into a spray of sparks as someone threw several handfuls of sand onto it. The campsite erupted into pandemonium—people dashing this way and that, shouting, laughing.

Raba scrambled to her feet and started running. She collided with someone else. He grabbed her arm and pulled her along with him into the brush. The man stumbled, accidentally or deliberately, and they went crashing to the ground, rolling over and over together. *On purpose, on purpose,* she thought as they tumbled, for they were missing the punishing spines of the saltbushes.

They came to an entangled halt. Her leg was wrapped tight between hard, denim-wrapped calves. Her own panting breath was echoed out-of-rhythm by a broad, heaving ribcage. Pulling away a little she found herself looking down into Migay's face. He looked back at her with equal surprise; he hadn't known whom he'd managed to grab.

He grinned and rolled over so that he was on top. His torso pressed against her, sinuous as a snake. "How does little Raba like not being so little anymore? When I first saw you back there I'd forgotten you'd grown up to be a woman already."

Raba flushed and scrambled out from under him. This wasn't how she'd imagined things; being laughed at by someone who'd always been like an older brother to her.

"Hey, why are you so shy? You're all grown up now." He tilted her head into the light. "Why are your eyes all full of tears then, just like a little girl's?" he teased.

At that the tears flowed down her cheeks. Completely crushed, she turned, shoulders bowed, and started trudging back to the half-extinguished fire.

"Raba, what's wrong?" He caught her arm and pulled her around.

"Nobody's been around since my rites," she managed to mumble. "I'm not a woman yet. I don't know anything about this sweetheart business." She gestured awkwardly at the couples pairing off into the dark in the aftermath of Kunja's drama.

"Ahh. Now I see." He held her face in his hands and wiped away the tears with his thumbs. Then he hugged her and laughed. Raba was aware of him as warmth, muscle, and dusty skin. "When I was first a young man—I mean really a young man—after my second initiation, you were just a little girl hanging around Sister Djilbara's tent. Now here you are a grown young lady, and I'm still a young man . . . I think." He let her go to do an imitation of a hobbling old man. Raba giggled. "I'm lucky," he said. "That is . . . if . . . do you think you could like me that way?"

Raba looked at him and smiled. "Yes, I think I could do that," she said.

He pulled her to him in another hug. His fingers trailed along her ribs, gently grazed the side of her breast. "You know," he said, cradling her head in the curve of his collarbone, "sometimes it's good to learn things with old friends." She nodded against him. He took her hand and guided her out into the dark. "For example," he said, "I just happen to know of the nicest, softest sand hollow in the whole Outback, just big enough for both of us."

The Emu Ceremony
1958

Men were coming from far away bringing objects for the special Emu spirit-seeding ceremony, trying to rectify the scarcity of the great birds for the last two years. The closer the men came to the settlement, the more Raba dreamed. Each morning she woke less and less fully. Her spirit stayed *badundjari* even when it remained in her body. The waking life became haunted and insubstantial to her.

She watched herself forming words that spoke and answered questions asked by the thin and transparent forms of her teachers, friends, and family. She strained to see people; the shadows of ever more numerous spirits solidified and blocked them out, commanding her attention.

"Raba, listen to me," came Djilbara's worried voice. The *Wuradilagu's* wholeness and reality penetrated Raba's consciousness like a shock. "Try to wake up. If you can't, go further into the dreaming and bring something back we can use. Ask for help; a song, a weapon, anything."

Raba anchored herself to Djilbara's clarity, feeling awake only within the woman's sharp focus.

"The other day I woke up to find myself waving my hand at Dhuma," she said, "as if he were a spiderweb I could brush aside. What is happening? Is this from any magic we've done? Is it something I did?"

Djilbara shook her head. "Someone long ago wove a power that's blocking the pattern of the Dreamtime here. We've come upon the knot it caused. I don't know how to deal with it yet in a way that won't cause too many other things to unravel."

"Someone drove the Emus away and they don't want to come back. Maybe the old men can . . ." Raba said.

"The old men were sung up into that weaving. Raba, please try to help me."

* * *

Raba spent more and more time in the clearness of the Outback. She could indulge in an illusion of normalcy there, for all of the spirits of the Outback had been drawn to the settlement. Clustered densely, trapped in a simmering anger, they waited for the messengers to arrive. Even from her place in the clean, empty sand, she sensed them writhing, trapped, throughout the fabric of the camp's being.

She drew an outline of her hand in the sand and placed her palm against it. Her hand sank first through sand and then into the dark tunnels of the paths-between. She groped around, her fingers gliding down the shapes of miniature trails, until she grasped the orphaned *maban*. She drew it out and laid it against her stomach, stropping it back and forth in familiar ritual. Heat soaked into her in an infinitely slow healing, the scars melting into a finer texture. It no longer burnt with a sensation close to charring. Four years of this had had its effect on the crystal, too. The oblong chunk had been honed to the shape of a crude blade.

She relaxed, her overcrowded mind drawing comfort from the blankness of the *maban*. She couldn't see the mission from here, but the miasma of spirits hovered in the air above its site. Like her, they were watching, impatient for the arrival of the men. The souls of animals, plants, stones, they had all been captured by the events.

Reflected in the *maban's* clear gaze, she saw refracted images of different perceptions. The old men, of course, were aware of the gathering of the spirits, and they rightly perceived that they were being drawn to welcome the returning Emu spirits. What the elders were strangely blind to was the anger and hysteria of displacement saturating that anticipation.

The spirits waited on the approaching Emus. Unwillingly drawn back, the Emus were returning in a fury. Boundaries of Dreamtime patterns were being ruptured and each creature's place within the origins of the world was dangerously fluid. Raba put the *maban* away. She dreaded returning to the camp.

That evening as she rounded the corner of the mission store in a haze, she almost ran into Marindi, Huroo, and Yemma laughing together as they came out of the building.

"Marindi, tell Yemma how we discovered that Yalapa was a two-snuff-box man," Huroo was saying, paying lip service to

clan taboos by invoking Marindi's name. But he was looking at
Yemma, really speaking to her directly. Yemma belonged to
the same totemic clan that Raba did. Raba fought back a small
wound of hurt. Huroo never made that kind of exception for
her.

Raba choked as a wave of nausea swept over her. Even
that slight deference through Marindi caused watching spirits
to glare. When Huroo laid an arm over Marindi's shoulder,
caressing her, Raba saw lips being drawn back from glowing
spectral fangs.

The trio caught sight of Raba. Huroo's face tightened and
he shifted so that the two young women stood between him
and Raba.

"Raba, are you all right?" Marindi reached out a hand to
her. Raba's queasiness was replaced by love and fear for the
other girl. Marindi was unaware of the agitated spirits pacing
in a circle around the group. As one of Huroo's taboo lovers,
she was a focus for their wrath. The trio became transparent,
frighteningly vulnerable. Raba cried out to the spirits, throwing her words like spears. "It's not fair. You don't understand
us. You don't care that ignorance can be innocent. Leave them
alone!" The spirits scattered. A look of fear passed across
Yemma's ghostly face. Then the plump girl resolidified into
flesh. Raba became conscious of the trio staring at her. The
embarrassed silence was broken when Huroo, his face stiffened into a mask, spoke. "Marindi, tell Sister Raba that if she
is feeling unwell she should seek help from the *Wuradilagu* or
the elders." He turned and walked off.

Raba felt a pain that was all her own, separate from the
turmoil infecting the camp. Huroo should have been a strong
element in the pattern of her life. Since his initiation two years
ago, he avoided her at all costs. She knew this was partly from
the fatal lack of knowledge about his true clan status, but it was
also for reasons she couldn't understand. Had she done
something wrong at some time in the past that made him hate
her? Was she flawed in some way that only he could see? There
must be some truth escaping her that left her blind and
helpless.

Yemma hurried after Huroo. Marindi still stood there, her
eyes filled with sadness and pity.

That night Raba fled into sleep, willing herself not to
emerge from *badundjari* at all. If her few waking moments

were to be so filled with a pain and confusion she could do nothing about, then she would stay on the edges of the Dreamtime. At least there she could roam freely and had some power.

She moved through a different Outback under a flatly black sky. A faint light glowed from the ground. It painted the undersides of objects with a silvery sheen, leaving upper edges dark, in an eerie reversal of the light and shadow of waking life. When Raba looked down at her own body she saw the same eerie lighting. Her flesh shimmered whitely, shading upwards to gray, except on her stomach, where the *maban's* power hadn't finished its work. There the small unhealed part of her center looked dull and flat, like the ghost of a hole.

Thunder rolled from beneath the ground. Boulders slowly throbbed and swelled, growing larger till they broke through their crusts to emerge as creatures. Elsewhere stone beasts sank back into the ground into dormancy. Pale spiders and moths drew lines of web and cocoon in patterns on the ground and through the air.

Raba wandered until she found a weaving of such density that the white strands clotted together to give off their own light. The design was ugly and confused. Hovering over it, a tall granite spirit pounded its anger into the ground. The pattern shifted with each vibration. Arachnid shades cast threads around its legs, trying to hobble it. It snapped the tender lines with ease. It kicked at the web. Other, smaller spirits were trapped there. They struggled feebly against their bonds. The spirit drew its birdlike neck up and twisted to look at Raba.

"Retreat, you who know," it hissed at her.

"Greatest of the Emu spirits, why do you do this?" Raba said, her indignation greater than her fear. "Look how hard the spiders work. Why don't you help them to put it right?"

"There is a place, an entity, in which I should be resting. They've given it to another. They've placed the effigy of the Goanna on the rock I should grow from. They poison me and tell me to grow scales rather than feathers. Look at their work; their task is to maintain the connection with the Dreamtime. Instead they've corrupted it, and now the rot must be destroyed."

"What is this resting place you speak of?"

"You are a path. Follow yourself till you find it," it taunted. Melting into the ground, it sank below the surface to become a deep hole, which quickly filled with water. Raba moved away as she sensed a *Wanambi* take possession of it from below.

She walked along the gray rock plain. Her feet slapped on the cool dry surface. The sound echoed emptiness in one spot. She picked up a rock and held it high over her head to smash down, thinking she might break through into the hollow space. The rock writhed in her hands, turning into a Kookaburra. Raba squealed and let it go. Laughing maniacally, it flew off. Now there was a thin crack in the stone. Raba ran one finger over it. She sang in the pitch of the Kookaburra's cackle, which did nothing. Then she repeated the tone of her own shriek. The crack widened. More lines branched off of it. The stone began to crumble. Pushing down on it with both hands, Raba almost fell inwards when it collapsed.

Below was a sunlit glade surrounding a billabong. No light from the scene reflected upwards into Raba's dreamscape. As she watched, Huroo burst from the water, laughing. His head was thrown back, the weight of the water washing his hair in ringlets down his neck.

Clutched under each arm was an enormous Barramundi fish. They would have been too large for him to carry in waking life. He threw them one at a time onto the banks of the billabong, then waded to shore after them. He flung himself on his back on the grass there and stretched, eyes closed in evident enjoyment as the sun's warmth dried his water-chilled skin, smoothing goose bumps to silkiness.

Raba watched, aching. It had been years since she'd seen Huroo open and relaxed. Whenever she was present he became tight and guarded.

She slid through the hole and landed lightly on her feet. Soundlessly she crept up and crouched by him. Leaning forward, she drew her hands through his hair and stroked his face. Tears stung her eyes. How long had it been since she'd touched him?

"Mmmm," Huroo murmured. "That feels good." He smiled, opened his eyes, and looked at her.

With a yell he was on his feet, and Raba was left with just droplets of water on her empty hands. The scene wavered as he tried to shift away from her. She weighted herself and held him fast as an anchor to the place.

"You can't do that," he yelled. "This is the one place you can't come to."

"You're wrong. This is the one place you can't run away from me," she replied.

He drew up images of Marindi and Ninual. "Raba, leave here. You're taboo." They spoke in Huroo's voice.

Raba wept. "Why do you avoid me? It's not just the taboos. You were my friend when we were little. You could at least still be my friend. What did I do?"

"Tell Sister Raba I can't explain it to her," he said through Marindi's lips. "She's too young. It's complicated and it would just confuse her." The voice deepened and changed. Raba couldn't quite recognize it, overlaid as it was with Huroo's, but it was familiar. Huroo's form began to thicken. Someone outside of the dream was weaving another skin around him.

"Huroo, what is that? You're closed in, as if you were wearing layers on layers of white-fellas' clothing." Raba tried to sing him in place, but he withdrew into the cocoon, diminishing. The figure of Ninual brightened for an instant. Startled eyes peered out at Raba and then faded. Walking in a dream of her own, the real Ninual had intersected with Huroo's for a moment. Huroo's dream began to blow away in tatters. Raba clutched at the pieces.

"Don't go, Huroo, please. I have to warn you. Don't go to the ceremonies tomorrow. It will be dangerous. The Emu spirit is angry."

"A Goanna has nothing to fear," came a last whisper through Marindi's lips.

Raba stretched along the underside of the night. Her veins forked out in a million paths. Spirits and others marched along their fine intricacies. Across her earthen body she felt the heavy tread of men, weighted down with small stones spectrally dense. The carcass of an Emu was slung between two of the men. Emu spirits followed behind. Raba realigned within herself and the path became a loop. The men were lulled for a while. One finally noticed their repetitive footprints, that they'd been walking in a circle. "*Wadjura* sorcery," he spat out, and they leapt away from her boundaries. Their approach resonated along other routes outside of her reach.

The sun rose and warmed her sinews and tendons embedded in the Land. She didn't wake, trusting an automatic pattern to propel her shell of a waking body to rise and dress itself with unfeeling fingers. The daytime was more like a dream than the night. Activities of people and spirits shimmered, flitted, and slid unsubstantially across her vision. She alternately tasted flavors of joy and wrath.

Numada rose with that first light of morning in elation. He felt as if he were the crest of a great wave, coursing over the Ocean. Today Huroo would be the axis on which the Dreamtime began to shift.

Creeping quietly from between his two wives and around the children, Numada dressed without waking them. He'd spent the night in a great dreaming; preparing for today, diverting that pest, Raba, from chasing after Huroo. The power of his dream washed over his family like a drug.

He pulled on worn dungarees, remnants of his few years on the stockman's circuit. Although stocky in frame, his body was tightly drawn in muscle to the point of leanness. He'd avoided the barrel belly cultivated by most prosperous men. His hair and beard were more closely cropped than the shaggy manes favored by many of the men in the settlement, and evenly shot through with gray. Yet the skin on his face was taut, giving it the smooth appearance of a much younger man.

Making his way southward through the camp to the well, he called greetings to other early risers. The well was already crowded with those busy in preparation for the great feast. Not the best of places to go *badundjari*, but it had to be here, where sixteen years ago he'd repeatedly made love to Huroo's mother and driven his dream-child into her.

He slipped into one of the surrounding clumps of gum trees and sat, comfortable in the deep litter of their crescent-shaped, aromatic leaves. Leaning back against a trunk, the sunlight filtering through the trees striped his body in a jagged pattern that matched the perpetually molting bark. He closed his eyes and flattened out, becoming a shadow on the living wood, no thicker than a single layer of cells. Soaking through it, the tree became a portal for him. He moved into an opaque, light-filled space, like diving up through a golden pool of the white-fellas' butter. On the other side was his own special place. In all these years the elders had not detected it. It was here he'd rewoven the underpinnings connecting the settlement to the Dreamtime.

He burst into this private, most protected of havens and cried aloud in shock. Piles of his weavings lay strewn about, unraveled. In the middle of the chaos a figure bent over, obscured in a heap of dark clothing and ribbons. It was pulling apart another one of his works and retying it in a new pattern with flying hands.

"Stop that!" he yelled, and tried frantically to pull the strands away from the apparition. Fingers not slacking in their pace, the thing threw back its head with a low laugh. He found himself staring into Djilbara's glistening, deadly eyes.

"You!" he hissed. "How?"

A moment ago Numada was invincible. Now a mere woman had penetrated to his most secret place undetected. Numada's life crumbled away from beneath him. He felt a terrible, overwhelming fear. This woman was monstrous, more powerful even than he. She had done what none of the elders could do. Wait, that had to be it. The reason was because she *was* a woman. He hadn't thought to protect himself from that avenue. His confidence began to return. He'd been careless, foolish, deservedly caught unawares. But now that Djilbara moved openly against him, he could deal with her.

He couldn't wrest the weaving from her. She was locked safely in a ring of charms. "Do you think that will stop me?" he sneered. He would leave her here and attack from waking life, or go to another refuge and weave around her, making this place her prison.

Gathering up an armful of the dreaming strands lying about, he made for the portal. It was blocked. A dense net of intricately knotted hair had fallen over it, sealing it shut. He snarled. Did she think that would stop him? There were many doorways from this place that led directly into his great dreaming. But each one, as he came to it, was barred.

He turned. Never ceasing in her reweaving, she watched him.

"So be it," he said. "We will match our skills here and now."

The pile of spectral fibers glowed at his feet. He began to retie his own knots to the Dreamtime, his speed as great as hers.

"Why?" she asked. "Can't you feel the spirits gathering? Can't you feel the Emus' anger?"

He laughed. "I'm well aware of their displeasure. What is it to me? I've already proved myself their master. Two years ago I challenged them, and they left rather than do battle with me."

"Yes," she said. "When Huroo went through his first initiation. How can you do this to him, make him your experiment? He won't make it through his clan initiation, even if he should survive today. You have other children. Why don't you release him and concern yourself with them instead?"

"They are like a family of shadows to me," he said. "It is Huroo that binds me. At first I only wanted to possess his mother. If not in marriage then at least in this secret, even from her. But my dreaming of him was so strong it became something else. I skirted through the edges of the Dreamtime and found its boundaries molten, malleable to my will. In a way, I have never left that dreaming. As Huroo grew in the womb, I grew."

He laughed as he retethered one line. "Just before he was born I was so afraid. Surely someone would see he was an Emu and know I was the father! I went into the hills again and dreamed layers of disguise as soft and protecting as swaddling clothes. Other children were born naked; not Huroo. For years I was always in terror, waiting for the day the elders truly saw him. That day never came, and my fear faded as I realized I had redreamed a part of the Dreamtime, actually altered its structure. And no one ever saw."

"I saw. I always knew," said Djilbara.

"But you did nothing. And over the years Huroo and I have grown, each in our own way. Now I'm too powerful to be stopped. I am the strongest of the Clever Men, and I have only a woman opposing me."

Djilbara looked startled, suddenly unsure of herself. "A Clever Man?" Her weaving faltered for a moment. "When were you initiated? You're never in the company of the others. When could you have learned their secrets? They would never have let you do this."

"I skirted through their dreams. They never knew I was there, learning from them. The path I followed was my own."

Djilbara trembled. "You're completely outside of the Law. Huroo will be destroyed. We'll all be destroyed. Can't you feel your scheming tearing our ties with the Dreamtime apart? We'll be lost."

Numada said nothing for a moment. With a deft twist he'd

retied the most ancient of the elders, Makwora, into place
again. Sweat wept down his brow into his eyes, almost
blinding him. The old one's consciousness had been awakening, which would have been disastrous. He cursed at the
woman's hindrance.

"Huroo is a pool whose waters go deep to the source of
life. He will survive and I will survive. Those who will be lost
in the transition are just passing reflections. I've dreamed the
camp on edge and today I will begin to spin it. By Huroo's clan
initiation, it will fall into place in the proper alignment for the
two of us."

"No, this is monstrous!" shouted Djilbara. "When it falls
all will shatter, including the two of you."

Numada laughed. "I defeated the great Emu spirits. Do
you think I fear you?"

Their contest reached an equilibrium. Numada chafed,
for if he were not trapped here he'd have access to other kinds
of magic and could easily defeat the *Wuradilagu*. But weaving
was the most ancient of women's skills—at this she was his
equal, if not his better. Well, let her delay him here. The
events he'd set in motion would still proceed.

All day Raba's spirit looked for Djilbara. At last she sensed
the *Wuradilagu*, hidden away somewhere, in a contest of
weaving skills with a demon. Her fingers were flying, un-
knotting his work and retying the threads to her own design.
But the *Wadjura* kept apace of her.

Raba couldn't sense enough to provide herself with an
inner visualization. She couldn't *see* Djilbara or her opponent.
Instead, she felt the *Wuradilagu* as a concentrated density, the
joints and knuckles of the woman's fingers and hands turning,
rolling, jabbing, tucking, pulling. Raba felt the *Wadjura*, too.
There was something she could almost remember about him.
He was almost familiar, but because she couldn't *see* him, he
stayed on just the other side of the edge of recognition.

The contest was so intense, so close. Raba wanted to call
out to Djilbara, but she was afraid that drawing the slightest
bit of the *Wuradilagu's* attention might tip the battle to the
Wadjura.

But what if Djilbara should lose? Now Raba noticed that
when Djilbara unloosened one set of knots and then retied
them, Raba felt a corresponding release and catching up
snugly into the right place of the flux of events in the camp.

And when the demon untied and rewove his knots, there was a loosened-bowels-illness sense of dissolution, followed by a strangled feeling, like netting pulled off its proper angle, till it choked rather than supported.

Djilbara must win! Raba decided to risk calling to her teacher. If she could help, even a little, it might throw the balance of the battle.

She pitched a query song along what she felt of Djilbara; along the inner lines of the woman's bones and joints, which were clicking and sliding against each other like polished wood. Raba sang her song into that pattern within Djilbara, so the *Wadjura* wouldn't hear her.

> Djilbara, Djilbara
> I feel you fighting
> Let my voice join with yours
> Let my voice strengthen yours
> Let my hands join with yours

If the *Wuradilagu* was startled, it was only for an instant. It didn't cause her to drop a single stitch. Raba sensed, for the first time, the stance of battle. Her teacher's focus, though concentrated, was not narrow. Djilbara was open and prepared for any attack, any new turn of events.

Raba knew Djilbara was aware of her, but the *Wuradilagu* didn't reply. Raba felt ashamed. How could she have expected her to? Her teacher couldn't call out to her in front of the demon. Then she felt a tightening in Djilbara's hands, calling her attention to them. The pattern of the *Wuradilagu's* flying fingers was weaving a message for Raba.

> I fight him alone to keep him at bay here.
> You must stay to watch the camp.
> You must stay to watch the camp.
> I fight him alone to keep him at bay here.
> You must stay to watch the camp.
> You must stay to watch the camp.
> I fight him alone to keep him at bay here.

Raba withdrew from Djilbara's bones.

People were singing to the Emu spirits, thinking their songs were received with favor. The visitors had arrived late, but now the carcass they'd brought was baking in a sand-bed oven. Elders shaved fragments from stones brought on many days' travel. These they buried throughout the surrounding desert as seeds the Emus would increase and multiply from.

By midafternoon the camp gathered around the cooking pit to dance and tell favorite tales. Old men sanctified the day's proceedings. The Emu spirits stood as tall and threatening as flood clouds over the settlement.

Raba gathered herself back into her body. As the sky darkened into night, ritual cooks began to serve the feast. They opened up the fire pit and drew away the leaves covering the roasted Emu. Tearing off strips of flesh, they served them to the laughing, hungry crowd. Only members of the Emu clan sat apart, with separate ritual foods, not tasting any of the steaming meat. To eat Emu would be the same as cannibalism, and worse. It would be the same as devouring their own souls. So none of them ate from the carcass, save one.

Raba watched Huroo accept a serving. She rose to stop him. His eyes met hers and she saw he remembered her intrusion into his dream. A few quick words to Guwara, seated next to him, and the bigger youth intercepted her, blocking her path. "Raba, I'd heard you were unwell yesterday. It's good to see you feeling better." Frantic, she tried to edge around him, but he took her arm and guided her back to her place. Over her shoulder she saw Huroo finish his portion. Raba yanked at Guwara, trying to pull away.

She felt the Emu seeds out in the desert erupt from their places and burst into flame. The sands themselves began to burn. Sensing this, the old men looked at each other, startled. The gathered crowd picked up their unease. Raba felt Guwara loosen his hold, then leave her.

Arching their chests, the great Emus hovering overhead drew back their wings. Raba saw powerful muscles stretched taut over bone, feathers blending up into the clouds. Wings began to beat, birthing frenzied winds. Sheets of fire raced across the Outback. Gray smoke boiled up into the sky. Women grabbed their children and ran back to the tents. Bells rang out from the mission. Milling uncertainly, men looked to the elders for direction. Spirits coiled and uncoiled in terror. Raba's vision darkened as Dreamtime and waking time flickered in and out of each other.

Huroo lay on the ground. His face was crumpled in agony

and bathed in sweat. Marindi and Guwara bent over him in perplexed concern. The great Emu spirits hissed upwards as steam, condensed, and pooled together as they trailed down from the sky. The liquid precipitated as flinty stone that grew into a single ominous bird. With slow but inexorable strides, it bore down on Huroo.

"Djilbara! Djilbara!" Raba screamed.

Djilbara and the demon were still *badundjari* together. They fought, pulling the weaving, stretching it, each trying to draw it around the fire in their own way. Djilbara's voice whistled to her from the flames. "I can't. I have to save the camp. You must save Huroo."

The pounding of the Emu's footsteps shook Huroo's body into spasms. His eyes were open and staring. Raba knew that he could see the spirit. She staggered to her feet and began to race across the clearing to him. She stumbled, hindered; small claws were scratching on her skin. Flowing across the ground, spirits were trying to crawl up her; their actions a mute insistence that she was a path they could escape by. Cursing, she shook them off.

Reaching her friend, she grabbed Huroo's feet and started to drag him off. Guwara and Marindi stood staring at her.

"Help me get him away," she yelled at them. Guwara grabbed Huroo's arms and they pulled him behind some tents. Blood trickled from his nose and mouth. He tried to retch, feebly, but the food stayed, eating its way out instead through his entrails.

The Emu spirit rounded the corner of the tents. Raba could see each stride pulling it forward from the Dreamtime, the discontinuity dragging on its feet like glue.

"We have to get that meat out of him. Force it out of his stomach!" she yelled frantically.

Guwara pushed on Huroo's abdomen with his hands, leaning all his weight into the action. Then he knelt on him, rocking back and forth with his knees. Huroo's whole body convulsed and his neck snapped back, but the poisonous flesh remained. Raba pushed Guwara aside and grabbed Huroo, shaking him. Helpless, she could see into him, see the ingested spirit etching through him like acid, burning its way out to join the greater spirit. Someone grabbed her, trying to yank her from him. She tightened her grip and watched her hands sink into him, as if she were a crystalline blade.

Marindi was tugging at her, crying hysterically.

"Raba, don't touch him. You mustn't touch him. You'll only make it worse. You know you're taboo for him." She tried to pull Huroo away from Raba.

Just then the Emu spirit reached them. Enraged at Marindi's contact with the youth, it kicked out at her. The blow caught her above the eye, opening a gash in her forehead. With the great bird distracted, Raba cut the rest of the way into Huroo. She felt as if she were her orphaned *maban*: clear and bright and mindless. She guided the meat back up through Huroo's digestive tract, drawing the spirit of it into herself. Trembling, Huroo struggled to his hands and knees and was finally able to vomit. A moment later he and Raba were both knocked flat as the Emu struck. Raba flung herself around Huroo and sang, her voice hoarse in an ugly scream.

> *Into me*
> *Into me*
> *Into me*
> *Follow me*
> *Follow me*
> *Follow me*
> *I am the path.*

He is mine, the Emu hissed. *He has always been mine. He is part of me. You cannot keep us apart.* But compelled against its will by the spirit she'd absorbed, it slid inside of her.

He will be yours, Raba promised. *But not like this, not to destroy. I will give him to you the way it was meant to be, so that you and he are one.* She led it further inside herself on a path that was a labyrinth and sealed it within. *I'll give him back to you at the place of your beginnings.*

The sands in the desert crisped, smoldered, and subsided. Somewhere Djilbara folded in on herself from exhaustion. Huroo lay on the ground, eyes closed, panting like a Dingo. Guwara held a sobbing Marindi. When Raba went to touch her face, the other girl flinched away in fear, but Raba persisted until Marindi let her explore the wound.

"It missed your eye. You're just blinded by the blood. Come with me. There are herbs in Djilbara's tent I can make into a poultice that will close and heal the wound."

She turned to Guwara. Nodding at Huroo she said, "Get him cleaned up and take him somewhere he can sleep undisturbed." She put an arm around the now unresisting Marindi and pulled her to her feet, supporting her. Unnoticed, the girls made their way through the still panicky camp.

Raba hardly felt Marindi's weight leaning on her. The stoniness of the Emu coursing round and round within her made each step seem like an hours-long task. She yearned to be away by herself out in the desert, in the cleanness of wind and sand.

Repossession

Huroo's guts were still drawn tight and aching the next day when he went in search of Raba. He found her in a curious place; out on the plain a considerable distance from the camp, sitting in reverie in an unshaded, absolutely featureless spot. If he'd approached directly from the camp, she would have been partially hidden by a slight swelling in the ground. But he came from behind at an angle, having looked for her first farther outwards and to the north.

He approached quietly and without stealth across scorched and blackened sands. Raba was staring in an unfocused way in the direction of the settlement. She held one hand to her stomach. As he came around her other side, he caught a glimpse of something bright and clear there. She turned to him and that hand left her belly to rest on the ground. He saw it resting palm down on the sand, nothing shiny in it. At the same time it seemed to sink past itself through the earth in a curious illusion. He blinked hard several times, eyes swimming. His vision cleared and he saw Raba watching him. One hand lay curled on her lap. The other was simply an empty hand, solid, beside her.

Her eyes were calm, unstartled, but he guessed that few people could walk up on her like that, even when she was deep in trance.

She said nothing. There was not even the anticipatory feel of waiting about her. She would sit here, silent, until he spoke or left.

Huroo shifted from one foot to the other. He didn't know how to begin. His deep urgency to find her hadn't considered or provided the words or thoughts he needed now. Thanking her wasn't enough. Nor was a simple apology; then all the complicated reasons an apology was necessary had to be dealt with. Until this moment he hadn't been aware of how much he'd hidden from himself, of the false distance he'd imposed between them. And yet, the unsettling vision he experienced moments ago reminded him in some deep place inside why he'd nurtured and encouraged that distance.

He looked at her in the simplest way, stripping away years of assumptions and defense. Raba, a slender young woman of fifteen. Like himself, she was dressed only in a pair of khaki shorts. They were too large. Her hips barely kept them from sliding off her body. Her belly was little more rounded than his own, lightly marked with its curious scarring. A hair-string belt crossed just below her navel. Her breasts were small but more prominent than he'd allowed himself to see before. Her collarbone cut a clean cliffline above them, with her neck arching above that. The wild darkness of her hair was streaked with sun-bleached russet. Her eyes were dark and calm. Her face matched their gravity, but in his memory's eye he saw that finely etched mouth split into a grin, the broad features of her face a lively landscape.

Why hadn't he been able to see her like this before? He'd watched the other girls grow up, accepting their changes with only the usual bumps and detours in his perceptions natural to his own growth. When Marindi blossomed he'd viewed the change with an embarrassed pleasure, which changed to simple enjoyment when he was old enough himself to see that that reaction was natural.

But Raba was different. He had kept her as a small child in his mind. When the other boys spoke of her as a lover, he was uneasy, even feeling a small horror, as if they were abusing the little girl that was his closest friend. When they hinted about her sexual responsiveness, he felt confused. He had withdrawn from her more and more, accelerating their separation by clan taboos.

Then there was the other side of her he was more aware of

fearing; the *Wuradilagu*, the woman of power and magic. He would be an old man before he lived as close to the source of things as she did now.

He didn't think of Raba as evil. But he knew she was willful. When she'd continued to pursue a connection with him, in spite of their eventual separation under the clan taboos, he'd feared her. He felt she was capable of deluding herself and using her gifts for dangerous indulgences. Dreaming, he met her frequently, always confronting him mournfully and accusingly.

But last night's events turned his beliefs upside down. He could see nothing that he'd done wrong, but he'd been punished fearfully for some inadvertent ignorance. Raba, whom he'd doubted, whom he treated so arrogantly, had helped him.

Clearing his throat, he forced himself to leap into words, stumbling stiffly through their meaning.

"Raba, I've treated you like a child. I've been the child. I lied to myself that I was a man, and could understand and take responsibility for the Law. But I was just using that as an excuse to drive you off. I blinded myself so that I couldn't see you.

"I don't know what I did that made the spirits so angry with me last night. I'm glad you saved me." He shook his head as if to clear away the memory of the night. "But I'm also glad because I didn't know there were these layers of lies inside me. Don't go away from me. I don't really want to drive you off."

Raba stood up. "Huroo, about last night. It wasn't anything you did that you could know about," she said softly. "You're so good, and you're careful about the Law." She hesitated before speaking again. "There are things we can't help, can't always understand. Sometimes I think we're like the white-fellas' jigsaw puzzles. We're those funny-shaped pieces. We don't know which way our ancestors and the Dreamtime are going to turn us to make us fit the whole, and what part of the picture we'll be, no matter how carefully we follow the rules."

Huroo felt despair. "Do you mean I'll never know when that will happen again? What I did to cause it? Can you help me?" He looked down at his feet in shame. "Would you even want to?"

Raba took his hand and smiled. "Maybe we can help each other, together," she said.

They started to walk in a roundabout way back to the camp. It was the hottest part of the day. Animals and birds rested in shade or their tunnel homes. Even the spirits of the plants were withdrawn into the quiet of their dark moist centers. Huroo marveled, for he sensed the heat only through these and other signs, without feeling it. Being with Raba felt like walking in a cooling shadow.

They approached the camp along the gradual downgrade that led to the communal well. Surrounded by boulders and sheltering mulgas and gum trees, it was still some distance from the crowded dirtiness of the settlement. No one was there. The Aborigines were of a like mind with the other residents of the Outback when it came to the midday sun.

While the well was still a long way off, a perception crept up on Huroo that he, Huroo, was somewhere behind them, very small, watching another Huroo and Raba walk along hand in hand. He watched them, detached, until they were almost at the well. Then he was back in his own body feeling himself being watched by the small spirit Huroo trailing behind them.

Raba stopped at the well and drew up some water. She poured it into one of several tin bowls lying around and held it up with both hands for Huroo to drink. He put his hands over hers and drank, not letting go. The structure of her fingers against the tin was a terrain of warm firm ridges dropping into water-cooled metal. He closed his eyes as the water slid down his throat. Across the few inches between them he keenly felt every inch of her body parallel to his own.

Lowering the bowl he met her eyes. Her lashes dropped as she, too, bent her head and drank. His hands slid along her arms to her shoulders. The small spirit loomed closer and closer. He knew he should speak and ask her about it. Finished drinking, Raba let the empty tin slide to the ground and rested her hands on his hips.

The gentle approach of the spirit became the pounding of heavier footsteps behind him. His stomach wrenched. He recognized the angry, birdlike tread from the night before. He pulled Raba to him convulsively, not knowing whether it was to protect her or to be protected himself. He forgot the spirit momentarily in the shock of contact with her skin. She was warm and cool at once. Burrowing against her he became aroused. He choked in horror, but couldn't stop moving against her. She didn't withdraw, but held him with a light touch.

The spirit's stride was so close it resounded in a throbbing that filled his entire head. Now he willed it to come. It must kill him before he broke the worst of taboos. How could he stay so aroused when terror was filling him, drowning and strangling him from within? Raba's face, trapped against his throat; her breath echoing on his neck; her breasts, alive with her heartbeat, gliding against him, were all exquisitely tormenting. He cried. Tears streamed down his face to join sweat in a conspiracy to help their bodies move more slickly together.

"No, no. I'm sorry. Don't let me. Please, Raba, help me . . ." he groaned. Her hands left him and he experienced an instant of hope. But she was unfastening the buttons of her shorts. In despair and pleasure he felt them slide downwards, the slight tooth of the fabric's nap a taunting promise against his calves. Then she made short work of his pants and they joined hers on the ground in an easy union.

He bent her back on the boulders ringing the well. The Emu spirit's breath blistered his back. The smell and coolness of the water below seemed a oneness with Raba's body beneath him. His erection was nestled against her belly. With another kind of shame he remembered some of the young men talking about her; how smooth her buttocks were, and the contrast of the scarring on her stomach. Now he felt that; the granular texture softly scratching in wonderful relief against the irritation of his erection, and at the same time goading it to greater aching. He moaned.

The angry spirit was kicking into him through his back. Ripped into, Huroo could feel it stretching its claws down along his thigh bones till they reached and filled his feet. His legs felt engorged with blood, which only served to heat him further and make him writhe more strongly against Raba. The Emu tore away at him, emptying him. Huroo felt the empty cavity filling with feathers. Raba slid up the boulder a little. Huroo ran his hands frantically up the inside of her thighs to find with a shock that she was softened and wet, ready for him. Raba pulled her head away a little to look into his face, waiting to find something there. Her features were blurred, as if he was looking at her through someone's eyes behind his own—

the Emu's. The vision sharpened as the spirit filled his skull. Raba shifted a little, still watching him. As the Emu took him, she slid onto him.

With a gasp he shoved into her, finding all his own heat tightly answered there. The Emu's angry stride echoed in his frantic pounding into her. He still wept, now because this was not the way he made love, in a mad rutting. He was used to pleasuring his partners with skilled tenderness. If he had to do this terrible thing with Raba, he wanted at least to give her the best of that. But instead he felt irritated with her because she wouldn't give him the distance he needed to draw back with each thrust and strike into her. Welding her body to his, she rode each movement with him. His irritation melted away as he began to discover her internal surfaces and rhythms with the continual contact.

Raba's limbs were supple against his, undulating with him in a dance of flesh in flesh and flesh against flesh. A ripple started at the base of her spine. He grabbed her there to support her. Her back slowly arched. He could see her face contort in a grimace and thought he'd finally injured her. But she drew her lips back in a cry of such joyous pleasure and release that it raced down his own spine to reverberate in his loins, swelling him, and he burst his own release within her.

Afterwards they lay together under the mulgas. Raba felt a kind of completion, a discovery of the beginnings and endings of her paths in Huroo. The years of self-doubt and undefined longings flattened like drought's dust under healing rains. She luxuriated in stretching fully against him, held loosely in the circle of his arms. The Emu was at rest, content, inside him. But there was a tenseness within Huroo himself that she felt. He disentangled himself from her and awkwardly started to sit up, pulling away from her. Then he changed his mind and drew her to him, holding her tightly.

"I'm afraid. Raba, forgive me. All we can do is wait for our ancestors to strike us down. I don't know why it hasn't happened already. To force myself as a lover on a woman of your clan . . . I love you, but I've destroyed you."

She stroked him gently. "Don't listen to your thoughts, Huroo. Listen to the spirits inside of you. Do you feel better or worse than you did last night?"

He was quiet for a while. His grip around her relaxed.

"Better, much better," he admitted. "I feel whole. As if my whole life I'd only had half my eyesight, and now I can see everything clearly."

"What do you see when you look at me, then?"

He studied her. "I see Raba. I don't see anything wrong. It's as if you're part of me." He let go of her and covered his eyes with his hands. "I'm confused. I don't see how that can be," he said unhappily.

She burrowed back into his arms like a small night animal into its den. "Do you trust me?" she asked.

"After last night? Yes."

"Do you understand that there are things I might know that you don't?"

"Yes," he replied. "Can you explain them to me?"

She hesitated. "I don't know it all yet, myself. But this I can tell you: there's confusion about your clan totem status. At least part of you belongs to the Emus."

"Why haven't the elders told me that?"

"Apparently they can't see it," she said.

"What should I do?"

"We both need to be careful. There are going to be a lot of questions after last night. We'll help each other as much as we can."

There was still a small core of unhappiness to him.

"Don't you believe me?" she asked.

"It's not that." He sounded embarrassed.

She waited.

"Raba, the way I was with you . . . that's not how I am as a lover," he said miserably.

She wrapped her legs around his waist and crowed with delight. "Oh, really? And how am I to believe that?" She licked the hollow at the base of his throat and trailed her tongue upwards to trace along his chin.

He shivered happily and drew her hips snugly to him.

"You'll just have to prove it, I guess," she said.

Rain

In the Outback rains came infrequently but with a hard violence. Storm clouds pregnant with tons of suspended water hovered, pressing heavily on the air trapped between them and the unyielding gibber plains. The atmosphere compressed into an essence of heat, dust, and unreleased power. Breath became hard to draw into lungs. When the sky finally ripped open, the water descended in sheets hard enough to bruise a man. At first miniature clouds of gold and red formed along the ground as the weight of the rain displaced dust and sand upwards, as if the rain and the earth were in the process of exchanging places. Then that fragile, dusty atmosphere was also beaten down. The Land drank in what it could—not enough—and drowned in the feast of water. Red claypans dissolved and ran like blood. The blackened sands, scorched months before by the rage of the Emu spirits, floated up and were skimmed clean.

The spirits within the desert plants at first retracted in shock. But as the moisture finally seeped down and bathed their parched entrenched roots, their long, still memories retrieved sensations of other such deluges.

When flash floods and mud flows snapped off their branches and trunks clean to the ground, their hearts, protected inside the Land, continued to soften and expand. Mummified seeds, dormant for years, swelled with moisture. When the sun returned, they would explode from the soil into a life of color and propagation as intense and almost as brief as the rain itself.

The lovers nestled together in a nest they'd constructed in the heart of a clump of cottonbushes. Raba listened to the plants and reported on their doings to Huroo. He sang a song for each place she told him of. Someday Huroo would learn the skill of making rain from the elder men. What he wouldn't learn from them was what Raba taught him today; how to divert gusts of it to areas that needed it—areas that Huroo by his birthright was responsible for.

After one of the song cycles, Huroo shifted and turned Raba to face him. "Enough of that for a while," he said, nuzzling her ear and the contour of her cheek. "We hardly ever get to be together like this, with everyone else holed up till the rain is over."

Raba laughed, put her hand on his stomach and braced her arm between them, keeping him at bay. "But that's why we're here," she said. "To play with the rains. So you can learn."

He brushed her hand aside and pressed against her. "There are other things you can teach me."

Raba continued to protest, but she found herself responding to him. She always did. Their nest was lined with dried tussock-grass. The moisture from outside, trying to seep through, released the latent fragrance in the matted stalks. The rain sang its own song onto the cottonbush leaves.

The water from all the millions of drops pooled together, gathering strength, becoming something larger. As she and Huroo made love, Raba felt that pattern beating into her, reflected in the two of them. Each time they were together in any way—talking, learning, or joined in passion—they became the beginning of something greater. And each time that process started where they had last left off, growing larger and larger. She sensed their togetherness as something so vast that they were as huge as the clouds. The thirsty Land inhaled and assimilated them in the ending of a cycle of a different kind of drought.

Huroo watched her, reading her changes in expression like a white-fella's map, a signpost on how to proceed. She smiled at him and slowly, so slowly, pivoted her hips against his. Huroo's eyes snapped shut as he fought for self-control. His fingers fluttered against her, the tips of the Emu's wings. Raba relaxed into the solidity and satisfaction of the Land.

Afterwards Huroo was uneasy. He hugged Raba to him hard, rocking back and forth in anxiety.

"I can't not be with you," he whispered. "And someday they'll find out about us. I'm afraid for both of us."

"We've been together for months now," she reminded him. "We've been very careful, but none of the elders are stupid. The best of them, the Clever Men and the Doctors, are as alive to the Land as I am and should be able to sense us just by placing the bottoms of their feet to the ground as they walk. But they don't. So the Dreamtime and the Land and our ancestors are pleased that we're together and are protecting us." She didn't tell him that there was someone or something else. Something hidden and watching that skirted, when they were asleep, on the edges of their dreamings together. Something that had drawn all the old men up together into a dilly bag of shadowy weaving.

"You must be right. You have to be right," Huroo tried to reassure himself. "There can't be any other reason the elders and the *Wuradilagu* don't know."

Raba hesitated, reluctant to draw Djilbara into the conversation. But she and Huroo were part of each other. To not alarm him with vague suspicions was one thing, but to not share certain knowledge was another.

"Djilbara does know," she told him.

Huroo's glowing chestnut skin paled. "Even if she is your teacher, how could you tell her?" he asked shakily.

Raba shook her head. "I didn't have to tell her. She knew the instant that we were together at the well."

They were both silent for a while; Huroo afraid of the answers to the questions in his mind, Raba aware of those questions and afraid of answering them, of endangering Djilbara.

"Raba, someday things will finally have to change."

"Yes, I know," she said. "When it's time for your second initiation, when you'll be made a full member of the Goanna clan. The Goanna spirits are going to be as unhappy about your being made privy to their secrets as the Emus were that you 'ignored' them and broke their taboos. But there's three or four years before that."

Huroo looked at her curiously, as if she were forgetting something. "But Raba," he interrupted, "what about you . . . ?"

She kept talking, wanting to finish. "Three or four more years to grow together. The Land will tell us what to do then. In the meantime the elders will give you a sponsor and the things he'll teach you are the things that all men must know."

"Three or four years," Huroo repeated. He looked pensive, anticipating being on his guard for that long a time.

Raba teased him to change the subject. "I know what's bothering you. It's how limited your choice of other lovers has become."

Huroo shot her a sour glance, then laughed ruefully. The girls who'd been his lovers when he'd thought himself a Goanna were forbidden to him now that he knew himself to be an Emu, and it was awkward refusing their advances. Those who should have been available to him as Emu were not because his true clan affiliation was a secret. This left him with girls from the few clans that were marginal to his situation, and Raba, with whom he preferred to be anyway. But that was dangerous, and the times they could be together were too few for either of them. Raba, on the other hand, had full access to all her proper clan lovers. She worked hard to make Huroo not feel neglected. But sometimes she couldn't resist teasing him when he lapsed into boasting about his earlier sexual reputation.

She touched his genitals. "Try to sing a song to the stones on the Emu's ancestor trail, so that they won't crack with the rains," she said. "See if you can sing while I'm doing this," as she began to stroke him.

Huroo struggled with the task for a moment, croaking out notes, then surrendered to her with laughing groans.

"The others aren't important," she whispered as he drew her onto him. "They're just part of the in-between times. The two of us together is the proper dreaming."

Djilbara rested in her tent. Her fingers, usually busy with herbs, weaving, and magic, lay stilled in her lap. Half asleep, she coasted the boundary between the Dreamtime and waking-life, not wanting to be fully in one or the other. She was enjoying the bonding and peace between the two that always occurred when Raba and Huroo managed to be together. She hummed a melody that had just come to her, a gift from the spirits. It echoed the melting together of the lovers and of the two existences.

Djilbara sensed the healing of Dreamtime wounds that long predated the arrival of the white-fellas into her people's lives. Her heart and then eyes filled with joy, spilling over onto her cheeks as tears. Slowly but inexorably the Dreamtime was merging with waking-life. *I will live to see it happen*, she thought with awe. *I will live to see our return to the Dreamtime.*

The rain had slowed and softened to a steady, lasting beat, pacing itself for its Walkabout across the Land. Djilbara still lay propped against her bundles of possessions, not thinking, the fabric of the Dreamtime pulled up about her like a blanket, when she felt something wending its way towards her. It was wrong. It felt like a fish in one of the great rivers to the north, swimming at the wrong time against the true, swift currents; making unharmonious gashes in the water's surface.

It came closer and closer, till Djilbara was able to call out "Come in," an instant before someone tugged on the tent flap.

Her eyes widened as Mitika entered. The younger woman's face was haggard, wet, and glowering, at odds with her healthy body, her pregnancy swelling against her soaked, clinging clothing.

Djilbara was surprised. Since Mitika had married Talbiri, she'd avoided the *Wuradilagu* at all costs. Whenever she or her children were ailing, she always requested that Raba come to help her. Djilbara acquiesced, understanding her fears.

Talbiri was a kind and gentle man. After living with Burunu's brutality, Mitika came to worship her new husband. But much as Talbiri cared for her and their children, the whole camp knew it was nothing like the love he'd held for Djilbara. He and Djilbara did nothing to pursue their old ways. In fact, they'd seldom spoken these last three years. But Mitika was still afraid and resentful.

"Mitika, what are you doing here?"

"I am carrying Talbiri's second child."

Although the young woman only stated the obvious, Djilbara felt a flash of pain. *Talbiri, it could have been me. Perhaps Raba was right, and I was blind. I miss you.*

But Mitika wasn't taunting her. Her eyes were defiant, full of fear.

"I'm sure you will have an easy birth and a healthy child," Djilbara replied.

"I have two children to care for, and soon this one, too. I need someone to help me."

Djilbara said nothing, waiting. The steady thrumming of the rain sounded a counterpoint to her enforced patience.

Mitika looked frustrated, tried a different tack. "My husband is a good man, the best of the hunters, and well favored by the elders. Sooner or later they will surely give him permission to have another wife."

Djilbara leaned forward slightly. Now they were coming to the heart of the matter.

Mitika fished for words, thought a moment, and then drew herself up in the posture of one woman confiding in another.

"He would wait, if I asked, and marry later. But then I'd be old and withered from child-bearing, competing with a young girl for his love.

"So I would rather he marry now, with a second wife closer to my age. We would be like sisters that way, instead of like a mother and daughter. She could help me with my children. And I could help her with her babies, too," she added as an afterthought.

"Why do you come to me?" Djilbara asked.

"I know who the second wife should be," Mitika replied.

Djilbara drew her brows up.

The younger woman visibly gathered her courage. "Talbiri's second wife should be Raba."

Djilbara drew her breath in a sharp hiss. A tremor ran through the Dreamtime. The rain outside faltered and gusted.

"Raba's fifteen. More than time enough for her to marry," Mitika continued.

Stunned as she was, Djilbara still marveled at the woman's cleverness. If Raba married Talbiri, Mitika could be assured that any remaining connection between her husband and Djilbara would be severed. Djilbara's love for Raba would make it impossible for her to intrude on the household in any way. And if Djilbara refused to give permission, Mitika's fears would be confirmed and she would openly take some sort of a stand against Djilbara.

The *Wuradilagu* sighed. Ironically, in a way she wouldn't mind if Raba was married off to Talbiri. For years she'd worried about Raba, if a marriage could be found for her that would be as protective and nurturing as Djilbara's first. Talbiri would love and take care of her, support her in her healing work. He wouldn't try to control or beat her. And although Mitika's motives in all this were purely selfish, Djilbara knew the young woman was genuinely fond of Raba and would work well with her as a co-wife. Even for herself she could accept this solution. To her surprise she'd never been completely at peace with the loss of Talbiri. This would at last lay all that to rest.

"Why have you come to me? Talbiri should go to Raba's parents for permission."

Mitika looked down at her feet. "I did go to Waku and Kultuwa first. They said since Raba is being trained to be *Wuradilagu* that only you could say when and who she should marry."

So. Talbiri didn't know of this yet. And Mitika had tried to get permission from Raba's parents first, so she could confront Djilbara with an accomplished feat. She must have hated to have to come here after all, so she chose the storm to come in secret to Djilbara's tent.

But it would be Raba who would refuse the situation. Now that she was with Huroo, she'd never accept anything else. Huroo. That made Djilbara think again. She looked at Mitika closely. No, she really wasn't all that clever. But Djilbara could think of someone who was.

She narrowed her eyes. "So, Mitika, you are so jealous of me that you cooked up this plot. No matter what you might think of me I'd never thought you'd use Raba in this way. You must have worked hard to think up this scheme."

"That's not true," Mitika said hotly. "I knew you'd think that, but it isn't true. It wasn't even my idea! I was with my relatives, trying to care for my babies while Talbiri is working at the stockman's. They suggested it."

"I don't believe you. Which relatives?" Djilbara challenged her.

"My cousins. Ask them if you don't believe me."

This was what Djilbara wanted to know. Mitika's cousin Danja was one of Numada's wives, and the other one, Lillibar, lived under his patrimony.

"Then I have accused you wrongly," she said in a mild way. "I will consider your suggestion."

Mitika was caught off balance.

"You will have my decision within a week," Djilbara said, dismissing her. In surprise Mitika stumbled back through the tent flaps. Djilbara saw her flinch as the storm battered at her back.

So. Numada's dreamings were inadequate to control the situation to his taste. He'd emerged again to maipulate matters more directly. She'd expected as much ever since Raba and Huroo had become lovers. But Djilbara never thought he'd attack through her own personal life. The rains sang back to her mournfully of a chance at the Dreamtime lost.

Arrangements

"No!" Raba was adamant when Djilbara told her. "How could Talbiri ask such a thing?"

"Hush. Talbiri knows nothing of this yet. He's up north at the cattle station." Djilbara wore a motley of bright scarves around a long shift. She retied a few of them and tucked them under her, shifting her seat on her bedding. Safer for Raba not to know Numada was behind this scheme. "This is Mitika's idea."

"Mitika. Then she's trying to throw me between you and Talbiri," Raba said. "Did she think I wouldn't know that? Did she think I'd make a pleasant addition to their family? I'd make her life such hell she'd be sorry the idea ever occurred to her."

Djilbara tried unsuccessfully to stifle a grin. "I don't think it will have to come to that," she said. "I'm meeting with the elders on this matter. There are many sound reasons for Mitika's request to be turned down."

Instead of being reassured by her words, Raba burst into tears. Djilbara was astonished.

"What is this?" She drew the girl into her arms. "You haven't cried like this since before your women's rites. These are children's tears." She wiped Raba's cheeks with the edge of a scarf.

"I feel awful about you and Talbiri," Raba sobbed. "It was bad enough you didn't end up together. Maybe if you hadn't taken me out for my women's rites at least Mitika wouldn't have gotten him. And now I'm being used to hurt you some more." She hugged Djilbara fiercely. "I love you. I want so much happiness for you; not all this grief."

Djilbara could feel power in those slender arms that went beyond the strength of muscle and bone. The breath and long-pacing of the Land were embodied in this woman-child. *This is the touch of the return Home*, she thought. She hugged Raba back. "Talbiri had the right to find a wife. And you *will* make me happy," she said. "Someday all this trouble will be a faded, laughable memory. Look at me." She pulled Raba away from her. "Look at me. Am I telling you the truth?"

Raba gazed at the *Wuradilagu* with reddened, puffy eyes. "Yes, you are," she said. "You really aren't upset at all."

"Not about Mitika and Talbiri, at any rate. Not anymore," said Djilbara. "However, this has brought up other things we've been foolishly ignoring for too long. This has made the elders notice you as marriage material."

Raba looked unconcerned. "That isn't a problem. I belong with Huroo." Catching the exasperated expression on Djilbara's face, she hurriedly added, "I know, no one can know that; not yet. We know how dangerous it is. We're very careful."

Djilbara sighed. "I'm afraid life isn't going to give you the time you need. I can make sure that you aren't married off to Talbiri, but now that you've been brought to the elders' attention they'll eventually think of someone to match you up with." She thought of all the small spells she'd scattered through the years—not to hide Raba, but to make her innocuous, so that the elders would think of her simply as the *Wuradilagu's* young assistant, and no more than that. She'd renewed and intensified the old dreamings when Raba and Huroo became lovers. But now Numada sundered those fragile veils with his machinations.

"You need to know what I'm going to say to the elders," she told Raba. "You won't especially like it, but it will buy the time we all need; you, Huroo, and myself."

Djilbara met with the elders two days later. The oldest men, the pensioners, didn't live in bush huts or tents like the rest of the camp, but in permanent concrete huts up near the missionaries' end of the settlement. The old men didn't particularly like the structures except for their durability and their location. It was good to be close to the white-fellas and keep an eye on their meddling. In the missionaries' eyes, the buildings were benefits awarded to the elders because of their age and government funding.

As Djilbara approached Makwora's dwelling, a pale figure slipped from the mission store shadows to join her.

"Missa Landell," the *Wuradilagu* addressed the white-fella woman formally.

"Djilbara," said the teacher by way of greeting. "Djilbara, I must speak to you."

Djilbara was willing to listen, but only if she could keep walking.

"Please, wait. Please stop so we can talk alone. There are all sorts of people gathered around the old man's house."

Djilbara turned to the white woman. "What is it you want?"

"It's about Raba. I know where you're going. I know they want to marry Raba off." The woman was visibly anxious. "I don't know how you feel—if you approve or are as upset about it as I am. But I wanted to beg you not to let them do it." As she saw Djilbara's eyes widen in surprise she repeated herself vehemently. "Yes, I *beg* you. You're Raba's teacher, too, so you must know how special she is. She's too young for this. She needs to be allowed to grow up more."

Putting her hand up, Djilbara stopped the white woman's flow of words. "Raba will not marry. Not yet."

Relief washed over Miss Landell's face. She didn't question Djilbara's surety. "She's almost out of our school now. The mission could protest, but we couldn't enforce anything. Raba can have a wonderful future. She could go on to medical school, law school, anything. She could be important to your people. I want to help you with her future in any way I can."

Again Djilbara cut her off. "Yes, Raba will be important to us all," she said quietly. "But I must warn you that her path will not lie through the white-fella's schools. Now that I've said this, can you still care about her?"

Miss Landell was caught off balance. She looked confused, but finally she nodded. "Yes, it's hard, but I can accept that the dreams I have for her may not be her future."

Now it was Djilbara's turn to be startled, until she remembered that the dreams Miss Landell spoke of, the white-fella's dreams, were no more than pictures they saw when they slept.

People clustered informally about Makwora's hut. Kultu-wa sat cross-legged on the ground, looking nervous and unhappy. Waku stood behind her, his legs bracing her back. Raba, of course, was in class at the mission school. There were a few other women waiting near a small fire pit in front of the hut, and a number of men. Raba's case was not the only decision the elders were passing judgment on today.

Talbiri had returned from the north and squatted across from Raba's parents. He received Djilbara's gaze calmly. She was proud of him for that; he could have looked embarrassed or defensive on Mitika's behalf. Djilbara had heard he'd been angry with his wife's meddling, but he hadn't abused her for her insolence. Now he waited for the elders' decision.

Migay lounged against the hut, his arms folded. Talking to him, trying to look nonchalant, stood Huroo. He was wearing mission school clothes, so he'd skipped classes or disappeared from a work detail to be there. As she came up to the doorway of the hut he turned. His eyes were tense.

Djilbara instinctively ducked as she entered the structure, as if it were a bush hut, although the doorway was more than tall enough to accommodate her.

Nine old men sat on the concrete floor of the one-room house in a semicircle, conferring with a couple about their son's upcoming initiation. Djilbara leaned against the wall, waiting till the council was ready to grant her an audience.

Three of the elders, including Makwora himself, were acknowledged Clever Men, or Doctors. The other six were also powerful in wisdom and magic, but without the special calling and training to be designated as one of the tribal shamans. All but Numada, who two months ago had become the youngest of the elders; Numada, who'd followed the path of the Clever Men on his own and in secret.

Eventually the couple left, and Makwora addressed Djilbara.

"*Wuradilagu*, a request for marriage has been made to the family of your apprentice. What do you think of this offer?"

Djilbara ducked her head in respect. "Honored father, I am of two minds about this. Talbiri was my lover and I know him well. I could not ask for a better husband for Raba. Also, if I oppose this match I know it will hurt my standing with some of the women in the camp, and therefore hurt my calling. They will say I have an ungenerous heart; that though I did not wish to have Talbiri as my own husband I am not willing to share him with others." She didn't look at Numada, but this was her acknowledgment of his threat.

"But in this case I must set myself aside. Raba is very gifted and will soon be ready to set out on her own as *Wuradilagu*. It would be inappropriate for her to be a secondary wife in a marriage, subject to the first wife's or wives' beck and call. She should be free to serve the community. She should be her husband's primary wife. Ideally he would then marry other women to help her with the household and her work."

All the old men, except Numada, nodded. It was a point well made.

"Talbiri is a fine man. But although he doesn't belong to a clan that would be taboo for Raba, he also does not belong to one of her 'spousal' clans either. He stands to her as a 'cousin.' Ordinarily this would be adequate if not most desirable in a marriage. But because Raba will be *Wuradilagu*, she should have the most propitious mate possible picked for her. I offer myself as an example. My first husband was from one of my spousal clans. After he died, my second husband was chosen for me on the basis of his youth, his strength, and his ability to provide—but he came from a cousin clan."

The old men nodded again. Looking around, they saw agreement in every face, except Numada, who tried to appear neutral. Makwora spoke. "Your objections to this marriage are well made. Another second wife will be found for Talbiri. We will search for a more appropriate husband for Raba." He turned to the other men, a signal to Djilbara that her audience with them was ended.

Several of them shifted from sitting cross-legged to crouching on their haunches. Djilbara could see that the concrete, although cooling, was harder on their old bones than sand or dirt floors. They were anxious to stretch and leave. Now was the time to get a quick agreement. She cleared her throat, regaining their attention. She wasn't finished yet.

"Forgive me, my fathers. The matter of the marriage is settled, but I have another issue in connection with it I would like your advice, and perhaps your permission, on."

The men looked at each other and reluctantly settled back into place.

Addressing Makwora, Djilbara's words were really for Numada's ears.

"Although this is a large settlement, with many women for

me to care for, it is also a center, through you, of healing power. And living amongst us is the only white-fella doctor within hundreds of miles. I am forty-one years of age—still young enough to bear more children if I wished it; young enough and strong enough to take care of my responsibilities here for a good many years. What I'm saying is this: there is only need for one *Wuradilagu* in this settlement.

"But in many other places there are no *Wuradilagu* at all. The white-fellas take away our young women and put them in their schools, so the girls don't have the chance to learn our people's ways.

"Within the next year Raba will have learned all that I can teach her. With your permission and approval I would like to send her on Walkabout to my first husband's family in the Oenpelli lands so that she can learn more from them. They took in my son Chivaree years ago and raised him well in the ways of the Land. After that a marriage should be arranged for her in an area that has need of her skills."

She'd said it all. This was her hidden dialog with Numada. If he would leave her and Raba alone, he'd think Raba would be sent safely away. There would be no need for him to keep plotting against them.

Makwora raised his eyebrows. "Raba has been helping you a good deal. Are you sure you can manage without her?"

"She's not the only child I've helped raise. There are other young girls who show promise. I'll choose a new apprentice. That one can grow into the skills as I age."

Shrugging, Makwora looked at the other men. "You seem to have this well thought out. We'll discuss it, but I see no reason why not."

As Djilbara left the hut, she caught Numada's eye. He ducked his head down, as if looking at the floor, and then up again, his features cast in a slight smile.

Numada Dreaming

Numada went to sleep that night content. Stretching out between his two wives who curled on their sides, facing away, to give him plenty of room, he looked up at the ceiling of the tent and smiled with satisfaction. His son, Huroo, would soon be safe from the girl's entanglement. And he, Numada, would no longer have to risk coming out of the shadows to protect his son.

He thought himself to the ocean, far away to the north. His nostrils flared as he smelled its saline pungency. Drawing in hard, deep breaths in a tidal rhythm, he pulled the scent inside of him. Its saltiness crusted along the surfaces of his organs, dissolved, and soaked in. He felt his whole body becoming muscular waves of water. He became the sea. It was his heartbeat, rather than the moon's, that generated its pulse.

Numada rested peacefully, lulled by his own rhythms, savoring the small sensation of all things finally coming to rest in him. Small streams joined larger ones, washing themselves into rivers, which fled down into him.

He felt for Huroo, somewhere way up in the Land. He would sing to the tides in Huroo's blood and pull him, bit by bit, as the waves washed in and out, down to the sea. Not only had he fathered Huroo, but he had dreamed him, and their pulses were interlinked in tidal attraction.

Bubbling upwards through subterranean lakes, he passed sleeping *Wanambis* whose skin rippled in serpentine irritation; the echo of his dreaming discordant to their own. Spreading himself thin as surface tension on these underground pools, Numada looked upwards from his *badundjari* state; the faint visual intrusion of the tent's ceiling where his human body still lay blended to become the vaulting of the underside of the Land. Here he floated, waiting for the pattern of Huroo's Emu stride to carry down to him through the earth. Hearing a faint, familiar beat, he sang along its rhythms, enticing Huroo down to the waters. Huroo didn't hear him. Two more times Huroo's dreaming footsteps came to him, bare wisps of sound, but he could not catch his son's attention.

Numada swelled with anger. Small waves began to slap against the caverns' walls. The *Wanambis* stirred, on the verge of wakening. Quieting himself, Numada flowed back to his oceanic source.

Huroo was with Raba again. Before in his spying on the lovers dreaming together, Numada had recognized her as a spirit interlocked with the Land. To find Huroo he first had to ferret out Raba, the path his son traveled on.

Numada stationed himself by all the rivers' mouths, hungry outlets to the sea. He glided just below the surface of the open waters, along the interface with the sky. The Land was scoured and dispersed by winds, washed and eroded away by the rains. Each entering particle prickled through Numada's vast, watery skin. And finally, grain by grain, tiny fragments of the dreaming Raba drifted into his domain.

He visualized fluid hands to cup and contain this minute portion of her. Laughing, he drew the flecks together, washing them clean, like one of the white-fella prospectors panning for gold. With only this much of Raba he would be able to enter her dreaming, and begin to extricate Huroo from his connection with her.

Numada sank his gaze into the handful. But the sands would not draw together. They remained separate, inviolate. He couldn't find a way to enter them. He looked within them and his hands began to shake in horror. The shiny, flinty surface was all Raba, but intertwined with her in the heart of each grain was Huroo. This was where his son had gone! This was why Numada had not been able to find him.

As Numada watched the sands became heavier. They sank through his cupping palms. He scrambled after them, but they settled to the ocean's floor. Numada's currents roiled, lashing up sprays of sand, but the grains of Raba's being sank beyond his reach. The Land's stony bedrock absorbed her, and she was gone. Numada crashed against it, trying to wear it away. The Land rebuffed him. He turned his attention back to the sea, to find new fragments of the girl. They had all sunk away. Nothing new came from the rivers; the stream beds took her in as soon as she washed along their lengths. The Land had taken Raba back, and Huroo with her.

Numada churned with storms, beating at the Land in his

fury, not caring this time what spirits he woke. He felt the Land beneath him becoming denser. It began to drop away. He followed after it first in rage and then in fear. It sank away too swiftly for him to keep up with. There was a sensation of physical release from somewhere far below him. It peeled away from him, forever. He floated, huge and alone, stretched thin in a black, starless sky.

Numada woke with his heart pounding against his imprisoning ribs. He shook, soaked with sweat, as if the ocean followed him. A last iodine-laden whiff of sea grazed his nostrils. He flinched from it.

He knew now he couldn't trust Djilbara's assurances at the elders' meeting. Even if she fully intended to send Raba away, it would make no difference. He had seen for himself that Raba and Huroo were inextricably intertwined. Forbidden to each other during the waking hours, they spent their lives together at night, welded within their dreams. The distance between the Oenpelli lands and the settlement would make no difference.

Numada rolled on his side. That brought him facing his younger wife's back. Not wanting to see another human being, he turned again, to his stomach, and buried his head in his arms.

Nothing had been right since the day of the Emu feast. He'd been so self-assured, having fooled great powers like the elders and the spirits, that it never occurred to him that someone as insignificant as a woman or a girl-child would see through him.

That morning he hadn't been able to recover from Djilbara's undetected intrusion into his reality and they'd fought each other to a standstill throughout the day. When the sands caught fire he'd watched in horror as the flames swept down on the camp, endangering Huroo. He and Djilbara had stopped struggling and swooped around the fire, trying to contain it. Fully engaged, he watched as the Emu spirit bore down on Huroo, and he'd howled in grief.

Suddenly the Emu spirit was gone. He and Djilbara stumbled into the vacuum of its absence. He felt drained and enfeebled. When he could finally extend his senses again, he searched for the spirit and found it trapped within Raba.

Off balance, doubting his own abilities, fearing the spirit's release, he watched helplessly the next day as Huroo went off in search of Raba. And felt time layer back upon itself, a many-folded dreaming, as Huroo's conception was reenacted and finally completed at the well.

Now the two young lovers drew closer together, and Numada's connection with Huroo became more and more tenuous. If he was not to lose the boy to Raba altogether, she would have to be extracted from Huroo's life. Numada made Raba and Djilbara his new study.

He was not unsympathetic to the *Wuradilagu*. As he proceeded with his investigation he found that she protected Raba much in the way he'd disguised Huroo. But there was no choice to be made. He and Huroo must survive.

Carefully unraveling the threads that hid Raba, he began to expose her, bringing her to the elders' attention. It would have been pleasant if she'd been married off to Talbiri, but Numada had expected Djilbara to block that move. The scheme was a twofold gambit, even so. It stripped Raba of her camouflage, thrusting her into the marriage market, and it served a warning to the *Wuradilagu* of how vulnerable she herself was.

He felt safe from Djilbara launching a counterexposure of Huroo. Any measure she might take risked Raba also. Numada had been pleased with the compromise she'd surreptitiously offered him at the meeting: a voluntary withdrawal of Raba in return for safety for her and the girl.

But his experiences tonight taught him that it was an empty promise. Raba and Huroo were unified more strongly than ever. If he were to regain possession of his son, Raba would have to be eliminated.

New plans began to float in Numada's mind. Smiling, he fell truly asleep, his decision made.

The Adversary

Hurrying back along her own tracks from the mission laundry where she'd been working, Raba stopped and smiled when she saw the footprint. Its owner had had to contort to place it so distinctly and at right angles to cover her own. Huroo was signaling for her to get away and join him. She dropped the pile of bedding she carried. Scrambling to pick the sheets up, she neatly erased the track.

When classes were over in the afternoon, instead of going into the camp, she perched her herb-gathering basket on her head and walked north from the camp, skirting the edges of gully-land. She stopped to gather seeds and plants now and then. A group of hunters passed, hailing her cheerfully. They were returning to camp with two fat wallabies and some lizards. Farther on she came across some of the younger girls, rooting in an old, rotted witchetty bush for grubs. She chatted with them for a while and then continued due north. She crossed a rocky stretch, where the earth's bones poked up through its flesh of sand, and cut to the east along it. From there she ducked southward into the gully-lands, walking on the windward side of the sand hills, so her tracks would blow away by morning.

Her legs tingled as the sands murmured to her through the bottom of her feet. Birds flew by occasionally, singing the songs that were their own chants to help keep the world in place.

When she reached their secret meeting spot, she found Huroo already there. He rose eagerly from where he'd been squatting. His eyes were happy, shiny as a river under the sun's light. His embrace was soft as feathers.

They made love on an old coat he'd brought and stretched out on the sands. Afterwards they lay intertwined, content. "Meet me again here this evening, *badundjari*," he whispered, nuzzling her ear.

Raba laughed. "The other girls tease me," she said. "They

say I never sneak out at night with them anymore . . . that all I want to do is rush to my bed early to sleep."

His nuzzling trailed down to her belly. The skin there was almost smooth, the scars nearly healed. Over the years the *maban* had almost done its work. "Don't you have a better time meeting with me dreaming than running off with the other men awake?" he asked.

Raba shivered under his touch in way of reply. They lay quietly for a while, comfort to each other.

"Djilbara's going to take me with her to the mobs down south past the sheep station soon," Raba said. "A big Corroboree is being held. There'll be other healing women there that she wants me to meet."

They'd had other conversations like this before, skirting around events still far away, but pressing closer and closer. Even with all the danger of their present circumstances, they wanted to cherish and stay in this first phase of their lives together, not think about the future.

Huroo hugged Raba. "I'll miss you. I'll be here when you get back from the Corroboree." Then his hug turned into an attack of tickling. "You're getting to be kind of a big-head girl," he teased her. "You're not the only one who's getting trained." Raba tried to fend him off, convulsing with silent laughter. "That's one of the reasons I wanted to meet you out here," he said. "I've got news for you, too. I've been assigned a sponsor to teach me before my next initiation."

Raba sat up abruptly. This was another fragile topic. If she left for the Oenpelli lands, who would protect Huroo from the spirits if he was forced to break taboo again during his next initiation?

He waved his hand against her evident alarm. "I know, I know, I won't actually take my second initiation; at least not here, not as a Goanna. But I'm to be a man, I can't not learn. And it would be more suspicious if I were the only one in camp to refuse or avoid his training. No other man has ever done that."

Raba sighed. "I know. It just scares me, because I know that sometimes you'll be in danger. Who did they give you to?"

Huroo grinned with pride. "Well, I wasn't actually assigned a sponsor. Someone came forward and asked to teach me. One of the most important men in camp. Numada."

Raba had been gazing off at the top of the gully. She

started at his words. "Don't be silly. He can't sponsor you. He's . . ." She stopped. She'd almost said, "He's your father." She turned and stared at Huroo. It was right there for anyone to see, but she hadn't known it until Huroo had said Numada's name. Why hadn't she seen it before?

"What do you mean?" Huroo asked. "Why can't he?"

Raba scrambled for an explanation. "Your sponsor should be your father's brother. Or at least a clan uncle."

"My father has only a half-brother. You know that. And *he's* much too young to sponsor me—he isn't even finished with his own final initiation. Anyway, the other elders gave their approval. It's a tremendous honor. It won't make a difference anyway. By the time my second initiation comes around, I'll have run away to be with you."

Raba was distracted. She wanted to get away by herself and think. "You're right," she said to placate him. "I think I'm just afraid for you to be so close to such a powerful man. It's even more dangerous."

Now it was Huroo's turn to look uneasy. "I'll be careful," he promised.

Raba stood and picked up her basket. "I'd better start back to camp. I have a long way to go around and it's getting late."

Still sitting, Huroo grabbed her ankle, detaining her. "You will meet me tonight, won't you? You won't hide in your dreams?"

Raba pressed his head against her thigh in an answering caress.

Retracing her roundabout way automatically, she was lost in thought. The old men played cards interminably, and, like their decks, her life was shuffled before her. Events fell into place: the enigma of Huroo's birth and the lurking menace on the edge of her dreams. The old barrier between her and Huroo now had a name: Numada. She understood now that Huroo's old avoidance of her had been deftly planted aversions.

She felt ill with fear. The solidity of waking-life twisted, distorted, laughed at her unsteadiness. Did Djilbara know? Raba remembered the night of the Emu feast and the unknown demon that the *Wuradilagu* battled then. She saw clearly the fine machinery that set in motion the request for her to be married off to Talbiri. Djilbara had known. Why hadn't Djilbara told her?

Raba cast her memory like a spear-thrower. It came back with a possible answer. She remembered a lesson Djilbara had given her in building spells to hide. She'd rebelled, preferring to fight or flee if the need arose.

"There are birds," the *Wuradilagu* told her, "that camouflage their young by having them simply hold very still when danger threatens, so that they seem part of the landscape. The chicks do not look at their enemies, nor think of them, so they won't smell of fear. Then the mother leads the hunters away. These spells are the same. You will hide by denying your enemy any power over you."

Was that what Djilbara had been doing? Hoping to leave Raba invisible through ignorance, while she, Djilbara, dealt with Numada? If so, Djilbara was wrong. It hadn't worked. It couldn't. Raba saw that Numada had been interwoven in the fringes of Huroo's life since his birth. Raba and Numada were bound to collide with each other, each of them so intertwined in Huroo. Her confidence in her teacher was shaken.

Should she tell Huroo? Was it fair to leave him in ignorance the way Djilbara had left her? All alone by herself climbing through the gullys, Raba shook her head. Huroo didn't have her resources of power to protect himself, and Numada's lie was the very foundation on which Huroo's life was built. He'd be shattered. Better to get him away from here first, away from Numada's influence.

Raba's anger at Djilbara was still unabated. But, shuddering, she had to admit to herself, that now that she knew about Numada, it was as if she'd drawn his gaze to her more clearly.

Sponsorship

The days descend, one by one, into an accumulation of weeks, then months. All things animate and inanimate in the waking-life interact. The culminations of their interstices percolate down to the Dreamtime, just in the way that runoff from the rains eventually seeps, distilled and intensified, into the water table. As groundwater can be drawn from the wells to be used by all, so the sustaining nature of the Dreamtime rises back up.

Djilbara thought of this as she pulverized curled-up chunks of dried clay that looked like peeled tree bark into a fine powder. Raba lay beside her on the white claypan, humming to herself as she waited for Djilbara to finish the task.

The *Wuradilagu* knew that time in waking-life and the Dreamtime were not only not analogous, but that time in the Dreamtime actually consisted of a different substance, had a different function. What happened in each place affected the other, but not necessarily at the same "instant." That part of the Dreamtime was unknowable. Those who dealt with the Dreamtime, who tried to keep the tenuous connection intact until the two existences could become one again—those like herself and the elder men—learned to ignore that element; meanwhile carefully tracking the sequence and duration of events in waking-life.

For the last few months, as she prepared Raba to leave the settlement, she'd felt events drawing together. An ominous pressure was building from the interweavings with the Dreamtime. At first she threw her efforts into outracing it. Finally she saw that she was part of a great current, and could only accept that for good or for ill, something cataclysmic was going to happen—was even now happening.

Djilbara rubbed the fine clay dust between her fingers, satisfied with its silky texture. Placing the grinding stone back in her dilly bag, she drew out a water bottle. She mounded the clay in the middle of the flat rock she'd carried in from the edge of the claypan to use as a mortar, making an indentation in the top of the heap. Into this small crater she dribbled the water, working the mixture into a gray-white wash. The water was warm from the sun's heat. As she spread the slurry onto Raba's face and chest, its temperature and satinness matched that of the girl's skin. They seemed to be the same thing, soaking into each other without boundaries.

Djilbara covered the left side of Raba's chest and almost all of her face. She was stretching to reach over to the girl's right side when she stopped, trembling. The white clay was meant to be a preliminary background on which brighter and darker designs and symbols would be drawn, nothing more. But where it spread Raba became insubstantial, disappeared. Her brown skin, where it wasn't painted, looked like it faded directly into the ground. Her dark hair was a corona lying empty.

Shutting her eyes against this vision, Djilbara raised her hands to her face, unmindful of the white streaks of clay her fingers left there. All her life, even when she was young and just learning, aware of how much she didn't know, she'd been unafraid. She'd known herself to be a sharp tool that could cut through the thick defensive layer of things to the secrets that lay within. She sensed the unsensable the way certain animals knew of the sweetness of water hidden far below under the bedrock.

Now she was half-blind. She could still sense things, but they rushed past her before she could cut her way to them. Or they proved impenetrable. Djilbara would see things like this vision and not understand them: Raba washed-out and as paper-thin in substance as the white-fellas, disappearing. She tried to grasp at the idea, but it faded away from her as Raba had seemed to.

She opened her eyes to find Raba staring up at her. The bright brown eyes destroyed the terrifying illusion. The contours of the girl's face leapt up at her under the thin layer of clay. Her flesh came alive again to Djilbara.

"Auntie? Are you all right?"

Raba hadn't called her that in months. Djilbara gave her the water bottle and turned away.

"Wash yourself off. We won't do that ritual after all today."

Raba touched her arm lightly in concern, but the *Wuradilagu* shook her head.

"What is it?" Raba asked.

So, Raba hadn't experienced the illusion. But she had seen the fear in Djilbara's face. Djilbara squeezed Raba's fingers where they still rested on her arm.

"There are too many things I no longer see clearly." She meant to speak normally. It came out as a painful whisper.

There was a moment of silence, then Raba's quiet voice. "Yes."

Djilbara sighed. "I'll be glad when you're safely gone to the Oenpelli lands within another passing of the moon."

"Me and Huroo," Raba corrected.

"No. That's too dangerous. If you both leave at the same time the elders will know. They'll track you down."

Raba looked at her, then answered indirectly. "Huroo is out learning with *him* again today."

Djilbara froze. Raba never referred to Numada by name. But since he'd been announced as Huroo's sponsor, it was obvious that Raba had known, finally, who her enemy was, and why.

"That's another reason, the most important, why you must go ahead of Huroo. Don't forget, you speak of an evil who knows who you are. Don't openly challenge it by taking Huroo away with you. It will have to attack you. You can't take risks. Even with my help, it's too powerful."

Raba bowed her head and slid water across the top of her shoulders. Her fingers caressed away the clay as the rivulets streamed down her chest. "That's why I *must* risk it," she said. "Huroo can't be left alone here. Not even for the shortest time."

Djilbara pitched her voice low and still. "Raba, I won't let you." Raba looked up and their gaze locked.

"You know it's beyond you. You just said so yourself," Raba said.

"Yes, but I know at least that much. And I can still stop you. You know I can."

Raba's face was expressionless, but her anger was palpable. At last she nodded. Relieved, Djilbara continued. "Look, it's only reasonable. If I can stop you, imagine what he could do."

Raba retreated into passivity. She stood up to go, leaving Djilbara sitting on the ground. "I will go without Huroo, but you are wrong."

Djilbara wanted to call out so many things to the retreating girl. That she would watch after Huroo and protect him. That Raba should trust her. But she didn't call. The trust was gone. It was more important to protect the two lovers than regain it.

"I had a dream for you," Numada told Huroo. They sat together in a shelter made by throwing some scrub over two big boulders in a gully. The gully itself offered sufficient protection from the sun—the crude structure was more to give them a sense of being enclosed together. Indirect sunlight filtered through the jumble of branches to cast their skin in shadows of light brown, dark brown, shimmering hypnotically as a faint breeze stirred the foliage. Numada sang:

> *This dream was meant for you to live*
> *A Clever Man, a Clever Man*
> *Like me you'll be a Clever Man*

He took out a vial, unstoppered it, and began flicking droplets onto Huroo. Clear and shining, Huroo could see it wasn't water, though. It looked like the crystal fragments he knew Raba to be made of, but liquified. Each drop struck separately and sunk in with a wet sharpness. They seeded within his skin and feathers like blades began to emerge. Huroo experienced a wave of fear. These were the feathers he always felt massed just under his skin, resting and waiting, since his transformation by the well with Raba. Now they bloomed all over him, the knifelike shapes spreading into quartz fronds. He looked at Numada anxiously. His sponsor's face looked unconcerned. Huroo remembered tales of Clever Men transforming into birds. Perhaps this was the change he'd just undergone. Numada still sang.

> *A Clever Man can fly the world*
> *Fly the world*
> *Fly the world*
> *Fly the world round.*

Yes, fly the world. I must go out and fly, Huroo thought. His legs grew long and powerful. His arms thickened into great wings. Bursting from the shelter, he leapt over the gully-lands in a few monstrous strides. Wings spread, he tried to soar like a hawk. But each time he launched himself he drove straight back to the ground. His legs caught him like springs and threw him back into the air. Finally he learned to stretch his legs out and lengthen his bounds. And he *was* flying, coasting far over the ground with each leap, his wings supporting and guiding him through each glide.

He could see so far. The Land stretched out before him like a sensuous lover. In its curves he could see reflected the sweetness and invitation of Raba's limbs. He rose and descended through thermal waves muskily scented with dust, wind-borne seeds, spores, all the scents of the Land, and it was as if he was smelling the richness of Raba's skin as they made love.

He felt things he'd never felt before. He could sense the echoes of the spirits of the Outback. Flying far below him were the small sparks of lesser birds. Unalarmed at his passing, they called out, accepting him.

Glinting like white-fella mirrors, distant springs and wells shone up at him. *Fly all you like*, they seemed to say. *For your soul lies safely in our watery depths*. He plunged into one. Its water was a joyful shock. The liquid crystals within him exploded into a million bubbles in reaction and burst him out of the water again. Throwing back his head he laughed, the sound emerging as a strange and wild cry. He felt as if he could never be contained again. He would find Raba and they would leave together, never going back.

Tugging at him, curbing him, he heard Numada's song.

> *Come back*
> *Turn back*
> *This is just the beginning*
> *There is so much more to learn.*

Reluctantly and dutifully he returned.

Numada waited for him in the shambles that was left of the shelter. He sang off Huroo's wings. They fell to the ground and crumbled. He taught the boy the cycle of songs to make them grow again. "This is the beginning of your training as a Clever Man," he told him.

"I'm too young," Huroo objected. "I'm not even ready for my initiation into my clan, let alone final initiation into manhood."

"Ahh," Numada smiled. "But those who are children of the Emu often show their gifts young."

Huroo quailed. He'd been tricked! He leapt up, believing for an instant that he could outrun the older man's powers.

"I've known about you for a long time," Numada said. "There's no need to be afraid of me."

Huroo was speechless with shock. This went against everything he knew. He was finally able to speak. "Does this mean the elders have known all along? That I've feared them needlessly? Why didn't anyone tell me sooner about my clan?"

Numada shook his head. "No, you were right to be afraid.

I'm the only one who knows. I'm the only one who understands. I want to protect you. Why do you think I asked to be your sponsor?"

Sitting down again, Huroo tried to order his thoughts. His world was turned upside down as effectively as it had been during the Emu feast. His mind couldn't encompass what this would mean to him. A fear knifed through him.

As if he'd spoken the question out loud, Numada answered that fear directly. "And I know about your lover. I know about Raba."

Huroo moaned, put his hands up to his face. Raba had done nothing but love him, protect, and teach him. Now he'd brought her into terrible danger.

Numada pulled his hands down. "I tell you," he insisted, "that I understand. I want to help you both. If I didn't I could have set the others on you a long time ago.

"She is leaving soon for the Oenpelli lands. She wants you to go with her, doesn't she?"

It seemed to Huroo that Numada's eyes sharpened as he waited for an answer.

"Yes," Huroo whispered in reply. "She's afraid of leaving me behind. But I've refused to accompany her. It's too dangerous. I've told her I'll come along later, when it's safe."

Numada appeared to be agitated as he thought for a while. "She's right. You should go with her."

"But how?" Huroo asked. "Even if we can leave from here without discovery, word of us will spread if we travel together. People will recognize us."

"You yourself are not what you appear to be," Numada said. "This is the result of a powerful dreaming, which can only be accomplished by spirits or men. It is beyond the realm of women. But it could be cast *upon* a woman. I could do the same for her, so that she will seem to match you. Then you'll both be safe."

Huroo came out of his stunned daze into relief and a wild joy. "Raba will be so happy to know we have an ally, that we're not all alone in this. I can't wait to tell her."

"No!" said Numada sharply. "You must not tell her!" Seeing the confusion on Huroo's face, the enthusiasm fading away, he softened his tone. "I told you I knew about Raba, too. She's hid herself all her life, like an overhunted animal. She wouldn't understand an elder helping her. It would just make her afraid."

He thought another moment. "I have a better idea. I'll teach you how to transform her. If her love for you is strong, and she's as selfless as she should be, there will be no trouble with the change. She's been protecting and teaching you. This way you can do the same for her, as a man should. And it won't needlessly give her any reason to fear. I'd guess she's been very anxious these past few months."

Huroo nodded.

"Then let's not give her more to worry about, shall we?"

Huroo beamed his agreement.

Proposed Diversion

Raba felt listless and depressed. Even being with Huroo accentuated rather than lightened her feelings. He sat behind her, rubbing her shoulders, trying to relax her. Not in a mood to be softened for lovemaking, she drew away from him with an irritable gesture.

"Raba, what's wrong?" His concern was so genuine that she sighed and made herself lean back against him.

"I just feel badly about going on without you. It's wrong. But with you and Djilbara both against me, there's not much I can do."

He drew his arms around her and laid his cheek against hers. "What if I were to tell you that I've changed my mind? That I'll go with you?"

She turned in the circle of his arms. "Really? Do you mean that?"

He nodded.

"That makes me feel better," she hugged him, "even if it doesn't make a difference now."

"Why not?"

"Because Djilbara is determined. She's even going to accompany me for a few days to make sure you're not tailing along."

"Your powers are stronger than hers now."

"Yes, and she's very confused these days, too. But even so,

I'd have to go my full limits, be willing to risk hurting her to use them. And I couldn't trick her. She's too smart, and she watches after me all the time."

"Even now?" he asked.

"Even now."

"I'll bet she doesn't watch me all the time, except when I'm with you," he said.

"No, I'm sure she doesn't." Raba almost gave a bitter laugh. Huroo was with Numada a great deal of the time, and the *Wuradilagu* gave the man a wide berth, as if they had some sort of pact.

"So I'll take care of it." He began to fondle her as if that settled the topic, and now they could get on with lovemaking.

"What do you mean?"

"I'll concoct a diversion for her. She won't even know. Now that I've been working as a jackeroo you wouldn't believe how skillful I am at cutting a single animal out of the herd."

In spite of herself Raba had to laugh at the analogy. "You'll be in for a rough time of it if you think of Djilbara as a sheep or a steer."

Huroo laughed at the image, too. "It will work. She won't be expecting anything, except from you. In the meantime I'll make myself scarce. I won't even be in camp when you leave. She'll think I'm off consoling myself somewhere."

"Consoling yourself? With who?" Raba attacked him, tickling. He tried unsuccessfully to fend her off. Then breathlessly, happily, they collapsed together.

Culmination

The day that Raba left was hot. The earliest touch of morning sun raged through the camp as searing as noon. There was no moisture; thirsty, the air lapped up sweat before it formed. Djilbara's skin felt like stretched parchment. She dressed in an underlayer of loose, ragged black clothes, and over that another layer of reflective white. When she emerged from the tent the light outside struck her eyes like a blow.

When Djilbara got to Waku and Kultuwa's home, Raba was taking farewell of her family. She and Kultuwa sat on the ground on the shady side of the tent, talking quietly. Waku and the boys were trying to pack a few more things into her already overstuffed dilly bag. Raba looked up as the *Wuradilagu* approached, nodded in acknowledgment, and turned back to her mother.

Waku greeted Djilbara respectfully. Dhuma was scowling down at his task. Then he looked up and grinned at her.

"How come your dilly bag isn't anywhere near as full as Raba's?" he asked.

"I'm going to travel with her just for the first leg of the trip. We're catching a ride with the mission truck as far as the crossroad to Kooniba Station. Then we'll Walkabout—I'll stay with her for a day or two till we're out of the white-fellas' ranch lands."

"Do you think Raba has to worry about stray white-fellas, then?" In spite of Dhuma's constant attempts to heckle his sister, there was genuine concern in his voice.

"Not really. That will be my time to say good-bye to her."

The boy eyed Djilbara's dilly bag speculatively. "Well, since you've got so much room, can you take some of these things?"

"Dhuma!" Waku scolded.

"Well, it's extra food for them both to eat. She wouldn't have to carry it for very long," Dhuma said defensively.

"That's all right, Waku," Djilbara said, as she took the wrapped parcels from the boy and slipped them into her bag. "He's right. I have lots of room to carry more things. I'm happy to share the burden."

Raba stood. "I'm ready. The truck will be leaving soon."

She's almost as tall as I am, Djilbara thought. *It's good there's this break between us. The next time I see her in the Oenpelli lands I'll be able to see her as grown.*

The whole family accompanied them to the mission. A crowd of laughing men were loading up the truck with work gear for the sheep station.

"Hold on while we get things rearranged and more comfortable. We don't usually have the pleasure of ladies traveling with us."

"It won't be that long a pleasure," Djilbara joked back. "We're only going as far as the crossroads."

Raba hugged her family and clambered up to nest in a pile of saddles. Balayang and Dhuma lifted her dilly bag to her. Kultuwa cried and Waku tried to look comforting rather than sad. Raba's face, calm and composed, suddenly yielded. "I love you. I'll miss you," she called down to them. Waku began crying, too.

Djilbara started to climb the side of the truck, two of the jackeroos giving her a hand up. A small boy came running from the camp. "Wait, wait," he yelled. "I've got to talk to Auntie Djilbara." She lowered back down from the truck. It was Baran, the son Mitika had borne to Burunu. He tugged on her clothes. "Wiradji is sick, Auntie. You have to come see him."

Djilbara felt a pang of fear. Wiradji was Talbiri's firstborn with Mitika.

Raba looked away from the little boy. She'd always cared for Mitika's children, but she hadn't spoken to the woman since the attempted marriage of Raba to Talbiri.

"We can't wait. The truck is ready to leave now," said one of the jackeroos.

Seeing Djilbara's indecision, Raba said, "Look, go ahead and take care of Wiradji. These things happen. I'll be fine. You know I'll have no trouble finding my way. I'll send word back when I reach the Oenpelli lands safely."

Djilbara still stood, trying to make up her mind. Raba leaned around to the cab and yelled to the driver, "It's all right. Let's go."

Coughing and cranky from the heat, the truck started up. It lurched off to circle around the camp to the main road. The last thing Djilbara saw was Raba's hand waving to her through a cloud of dust.

Mitika was sullen. She handed Djilbara the toddler and went back to the new baby she'd been nursing.

"What's wrong?" Djilbara asked, raising her voice to be heard over Wiradji's screaming.

Mitika cast her a scornful look. "Sick," was all she would say.

Baran proved more helpful. "He ate a whole bunch of white-fella teacakes Mother's cousins gave us. They were left out there," he pointed to a crate, "and then he started crying a little later."

The child's belly was swollen, but not enough to account

for his agony. She rubbed her hand gently over the skin. It felt hot to the touch. She scanned her gaze back and forth, each time sinking her sight in a little deeper. White-fella food lay there, lacking the glow of life that marked native foods. But it was more than just that. Even half-digested she saw it was spoiled. Was that because of the heat this morning? Or when it was baked were the ingredients already bad? How could such a small child be left loose around a large quantity of unwholesomely rich food anyway? She looked at Mitika. The young woman turned away and fussed with the baby.

Djilbara laid Wiradji down on some bedding. "Baran, look after your brother for a few minutes. I'm going to my tent to get some herbs and medicine. He'll hurt for a few more hours and then he'll be fine. Where is Talbiri?"

Mitika answered this time. "My husband went hunting with Migay this morning. One of the boys went to find them."

By the afternoon Wiradji slept comfortably and Djilbara was able to return to her tent. The driver of the truck stopped by to report dropping Raba off safely at the crossroads.

An hour after that Talbiri, accompanied by Migay, came by to thank her for tending to his son.

Djilbara couldn't accept his thanks graciously. She felt restless and unhappy. "I was going to accompany Raba on the first leg of her trip, until your child fell ill. He ate too much spoiled white-fella food." *Or was fed it,* she thought. She couldn't voice that thought, so she complained petulantly instead. "I don't know why Mitika called for me. She used to ask for Raba."

Talbiri hesitated, not wanting to bring up painful past events. "Raba is still angry with her. Besides, Mitika knew as well as anyone that Raba was leaving today," he reminded her.

"Even so, she'd call for Dr. Blackston before me. Then when I got to your tent she hardly said two words to me, not even to help with the child," Djilbara complained.

Talbiri and Migay looked at each other. They'd never heard Djilbara sound like this.

"Mitika didn't call for you," Talbiri defended his wife. "Her cousin, Numada, sent Baran for you."

"Numada," Djilbara repeated. The color leached from her face, leaving her bronze skin ashen. "He wasn't at your tent when I was there."

Noting her alarm, Migay tried to reassure her. "Tell my sister he didn't stay around. He took Huroo on a Walkabout. That's why she didn't see him."

Djilbara pulled one heavy foot underneath her, then the other, and rose. She could hardly stand. Tremors ran violently up and down her legs. Her innards fluttered like a flame. A fool. She'd been a fool.

"Run! Now!" she screamed. "Run to the elders and tell them to sense for me and follow—any way they can, as fast as they can."

Talbiri and Migay stared up at her as if she were mad. Her words shook in the air. "Now!" she screamed again.

When they'd left, running, she forced herself to stillness. In that stillness she cast about for the intersecting paths of Raba, Huroo, and Numada. Then she began to sing for herself the swiftness of birds.

Raba had backtracked for hours after the truck let her off. Now she waited uneasily in a sand hollow for Huroo. She could not be seen, but neither could she see any approaching danger.

She had troubling questions to ask Huroo. Was Wiradji taking ill the diversion he'd promised to rid them of Djilbara? She couldn't believe he'd do such a thing to a child.

Fretting at his lateness, she listened to the sands. They murmured, trying to speak to her, trying to warn her. Something muted their voices, like a blanket of water between her and them. Even so, she sensed a force approaching. She wanted to jump up and flee. She felt Huroo nearby, too. It would be close. It was all she could do to hold herself there for him, to trust he'd arrive first.

"Raba, are you there?" She heard his muffled voice over the rise. She stood, almost weeping with relief. First she saw his forehead, then his eyes, bright and dark, and then his mouth, smiling as he mounted the crest. Then his chest, his arms—she froze. Huroo was holding a power board in his hand.

His words carried clearly through the still air. "Raba, I have a way for us. No, stay there, don't move," as she started to back away. "This will change the way you seem, just the way that I'm changed, seeming Goanna instead of Emu. It's men's magic. That's why you didn't know about it. Numada showed me. I know you don't trust him, but he knew about us already. He understands and wants to help us."

As he spoke Raba thought swiftly. She knew what was really going to happen, and that Huroo didn't know. She began to go *badundjari*, keying her form into sand grains. Transformed into crystalline particles, the blast might go through her. Raba's shell-like connection to the waking-life rippled to the desert floor like a shed snake skin. Her hand brushed her stomach. Was her center healed enough to transform completely with the rest of her? Her flesh shimmered there, trying to match, almost making it, then turning into the stubborn, black, leathery opacity that had given her away to the elders at the initiation years ago.

Her mind cast about frantically. Her *maban*! Perhaps it would deflect the blast. She dropped to her knees, keeping her eyes fixed on Huroo.

"No, don't move about like that," he called. Uncertain, he lowered the end of the power board. He looked behind him as if for advice, and Raba knew that Numada hid close by.

She slapped her palm against the sand, leaving a picture imprint. Her fingers sank in. Their tips traced trails in the passage in-between. Heart drumming in her chest, her hand closed on cool, smooth hardness. She withdrew the *maban*. Hiding it in her palm she slowly stood, drawing it up through the sweat on her calf, thigh, hip, till it rested against her belly. She exposed the length of the blade.

As she stood up into her full height Huroo called out, "That's better," and raised the power board again to aim. The sun caught on the *maban's* edge and reflected up at him. A band of light streaked across his face. He flinched and cocked his head away from it as he adjusted his aim.

Raba blanched. What if the *maban* didn't absorb the energy from the power board? What if the power bounced back at Huroo as the sunlight had? The blade slipped from her nerveless fingers. It slid back down the trail of her body. She looked down and numbly watched it catch on an edge in the sand, turn over onto the trace of her handprint, and slowly sink from sight.

Huroo was chanting the brief song that would ignite the board. In the instant before it fired Raba felt it draining substance from everything around them. Its energy crested to an overflow. She felt slow, sluggish, as if she had all the time in the world to grieve for Huroo afterwards. Then the board glowed. The blast must have been swift, but Raba saw the searing brightness coming towards her like the sun on its slow daily stroll.

"No, Raba, no!" came a cawing shriek. From the edge of her vision Raba saw something black and white, tattered, all rags and feathers, streak across the sky. It flung itself between her and the light. For an instant its silhouette glared with a corona as it drew the fire to it. Then it fell, writhing, recognizable, to the ground.

"Djilbaraaaa!" Raba screamed. She ran, stumbling, her eyes dazzled to blindness from the glare. She skidded and almost fell on top of the twitching form. Trapped power still raced through the *Wuradilagu*, animating her limbs in a ghastly palsy. If it could be drained away—Raba seized Djilbara's shoulders with both hands, and was thrown backwards by the force.

Then Huroo was there holding her. "Raba, it was a mistake. It was to change *you*. It wouldn't have hurt you. It wasn't meant for Djilbara. Oh gods, Numada, come help," he yelled.

She wrenched herself free and scrambled back to Djilbara. Drawing on all her power, she tried to find a way to contain Djilbara's spirit. Some peripheral part of herself felt Numada approach; felt his fear, his trying to pull Huroo away. Then others arrived, more and more. But it was as if Djilbara was her universe, and the men were the faintest, most faraway stars in the sky.

If only the fire within the *Wuradilagu* would abate, she could snatch the remains and heal them. Ghostlike voices, arguing, came to her.

"The woman and her apprentice tried to ensnare Huroo into breaking taboos, perverting him with women's magic," said Numada. There was a cry of protest from Huroo, which someone stifled. Talbiri and Migay called out, challenging. Numada continued. "Raba tried to seduce him, though she's from a clan forbidden to him. As his sponsor I had to protect him." There was an uneasy murmur from the old men.

"Not true." Some vestige of Djilbara struggled free from her body as a clear, light voice. "Look at Huroo; truly look at him. See him as he is, an Emu." Even from the center of her fugue Raba could feel the old men's powerful gazes focusing on the youth. Years of spells and disguise unraveled and shredded away. The elders' murmuring became angry. "Now look at Numada." The voice faltered, then strengthened. "He is not the boy's sponsor. He is his true father."

"No!" Huroo said. Raba felt Numada reaching to him. Huroo backed away, repulsed. He turned towards her. "Raba, I . . ." he started—then men blocked him away from her, forcing him back towards Numada.

The power was draining from Djilbara, leaching harmlessly into the Land. In its wake it was leaving a husk, and Raba knew she could not keep her teacher from dying. Hands tugged at her. She shook them off. Now was the most important time. She could at least follow Djilbara's spirit, mark it, and nurture it to its next life.

But the *Wuradilagu* fragmented. Some of her, with her blood, sank away into the sands. Some steamed up through her charred skin to disperse into the air. Time telescoped for Raba and she remembered the lizard she'd killed the last day of her childhood Walkabout. Like it, a last hard core of Djilbara stayed for a moment, watching her, loving her. Then it relaxed, faded, and was gone.

Hands forced Raba away. A voice clanged like a cracked bell, on and on and on. She recognized it as her own. The last image her eyes would accept was of Talbiri lifting Djilbara up, slowly, gently; cradling her body as he carried her back to camp.

Retribution

Raba woke to morning light. Or rather, she didn't wake, for waking was to be asleep and then emerge from dreaming to waking-life. Instead, she came from one flattened undreaming place to another. Her eyes were open and could see and she seemed to have some thought, but her thoughts had the flavor of the flat undreaming.

Her arm was stiff and sore. Tightened and resisting muscle had been penetrated by a feeding sharpness that had

fed *into* her, not from her. Raba felt it as the fanged ghost-
mouth of a tributary where streams of a white-fella drug flowed
into her.

That was who she seemed to be right now. Not Raba, but
a system of chemical rivers propping up and supporting her
unfeeling body. Moaning in anguish, she tried to flee the
sensation of separation from herself by rolling away from it. As
she turned over and over she became more and more wrapped
in a substance that clung to her. She began to slowly fall. Only
then did she realize that she was lying on a white-fella bed and
she was sliding off of it, tangled in sheets that dragged on her,
slowing the fall.

Was she back in the dorm room? Truly looking for the first
time from her skewed perspective near the floor, she could see
that, no, it was too small for that. Both nausea and relief swept
over her. The dorm room would have seemed cavernous, too
vast for her shocked system to absorb. As it was, the small
infirmary room was queasily large.

She sank to her knees on the floor and, wormlike, burrowed out of the sheets. Rocking back on her heels and
pushing up with her hands, she gingerly achieved a crouching
position. The drugs seemed to pool down to her hands and
feet, numbing her extremities and leaving her head temporarily light and clear. Like tide waves the drugs struck the final
barriers in her fingers and feet. Not finding an exit there, they
turned and swept back up. Trying to escape, she clutched the
bedding hand over hand, pulling herself upright. She leaned
hunched over against the bed, in no hurry to make further
movements.

What had happened? She remembered. Djilbara. Djilbara was gone. Raba observed herself curiously. There was no
pain, just vacuum. The substances in her bloodstream ebbed
into that abyss. Dimly despair began to percolate up in its
stead. She willed the drugs back, overtaking the emotion with
their returning surge. That was better.

The chemicals allowed her to function, albeit as peeled,
separated layers. She felt like the ancient mission truck; great,
heavy, clumsy, fragile machinery, barely functioning, connected by hesitant gears. But that was preferable to being a
single raw, shrieking entity.

Raba took one step, then another. There was nothing to
be afraid of anymore. Everyone—the old men, the whole

camp—knew the truth now. And also there was nothing that mattered either. Djilbara was dead. Raba felt lighter and lighter, disconnected from the camp. The gear that turned and kept her here in place was broken. She would simply float away.

But there was more. She remembered. There was still Huroo. A small pulse began to beat deep within her. In wonder she recognized it as hope. She tried to sense him. There were traces, no more than a day old. He'd been brought back to camp and then left again, surging and ebbing like the drug tides within her. She couldn't detect him any further than that. The drugs restricted her abilities. There was still Huroo. They could still be together. It hadn't been his fault. He was innocent. She'd find him and explain. They would heal each other.

She began to walk. Each step was deliberate. The muscles in her thigh contracted and pulled her knee up. Then the lower part of the leg swung forward and her foot descended, solidified on the ground, and braced to support the next step. She reached the door to outside without meeting anyone. It was as if she were a ghost. Where was everybody? She sensed the whole camp grouped together to the east: ahh, Djilbara's funeral rites. Later they would be back to burn the *Wuradilagu's* tent. That meant Raba had been lying in the white-fella's domain filled with white-fella medicine for at least two days.

The faint track of Huroo's presence departed to the southwest. Raba floated along it through the settlement. Near the edge of the camp she came upon a solitary figure. A naked woman sat as rounded and quiet as a rock. Raba could feel the Land reaching up through her, slowly claiming her for Itself. The woman turned to look at Raba. It was Huroo's mother. Their eyes met. *How curious,* thought Raba, recognizing the same sort of functional madness she herself was experiencing. *Did the white-fellas drug her, too?*

Raba studied the woman. Her ripe, middle-aged lusciousness had withered overnight into the soft dessication of old age. Yet the vulnerability now exposed echoed back along her life, and Raba saw in it the image of the tender young woman Numada had loved so desperately.

"Where did Huroo go?" Raba asked, although she could detect perfectly well the path he'd taken. But it seemed only properly ritual to ask his mother.

Huroo's mother pointed the way, then withdrew back inside herself.

A little past the camp another pair of footsteps converged with Huroo's. They were Numada's, driven forward by others.

No matter, thought Raba. It was clear Numada and Huroo had been forced to leave together. But Huroo knew the truth now. Numada could no longer stand between them: he was a vessel empty of power. Huroo would not stay with him when she came for him.

She followed the tracks a way outside of the camp. Suddenly she stopped, leaning down to study them closely. A keening noise broke from her and she crumpled to the ground like a spear-shot bird. Her cheek rested against the sand and she willed herself to become sand herself, to mingle with it, feeling nothing, forever. The drugs were gone. The hope was gone. Anguish and vacuum welled up, laughing, to claim her.

For merging with Huroo and Numada's tracks, obscuring them, were the wispy not-footprints of the *Djinagarbil*, the featherfeet killers.

Makwora

Makwora crouched on his heels before the blackened remains of Djilbara's tent. He had seen her die and knew her ghost would not be returning to haunt its former home. But tradition still had to be preserved. The other tents nearby were drawn back to safety, not just from the great fire, but more in fear of the dead woman.

Scratching into the ruins with his digging stick, used more frequently for years as a cane, he sighed. He wished her spirit *would* return. There were so many questions only she could answer.

Makwora felt forlorn in his great age. The oldest lore said that men were born from the Dreamtime many times into the waking-life. When they were infants, their spirits were still not far from it. As children they grew away from it fully into waking-life. As a man became old he grew closer and closer again to it, until with his death he was released back to his home.

Makwora shook his head. Perhaps he was so close to his own return that he could no longer see the waking-life clearly. But he knew that as an excuse. For years there had been tumult. He and the other elders had put it down to changes in the Dreamtime: powerful changes, hopefully for the better, brought about by the unprecedented concentration of the Law and knowledge in the settlement. Since the Dreamtime was unknowable rationally, they had accepted, and not looked for other sources. And so Numada had worked his tricks and almost destroyed them all.

He remembered the night of the Emu reseeding when the desert caught fire. The *Wuradilagu* had known so much but didn't come to them. He couldn't blame her for that. Women had no reason to trust men, the thieves of the great magic originally theirs.

His hands clenched the digging stick. There were so many places where this tragedy could have been averted. When Huroo was first born, Numada could have come forward and claimed patrimony. There would have been a small scandal, and undoubtedly a spear duel, but those were the usual petty concerns of waking-life. Numada and Huroo's mother were not of opposing clans. There was no reason for the Dreamtime to have been defiled, except for Numada's prideful madness.

What of Huroo? What had the Dreamtime meant him to be? Only a foil for Numada's psychosis? There had been so much potential in the boy. Makwora almost regretted sending him out with Numada to die. But to the very end Numada had laid claim to Huroo, and the elders saw them as inseparable. Huroo would always be tainted. He had to be destroyed with Numada.

The old man wanted desperately to ask Raba what she knew of all this, what her part had been. There was more to her, too, than they'd ever guessed.

But she was gone, disappeared. After she'd been found, collapsed, at the edge of the Outback, the white-fellas had taken her again. Waku and Kultuwa, bitter with the elders and the camp, had helped one of the missionary-teachers spirit her away. In an angry scene Waku declared he would not let his daughter be murdered as Huroo had been, that Raba was finally protected. He then took the rest of his family and left the camp.

Had some important conjunction with the Dreamtime been missed, or simply disaster narrowly averted? Makwora pulled himself painfully to his feet. If there were answers in the forlorn charred scraps of tent and clothing, he could not see them. He knew with relief that his own death would come soon. Perhaps all would be clear to him the other side of the Dreamtime. But for now, he was tired. It was hard to care anymore about the rest.

Interim Whiteness
1960

Sight consisted of a singular, infinite paleness. There was no sensation of temperature. Raba felt no hunger. She thought she remembered times of great, unrequited thirst that came, went, and would come again, as if she were the geographical site of a drought, but not now. Sometimes there were noises, but they were being heard by someone else. At times she was aware of things being pulled tight against skin, but against someone else's skin, not hers.

In lazy moments it occurred to her that thoughts and feelings should be struggling to swim up and disrupt her placid, glassy exterior. They never arrived. She assumed they'd departed for more promising waters. Every once in a while, out of mild curiosity, she sank to the still depths to see if they hid there. They didn't. Empty, content, she rose back upwards to float suspended in the pale light.

"What in the Lord's name is she doing in restraints again?"

She didn't know what the words meant, or who spoke them, but the voice resonated with familiarity. Raba tried to hum its cadences, just to herself, deep within her skull. It didn't sound like anything. She lost interest and stopped.

"You know you're not supposed to be here now, mum. It's not visitor's hours." A man's voice.

"If I didn't come now I wouldn't catch you people out. Take those things off her. You know you're not supposed to do that. She's not violent. Did the doctor sanction this?"

Raba noted with interest that the sense of fabric being eased away from someone else resulted in a lighter texture in the air surrounding her.

"We *have* to wrap her up, mum. Otherwise, when her medication's wearing off and it's too soon to give her more, she starts in crying. She huddles in a corner and sobs as if her heart were breaking, even though at the same time she looks unconscious. It makes the other patients get that excited. Never seen anything like it. We have all kinds of bloody hell (begging your pardon, mum) busting loose here all the time that they pay no mind to. But once *this* one sets in weeping, the rest of them go buckjumpers. If we wrap her up, she's just quiet and fine—everyone happy.

"And look here, mum, about putting her up by herself . . . it's safer for her. I know you don't want to hear this, being a missionary and all, but you've got to look at these people here. Their minds may be off somewhere past the other side of the black stump, but their bodies still go on. The men's corridors aren't barricaded and sometimes those blokes get in here. They don't know right from wrong no more, if they ever did, and she's real young, if you catch my drift."

The woman's voice still bristled. "She's supposed to be here to get better, not to be tied up and drugged for the rest of her life. Look at these sores from the straps . . ." The voices lost their interest, and Raba let them fade away into the peaceful thinness.

Raba found herself standing, leaning up against a wall. She was in a corridor that opened onto some sort of dayroom. The walls were painted a cream green up to her shoulder, then a cream yellow up to and including the ceiling. Looking down, she found she wore a loose, green smock a shade darker than the walls. Scattered around the room were other Aborigines, all wearing identical smocks. Was she in a new school?

But the women were all too old for that. A few looked ancient. Mostly they stared ahead dully, or talked to themselves in a monotone.

Someone standing next to Raba was talking like that. Raba shifted her weight to turn and look.

The sight jarred her. Instead of a numbed Aboriginal woman in shapeless clothing, the speaker was Dorothy Landell. With her pale skin and clean, tidy, street clothes, she provided a shocking contrast to the others. The only thing in common was the monotone talking, on and on, and a somewhat glazed look in her eyes.

"So you see, now that you're off the drugs, when you get well, you can come home with me. I have a lovely flat with an extra bedroom and a room already set up . . ."

Raba filled with a terrible anxiety. Something was all wrong with the setting and the circumstances. The room seemed peaceful enough, the voices no more than harmless, dull, static, but it was all wrong. Although the static remained at the same level, the more she listened, the more it bothered her, becoming important for some reason.

She noticed the room's warmth, and began sweating. The heat gathered in her body as she became more upset. To her great relief, bits of the scene started whiting out. The noise died down to a pleasant hum.

Just as she was settling into interior comfort again, an unexpected stab of panic launched her fully back into the room. She couldn't leave; not until she knew what ailed Miss Landell—why her white-fella teacher was also stranded in this place. She had to find out what was wrong with her.

Miss Landell still droned on. "I know you're not aware of it, but you're actually functioning again. I know if I just keep coming and talking to you . . . the doctors say with a bit more reemergence you could . . ."

Raba cleared her throat, a physical gesture to give her resolve to speak. How long had it been since her mouth had formed words?

"What?" she asked Miss Landell.

The woman's monologue stopped dead. Awareness shot back into her eyes. Raba felt relieved.

"What?" parroted Miss Landell.

"Miss Landell, why are you here?"

The woman's reaction was completely unexpected. She started shaking. Her whole body became a stutter. She looked as if she were trying to say something, but she couldn't get any words out. She stared at Raba. She finally whispered, "Raba? Are you here?"

Raba looked around herself. What a strange question! "Of course I'm here," she said in some confusion. "Are *you* here?" she asked gently, cautiously, not sure what state her teacher was in.

Miss Landell started crying, alarming Raba again. She tugged her teacher towards a chair. "Come sit down till you feel better."

Men wearing all white trotted up the hall towards them. "Help us. Miss Landell's not feeling well," she called to them. But when the men arrived, they grabbed her instead.

"What are you doing?" she screamed at them. Everything was wrong. They were dragging her away, not helping Miss Landell at all.

Miss Landell yelled, too. "Let her go! She's all right. Can't you see that?" She yanked one man's hands free of Raba. "She was just worried about me. That's why she was making a stir."

The other man didn't let go, but he stopped pulling at Raba. The two men stood, looking upset and confused.

"It's all right," Miss Landell reassured them. "We're going to sit down together over here. I want you to fetch Dr. Mackenzie."

When they'd left, she faced Raba. "I scared you, didn't I?" Raba nodded.

"I didn't mean to. I cried because I . . ." Miss Landell shut her whole face up tight. Tears were leaking again from her clenched eyes. Inside, Raba felt herself hopping and dancing in distress. She'd never seen her teacher like this before, with her face all folded in, crying.

Miss Landell blindly reached out to Raba and found her hands. "Bear with me a moment, dear," she gasped. She drew a handkerchief from a pocket with one hand. Mopping her face with the fabric, she began to giggle. "I know it's ridiculous, but I'm crying because I'm so happy. You've been gone so long. Having you come back so suddenly, all at once, caught me unprepared."

"Gone? I've been gone?" asked Raba. "Where?"

"Look around you. Here. Do you recognize this place at all?"

Raba looked. She didn't, but at the same time it wasn't unfamiliar. Puzzled, she answered, "I don't know. I was gone somewhere and just came back here? Where was I? How long was I gone?"

Someone came up behind Raba. Dorothy Landell waved them away. "You've been gone for well over a year, dear, in this place. Your parents found you collapsed at the edge of the settlement. Apparently one of the boys, Huroo, had died out in the desert and you'd just found out. It was too soon after . . ." she let the words trail off. "Anyway," she picked up again, "they asked me to take you away from there, get you help, so I brought you here. Until recently, when I got these people to stop medicating you, I felt I'd betrayed them—that more harm than good was being done." She shot a venomous glance over Raba's shoulder to whomever stood there.

Raba remembered Huroo and Djilbara. A small shaking started up a rhythm deep inside her. "Do my parents come to see me, too, like you do?"

Miss Landell dropped her eyes to look at the floor. "No, I'm afraid it would be too far for them even if . . ." She looked up again. "They asked me to take you far away from the settlement. I think they believed it would help if you were as far away as possible from the . . . source of the pain," she ended lamely.

Raba nodded to herself. That, too, of course, but what her parents must have wanted more than anything was to hide her from the old men. So that she wouldn't end like Huroo. Miss Landell had said "I think they believed." Why didn't she know what they believed now?

"Now you can tell them I'm getting better?"

Miss Landell's gaze rushed back to the floor. "They're gone," she almost mumbled. "They went while I was bringing you here. I've since left the mission, but I'm still in touch. So far they haven't returned."

Raba knew enough about white-fellas' thinking processes to recognize Miss Landell's pained and embarrassed reactions. Her teacher believed that Waku and Kultuwa had abandoned her. The tremor in Raba grew stronger. Her parents had fled to protect her. Perhaps by then they'd needed to protect themselves, too. Her rash plans to escape with Huroo not only lost her lover's and Djilbara's lives, but had turned her parents into exiles. The vibration inside her ate at the edge of her vision. To Raba's great relief, Miss Landell's face, the room—everything—began to pale and fade.

"Raba? Raba?" Miss Landell's voice was shrill. Raba felt the woman's palms seize both sides of her face, plumping her cheeks out around them. Along with her sight, that sensation numbed away to a pleasant haze.

"Raba! Don't go away again!" The sharpness of Miss Landell's voice cut through to her. Raba's vision cleared enough to see her teacher's livid face again. It twisted with such anguish that Raba couldn't comfortably sink away from it. She started to slide off. The awareness of the pain she was causing, the knowing and uncaring cruelty of it, pulled her back. Raba struggled to return to her silent peace. But she couldn't make herself hurt Dorothy Landell. She couldn't make herself not care. She reemerged to face the woman's frantic eyes. Dorothy saw. She grabbed Raba, hugging her fiercely.

Raba found that she apparently spent a lot of time sitting on her bed. She shared a room with two other Aboriginal women, both of them as vague and buried inside as she had been. Their plain, iron-frame beds lined up in a tidy row against the wall. The air smelled strongly of disinfectant masking the odors of indifferent bodies. All in all, it reminded her of the mission school dorms, but smaller and with a different slant to the smells.

Miss Landell joined her there a week after Raba's awakening in the corridor.

"I hear you've seen the doctors several times in the last few days. They're very happy with your recovery."

The doctors had talked to Raba, asked her simple, polite questions. When she answered they didn't look at her. They didn't even seem to be listening. They busied themselves writing on pieces of paper pinned captive to clipboards. Then others came, not doctors, and did other things, not talking. A band of cloth was wrapped around her arm. It turned out to be less a strip of cloth than a deflated tire. They pumped it up, squeezing her arm, then deflated it again. They shone bright lights in her eyes. She coughed for them on command, although she didn't feel crook.

The only commotion occurred when they jabbed a sharp needle into her arm. She yelped, but from expected pain, not surprise. It had looked as if it would hurt. What she was unprepared for, though, was the attached tube filling with liquid red. Something about the sight of her blood leaving her body, to be taken away and lost among the white-fellas, filled her with horror. Shrieking, she yanked away. The nurse administering the test, lulled by Raba's cooperativeness up till then, was caught unprepared for her reaction. The needle jerked free. Blood dribbled down Raba's arm. She grabbed at it frantically with her other hand. The nurse yelled. Men came and held her down while the nurse lanced her again, Raba howling the whole while.

"I think she's going off again," said one of the men.

A doctor came in. He opened one of Raba's eyes wide with thumb and forefinger and peered at her. He chuckled, and Raba felt the men's and nurse's irritation shift to him.

"She's all right," he said. "Undoubtedly she's never seen her blood being drawn before."

"It's not as if she's never been injected," the nurse snapped. "Whenever we couldn't get pills down her, we medicated her with shots."

"True," said the doctor. "But she was hardly aware of what was going on then, was she?"

Now all of that seemed to be over. Raba wondered if they'd told Miss Landell what happened. Her teacher didn't act as if she thought Raba had relapsed.

"They want to observe you for another month," her teacher said. "Then you'll be released into my custody."

Raba dreaded what the woman would say next—about returning to the settlement; returning to all the things Raba had fled there.

Miss Landell seemed to see the fear. "We won't be going back to the mission," she said, "unless word comes that your family's returned. Or unless you really want to go back. Those are your people, and I won't stop you if that's what you wish."

The desperation in Raba's eyes answered her more eloquently than words.

"Well, then. I'm still involved with the church, but I've left missionary work. I moved to Broome, a small city near here. I think you'll like it. I've got a job teaching. If you want to, I thought I might tutor you; catch you up on schoolwork, maybe get you ahead." She watched Raba carefully.

Raba thought about reading again, the little bone words building skeleton sentences. It would be something growing in her life again. She could learn new things; things different and apart from her past.

"Yes, I want that," she said.

"We could prepare you for the University, if you like," Miss Landell said. With Raba's assent it had become a joint endeavor. Raba nodded.

Miss Landell warmed to the subject. "You'd have no trouble getting in. You always were the brightest student I've ever seen. Money won't be that much of a problem. The Church would put up some. Native Australian scholarships often go begging for qualified takers. We could find you a work grant, too."

Raba kept nodding, mesmerized by Miss Landell's dream for her.

"You can do anything you want to with your talents. There's medical school, nursing, any of the healing arts."

Healing arts. Raba experienced sharp tugs of distress. Images of Djilbara flickered painfully across her retinas. Her eyes began watering. Her stomach burned. She mewled.

The sound brought Miss Landell up short in her headlong rush of words. She saw Raba shaking her head back and forth. Tears welled over and splattered down the girl's cheeks with the motion.

"I'm sorry, dear. That was terrible of me. How could I be so thoughtless, reminding you of Djilbara like that?" She put her arms around Raba as the girl rocked on the bed, sobbing. "Not medicine, then. Anything else. You always loved history, didn't you? So perhaps history. Or math. Or writing. Don't let it be spoiled just because of my careless words. Please, please, forgive me."

Raba couldn't afford to let remembrances of Djilbara spoil Miss Landell's plans. Where else could she hide safely, from her past, and herself, but in the white-fellas' world?

Interim:
Academic Beginnings
1963

Balancing her tray of food, Raba negotiated the crowded dining commons in search of a quiet, solitary place to eat. It was her first week alone at the University. Dorothy Landell had left after spending several days getting Raba settled in her new surroundings.

With Dorothy as a companion, the University, though large, had bustled unthreateningly. Now, alone, Raba felt overwhelmed. Her monastic, cell-like room became her refuge. She darted out of it to classes and meals and back like a lizard scurrying to the refuge of its burrow.

When in the classrooms, transfixed by new knowledge, she forgot to be anxious. Morning lectures over, though, she faced meal times. This was where she felt most conscious of her singularity, of being alone. The worst, however, was that she was not really alone. The first day Dorothy had taken her to the dining commons, Raba saw them: other young Aborigines, about ten or sixteen of them scattered among the tables in groups of three or four. She clutched her tray to hold herself from shaking. Staring down at it, she pretended she didn't see them. Surely they would notice her. Could they feel her, sense the wrongness of her, and that she was different even from them? As long as Dorothy stayed, Raba hid behind the older woman's presence.

Now that she was on her own, she felt their occasional curious stares. Raba found a place at the end of a long table. The other end crowded over with a mob of young white-fellas. Eager to pack as tight as they could together, like a knot of swarming bees, they'd left the other half of the table empty. When Raba sat, they favored her with an uninterested glance, then ignored her.

167

Raba had half-finished her meal when someone tapped her on the shoulder. She turned to face an Aboriginal girl; much taller than she was, but about the same age.

"G-dye," the girl said. "We were wondering if you'd like to bring your tucker over and eat with us." She waved towards a small, round table with three other Aboriginal students sitting around it—two other girls and a boy.

Raba looked at her. She sensed nothing—no bristling, no hidden menace. Raba couldn't understand the girl's lack of reaction. Raba was conscious of herself, knew that she exuded through her very pores the years of isolation, the betrayal and exile of her family, the destruction of Huroo, Djilbara, and even Numada. This student should be cringing away from her, or challenging and attacking, anything but bending over like that, smiling.

The girl began to fidget, uncomfortable in Raba's long silence. Raba found that interesting. At the settlement answers often took a long time coming, and were patiently waited for.

"What is your clan?" Raba asked suddenly. This was a crude, abrupt way to find out, not customary at all. Under the circumstances she could see no other way to find out this necessary information.

"What?" said the girl.

Raba repeated the question.

The girl looked confused. "I'm from Sydney," she said, as if that were an answer.

Raba kept studying her. She really didn't know. She was like a wrong-color white-fella.

The girl was now thoroughly nervous. "So would you like to join us?"

Raba looked down at her food. "Oh. I'd finished. I was just about to leave. Thank you, though."

The student also looked down. Raba's plate was still half-full.

Raba flushed. "I'm not as hungry as I thought."

"Some other time then, maybe." The girl hurried back to her table.

Raba picked up her tray to make good her lie. If all the other Aboriginal students were like that she was safe! Fear shed off her like sweat. She felt a relief so great she almost could have called it joy.

But underneath that was a small, hard sadness. She was safe, but only because the other students had lost what should be theirs. Perhaps she was wrong. Perhaps they were only muted. The sadness softened a little. But if that were true, if she joined them, became friends, they might slowly come awake and sense her. She couldn't risk that. She didn't want to be known, and she didn't want to remember. Alone, she walked out of the dining commons.

PART II

Reawakenings
December 19, 1974

The dark brown woman finished marking the test in front of her, and reached across the oak desk's golden surface for another one. It bumped against her name plaque, turning it slightly so that she caught an oblique glance of her name: R. Landell. She turned the plaque around again. Leaning back in her chair she read aloud the student's choice of a title for the essay question: "Making Right Merry in the Time of Du-Barry—an Analysis of Entertainment and Economics in Medieval France."

Sunlight leached through venetian blinds to cast white bars on the surface of the desk and the piles of papers. It exposed dust motes floating in the hot, still air in suspended stripes as if they were an aerial core sample on display. Outside, sprinklers scattered light-brightened droplets on velvet green lawns, chugging in patient rhythm. Their atonal song was more engrossing than the student's paper, distracting the woman from her chore.

She sighed. It would have been a misleading sound, if there'd been anyone else there to hear it. But the other three desks in the department office were empty. The campus was deserted for the Christmas holidays, students and teachers alike off with their families or to the beaches to cope with the summer heat. She liked the solitude, the cessation from undergraduate bustle. Her sigh exhaled slow luxury more than boredom. Interlacing her fingers so her hands became a cat's cradle, she stretched arms grown soft from academic disuse overhead, turning pink palms up to the ceiling.

Footsteps echoing down the hall and past her door didn't disrupt her reverie. During school breaks groundsmen and caretakers emerged from their closets and basements like nocturnal animals to take possession of the University; scurrying to prune, build, make repairs, and disappear again before the students returned.

But when the footsteps stopped and retraced their path, she took notice. They were too light-textured to be McVey, this building's custodian. The sound stopped in front of her door, hesitated. When the expected knock came, the woman also hesitated before answering. She felt a flash of humor at the pattern of the situation, and wanted to throw its rhythm off by not coming in right on her cue.

"You may come in," she finally said.

The door opened. A cap of light brown hair, bisected by a narrow, pale face, peered around it.

"Miss Landell?"

The woman nodded.

A slender, rather androgynous young woman slid into the room. As she moved to sit down, the girl's grace and quicksilver narrowness made Landell conscious of her own stolid form. Years of physical dormancy had thickened on her body like the layered rings on a tree.

"What can I do for you?" she asked.

"My name is Gwyneth Nemane. I was hoping you could help me with some research for a semester paper."

"You aren't one of my students . . . ?" This was framed as a question. Her Intro courses consisted of lectures with students crammed into the massive halls like lemmings.

"No, this is a paper for Dr. Glenhollie."

Leaning back in her chair, Landell folded her arms. "Dr. Glenhollie teaches in Anthropology," she said firmly. She pointed to the door, swung inward to the room now, its chipped gilt lettering clearly visible. "This is European History; specifically the Medieval Studies Department."

Gwyneth squirmed a little. "Well, yes, I know. My paper is on the impact of assimilation on native Australian culture."

Landell stiffened, saying nothing, giving the girl no openings. Time stretched between them. She expected the increasingly nervous student to finally blurt out, "and you're an Aborigine." Then she would order the girl from the room.

But this one had more presence of mind. She was smarter. "I looked up your faculty bio. It says you grew up in a missionary settlement. I thought you might have had access to

the old stories and ways, seen the changes as they happened."
She spoke calmly, but she'd drawn a charm necklace from
where it nestled inside her blouse and worried it through her
fingers.

Nerves sent prickling warnings up Landell's spine. The
faculty bios were supposedly public, but they were buried
away in the reference library. It was doubtful anyone had
looked at hers since its submission when she made the
transition from graduate student to lecturer.

Her voice became very quiet, very still. "I was raised and
educated in a missionary school. If your paper was an analysis
of Deuteronomy or Psalms I might be able to help you. But it's
not, so I can't. Dr. Glenhollie will have to give you better
suggestions on appropriate people to interview."

The girl wasn't immediately cowed. She stared at Landell
intently. The teacher noticed the girl's eyes were a bluish gray
that echoed the silver of the charms on her necklace. The
student narrowed her pale lips into a stubborn line.

"You don't understand. I need to talk to you. There's more
to it . . ." she began to speak forcefully, her shy deference
vanished.

"Good-bye, Miss Nemane."

The student's mouth snapped shut. Landell could see
anger struggling under the surface of her features. It wasn't
strong enough to do battle against the teacher's stony gaze. The
girl gave up. When she reached the open door, she turned and
drew breath to speak again.

"*Don't!* Just don't," the older woman said.

The girl shrugged, turned, and left.

Shaking her head, the woman thought, *bloody students*.
She'd been approached time and again over the years, and
she'd never felt like anything more than an easy tool they
wanted to use to finish up a quick term paper. She couldn't
retrieve her past for herself, let alone for them; a past they
didn't care about and wouldn't have understood.

Her irritation faded and she shook her head again. There
was something about this student, though, that had especially
bothered her. A chill rippled her back.

When the sun sank low enough so that only the upper
walls of the room still showed bands of light, she filed away the
corrected test papers, packed up her briefcase, and left the
building.

Outside she felt, as she had many times before, the eerie artificiality of the verdant grass, lush in the very last of the Dry. Already thunderheads coasted the bright blue sky. Their gathering electricity lanced through the oppressive heat. It would still be days before they erupted into spectacular displays of thunder, lightning, and the intermittent hard showers that brought first growth to the wilds; predecessor to the long steady soaking of the Wet. Everywhere the white man hadn't touched, the grasses and bush of the Land waited, patient and parched, on the promises the Land had given them.

Intellectually she knew that here the blades of grass, glowing an unreasonable shade of jasper as the sun touched them, were real, were alive. But in her heart she couldn't accept them as living things. She liked the lawns because they were a beautiful fantasy actualized, proof that the harshness of life could be kept at bay.

Her flat was a simply furnished studio apartment in a graduate student and faculty housing project. As was her custom, she fixed a simple supper on the hot plate and ate it reading the afternoon edition of the newspaper. Afterwards she walked down the hall to the public phone for her weekly call to Dorothy.

"How are you, dear?" the voice crackled and flickered over the long-distance lines. Dorothy never called her anything but "dear." Once she'd almost joked that she was going to change her first name legally to Dear. She'd kept the thought to herself, afraid of hurting her namesake's feelings.

"I'm fine," she answered. "I'm still finishing up midterms, but it's going well. Although if I get another cute or pretentious theme, I'll scream."

The woman on the other end of the line groaned laughingly. "Me, too, although second-form students don't write as complicated papers as your University crew. But they make up for that with abysmal grammar. I haven't seen so bad since you yourself were in . . ." she trailed off awkwardly from almost mentioning those times they never talked about. She tried to pick up the conversation. "Do you think you'll have time to make it up here at all over the holidays?"

"I doubt it. I'm behind on the deadline on that article for the *Sydney Review*. If I don't publish more I'll never get booted from assistant to full professor. But I promise to visit next semester break."

"That's all right, dear. I understand," Dorothy Landell said.

"No, really. I'd like to go on a big shopping trip with you. Hints have been dropped around the department that I'm looking a little staid. The other faculty members feel I could use a new wardrobe."

They both laughed at that, knowing how spare her lifestyle was. They spent a few more minutes chatting about students and the ins and outs of school politics. After hanging up she returned to her room and her evening routine; putting a billy on to boil for tea, nestling into her one well-padded armchair. Like a patient pack animal a small table stood beside it, burdened with a pile of reference books and several notepads and pencils.

On Christmas Eve she called Dorothy again. Christian holidays meant nothing to her personally, but they were focal points for her old friend and mentor.

The hallway echoed with emptiness. Glad for that, she padded down to the phone. These last few weeks of the Dry had seemed closer, more dense than they ever had before. A depression had settled in on her, languid and heavy. The absence of people relieved the symptoms.

"Are you sure you're all right there, dear?" Dorothy asked. "The University must be a ghost town by now. I worry about you."

"I'm fine. There's still a mob of people hanging out here," she lied.

Back in her room she felt exhausted, as if she hadn't slept in days. In spite of the heat she drew out extra covers for her bed and burrowed into them like an animal gone to ground.

She woke, gasping, to a room devoid of air. The instant before waking she'd sensed a blow flatten the atmosphere. Something struck hard, driving the air before it. Her mouth opened and closed like a dying fish, trying to find breath enough to fill her collapsed lungs. Back arching in a bow, she twisted on the bed. Somewhere in an unimportant place beyond her panic, her eyes registered the faint light of early morning barely graying the dark of the room.

A moment later wind exploded into the vacuum, rushing into her open mouth, pumping at her like a bellows. Grateful at first to be breathing again, her gratitude changed to pain as the sensitive skin inside nostrils and throat was stripped raw by the blast. She turned on her stomach. Eyes shut tight, she buried her head in the pillow. Fabric flapped wetly with each exhalation as blood from a nosebleed seeped down to soak the pillowcase. She clung to the bedding, terrified.

Behind the wind came the furious power driving it. It loomed somewhere far above, the presence of a fast-moving multitude. As it passed she sensed it as a song. *Raba, Raba, Raba, Raba,* it babbled on and on. Nearly paralyzed, she managed to moan. Inside she was shrieking. The barriers to her numbed, carefully anesthetized past crumpled.

She remembered being a child again, lying on a simpler bed even than this, tossed and bucked about as her dormmates lay in fitful slumber. The *Wanambis*! This time was the place they'd disappeared to, so long ago! She felt them sweep now across the ceiling of the sky, trailing threads to the Dreamtime behind them, like spiders trailing their silk, looking for a focal point to retie their weaving. Somewhere, over her horizon, at the far edge of the Land, they found that rebinding spot, and plunged to earth.

Raba felt things shatter and burst. Buildings flattened. People were dying, their consciousness violently centrifuged from their bodies. *Oh my god—dying, dying,* she thought. In her memory Raba saw again Djilbara's soul chasing up and down her burned body—trying to find a way to stay, trying to find a way to leave.

In the here and now massive objects blew away as if they were fragile insects, as the *Wanambis* retied the moorings to the Dreamtime in the barren, vacated spaces.

The great serpents finished their task and departed. As they whistled by overhead again they laughed her name, aware of her far below them. *Raba, Raba, Raba, Raba. So here's the time you slipped away to. Raba, Raba, Raba, where's the song you promised?* She forgot to fear for herself. Raising up on the bed she screamed hysterical anger at them for the destruction they'd left behind. They must have heard her, but they did nothing to retaliate. Their merriment echoed long after they'd disappeared down their own pathways.

Raba lay there all day. Looking out the window she saw that not a single leaf on the trees swayed in the still heat. But her body felt continually buffeted by winds, as her long suppressed childhood resurfaced and washed over her in successive waves. She couldn't absorb it. Curling in on herself, she moaned with nausea.

Sometime in the middle of the day she crawled to the bathroom. Hoisting herself to drape over the edge of the sink, Raba jammed her upturned face under the faucet. With shaking fingers she managed to turn the tap on. A spare dribble washed the inside of her mouth. She gulped convulsively. At first the water felt wonderful coursing down her raw throat. Then another wave hit her and she retched it back up. She sank to huddle on the floor, crying weakly with frustration.

She crawled back to the bed. When she got there its surface was too enormously distant to even contemplate. The air was cooler down on the floor, anyway.

The attacks abated somewhat by evening. Raba forced herself upright by pushing against the wall. Leaning on it, she could slide her body along. In this fashion she struggled into her bathrobe, got out through the door to her flat, down the hall, and, bracing herself, even down the steps to the front stoop. She had to know that what she was experiencing was an aberration. It had to be her personal psychosis—she wanted the rest of the world to be as serene as the expanses of lawn outside.

Leaning down to pick up the newspaper was the worst part. As the blood rushed to her head, her vision flickered in sheets of burgundy. She stayed in that awkward position, bent over and clutching the paper, until her head cleared. Clenching the paper under her arm, she hauled herself back up the stairs, pulling hand over hand on the bannister. She was grateful there was no one else in the building to see her.

When she got to her room she sprawled on the bed, panting. Finally she unfolded the paper.

The headlines took up half the front page.

DARWIN DESTROYED!!

CITY ANNIHILATED BY MONSTER CYCLONE
ON CHRISTMAS MORNING
THOUSANDS HOMELESS
AT LEAST FORTY FEARED DEAD

Raba threw back her head and wailed.

Office Fugue

Over the next two days she retained little consciousness of her surroundings. Occasionally she'd find herself on the toilet, or drinking from the sink like an animal at a billabong. Everything she'd been, everything she'd learned as a child, battered at her to be let in. Nothing assimilated. Memories, lessons, and dreams shimmered and slid past each other like colored oil droplets in water. In a state of shock she felt numb and passive to the process.

On the third day Raba woke up pressed to the glass of the window. How long had she been standing like this? She whimpered with fear. The air inside the room smelled hot and stale. She stank. Her bathrobe felt like an old skin that needed to be shed. If she could only get out of this room, get outside where the air was fresher.

Hands shaking, Raba untied the robe. She wanted to bathe, but that seemed too hard. By sitting on the bed she was able to struggle into underpants and a blouse. She gave up on a bra—it was too complicated. She pulled a skirt from its hanger, wrenching off a button in the back. When she tried to jam her feet into shoes her heel caught. She drew a finger along an edge to slide her foot in. Just as she was leaving she remembered her keys, snagged them, and put them in her blouse pocket.

On the stairs, she leaned on the bannister and wall again. At the bottom, through the front door, the world opened up to vastness before her. She hadn't taken into account that she'd have to make her way into it unsupported. Drawing a deep breath, Raba launched herself from the building.

The cobalt blue sky was so shiny it glared. Thunderheads piled up in sooty contrast, their blackened edges thrown in sharp relief against the blue. Raba almost giggled. She felt as if she were floating. The ground and her feet argued over where they should meet. She would take a step, expecting to connect with the asphalt of the path, which then fooled her by being several inches lower. Her leg plunged into the difference, jarring her spine up to her teeth. She regained her balance by swaying a moment.

Halfway across campus, the Dry decided to end. A massive bank of clouds ripped open. Sheets of water poured over its edges, driving hard to the ground. Lightning strobed the sky. Raba gasped with shock. In less than a minute she was soaked through, her clothing glued to her body. The water weighted her down. No longer floating, she struggled just to lift her feet. She trudged the rest of the way to the History building.

Inside, she tried to remember if there was a sweater or some sort of wrap she could change into in the office. In spite of the still tepid air, she shivered. It didn't make sense to her that chilled and clammy as she was, her earlobes burned like fire. The bottoms of her feet were sore. She fumbled taking her keys out of her blouse pocket. Then through vision swimming with a gray-brown haze, she saw that the door to the office stood ajar. It should have been locked. There could be only one explanation. She faltered, not wanting to face any of the custodians right then. But she felt so tired, so heavy—she had to go on—it was such a short way.

As she entered the doorway she dimly perceived a figure swing around in the chair in front of the desk to look at her. It was the girl who'd wanted to interview her. How had she gotten in? Had McVey let her in? Raba ignored her. All she cared about was making it to her desk.

She lowered herself into the armchair, sinking into the bottom of it. She kept sinking. Her eyes burned with dryness. If only she could close them for just a minute to refresh them. If she could just blink a few times she'd be fine. She closed her eyes. She sank.

Then she flung her head against the back of the chair, her nostrils burning from a smell as assaultive as a knife. Her eyes watered as she tried to push away from it. Blearily she saw the girl perched on the desk before her, holding out a bunched-up white rag.

"Sorry," the girl said, lowering the cloth. "You passed out. I didn't have any smelling salts, so the janitor gave me a soak of ammonia."

Raba's vision swam. The girl raised the rag again and Raba

flinched. She waved the rag away feebly. "I think I'll be all right now," she said.

The student studied her for a moment, then leaned over to chuck the cloth into the wastebasket. "Maybe you won't faint again, but I don't know about being all right." She hopped off the desk, bent over Raba, and began unbuttoning her soaked blouse.

"What are you doing?" Raba asked as she tried to bat the girl's hands away.

"You can't stay in those wet things. They've got to come off. I've got a light jacket I can tuck you into."

Raba looked at her narrow frame doubtfully. The girl caught her gaze. "Lucky for you students favor second-hand baggies." She had a handful of paper towels she must have gotten from the restroom, and proceeded to blot Raba dry with them. Raba self-protectively covered her arms over the scarring on her stomach.

"Stop that," the girl said as she untangled Raba's arms. She bundled Raba into the jacket.

"Okay . . . now . . . up!" she ordered. Raba groaned and struggled weakly against her, but the deceptively slender arms tightened around her shoulders like a vise, and she was hauled into a slumped standing position. "Good so far. Next, the couch," the girl said as she steered Raba to a venerable old sofa, its tweed worn thin by years of waiting students. They teetered there for a moment while the girl slapped her palms against the wet skirt girdling Raba's hips. "This won't do," she said. The skirt hit the floor at Raba's ankles with a wet flap. A light push slumped her onto the sofa. The girl was at most only an inch or two taller than Raba, so her jacket, although oversized, barely covered Raba past her crotch. Raba felt ridiculous and vulnerable, but now she was shivering too hard to protest any further.

The girl stood back and appraised her. "You're turning blue. Something has to be done about that. I'll be right back. Get some sleep in the meantime." She started to whip out the door.

"You . . . stop . . . you can't," Raba stuttered through chilled lips.

"Gwyneth, my name's Gwyneth. Go to sleep. I'll be right back," the girl repeated, and she was gone.

Raba looked down the length of her body. Her legs

seemed improbably long, impossibly bare, densely studded with goose bumps. What if the janitor walked in? Her bones were made of ice, the chill seeping outwards into her muscles. A spasm of shivering jarred her. Sleep? She was too cold and miserable, too afraid to sleep. But exhausted, she found herself, over and over, jolting up out of a slow drift.

When she woke she felt enveloped in warmth. A gentle friction took the last of the cold from the tips of her fingers: someone was rubbing her hand. She opened her eyes. Her body was no longer exposed—she lay covered up to her chin by several overlapping plaid blankets. The girl, Gwyneth, had extracted one of her hands and was chafing it between her own.

When she saw Raba's eyes open, she smiled. "Do you think you're ready to take on some fluids?" she asked.

Gwyneth had a billy boiling on the hot plate the faculty used for morning tea and coffee. She threw a handful of tea in, then swung the billy in gentle circles, settling the tea. She poured some into a cup, and on the hot plate replaced the billy with a small saucepan. Swirling the filled mug slowly, she let the infusion gain strength. When it cooled sufficiently she propped Raba into a sitting position, bracing her with one arm, and fed it to her slowly.

It didn't taste like tea. Wet flakes and shreds of herbs covered the bottom of the cup with dark green. As she drank, Raba watched them tilt towards her mouth with small, eddying currents. Each separate herb sought aching parts of her body and drained away knots of toxins. Raba looked upwards. She was afraid to look down, afraid to see the fluid moving through her, healing her, glowing through even the opaqueness of the blankets. She concentrated on the heathery stitching of Gwyneth's sweater. The charm necklace spilled over its edge. Its pieces melted in silvery light: a flower, a moon, a twig, a tree. A flower, a moon, a twig, a tree. Raba drew them over and over again through her mind the way Gwyneth had drawn them through her fingers, finding in that rhythm a comfort from the terrible return to awareness.

When she'd finished with the tea, Gwyneth wiped the lees into a wastebasket. She returned with the cup refilled, this time from the saucepan. "That was for mending," she said, handing the mug to Raba again. "This is for strength."

Raba leaned her head over the cup, bathing her face in rich vapors. The new liquid was a simple beef broth.

"What do the custodians think of all this?" she asked between sips.

"Nothing," said Gwyneth. Seeing Raba's raised eyebrows, she elaborated. "Oh yes, I spoke to them. I told them we were working on a mammoth presentation that had to get done over the hols; that there were going to be papers scattered all over the floor for days and if they touched anything there'd be hell to pay. Believe me, they won't want to step foot in here. I said we'd be responsible for having it all tidied up when school starts again."

Raba had trouble picturing McVey, a stern and compulsive worker, being put off so easily. Gwyneth turned on the desk lamp, her back to Raba. Faceless for the moment, she became a shifting, unidentifiable presence. Raba shivered. But then the student turned, with her normal white-fella wedged face. The impression passed. Perhaps she did fool the custodian. Remembering Gwyneth's persistence, Raba had to admit it was possible.

She finally noticed that Gwyneth was turning on more lamps. No light came through the windows. Fear gripped Raba. How long had she been here?

"Night of the same day?" she whispered. Gwyneth nodded. Raba felt relieved. At least she hadn't been collapsed here for all that long.

She struggled to sit up. "Good," she said. "I can get back to my flat now."

Gwyneth stopped her just by putting a hand out. "See?" she said, as Raba fell back. "You're still too weak. You feel better right now, but that's because you're in the lull between the chills and the heat to come."

Gwyneth was right. Before daybreak Raba woke to blankets soaked in sweat, consumed by a heat so intense that the chill of the day before would have been welcome in comparison. She drifted in and out of fevered fugues. Sometimes Gwyneth was there when she was conscious, and other times she was not. And sometimes her wraithlike presence couldn't be separated from the fabric of Raba's dreams.

Raba rose out of her dreams thirsty, so dry she cried petulantly in parched, tearless sobs. When Gwyneth was there she handed Raba glass after glass of water and cup after cup of medicinal tea. Raba drank until her belly swelled, and still her thirst wasn't quenched.

One morning she woke feeling as if she had passed finally beyond the realm of thirst; that she had transformed into the radiant source of heat itself. Gwyneth slept, draped in a chair pulled up nearby. The girl's face was the same hue as the pale light washing the surfaces of the room. Circles the color of fading bruises pooled under her eyes. She stirred and woke, as if Raba's scorching stare was the first warming touch of the sun.

"Happy New Year's Day," she said, stretching. Then she leaned forward, studying Raba. A line drew up between her eyebrows. She frowned, but said, "I think the fever's beginning to break." One hand reached out to touch Raba's brow.

Go ahead, thought Raba. She felt silently hot, like an empty frying pan left forgotten on a grill, ready to singe the unwary. The girl's fingers pressed against her forehead, and with a shock Raba felt them drawing the heat up and out of her. Gwyneth's face registered no reaction. "Yes, you definitely feel cooler," the girl said.

Raba trembled. She'd experienced nothing like that since Djilbara died. But a white-fella girl? It didn't seem possible. Gwyneth acted as if nothing had happened.

The next day Raba felt stronger. "It's time to get you back to your place," Gwyneth said. "I think you're well enough to manage now, if you take it easy for a few days." From a cardboard carton of supplies she'd brought in she pulled out Raba's clothing, washed and moderately well-ironed, with only a few crease marks from being folded up into the box.

When Raba was ready they walked together across the campus. Gwyneth rested one hand under Raba's arm when support seemed needed. When they got to the fork in the path that led to Raba's flat, Raba hesitated, fearful that Gwyneth would somehow already know the way there. But Gwyneth just looked at her, curious, waiting for her to indicate which way they should turn. "This way," Raba said.

They stopped so she could rest a moment.

"Why?" Raba finally asked.

"Why what?" said Gwyneth.

"Why the last few days?"

Gwyneth looked down at the path and smiled to herself. "I'd come back to the office hoping to catch you in and try one more time to talk you into helping me. You looked terrible, you know. Deserting you sprawled out over the desk—I couldn't have done that."

"You should have called McVey. He would have had me taken to the infirmary."

"The infirmary," Gwyneth snorted. "Have you ever spent any time there? They wouldn't have taken care of you. A couple of aspirin and you're left lying there, to get better or not on your own."

Raba had nothing to reply to that.

They reached the apartment. Raba rested midway up the stairs. Breathing came hard and the muscles in her calves felt watery. The door to her flat had several notes taped to it in the building superintendent's handwriting. "Your mum called," they said. Since she shared Dorothy Landell's last name he'd assumed she was Raba's mother. Raba almost smiled. If he ever met Dorothy, fair-skinned as goose down, he'd be shocked.

She tensed as Gwyneth unlocked the door for her. Was it as wretched inside as she remembered it last?

The apartment was stale and close, but any carrion smell of illness had gone in the intervening days. The bed looked like an animal's wallowing hole. The bathrobe lay at its foot, and the newspaper . . . Raba wanted to turn and run. The days of fever at the office had let her forget. The newspaper was scattered on the floor. Other than that, things weren't too bad.

Gwyneth propelled her to the armchair. Raba couldn't stop staring at the newspaper. Seeing where her gaze fixated, Gwyneth quickly picked the sheets of paper up, folding them as she went. The newspaper got smaller and smaller, a disappearing origami, until tucked up, it vanished under Gwyneth's arm.

Then the girl made the bed and hung up Raba's bathrobe. "I'm going to tidy up the office now," she said, reassuring Raba that all traces of the last week would be erased. "Are you going to be all right?"

Raba nodded.

Gwyneth backed out of the room.

"Wait," Raba called after her. The girl poked her head back in. "Thank you," Raba said. Gwyneth winked at her.

Fully clothed, Raba lay on top of the bed. The light in the room fluctuated between bright and gray as thunderheads passed under the sun. At one point rain spattered in a racket against her windows.

An hour or so later she heard another sound; the soft knock she recognized from the first time Gwyneth had come to her office. She ignored it. After a few minutes it repeated itself. Raba waited. Then, feeling ungrateful, she swung her legs down from the bed. A note had been slipped under the door. "I came by, but you were asleep," it read. "I left something for you outside."

Raba looked out. A shopping bag with basics in it—eggs, milk, tea, tins of soup—sat there. "Save for Miss Landell" was scrawled on one side.

The Moon and the Crossroads

The semester began early in February. By then the erratic spell of lightning and thunderstorms had settled into the long, steady soaking of the Wet.

Raba trudged each day to work under perpetually weeping gray skies, her black umbrella no more than a thin skin between her and the rain. Her shoes were ineffective against all the water.

Each day she stopped in the hallway with her hand on the office doorknob. If the Dreamtime existed in the same moment as now, if time flowed in and out of itself like the tides in an estuary, would she open the door to find a dark, deserted room with a solitary figure huddled on the sofa? But she would enter and find the room warmly glowing. The three other teachers made the place appear happily crowded. George Collins would be dashing about—a bleached-looking young man with a tall, thin, rubbery body. Joan Petrini had been to the beach over the holidays and returned deeply tanned. To Raba she seemed a riot of color: bright blond hair, bright blue eyes, bright brown skin, a raucous print dress. John Noddy, head of their little department, sat stolidly behind his desk, as always.

Raba felt as if she were sitting back in the dimmed seats of a cinema, and the office was the bright, active surface of a movie screen.

She expected each day to find Gwyneth waiting for her at

the office or at one of her classes. With more and more of her old way of being coming back, Raba dreaded being queried or picked at about the past.

The weeks passed and Gwyneth didn't appear. Raba began to relax and enjoy her rediscovered awareness. The Land, under its mantle of water, sang to her again, softly and indistinctly. Trees and plants drank in the rain's gifts. The birds, drenched and happy, continually shook out their feathers and bounced on the ground ferreting out new food; their lives made again an interconnecting pattern for Raba.

There was no need for her to think about the other part of things: spells, her people, rituals to keep the Land in balance. All that had gone along without her for fifteen years. A burden had been taken from her. She didn't have to think about the past, but it had returned to her to let her live in the present.

Still, when she finally returned Dorothy's calls some of the old fears returned.

"I've been so worried about you, dear," her old teacher's voice sounded faint. Phone lines operated at peril during the storm season. "I kept trying to call, but you were never in."

"I came down with the flu and checked myself into the infirmary," Raba lied. If Dorothy knew about her collapse and the dreamlike siege of illness in the faculty office, she'd be horrified. She'd remember how Raba had left the mission, and the year and a half of white rooms afterwards. "I know I should have had the nurses call, but you know how it is; when you're feeling sick and miserable you don't think of anything else."

"Are you sure you're all right?"

"I'm fine now. It wasn't bad, and I lost some excess poundage. Now we'll really have to get together for a shopping spree, to celebrate my lovely new figure," Raba joked.

"I'm not reassured." In spite of the poor connection, Dorothy's voice came through crisply. "I think I should catch a train and come see you."

"Don't you dare," said Raba. "Classes are starting and you'll make the trip just to find out how busy I am. And you can't desert your own students."

"Well, if you're that adamant, you must be all right. I'm afraid I've already been neglecting my students; I've been so involved with relief fund efforts for those poor people in Darwin."

Raba shook. She didn't want to remember that that was

what had brought her back. That was the other side of the pleasure in life she'd returned to. She began to sweat. She thought of quiet white rooms with no pain in them, and wanted to hide again.

Her relief that Gwyneth had not returned faded. At unexpected moments she found the girl creeping into her thoughts. Telling herself that if Gwyneth still needed help she knew where to find her didn't quell small eruptions of guilt. It was as if she were haunted by the girl.

Raba remembered dreamy sequences of being fed soups and tea during her illness. Gwyneth might come from a well-off family, but she was just as likely student-poor. For all that Raba knew, Gwyneth might have seriously strained her living allowance to nourish her. Gwyneth had watched after Raba and cared for her. She had shared in every way.

Raba flinched. The white-fella child of a culture whose basic dogma was selfishness had shared with her, and she'd refused to share in return.

Remembering how Gwyneth had looked up her faculty admissions file, Raba decided that turnabout was fair play. She went to the registrar's office and requested to look at the girl's transcripts, telling herself it was only because she wanted to track Gwyneth down. She didn't want to admit to herself that she was approaching this in the way that she'd been taught to hunt dangerous quarry as a child; with as much knowledge beforehand as possible.

"Gwyneth Nemane?" the assistant registrar said. "We don't have any students registered by that name. The closest we have is a Diana Nemane. And yes, she was in Dr. Glenhollie's classes last semester."

"Last semester? What about now?"

"She was signed up for this semester, too, but transferred out at the end of the first week. Here, you can see for yourself," the man said.

Whether Diana Nemane was the same person as Gwyneth or not, she had been taking Dr. Glenhollie's classes. More than that, the records showed that her first year in school she'd been enrolled in one of Raba's introductory History courses, one of those classes held in the enormous lecture auditorium, where masses of students blended together in a faceless sea.

Diana Nemane's first two years at the University were

primarily filled with prerequisites, but her electives in Botany suggested an eventual major in that field. However, in her third year her interests switched and she declared for Anthropology. Now she had dropped out of her finishing project course.

Raba felt relieved. Even if the girl was Gwyneth, she was no longer writing that paper for Dr. Glenhollie. There was no need to keep searching for her. Perhaps she would come across her again someday, and then she would try to find a way to repay the girl's kindness.

One evening after classes there was a lull in the ceaseless rain. Raba laughed to herself as she hurried back to her flat for a couple of string bags. One of the earliest lessons of the bush was to try to take advantage of any surprise opportunities the Land might send you. In this case that translated into a chance to bring home groceries without her or them getting soggy for once.

She walked the short distance across the grounds to a convenient store. As she left the shop with a filled bag in each hand, a waxing, almost full moon rose into the clear black sky, as if the moon man had driven away the cloud banks with his brightness.

Others strolled about, too, taking advantage of the rare surcease to get errands done or simply enjoy the evening. The trees dropped excess water in luminescent barrages. Saturated lawns mirrored the moonlight.

Raba noticed a young woman standing in a crossing before her. Although the girl faced away from her, towards the moon, she looked familiar. She looked like Gwyneth. Raba slowed, then stopped. It was Gwyneth. But the familiarity lay in more than just recognition. Gwyneth stood so simply, so open. There was a feeling of drawing between her and the incandescent disc, as if they sang to each other in voices no one else could hear.

Raba watched transfixed. She had stood just that way in the desert as a child when she and Djilbara had gone to fetch Mitika. And she had sung to the moon, wondering if there were other women in other lands singing to him, too.

Her heart beat percussively against her chest. She felt like crying. After all these years, years too late, would she find her childhood daydream true?

Gwyneth turned, her face relaxed and unremarkable. Seeing Raba she said, "Gorgeous night, isn't it? Beautiful moon. It really catches your eye."

Raba's heart tried to slow down. *Yes, let the world be ordinary,* she thought.

"You don't seem surprised to see me," she said.

Gwyneth shrugged. "I expected I'd run into you again someday," she replied.

"I thought you'd come back," said Raba. "I thought you'd still want help on your paper."

The girl looked embarrassed. "I couldn't do that. Seemed too much like expecting gratitude, expecting you to pay me back. I took care of you because . . . it was important. Not because of the paper. The paper was important, too, but not that important."

They stood there awkwardly for a moment, empty of words. "Look," said Gwyneth finally. "Would you like a beer? We could go to the campus pub. It'd be better than just standing here."

Raba couldn't walk away from the girl. "All right," she agreed.

The barkeep greeted them with a cheery, "G'Dye, ladies. Here for a beaut drop? What would yer like?" Gwyneth ordered a tankard and Raba asked for a stubbie. While he was drawing their beers, a student to Raba's left at the bar pushed his own tankard forward to be refilled. "Hey, Bert, are you having a bit of a bludge there, filling those so slow? I've got an empty here myself."

"Leave off, Alfred, you bot. I'll get to you when I'm done."

"Don't I get priority here? I'm just back from trying to help rebuild my old man's place. I need some suds for comfort."

The bartender handed Raba and Gwyneth their drinks, then reached for Alfred's tankard.

"That's right, Alf," he said. "I'd been wondering why I haven't seen your mug lately. How is your dad's place?"

The young man looked glum. "About like the rest of Darwin. Flatter than three-day beer. My dad hasn't been so crook since my mother died ten years ago."

"Let's get a table," Raba said to Gwyneth. She wanted to get away from the sad young man.

When they were seated, Raba leaned forward, forearms braced on the table. "I looked up your records," she said. "Why did you tell me your name was Gwyneth?"

The girl didn't look surprised. "Because Gwyneth is my name, my real name." She buried her narrow upper lip into the head of foam, then chased her tongue after the suds left there. "My family immigrated from Wales when I was eleven. Before that, for the primary grades, I had to go to an English school. My very first day of classes, when I was so high," she held her hand off the floor to illustrate, "we were told, no, *forbidden* to speak Welsh. If a teacher should happen to hear us speaking Welsh, even out of school, in the village we lived in, we'd be punished. They couldn't abide Welsh names. There wasn't much they could do about changing our surnames, so they demanded that we change what they called our 'Christian' names. We either decided on one for ourselves or they gave us one. I chose Diana. After my family moved here it kept following me around on my transcripts, although I went back to Gwyneth. They did that to your people, too, didn't they? Made them take English names, sometimes both first and last? Landell's not Aboriginal."

This was all said casually, as if only to note a point in common. But beneath the conversational tone Raba detected for the first time a hint of something that wasn't elusive, that was solidly Gwyneth. *We are alike*, it pleaded. *What was mine was taken away from me, just as surely as what was yours was taken away, too, and by the same people.*

It would serve no purpose to explain that Raba had chosen Dorothy's last name for herself, to hide from her own people and her past, so Raba didn't address the issue. "You must have been happy to leave, then," she said.

"No!" came the vehement answer. Then, with more control, "At least, not at first. I was glad to leave the school, but I hated leaving my home, leaving Wales." She spoke in the same tones that Raba would have used to speak of the Land. Then the familiar nonchalant Gwyneth was back. "Of course, I got used to it here after a while." She took a deep draught of her beer. "Kids go through that, moving and all. Now I couldn't imagine going back."

Raba didn't believe her.

Gwyneth grinned, a strange, horizontal gesture across her narrow face. "I must confess, though, that after all these years

I still haven't adapted to the way Aussies talk. The most I can manage is a 'G'Dye.'"

Raba allowed herself to return a small smile. "Why did you drop your Anthro course? I expected you to come back and ask again for help on the paper."

Gwyneth waved one hand. "It doesn't matter. I wasn't sure if I really wanted to major in Anthro after all. If I'd taken that class I would have had to finish up in it," Gwyneth evaded her.

"It had to do with the paper, didn't it?"

Gwyneth looked down into her half-emptied tankard. "Well, the whole course culminated in that assignment. I'm one of those people who if I can't do something the way I want to, I won't do it at all." She glanced at Raba and then away again. "I'm not saying that to make you feel bad, you know. That's why I stayed away."

"I guessed that," said Raba.

"You had every right to turn me down." This was said almost defensively.

"Why don't you tell me about the paper? What you wanted to write about."

"It was about Aboriginal folktales, and the impact that the white culture has had on them. Coming from a settlement like you did, you'd know which ones the missionaries had banned, which ones they changed, and which ones your people changed themselves to avoid conflict with them. It happened in Europe, too, you know. The Church turned all the old nature gods into the Devil and his demons to kill the ancient religions off."

"It seems as though your basic premise is that any change in the folktales is bad. Do you think they become 'impure'?" asked Raba.

"Don't they?" Gwyneth challenged her. "Each little bit takes them further away from what they really are, or were. Most stories I've researched are about the Dreamtime, your ancestral past. So each little change takes you further away from your history, and dilutes and taints it."

"We've always used the Dreamtime to explain and guide our lives by," said Raba. "It's not a comparison to a fixed point in the past. Both the present and the Dreamtime are always changing. They affect each other. So the stories also change."

"But don't you see?" said Gwyneth. "Say that I concede

your point. If your past can change, and this present can affect the past . . . just look at this present. How good can that be? Aren't you worried about the Dreamtime itself being damaged?"

They both considered that soberly for a few moments. Gwyneth ordered another round of beer.

"But it's not quite like that here," Raba tried to explain to the girl. "The European culture doesn't have to deliberately change our stories. Where the mobs are broken up and taken away from the Land, they lose their hearts and the stories simply stop. Where I grew up the missionaries couldn't change our stories, because none of them, not one, learned our language. That suited us just fine. We were saved by their stupidity. We all learned at least pidgin English. By not giving them a reason to learn our language, we kept our own existence separate and apart from them. Look, is it really too late for you to do the paper this semester?"

"Probably. I've missed a lot of lectures."

"Unless you're already set on another major, I'd be willing to talk to Dr. Glenhollie for you. Let's rework your theme and I'll help you on the paper, if you'd still like to. At the worst you might have to go to some make-up lectures the beginning of next semester."

"Are you sure you want to do this?" Gwyneth asked.

"Yes, very sure."

Gwyneth hesitated, but Raba felt the girl had known that this was how it would turn out all along. "All right then. Thank you," she said.

Turning Point

Sometimes they met to work on the paper in the office and at other times for tea or over lunch. Gwyneth jotted notes, trying to keep food off of her memo pad. Far-sighted, she wore glasses for close work. It amused Raba to watch the girl unconsciously juggle pen, paper, food, eating utensils, fidget with her glasses, and draw her charm necklace through her fingers as if she were counting prayers on a rosary.

The office provided its own entertaining disruptions. One time George Collins ducked his head in. "Sorry to interrupt during your consultation hours, Landell. Is it all right if I slide in for a moment? I forgot my briefcase," he asked.

"Of course, George," Raba said. After he left she commented, "If I had to describe George to someone from my settlement, I'd tell this story:

"In the Dreamtime there was a great frog, Tiddalik the Floodmaker. He thirsted, so he drank all the water and caused a horrible drought. All the other animals tried to make him laugh to release the water, but they failed. After a long time, Nabunum the eel finally succeeded by dancing himself into ludicrous shapes. George—the way he looks and moves—has always reminded me of Nabunum. As it was in the Dreamtime, so it is now. That's one way Dreamtime stories are kept alive today."

Gwyneth grinned. "In that case, that makes out your boss, Professor Noddy, as Tiddalik." They looked at each other, started giggling, then burst into laughter. The image of Noddy, always sitting squatly behind his desk, with George gyrating in front of him, was too perfect.

But there were times Raba could feel Gwyneth leading in other directions; away from the topic, away from the traditional folktales. She'd ask about life in the camp. She'd ask about love stories. "Did you ever have any boyfriends?"

They opened the dorm windows as quietly as they could. Raba shimmied out before the other girls, head first, checking to see that the watchdog missionary-woman was gone. Above her moon man shone full. His white light stroked her limbs. She leaned against the building, soaking in the silver, as if her pores could drink it in like liquid song. "Psst! Raba! Is it all right? Come on, the boys are waiting," an impatient Marindi hissed. Yemma got stuck as usual, her plump legs too short to clear the window. They pushed and shoved her, their chests aching from suppressed giggles. When they got out into the bush they released that pressure with gales of laughter, then hurried on to the campfire the boys had waiting.

The remembrance was pleasant. It felt good to be remembering again. But then she became afraid. The enjoyable memories were indivisibly linked to the agonizing ones.

"I told you," she said to Gwyneth. "We were put in missionary school and essentially out of camp life at a very young age. I left before I would have rejoined the culture."

"Sorry, I forgot," Gwyneth said. "I just asked because I wondered if you'd ever had any children."

Raba froze. The muscles along her back tightened. Why would Gwyneth ask that? Then she remembered Gwyneth undressing her, the scars on her stomach. "Do you see any children following me around?" she snapped.

Gwyneth's expression, sharp behind the lenses of her glasses, dimmed and retreated as if by command.

The next day she intercepted Raba on the way to class. "I was rude yesterday. I apologize."

Raba drew a shaking breath. "Accepted," she replied. "But I can't do any more for your paper. I just don't have any more examples of the kind of material you need. It's time for you to go elsewhere."

Gwyneth looked alarmed. "But you've helped so much. Look, I know I've been going about it all wrong. Can't I at least bring what I find to you, have you check it out?"

When Raba didn't answer she seemed crushed. "It's because I've been such a pain, isn't it? Look, I brought a peace offering." She held out a small tin box. "Knowing you liked tea . . . this is a blend I made up myself."

The lid opened easily. Raba lowered her face to the mixture. It smelled lively and strong, as if the leaves still drew blood from the plant. "Is this the same brew you gave me when I was ill?" she asked.

Gwyneth shrugged. "Some of the herbs are the same, but not all. This is for pleasure drinking. The other was for healing; just a bit of wort-cunning."

"Wort-cunning?"

"That's what an old neighbor of ours in Wales called it. You know . . . old wives' tales. It's just an old Welsh recipe. Please, what do you say? I promise not to be a boor again."

She looked such a picture of misery that Raba relented. After all, was she any more tactless and rude than any other white-fella?

The research ended before the Wet finished. On a day heavy with rain Gwyneth brought a first draft of the manuscript to the Medieval Studies department. The only other person there was Professor Noddy, entrenched behind his fortlike desk. He barely looked up.

"Here it is," Gwyneth announced. "Ready for your inspection and comments." She dropped it foursquare on a pile of papers Raba was correcting.

Raba's face stayed downturned. She looked at Gwyneth by rolling her eyes alone upwards, giving her face a disapproving expression.

"All right, I'm being a little cheeky. I'm just so happy it's done." The girl plopped herself into a chair in the same way she'd disposed of the paper. "You can look at it, mark it up, tell me what you think. And then I'll type up the final draft and be done."

Raba studied her. Gwyneth's high spirits were genuine enough, but the cause of the elation seemed disconnected somehow from the paper. Gwyneth's body fairly hummed with energy. Raba wouldn't have been surprised if the girl were to rub her arms or legs together to produce a cricket's song.

"So you'll be done; then what?"

Gwyneth exaggerated being taken aback. "I'll become a world famous anthropologist, of course, and have a wonderful excuse to hang around anywhere I want to. I'll be able to do all sorts of wild things under the respectable cloak of anthropology. Orgies, smuggling, you name it."

Raba looked nervously at Professor Noddy, who seemed wrapped up in his work. "With an attitude like that, you hardly need to bother with the pretense of getting a diploma," she said stiffly.

Gwyneth looked nonplussed for a minute, but she was unquenchable. "Our next meeting will be our last one," she said. "That's worthy of a celebration."

"Are you sure a celebration will be in order?" Raba lowered her voice. "Maybe I won't like your paper. There will go your fine career."

"I have every confidence," said the girl. "One way or the other, we should commemorate the occasion. I propose a picnic and an excursion. I'll take care of everything." She vibrated with feyness.

Raba was both amused and alarmed by her. "A picnic in this weather? I don't think so."

Gwyneth placed both hands on the desk and loomed over her. "Don't you trust me?" Raba backed away from her. The girl hovered oppressively close. Gwyneth's necklace slid out of the neck of her blouse and swayed forward. Light from it pulsed across Raba's eyes. She flinched. "What's that?" she asked. All she could see was radiance.

Gwyneth folded her face into a premature double chin to see what Raba was looking at. "Oh, that. It's a new charm. Do you like it?" She jutted her chin forward so Raba could see it clearly. A small sliver of quartz, it cast improbable sunspots on Gwyneth's throat.

In spite of herself, Raba's hand drew forward to touch it. The backs of her fingers brushed against Gwyneth's throat in grasping it. A pulse beat hotly at the soft base of the girl's throat. It connected to a cooler rhythm from the crystal. In breaking between the two, Raba felt their cadences transferring into her through the tips of her fingers. A dull thudding began in her far below, behind her scarred belly. She wanted to pull away her hand; it seemed glued to the charm. Her arm felt heavy and tired, but its weight couldn't drag her hand free.

"So you will come?" Gwyneth's voice floated gently above the small drama. "You can critique the paper over lunch and then we'll go play. We deserve to kick up our heels. How about next Friday? You don't have any classes after the morning lecture."

Raba felt ill. She tried to look up, but her gaze fixed on the necklace. With her peripheral vision she could sense Gwyneth's eyes looking down at her with the same tenderness as her voice.

Sweat crawled through Raba's hairline. It was very important to speak. "Yes, I'll be happy to go," she made herself say. She was panting.

Gwyneth leaned back and away. With great relief Raba watched her hand fall from the necklace. It seemed to descend in slow, silent motion, beyond her control. Detached, Raba waited for it to strike the desktop with force, anticipating the pain that would make everything seem real again. Instead it settled softly, naturally, with no sensation whatsoever onto the oak surface. Her stomach bounced hollowly a few times.

"Good. It's all settled then. I'll meet you at your place on Friday after your class." Gwyneth left.

Raba sat staring at her hand for a long time. She risked a glance at Professor Noddy. He remained oblivious. This unnerved Raba. Once again her unreliable perceptions had betrayed her.

* * *

Raba had no intention of meeting Gwyneth. The day of the picnic she ended her class early and headed across campus. A note already pinned to her apartment door apologized to Gwyneth for not making it, and told the girl where she could pick up her paper.

Rain streamed down the sky's face. Raba clutched her umbrella in one hand and the term paper in the other. She intended to drop it off at the Anthropology department and then hole up in the library the rest of the day. That last time with Gwyneth had been too unsettling. She still didn't know if it was part of the trauma she'd experienced during and since the *Wanambis'* return, or if it had something to do with the girl herself. If the former was true, she knew she was being unfair to Gwyneth, but she couldn't dismiss the sense of horror that haunted her.

Feet slapped wetly towards her. Another black umbrella bumped against hers in a friendly manner. Gwyneth's face ducked below the rim to peer at her. Today her eyes reflected the gray-blue of the weather.

"Oh good," she said. "I'm glad I ran into you early. I just stopped off at the department to pick up our lunch; they let me keep it in their pantry this morning." She dangled forward a sturdy plastic bag with handles so Raba could see it. "I was on my way to your place. Now we can walk over together." She cut Raba back on the path as cleanly as any sheepdog.

Of course. Raba felt stupid. If she were going to run into Gwyneth anywhere, it would have been near the Anthro building. But shouldn't Gwyneth be almost to her flat? She thought she'd figured out the timing precisely. But it seemed logical that the girl was on her way over now, except that Gwyneth had said she was early. How could she have so grossly miscalculated? The more Raba tried to order the sequence in her mind, the more it distorted, as if she were trying to view events in a series of funhouse mirrors.

This was too much like the other day. She wanted to get away. "I have your paper here." Raba tried to pass it to Gwyneth.

"No, no, you keep it for now. Wait till we get to where we're going."

"But Gwyneth, it's raining. We can't go anywhere to picnic. I've written comments throughout the manuscript. That's all you need. There's no reason to go to all this bother."

"Of course, it's raining," Gwyneth said. She put her hand on Raba's arm, still steering her. It was the touch of a perfectly ordinary hand—a little cool from the rain, but warm beneath that. "It's always raining this time of year." She looked at Raba as if she were a bit daft. "That doesn't have to stop us."

What is wrong with me? thought Raba. *It's not Gwyneth. It's my own past erupting, without control.*

"I know it seems weird," Gwyneth startled Raba by dovetailing with her thoughts. "But," she continued, "there's picnics and there's picnics. You have to remember that I come from a country where it rains all the time. You learn how to be creative about these things."

When they got to the flat, Raba pulled down the note she'd left on the door, crumpling and trying to palm it before Gwyneth noticed.

"What was that?" the girl asked.

"A note for you in case I missed you." Raba only partially lied.

"That was nice of you." When they got into the flat Gwyneth said, "You'll need to change into knock-about slacks and walking shoes. Bring a jacket and a cap or hat if you've got one."

"I assumed we'd be picnicking inside somewhere," Raba said as she pulled on some pants. She was still thin from the illness and they fit loosely, settling down onto her hips.

"We will be inside in a way," Gwyneth replied. "But there's still the getting there."

They caught a cross-town bus, Gwyneth paying for the fare. "This is where we get off," she said when they drew up to a sprawling, old-fashioned fortress of a building, surrounded by extensive grounds.

"It's the Metropolitan Museum." Raba tried to descend the bus steps and open her umbrella at the same time.

"That's right. Surely you've been here before."

"Just a few times. When I first entered the University." She couldn't describe to Gwyneth what it had felt like to be a young Aboriginal woman from the Outback facing that imposing edifice for the first time.

"Well, I come here constantly," said Gwyneth. "It's one of my favorite haunts." Gwyneth wasn't bothering with her umbrella; she'd pulled a tweed cap snugly onto her head. "No, not that way," she called as Raba headed up the drive towards the main entrance. "That's for later. First we eat, go over the paper, and celebrate." She set off on one of the garden paths to the side. "Walk slowly. Take your time. Enjoy the plantings." Jaunty in her cap, she used her folded umbrella as a walking cane. With her other hand she swung the plastic bag in time to her sauntered pace. Raba found Gwyneth more interesting than the predictable English gardens.

They turned onto an aisle flanked by thick hedgerows. Rain started driving down so heavily that the view of the end of the path was blurred, gauzed away by the effect of millions of droplets of water exploding back upwards.

Gwyneth stepped off the walkway among some flowerless rose bushes, as if to inspect them. She looked around as if to see what nearby beds had to offer.

"Nobody around," she said.

Raba's umbrella was soaked through. Water pooled along its shaft and slid down to her hand. "I can't imagine why," she said.

Gwyneth ignored the sarcasm. "Wait just a minute. Then tuck up your brolly and follow me."

Raba twirled the sopping vanes, spinning away some of the excess moisture. When she looked back, Gwyneth was gone. Raba blinked. Where had she vanished to? The path was still empty. Gwyneth's footprints ended in mucky dirt a few steps past the rose bushes. The hedgerow looked impenetrable.

But from behind its thick foliage came Gwyneth's impatient voice. "Come on, what are you waiting for?"

Raba stepped into the girl's footprints. From there she could see a dark, cat-sized opening in the bushes. She enlarged it by poking the spiked end of her umbrella through first. Then she bent over and burrowed her way in. A few leggy branches obstructed her way, snatching at her. The bulkiness of Gwyneth's manuscript, wrapped up and tucked into her jacket for protection, made the going awkward at first. But once she struggled through that first layer the space opened up. Tightly woven outer branches formed a facade concealing a dim, chapel-like heart. A soft, thick mulch of dried leaves covered the ground. The rain couldn't breach the outer hedge, but moisture-laden air released an aromatic perfume from the matlike floor.

Gwyneth had spread out a woolen shawl as a picnic

blanket. Bread, cheese, cold chicken, fruit, paper plates, and a thermos followed one another out of the plastic bag. A tin plate held a small candle. The light from its tiny flame barely illuminated the reaches of the live wood vaulting that cradled the two of them.

"Isn't that dangerous in here?" Raba indicated the candle.

Gwyneth barely favored it a glance. "It's on the throw, not on the leaves, and we're not going to knock it over. The flame never gets tall enough to reach the branches. Let's eat. I'm starved."

"How did you find this?" Raba asked as Gwyneth cut off chunks of cheese and bread with a handsome, black-handled knife.

"I was walking around the gardens one day and saw a white cat that kept disappearing and reappearing mysteriously all along the hedge, without rustling any of the leaves or branches, so I never knew where it was going to come out. It was like magic. I had to find out what was going on, so I plunged in after it. At the time I thought how it was like Alice following the White Rabbit down the hole. Since then I've explored all the rows; I know all their hollows. I think of them as my sanctuary."

This was a new Gwyneth for Raba. Over the weeks she'd come to know a girl who was relentlessly, ambitiously studious. A girl who never mentioned friends or any sort of social life. Even sitting with her in this improbable place, Raba had trouble grasping the idea of Gwyneth as a solitary adventurer, roaming free of the University confines to explore.

In the past she'd resisted all of Gwyneth's attempts at comparison between the two of them. Now she felt a small twinge of jealousy, realizing that in some ways she had unconsciously drawn her own parallels. She'd become smaller and smaller within the boundaries of her academic life, like a nut drying and shrinking within its own shell. She'd assumed Gwyneth was the same. In reality Gwyneth had found ways of rejecting that confinement.

"Aren't you hungry?" Gwyneth asked. Raba realized she'd forgotten to keep eating. She noticed the food on her plate for the first time and found she was famished.

Gwyneth finished. She scanned Raba's comments on the paper while Raba ate. The chicken shredded in moist, savory strips. Steeped in a slightly salty marinade, its flavor played against the bland smoothness of the cheese and the porous nuttiness of the bread. Gwyneth poured a cup for Raba from the thermos. Raba expected tea, but the liquid was cool and clear, golden of tint, with an alcoholic aroma. "Wine for lunch?" she asked.

Gwyneth looked up from the paper and grinned. "Why not?" she replied.

Gwyneth started writing notes in the paper's margins, giving Raba more of an opportunity to study her. At this moment she seemed nothing more than a pleasant, bright girl whose company Raba enjoyed. Raba was ashamed of the unease she'd felt towards her. And without Gwyneth as a scapegoat, she had to fear for herself.

They discussed the paper for a while, then Gwyneth packed up the picnic things. Wetting her fingers she pinched off the flame from the candle wick. The light played for a brief instant around her fingertips. Kneeling, they shook out the shawl together in the nightlike darkness.

Gwyneth crawled out first, checking to make sure that no one else was on the path. When Raba emerged, Gwyneth held out one of the umbrellas to her.

"Now for the second part of the day," the girl said, "the excursion part." She led Raba around the grounds to the front entrance again. "Did you know that this is the next biggest museum in the Western Territory, after Perth?" Gwyneth paid for both their entrance tickets. "The day's still my treat."

The building formed a labyrinthian homage to all that was Australia. They went through room after room. There were displays on colonial history, native botany, agriculture, Aboriginal crafts, animal life, the oceans, the Great Barrier Reef, and industry. One hall was devoted to extinct animals, their reconstructed skeletons embellishing the space like dense and weighty old lace.

One tableau depicted a dragon-lizard the size of a truck hunched over its prey, an extinct giant kangaroo; the two animals so different in life, but here abstracted to complementary patterns of rhythmic white bone.

Raba recognized within the bones spirits she'd met out in the bush when she was a child. It was strange to see their shells here; to realize they'd once gone cloaked in flesh.

When the bells tolled closing time, she and Gwyneth hadn't gone through half of the exhibits.

"Damn!" said Gwyneth. "We haven't seen the best ones yet. It isn't fair. Look, I'll tell you what. I'll show you a trick I know." She herded Raba into a small room full of old oil paintings. A colonial period cabinet stood by the single window. Gwyneth tucked the umbrellas and picnic bag behind it. The hutch had a wide lip girdling its front. "You sit here," she instructed Raba, "and hold very still. If anyone comes in, don't move. Don't even think about them."

"What are you doing?" asked Raba.

"We're going to stay afterwards for a little while," replied the girl. "Now, I'm going to perch here in front of you," she said as she arranged herself.

"This is not going to work," said Raba. "We'll be caught."

"No, we won't. And even if we are, we'll just say we were talking and didn't hear the bell."

Raba, afraid that Gwyneth's plan might actually succeed, stood up. "That's just what I want, to be locked up in a museum overnight."

Gwyneth pulled her back. "Sit down. Don't you think I know ways out of here?"

That gave Raba pause. Her image of Gwyneth as fey sprite, intrepid explorer of hedgerows, shifted to a more sinister one.

Raba faced the window. Instead of focusing on the grounds outside, her gaze rested on the surface of the glass. She looked at the room reflected back at her as if it were one of the paintings on the walls. There had been no sunlight all day. The varying intensity of the storm mottled the room in a dim version of the shifting light display of a sunnier day.

She felt completely abstracted and apart from the scene. Gwyneth sat so quietly beside her that there was no sense of the girl. It was as if she had vanished.

An elderly white-fella, stooped and wearing a museum guard's uniform, entered the left-hand side of the glass painting. His face looked lined and varnished, like the room's pictures. He walked across the composition slowly, without reacting to his viewers, and departed through the door on the upper right-hand side.

The two of them sat for timeless moments. Gwyneth reasserted her physical presence by stretching, startling Raba. "I do believe we're in the clear," she stated, grinning.

Frightened and angry, Raba grabbed her arm. "How did

you do that?" she demanded. Gwyneth pulled away with a laugh, but Raba saw fear there, too. Fear of what? Fear of her?

"I didn't do anything. We just held very still, sort of denied our own presence. Do you think I made us invisible or something? It's always amazed me what people don't see, if you don't draw their eye. Besides, I told you I knew the place well. Ninety percent of their guards are old and near-sighted. Come on. We have to see all we're going to in the next hour. We can't switch on any extra lights once the last of the daylight is gone. It would draw attention." She skipped out of the room.

Raba stayed behind for a moment, still shaken and bristling. If Gwyneth had been born an Aborigine, she would have made a frighteningly good hunter. Game would never know when it was being stalked.

Raba couldn't enjoy the rest of Gwyneth's tour. Sensing her reluctance, Gwyneth became more subdued and finally seemed to give up on the enterprise.

"All right, we can go now," she said, "after just one more room. It's my favorite. I never leave here without visiting it; it's so beautiful. It's pretty new, just a couple of years old. I bet you've never seen it before. You'll love it."

Raba doubted that. She just wanted to know a safe way out, and to no longer be Gwyneth's hostage in play.

They went down a rabbit's warren of halls that led deep into the center of the building, to a room with no windows, totally enfolded by the museum. It had its own set of heavy oaken doors. Gilt lettering over the door frame reminded Raba of the sign on her office door. But here the script was larger and unchipped. It said Gem Hall.

Inside were free-standing glass cases set on handsome walnut stands. Hidden lights were expertly placed. The transparent gems resting on black velvet within looked as if they floated in space, glowing with their own internal light.

Gwyneth was right. It was ethereally beautiful. It also made Raba uneasy.

"Come on, come on. You have to see this." Gwyneth tugged her into the room. Inside, Raba felt surrounded. These were little pieces, like bone splinters, of the Land itself. She walked gingerly, as if her footsteps could waken them.

Gwyneth hauled her before one particularly large case. "Isn't this wonderful?" The display held an enormous crystal, clear and bright as water. Light swam and dove along its sharp inner surfaces. Raba was transfixed, numb. With mute eyes she read its plaque.

Largest Single Quartz Crystal Mined
in the Northwestern Territories
Excavated from Penbarley Mines in 1943
Donated by Mr. and Mrs. Wendell Coombs

Her eyes swam from the light shifting within the quartz, dazzling her retinas and making her tear glands well up. It was as if the gem were coming alive.

Raba, Raba, you've come back to the path. It's time to finish changing. It's time to become the path.

Every pore of her skin rippled; every hair on her body erected. Her gaze was trapped inside its facets, gliding back and forth along the mirroring angles.

She heard a heavy, slamming noise. An instant later it penetrated; it was the sound of the oak doors shutting.

"Gwyneth!" she screamed. Something released in her and she raced back to the entrance of the room. She pulled frantically at the door handles. They were locked. "Damn you! Let me out of here!" She pounded on the wood.

The girl's muffled voice sounded distantly from the other side. "You have to stay in there. I can't let you out till it's over. It's for you." Gwyneth said more, but it came indistinctly as the voice of the crystal gained strength and drowned her out.

Raba, you must finish being born. It's time to begin to bring your people's song Home. You remember how it hurts. You know that doesn't last. Push forward into it as you did before. The pain is here, too, on this side.

Raba turned back into the room. The crystal glowed, its light pulsing along the walls. She was being drawn to it. Light burned through her, hotly at first, and then with a cleansing sensation as the crystalline cells of her body aligned to let it pass through. The light met the remainder of her scarred skin. Heat began to build up on her skin's surface, soaking through to the tender organs behind it. The cavity became a heat sump. Her intestines started boiling away into flecks of blood and flesh.

Raba dropped to her knees in agony. This was worse than when she was a child and had been attacked by the sand. The light ate away at her, etching into her like acid. She rolled onto her stomach, trying to protect herself. That only allowed the light to penetrate more easily through her already transformed back. The picnic lunch started to come back up through her digestive tract. For a moment she tasted the acidity of vomit. Then that, too, was corroded away by the light.

She pulled herself along with her forearms, trying to crawl to the door. The cells of the skin on her belly ruptured. Blood soaked through her clothing, so as she dragged herself across the floor she could feel a wide, red, paintlike swath being left behind her.

Just a little while longer, Raba. A while longer, the voice coaxed.

In her mind Raba was shrieking back at it. *I'm not a child anymore! I can't endure this. This time you're killing me!*

But the voice wouldn't hear her. The light kept feeding. Her nerves palpated in agony, sizzling, charring, before they, too, were mercifully consumed. She reached the door knowing that she wasn't going to survive this transformation. She was dying. She was detaching, becoming heavy and clear like the quartz. With her face pressed to the bottom of the door, Raba tried one last time to reach Gwyneth.

Her voice was a faint whisper, but it carried like the crystal's voice. It was becoming the crystal's voice. She could feel it reaching Gwyneth. *Let me out, please, Gwyneth. For god's sake let me out. I'm dying.*

As Raba abstracted farther and farther from the pain, her senses stretched outwards. She could feel Gwyneth through the thick oak. It was as if with her fingers she could touch the girl's body huddled there, helping to brace the door shut. As clearly as if she were on the other side, watching Gwyneth, Raba knew the girl lay curled in a tight ball, her hands pressed tightly to her ears, sobbing, screaming, trying to drown out Raba's insidious crystalline voice.

Then the light punched all the way through Raba and she felt herself fly away on its song.

Her body was being dragged again, this time on her back. Someone had her by the arms: Raba was aware of the bowstring-taut pull down through her armpits. It didn't hurt. Nothing hurt anymore.

Whoever pulled her was moaning. Raba would slide, stop, start up again with a jerk. The series of motions interested her. The sound began to form into words: "Please be alive, please be alive, please be alive."

A mild illumination crossed the surface of Raba's eyes, marking her uneven progress. She was being pulled under the windows of a hallway. Light passing through them gilded her in a ladderlike pattern. It didn't come from the moon. The clouds were too thick to let the moon through.

Finally she recognized its source as the white-fellas' city casting up its artificial glare to the underbelly of the sky. It caught there and bounced back down through the windows.

Her erratic journey stopped in the largest patch of light. Something waved in front of her unblinking gaze. "Oh shit!" came Gwyneth's voice, hoarse from crying.

Hands ripped her clothing open. Gwyneth's hair first tickled and then caressed her as the girl pressed her head to Raba's chest. She must have found a heartbeat, for there came a whistle of relief. Raba's slacks were unfastened and yanked away from her stomach. Frantic fingers brushed against her. Raba felt sharp, granular motes rolling off her stomach and down between her hips and the pants. "What the . . . ?" the voice asked itself. The girl's palms stroked Raba's belly free of the grains, then kept stroking the skin as if they were searching for something that had to be there.

Raba knew what those hands sought and didn't find, what they couldn't believe. The scarring was gone. Her stomach was as seamlessly smooth as glass.

Then the hands cupped her head. Gwyneth's face loomed into view, like some great planet. The girl's eyes were almost swollen shut. Raba knew her own eyes stared wide open, serene and unblinking. "Are you all right? Please let me know you're all right." Gwyneth's voice quavered with fresh tears.

Raba felt like a heavy stone resting on the bottom of a tranquil well. "How did you know?" she asked.

"Wha-what?" Gwyneth's grip wavered. She almost dropped Raba's head back onto the floor.

"I said, how did you know? How did you know to do that?"

Gwyneth couldn't answer. She began to laugh. The laughter dissolved into hysterical sobbing. "I want to get out of here. Can you move? Let's go," she said.

Raba smiled. Quiet and heavy, she didn't mind lying on

the floor. A lifetime of a few short hours ago she had wanted to leave, but Gwyneth wouldn't let her. Now let Gwyneth wait.

"Please," the girl wailed. "Outside I'll tell you anything you want to know."

Rolling over, Raba crouched and pulled her clothes back together. Gwyneth hovered over, trying to help pull her up. The girl was shaking so badly she slipped and almost fell herself. She sidled under Raba's arm to brace her, but Raba found herself practically carrying Gwyneth instead, tucked up under one arm like a chick under its mother's wing.

"The umbrellas and things," said Raba. "We have to get them."

"Leave that stuff," the girl said. "People forget their brollys in places like this all the time. I'll come back later and pick them up at the lost and found. Let's just go."

"Your term paper was in the bag, wasn't it?" Raba reminded her. "Even if it was just some sort of excuse to get at me and you don't really want it, your name is on it, isn't it?"

Gwyneth put a hand to her face and groaned. They backtracked to the painting room and retrieved the bag. Supporting each other, they didn't have enough hands to cope with the umbrellas, too, and left them to appear forgotten.

"Now let's see you get us out of here." Raba felt insufferably cheerful.

"We want a side door, facing the gardens." Gwyneth pointed the direction. "There's a night watchman, but he always stays in his office next to the front entrance."

At the door Gwyneth pulled a short, narrow rod from one of her pockets and inserted it into the keyhole. Raba sensed Gwyneth sending small surges of power down the rod. The girl didn't pick the lock in the usual sense. She wasn't looking to poke and pry at the mechanism until it slid open. Rather, she glided a charge from her body along the tool to syncopate with the key form and the alarm system. But, shaken and weakened, she pulsed unreliably. The more difficulty she had, the more hysterical and ineffective she became. Taking a deep breath, she steadied herself, aligned with the lock, and pushed the door open. Her energy wasn't strong enough. At the last instant it ebbed. Alarms started ringing.

"Oh bloody hell!" she gasped as she plunged through the doorway, falling to her hands and knees. Raba slammed the door shut and yanked Gwyneth to her feet. Half-carrying the girl, she ran as best she could into the cover of the hedgerows. When they reached the sanctuary she shoved the younger woman in forcefully, unconcerned whether Gwyneth was being scratched by the initial barrier of branches. They huddled together in the close heart of the bushes, listening to doors opening and shutting in the museum, watching lights being flashed off and on. After a long time the commotion subsided.

Gwyneth braved a whisper. "They've just checked the outside, to see if the building was breached. There's nothing for them to find that way, so they'll think someone tried to break in and was stopped by the alarm. That is, until tomorrow, when they find . . ." she stopped, shuddering uncontrollably.

"Now! Now you're going to tell me," said Raba.

Gwyneth began to cry again.

"Stop that!" Raba shook her. "It's not that I'm angry at you, though I am. I want to know. How could you possibly know to do what you did. *Why* did you do it?"

Gwyneth waved a helpless hand, indicating she'd talk if she could. When she calmed she began to speak in a throat-stripped voice.

"You've seen my transcripts," she said. "So you know my freshman year I took one of your basic lecture classes. That first day I perched way up in the auditorium with about a million other people. You walked into the hall and up to the lectern. You looked so tiny, way down there. It was like looking down a tunnel lined with people. And you . . . I couldn't believe it . . . you," she was at a loss for words.

Raba waited her out.

Gwyneth took a deep breath and tried a different tack. "Do you know what a speculum is?"

"It's Latin," said Raba. "It means mirror, doesn't it?"

"Well, yes, it can be a mirror. It can be a lot of things. To certain people a speculum is a way of scrying, or seeing. It's a tool, to see things that can be revealed. Crystal balls are the best known, but mirrors, shiny black stones, a dark bowl filled with water, all do very well. What I was trying to find a way to say, was that when you walked into the lecture hall . . . you were a speculum."

She sensed Raba's disbelief. "A living speculum," she

insisted. "All these images were moving across you. It was like watching a deep lake with the reflection of clouds moving across its surface."

"What kind of images?" Raba was fascinated, and afraid.

"Nothing definite. Shapes . . . strong shapes with will and purpose, but so vague and changing I couldn't grasp them."

The girl exhaled a tremored sigh. "Anyway, I'd never heard of, never even *imagined*, something like that. It was beautiful, and it was terrifying. Just as strange was that you didn't seem to be aware of it at all. No one was, except me.

"All my life I've been able to see and sense things other people couldn't. I've been so alone, searching for others like me. It was all right in Wales, because the place was like another 'person.' The trees and wind and rocks and rain were enough. But when we moved here I felt completely cut off, starved.

"And then, in that class, there you were." She started to cry again, but this time they were tears of fury. Her words came out as cracked agony. "And you didn't even know. Damn you, you didn't even know! I couldn't believe you could be so unconscious." She choked, trying to regain control. "That class drove me crazy. I'd go every day, just to watch you, trying to understand. I never could pay attention to those stupid lectures . . . I'd have to get notes from the other students just to pass the tests."

Raba interrupted. "So afterwards you dropped the whole thing. You never took another course from me."

"No, I never took another idiotic class in Medieval History," Gwyneth agreed. "But I didn't drop the other.

"I'd been planning on majoring in Botany at the time. I like plants, and herbal healing is one of my strengths. After your class I mulled things over for a semester, tried to get past the anger and confusion. That didn't work, so I decided I'd find out what I could; maybe find a way to connect with you. I switched to Anthropology, focusing on Native Australian culture. I learned a lot, but nothing that explained you.

"Then, last semester, I felt a tremendous urgency building. There are slots between times, and something seemed ready to burst out of one of them soon. There was a lot of focus towards you in it.

"I needed to write a project paper anyway, and it seemed

like the perfect way to approach you. That first day in your office you were cold, academic, and self-protective. And as usual, completely unaware. You didn't seem to feel the tremendous pressure going on all around you.

"When I woke up on Christmas day I knew everything had exploded. I caught the early news about Darwin and knew that was it. I started to haunt your office. I didn't know where you lived and just hoped you'd finally show up there."

"Why?" asked Raba.

"I was scared for you. The changes I'd sensed were so violent I figured even you couldn't hold them off or ignore them. I was right. When you finally showed up you were shattered. All the things you'd kept at bay had broken through and torn you apart. Just physically speaking, you were pretty ill."

Even in the dark Raba could feel Gwyneth's smile. "This will sound horrible," the girl said, "but I was so happy. After all that time of being bewildered and helpless, I could finally *do* something. I could heal you, take care of you, have a reason to be near and watch you."

"Some caretaker," Raba cut at her. "Taking care of me just to try to kill me tonight."

Gwyneth answered her back with more than equal anger. "It was to make you whole, goddammit. The first time I saw that crystal I thought of you, that it was like a part of you calling for you.

"I played with you for weeks, trying to get you to recognize yourself, drawing back when you got stubborn or suspicious. Finally I knew I just had to get you to that stone. I tested my theory out with the quartz charm." She chuckled. "Bingo! It plugged right into you. I knew I was right."

She sobered. "But locking you in, hearing you screaming . . . I wasn't so sure I was right, then. But it was too late." She began trembling. "Then . . ." She was sobbing, ". . . when I opened the doors and saw all that blood, all over you. Blood on your stomach, on the floor, coming out of your eyes and nose and mouth . . ." She turned away from Raba and clutched at the hedge trunks, breaking into a high, thin keening.

Raba pulled her away from the wood and held her. "Hush, hush. You don't want them to find us now, do you?" She sighed and laid her cheek against Gwyneth's neck. The girl's body was shaking like an earthquake. She rocked her until the tremors eased. Then she sighed again. "And I guess you were right after all."

Exhausted from crying, Gwyneth slept. Raba stayed awake, cradling the girl, exploring the completeness in herself. She felt such a clarity and weight that it was as if she would never have to think, to rationalize, to climb the twisted ladder the white-fellas called logic again. She was in a state of rooted perceptiveness, of just being. Gwyneth felt fragile in her arms. Raba wondered if this was what a tree sensed when it held the light, small life that was a bird.

She tried to imagine what it was like to be Gwyneth; to be blessed with the spark the girl contained and cursed in not having it grounded in anything. When she, Raba, had been a child she'd felt different from others and had fought her own little rebellions. Now she saw that her differences had been a matter of degree. All of her people who still lived with the Land were connected to it, the Dreamtime, and each other. The ones who had been driven away and dispossessed of the Land by the white-fellas; the sad empty people whose gaze she avoided meeting on the urban streets—Gwyneth reminded her of them. But, frightened and confused, with *her* Land thousands of miles away, Gwyneth at least continued to fight. Raba brushed aside a wave of Gwyneth's fine hair where it folded across the girl's face.

Raba at last saw the depth of the tradition the elders tried to preserve. She even had an inkling of Numada's alienation and his desperate attempts to realign matters according to his own vision. She felt overwhelmed by pity for him.

What would it have been like for her not to have had Djilbara or Huroo in her life? Or her family or the rest of the settlement? Now it was Raba's turn to find herself on the edge of tears. The years of isolation and self-imposed numbness in the white rooms began to drop away. All the pain and loss of her teacher and her lover seized Raba, eating into her like the acid light of the great crystal. She bowed her head and wept, but she accepted the pain, because it could not be separated from the love for them that had been returned to her, and she would not lose that love again.

Old Lessons, New Lessons

In the morning they untangled themselves and picked flakes of dried leaves from hair and clothing, trying not to look too disreputable before they crept from their hiding place.

As they scuttled past the museum entrance to the bus stop, Raba felt Gwyneth clench into a knot of panic.

"Why are you so afraid?" she asked her.

Hunched over in her damp, rumpled clothing, Gwyneth looked like a scavenger dog. "The museum doesn't open till ten," she said in a low voice, "but the staff will start arriving any minute. When they do and find all that blood . . ." She let the thought dangle. Her eyes, as they risked a glance at Raba, were miserable with shame. Raba started laughing. She knew it was cruel, but she couldn't help herself. "What blood?" she asked.

Gwyneth cowered before Raba's laughter.

"No, really," Raba said. "Don't you remember searching for wounds on me in the hallway? Did you find any?"

Awareness grew in Gwyneth's eyes. "No," she said. The words came slowly as she ordered her thoughts. "I expected blood, but instead you were covered with sharp . . . like little sharp grains of sand, or granules of glass. Do you mean that's what they'll find?"

Raba nodded.

Gwyneth smiled and began to straighten into her clothing. "They'll find swaths of sand-stuff all over the place, and that's all?"

Raba nodded again.

Gwyneth began to laugh, too. "And our brollys. We mustn't forget the brollys."

Gwyneth revived a little, but on the bus she still contracted with hunger. She nibbled on scraps of bread and cheese left over from the picnic. She offered Raba some, but Raba had no interest in food.

When they got off at the University, Raba walked

214

Gwyneth to her dorm room, half supporting the girl as Gwyneth had once supported her. Raba felt the Land's strength flowing into her with each step.

Gwyneth lived in a room on the fourth floor. Almost carrying her, Raba was grateful that the dorm had an elevator. She'd never been to Gwyneth's place before.

As an upperclassman Gwyneth rated a single room with its own bathroom. Raba expected furnishings as spare as her own—a typewriter, scores of books, not much else. She didn't expect the lively clutter that greeted her. Three banked rows of potted plants crowded the space beneath the windows, taking advantage of as much sun as possible. Bundles of drying herbs and bright glass balls hung down from the window frame. Some of these globes sported shiny mirroring colors. Others glowed prismatically clear. They caught the sun and striped the room with rainbowed bars of light. Two were of smoky, intertwined colors, like giant childrens' marbles.

Typical student bookcases of old wooden crates, and shelves of brick and board lined the walls. The top surfaces of these functioned as display areas for a casual assortment of stones, feathers, and seashells.

Gwyneth rushed into the bathroom. "Do you realize how long it's been since we've seen a john?" she asked with a grimace.

"Since yesterday evening at the museum," said Raba.

The room didn't have a kitchen, but it did boast a hot plate. While Gwyneth took care of her needs and showered, Raba put on the billy to boil. Search as she might, she couldn't find any tins or cartons of tea.

Gwyneth came out of the bathroom in a blue terry cloth robe, blotting her hair dry with a towel. She gestured at the housebound vegetation. "If you're looking for tea, I take it straight off the bush—more like an herb soup." She reached among the pots, pinching off shoots from different plants until she had two fistfuls, and threw them into the billy. "That should be good for what ails us," she said.

"What are those?" Raba gestured at the hanging globes as Gwyneth poured two cups of the brew.

"Most people hang them for luck, or because they're pretty. You don't see them much here, but they're common back in England. It's said they distract the Evil Eye, sort of suck in evil influences. They're called witch balls."

"Is that why you have them?" Raba asked.

"Yes." Gwyneth handed her the tea. "And also because they can be used to focus your gaze and thoughts."

Raba thought of the great crystal the night before, the way she'd been drawn to its brightness. "And you, are you a witch?" she asked the girl. "Is that how you know how to use them? Is that how you knew to trap me?"

Gwyneth hesitated before answering. "I'm not sure just what I am, if there's even a label for it. I told you I grew up lonely, inside myself. My family loved me, I suppose. It's just that I knew I was different from them. Before we moved to Australia I met an old woman from the next village. She was aware of me and sought me out and taught me a lot of things. Being taken away from her was very hard." That made Raba think of Djilbara. "Anyway, the year before coming here to college," Gwyneth continued, "I worked as a waitress to save up some money. During that time I met a coven and joined it for a while."

"A coven? Here in Australia?" Raba had thought that now that she was grounded in the Land that she would be unsurprised by anything, but she found her heart quickening. It would be her childhood fantasy come true, to find groups of white-fella women who knew the old ways.

"What were they like? Are there many of them left?"

Gwyneth looked at Raba with a puzzled expression. "Oh yes, there are still plenty of witches about," she said. She picked up a couple of apples and began to slice them. "They're people, just people." She laid the slices into a black glazed bowl as she cut them. "Very nice people, to be sure. Mainly they're trying to keep, or get back to, the benign sort of nature worship that Christianity did such a good job of destroying."

"But what do they *do*?" Raba asked.

"Well, magic as they taught it to me is the process and art of effecting changes through an act of will. Spells and charms are tools for becoming aware and developing your own focus and inner powers. They used their skills for healing and for trying to achieve a balance with nature."

Taking a few apple slices for herself, she handed the bowl to Raba. "The coven I met here was having a hard time of it. Nature is supposed to be nature, but Australia is a law unto itself. There were too many things foreign to the coven and they couldn't figure out how to integrate here—which was hard on a nature cult. They simply didn't know what to do, although they tried. That's one of the reasons I left them.

"When I started studying Native anthropology I saw that your people had it covered—had it all balanced out already. The white witches have no place here. It's quite sad. They have the best of intentions, but no way to interact with the environment. They're quite stranded. They'd have to become Aborigines themselves."

Raba wasn't hungry. She looked down into the bowl. Gwyneth had dissected the apple horizontally, so the seeds in each slice formed the pattern of a five-pointed star. The core in the middle formed a sunburst center. The fruit contrasted creamily against the black glossiness of the bowl, separated from the darkness only by the thin red line of skin drawn around each piece.

"I'm sorry if what I've said disappoints you," Gwyneth said. "I can show you what they taught me. You can decide for yourself if it's useful."

In the days that followed, Raba thought at first she'd lost the need to eat. Every step she took, each time she touched her hand to the ground, or whenever she lay down on the greens, feeling her back growing deeply into the earth—all these contacts with the Land fed and sustained her.

But then she found herself compelled by desire, not hunger, to find the foods of her childhood. The Land demanded to become a part of her in that way again, too. At night she searched lonely stands of native trees for the small plants and animals her people had eaten.

These small, isolated islands of the Land spoke to her. *Raba, help rejoin me. Stranded here, I am dying.*

"What can I do? You are trees, and Land, and rocks, and animals. You may be just a little plot of Land, but more than I could possibly carry away."

You can, you will, bring the Dreamtime back to nourish my roots. Dissolve the poison emptiness surrounding me. Take from me what you need to grow strong. Do not forget me.

Raba ground native grains in a mortar and pestle she bought from an apothecary and cooked seedcakes on her hot plate. With each bite of food, each creature and plant she consumed claimed her for itself and participated in her growing strength.

Michaela Roessner

She also thought she would be beyond the need to sleep again, as if she were some small, mobile eruption of the Land. She could just draw energy from its vast resources, like a plant draws water from the ground up through its roots.

But as the weeks passed, she found that although she didn't tire, she would suddenly be immersed in sleep as the Dreamtime asserted its need for her to return to it. Sometimes this meant actually sleeping and going fully *badundjari* into her dreams. At other times the Dreamtime superimposed itself over her waking life. The two realities swirled about each other like the smoky colors of Gwyneth's favorite witch balls.

When this had happened to Raba as a youngster, she'd been disoriented and confused. She'd needed Djilbara to guide her clear. Now, made whole, she swam between the simultaneous separated experiences as if they were interlacing cool and warm currents in a billabong; both to be enjoyed, neither impeding her.

The damp heat of the Wet lightened into the beginning of the Cool. Raba coasted through the last of one semester's classes and into the beginning of the next. Where before her work had given her solace in isolation, now teaching university students about their dead past distracted her. She wanted only to be involved with her own learning.

She and Gwyneth spent long hours together in a state of mutual excitement, comparing hard-won knowledge.

"Spells must be repeated three times," Gwyneth told her one lunch hour. They sat on a small patch of lawn enclosed by a skirt of rhododendrons. Gwyneth licked clean a spoon she'd been eating with. Using the handle end she drew three concentric circles in the sand at the flowers' feet. "See how each repetition builds around the one before, like stone-throw rings in a billabong?" She erased part of each circle and reconnected the lines so they formed a single spiral. "And in this way each repetition leads into the next, so it really is an ever-expanding whole. That way the power of your thought grows."

"Our chants are something like that," Raba said. "We repeat phrases many times. Variations of a word or two are added, and new material inserted, but the pattern must be continually reinforced. It's like having a weaving that begins so open structured that it's almost just the idea of a weaving. Then by adding more and more threads it gains in structure and strength and becomes a durable reality."

Gwyneth grinned in delight. "Spells to wear!" she said. "Spells . . . clothing . . . ," she mused more thoughtfully. "They can be alike in other ways besides structure. They can warm and protect you."

Raba remembered the spells Djilbara had woven around her, and the spells Numada had hidden Huroo in. "Yes, both for good and ill. They can hide you from others; that can be bad. They can constrain and inhibit you like tight clothing. They can trap and immobilize." The time she'd spent in the sanatorium, had that somehow consisted of a spell she'd cast, to hide away from herself and the world?

Gwyneth must have sensed her melancholy. She reached over to touch Raba's hand. "I wouldn't let you be trapped like that again," she said in a soft voice.

Again? Raba felt uneasy. What did Gwyneth mean? Did she somehow know about the sanatorium? No, that wasn't possible. Gwyneth must be just taking Raba's words at face value, that Raba was describing something she'd experienced. Or maybe she meant that period of time when she'd been unaware and Gwyneth had known what she was.

Raba pressed Gwyneth's hand in return and tried to smile. "Surely after everything that's happened, that won't be a state I'll return to."

Raba told Gwyneth stories of the Dreamtime, and the Aborigines' desire to reclaim it.

"Did you know we have a sort of Dreamtime, too?" asked the girl. "Or at least *had* one. It was called Annwn, the unworld. Nowadays most people like to say it constituted the Welsh version of the afterlife, like the Christians' heaven. But it wasn't. It was no less real than this world, and to pass between it and this world was an easy and normal thing to do. When I hear you talk about the Dreamtime I wonder if the knowledge of Annwn dates from a time when it had just begun to split away from this existence."

Gwyneth described for Raba the superstition of witches flying. "It's not as if we really get on broomsticks and sail off under the moon. Only part of us goes traveling. That part is called the fetch."

"We call it going *badundjari*," said Raba. She remembered Djilbara flying, all feathers and tatters, between her and searing light. That had not been just a part of her teacher.

It was night in waking-life. *Freed from linear time, Raba coursed through the interface with the Dreamtime as if exploring the contours of her own body. Here rose a prominence as familiar to her as the crest of her cheekbone. There flowed a riverbed formed by two hero-brothers in battle that duplicated the line of muscle meandering along her shoulder blades. Small pitted formations, waiting to be filled, ached as if she were teething. These sensations followed her until her dreamings were plagued by a desire to relieve them.*

When Raba woke she knew what the Land wanted of her, but she hesitated, afraid. She wished just to continue learning, letting the Land grow her like some docile white-fella crop. Unable to make herself take action, she tried to avoid sleeping; drinking coffee, forcing herself to stay awake. In the end she couldn't refuse to sleep when the Dreamtime called her.

The crying of the small hollows persisted. Her dreams filled with irritation. Raba tried to walk in valleys where she couldn't see them, afraid she'd find them growing ever larger, threatening to swallow her with their need. Finally she looked again: They'd become smaller, shrinking, their voices weakened and pain-filled. "Raba, you must act," they cried to her. "I cannot," she told them. "Once I thought I knew enough to act and I lost Huroo. Once I thought I knew and I lost Djilbara forever. I couldn't survive losing again. I can't make myself return to my past." "Your past is still here," their fading voices whispered. "We've been waiting so long for you to retrieve us. Do you want to lose us, too?

Tormented, Raba made her decision. When she awoke, she decided to test herself first. Putting some seedcake batter in a bowl, she sat on the floor of her apartment. She placed her right palm against the wood. Dipping the fingers of her left hand into the bowl, she drew around her other hand with the gruel as if it were a grainy impasto. Even before she completed the outline she felt her right hand sink into the spaces in-between. Something that looked like skin, her body's tie to the waking-life, curled in transparent shavings at the juncture of her hand and the floor. Raba felt as if she were immersing her fingertips into an electromagnetic bath. Forces tingled and tugged at her, pulling her hand down the passageways. The calls she sensed were from farther than her hand could reach. She withdrew it.

She pushed away an area rug, clearing more space. Then she shed all her clothes. Taking a piece of chalk, she sat again and awkwardly traced around her whole body, stretching to reach around the ends of her toes, switching the piece of chalk from hand to hand to circumnavigate her arms.

Raba stood up to evaluate her finished silhouette. Except for the thin, wavery quality of the line, it looked like the outlines drawn around murder victims; two-dimensional monuments commemorating their passing after the bodies have been hauled away.

The thought gave her pause. "Stop it! It's not going to be like that," she admonished herself.

There wasn't much seedcake meal left. Raba stretched it further with tapwater. When she smeared it along the chalk line, it left a faint pale yellow wash as delicate as a watercolor.

She knelt into the corona shape and lay as carefully as she could within its outline, face down. Since she'd drawn the form face-up her hand positions were reversed. She twisted her arms till the backs of her hands rested flat against the wood. Taking a deep breath, Raba turned her face to the floor. Her nose bumped on the wood and she pulled back in a reflex action. Countering her motion, she felt a sucking sensation along the sides and bridge of her nose. She'd begun to sink through.

For a moment in the matte blackness Raba experienced the vertigo and panic she'd felt when she first entered the passages in-between through the self-portrait in Arnhem Land. That passed as she remembered all the times after that she'd returned to explore. She began to glide through the narrow, airless, endless channels. Small sensations tugged at her, each an individual plea for help and retrieval from points beyond the passageway walls. For this first return, she let herself be drawn by only one of them; the smallest one.

It led her through a maze of turns, ascents, and descents. As long as she let herself be guided by its call, she strode freely, only bumping into substanceless walls when her attention lapsed. She found herself at last standing over a point where the pulse beat strongly, resounding through the bottoms of her feet. She moved her toes against the passageway, as if it were sand she could wiggle her feet into. It flexed, then crumbled and began to give way. She shuffled in place down into it. Underneath the passageway she felt actual sand. It startled her to return to sensations of real things against her skin. Then a breath of cool air glided against the soles of her feet.

She kicked upwards out of the sand into night. She stood in a broad indentation in some dunes. Its sides rose, steep enough to block out the view of any surrounding terrain. It could have been a bowl-shaped universe of its own, its only other component the silver-flecked night sky.

Raba had been there just once before, during the day. Here she had waited for Huroo that very last time. Her heart numbed.

The place looked quiet and ordinary, and felt so empty; impossibly distanced by the years from those terrible events. Raba felt rage sparking, that this place should seem so innocent. She wanted it to bear some indelible mark commemorating her loss and her grief. She screamed her hideous pain and anger to the night sky. The shriek rang, cutting and final as a thrown spear.

Something responded to her from a place near her feet, echoing her pain—the voice that had called her here. It was a small knot of wood. She picked it up and it nestled into her memories: a friend from lifetimes ago, it was the wooden burl she'd found on her childhood Walkabout with her family and Djilbara. How had it come to be here? She sat down, cupping it in her palm, and remembered.

The day she'd left the settlement for the Oenpelli lands Raba had carried a dilly bag holding her personal totems and things useful to a budding *Wuradilagu*. She'd never thought of what became of it—whether the men had brought it back with them or left it, whether her family had reclaimed it.

She stood up and searched, but no other traces of the bag remained. Just the small wood spirit, who had patiently waited for her return. It must have been thrown free of the dilly bag that day.

She went back to the place where she'd emerged from the sand, clenching the whorl of wood in one fist, aware of another point gaping like a small well into the passageway. She ignored it. That marked the spot where the *maban* had slid away from her. The *maban* was one of the other voices that called her. "Only one of you at a time. My heart cannot take a heavier burden than that yet," she murmured. She dove headfirst into the spaces in-between.

She wasn't there to see the grains of sand in the depression slowly absorbing the still-echoing resonances of her cry. She wasn't there to see their internal structure shift and change to trap her song of pain and bounce it back out and through their transformed facets as light, so that the place became forever a luminous cup, testament to her grief.

Interior Searches

When Raba emerged through the floor of her room, daylight startled her. Trying to cope with the disorientation from the light and the itching and soreness of fitting back into herself, she felt like a snake shedding its skin in reverse.

Immersed in the process of return, it was several moments before she turned her head and saw Gwyneth. The girl stood flattened against the wall; her face pale, her lips a bloodless blue, her eyes glazed with horror. How had she gotten in? Then Raba remembered Gwyneth's trick with locks.

Raba turned her head from side to side, searching, all too aware of how vulnerable she was at the moment.

"What is it?" she whispered to Gwyneth.

Speechless, Gwyneth shook her head wildly.

Raba finished filling in. Mobile again, she began to sit up. Gwyneth's eyes bulged. Moaning, she pushed against the wall even harder, as if she were trying to pass through it. Raba reached out to her. Gwyneth jerked away from the outstretched hand.

"What's wrong? It's just me."

Gwyneth choked. "Is it?" she asked, but color had started returning to her face. "It really is you, at least as far as I can tell." She still sounded unsure.

"Why are you acting like that? What did you see?"

Gwyneth answered cautiously, still keeping her distance. "I saw sort of a husk, or three-dimensional shadow, transparent and quite shallow. I didn't know what it was. Then all of a sudden I could see you inside of it, as if you were coming up into it from underneath. I thought that maybe you'd gone off . . . somewhere . . . and that it was some awful thing waiting for you to return. And then you got bigger and bigger inside of it. And then," she shuddered, "it became you. I thought it was something else pretending to be you. When it . . . you . . . spoke . . ." She paled again.

"I was returning from going *badundjari*," Raba tried to reassure the girl. "You said that witches do the same thing."

"Not like that. No witch that's sent off their fetch looks like that. Is that what's left of Aborigines when they sleep?"

Raba remembered the mission school and the comings and goings of her dormmates when dreaming. "No," she said. "I think that to most people they would seem to be sleeping normally, but with many dreams. Someone with your capabilities would notice that they'd be off somewhere. There are a very few, powerful, mostly old men who go *badundjari* in ways like mine." *But none of them*, she thought, *have traveled the paths in-between. Not to my knowledge, anyway.*

"Why are you here in the first place? Why did you break in?" Close as she and Gwyneth had become, it made her uneasy that Gwyneth would enter like that.

The girl blushed. "I came over to see if you wanted to go to the cinema tonight. It's almost as fast to walk over here as to call and wait for someone to pick up the hall phone. And this way, if you weren't in, I could leave you a note myself."

"So you knocked, and I didn't answer," Raba said.

Gwyneth nodded.

"Why didn't you just leave a note?"

Gwyneth raised a hand clenching a couple of scraps of paper. "I started to," she said. "Then a phone message came for you and I said I'd tape it to the door with my note. That time I stopped to see if I could *feel* into the room. You definitely weren't in there—not sleeping that I could tell, or in the shower. But the room wasn't empty, either. I got really nervous and decided to come on in."

She handed the notes to Raba. "Who's Dorothy?"

Raba looked at the messages. One was in Gwyneth's handwriting. The other was from the building superintendent. She was relieved to see that this time he'd written "Dorothy called, call her back," rather than his usual message of, "Your mum, Dorothy, called." She smiled. He and Dorothy must be getting pretty cozy on the phone.

"Dorothy was my teacher at the settlement," she told Gwyneth. "She sponsored my getting out of there and on to the University. We still keep in touch." Raba felt no compulsion to tell the girl any more than that. She didn't want to think that it was a matter of distrust. There were blank and nebulous spots in Gwyneth's past, too. Raba preferred to think that they were assuming a mutual respect for each other's privacy.

In spite of that, she said, "I can't go out tonight. I've got some papers to evaluate and an article to draft." Raba heard the stiffness in her own voice. She wanted Gwyneth to be aware that the girl had crossed an invisible boundary.

Gwyneth got the message. "Maybe in a couple of nights, then," the girl said. "Truth to tell, I'm not up for it anymore myself. That was a shock to my system. I'm sorry I barged into your digs; I was just worried about you."

Raba softened. She knew that if she sensed something possibly threatening to Gwyneth she would do the same thing. Had there ever been a friendship like this before?

"I'll tell you what," she relented a little. "We'll go out the night after next. I'll have all my paperwork done by then."

Later Raba regretted her promise. The thought of going to the cinema distracted her, filled her with dread. It would be the first film she'd seen since the *Wanambis* destroyed Darwin.

She possessed a fascination for the cinema that dated to the episode at the settlement between the Aboriginal men and the missionaries over the documentary shown at Coober Downs. It was precisely that incident that in large part had triggered the *Wanambis'* actions against Darwin. When she thought of films now, she associated them with wind-blown destruction, with uncaring death.

The movie Gwyneth picked for them was an old import from England, *The Lady Killers*, a very British comedy about a gang of inept mobsters trying to do in their elderly landlady. The slapstick humor, the alien setting, the British quaintness, gave it a sort of flattened cartoonlike charm that ordinarily Raba would have enjoyed. She couldn't concentrate on it, however. Gwyneth picked up her unease and kept casting furtive glances at her during the funny parts to see if she was reacting to them.

On the way back, Raba thought they'd stop at the pub, their usual custom. Just then, a beer seemed like a good notion. Gwyneth had other ideas.

"Let's go back to my place," she said. "I've got something I want to show you."

At her flat Gwyneth lowered the blinds. The apartment was less cluttered than usual. Gwyneth directed Raba to sit in a chair. Then she lightly drew a large triangle on the floor with a piece of charcoal. Carrying her black-handled knife, a small glass jar, a ball of blue beryl, and a purple scarf, she stepped inside it. She began to trace around the charcoal line lightly with her knife. A chill crept over Raba. There was a strong resemblance to her own actions the other day in preparing to go *badundjari*. Gwyneth sat crosslegged in the middle of the triangle. "Now I'm going to show you our version of going *badundjari*," she said.

It was as if Gwyneth needed to make things equal between them. Raba felt agitated. "Gwyneth, this isn't necessary."

Gwyneth's eyes were all innocence. "It's all right. It's nothing nearly as shocking as what you go through." She placed the beryl ball in front of her and sat quietly, reflectively, for a few moments.

Raba expected her to break into a chanting spell after that. Instead Gwyneth picked up the purple scarf and twisted it until it was like a length of silky thick rope. She clenched it between her teeth, each end hanging bannerlike down along either side of her face.

Then she picked up the jar and opened it. It contained a pungent-smelling salve. Gwyneth scooped out dabs of it and smeared it on her pulse points: her temples, the base of her throat, wrists, and the inside of her elbows. With a careful, respectful motion she recapped the jar. She returned to gazing at the beryl ball. Suddenly she began to twitch, her spine jerking in a series of violent motions. The girl's eyes and head rolled back as she gave an extenuated groan. Her teeth ground into the scarf. She pitched backwards and writhed on the ground for a few moments. Then her eyes closed and she lay still and vacant as a corpse.

Every hair on Raba's body bristled erect. Her first impulse was to jump up when Gwyneth's system went into trauma. Ruefully she remembered her own reaction to Gwyneth's intrusion at her flat. Raba held her place. Gwyneth must have done this any number of times before.

She watched Gwyneth closely. The role of the purple scarf

seemed simply to keep the girl from swallowing her tongue. The beryl ball must be a focusing object. It was the salve that caused the seizure.

Raba tried to see if Gwyneth's fetch left the girl's body. But what she saw was as if some portion of the girl burrowed deeper and deeper into herself, vacating the outer premises of the flesh that housed it. It diminished until it appeared to vanish.

Gwyneth lay that way for a good hour, with Raba watching intently the whole time. Raba abruptly realized that she'd been staring only along the route Gwyneth appeared to have left by. At some point the girl had already partially returned, seeping back in a diffuse pattern all along the dorsal surfaces of her body. Now she rested there in a shallow layer similar to sleep.

Gwyneth awakened several minutes later. Disoriented, she rolled up to a sitting position and sat blinking. Seemingly oblivious to Raba, she lurched to her feet and made her way unsteadily to one of the shelves, picked up a small, purple-bound notebook, and wrote in it briefly. She turned and leaned against the shelving.

Gwyneth appeared to be more composed, so Raba risked speaking. "Are you all right now?" she asked.

Gwyneth looked up at her, smiled weakly, and nodded. "Can you talk about it?"

Another nod, then Gwyneth cleared her throat, making a sound like cobwebs being brushed aside. "Did you see anything?" she asked Raba. "Did you see my fetch leave? Did you see any part of my journey?" She pulled herself up to perch on the counter.

"I'm not sure what I saw," Raba said carefully. Gwyneth seemed to be asking for an elaborate confirmation. "But yes, part of you was gone. Where did you go to?"

Gwyneth looked thoughtful. "Before this, it was always to some place, and things would happen with people I may or may not know. I'd learn something and bring it back with me.

"But this time was different. It was the beginning of the longest trip, as if I were going to be traveling and traveling and not coming back, because eventually at the other end was Home and once I got there I'd never leave again. But once I launched myself, knowing this, it was as if I were a bird flying over the ocean, with all that vastness below me, and not knowing where to go. The winds over the waters were high and strong. I could have sailed on them forever. I felt as if they could have carried me for all time, never dropping me down to the waters below, and I still wouldn't find the way Home. But if I *were* to find it, that's how it would have to be."

Raba remembered her childhood when she had flown the winds to the edge of the sea, and the choice she'd almost made to leave. If she had, would she still be floating on those currents, seeking a way to return Home?

"Raba . . ." Gwyneth retrieved her attention. "Raba . . . help me."

"Help you? How?"

"You live on the boundaries of your Dreamtime. All of your people know of it, know there's a chance of getting back. Help me find the way back to mine."

Raba was troubled. "Gwyneth, I've just barely been returned to myself. I'm still regrowing. And I've never made it all the way back to the Dreamtime. I wouldn't even begin to know how to help you."

"But I helped you, and I didn't know what I was doing either," said the girl. "And I was really scared for both of us a lot of the time. I also knew that there were things that had to be done, that I was being drawn to do.

"Do you remember when we met that night with the moon, during the break in the rains, and went to the pub for the first time, afterwards?"

"Yes," said Raba. She felt as if jigsaw pieces were being drawn closer and closer together, the space and air between them growing less and less, and they were about to be snapped together perfectly, presenting an airtight interlocked surface. She felt as if there wasn't enough air to breathe.

"Do you think it was an accident that we met under the moon, in a crossing?" Gwyneth continued. "European witches meet at crossroads as a drawing together of power. I was working with the moon to call you. I knew that *you* were a path. You can lead me, even without knowing how to. You can find the way for me."

Raba was stunned. Since the museum she'd assumed that she was the strong and grounded one, and Gwyneth was fragile and floundering. She felt like a fool.

Gwyneth had acted even when she was afraid, trusting her instincts, and she'd been right. The girl had known all along how things fit together. Raba had thought herself the wiser one since the night at the museum, but she hadn't even seen the obvious in hindsight. A fatal flaw in her judgment still followed her through her life, from her youthful decision to trail the old men at the initiations, which luckily had turned out well, to her plans to escape with Huroo, which had not. Had Gwyneth ever brought death to loved ones? In spite of the girl's recklessness, Raba doubted it.

Gwyneth looked at her expectantly, eyes full of hope. How could Raba deny her a chance to return to her own Dreamtime?

She was finally able to draw a deep breath. "All right," she said. "When do you want to do this?"

"Now." The girl leapt down from her perch, all smiles.

"Right now?" Raba was incredulous. "After what you just went through? Aren't you still shaky?" There was something that disturbed her about the whole salve business. "And it's so late, Gwyneth."

Gwyneth brushed her objections aside. "I'll be fine, and you don't need to sleep much these days anyway, do you?"

Raba felt chilled. How did the girl know that?

Gwyneth continued. "We should do it right away while the journey is still fresh inside me." She bustled about, erasing the charcoal line, moving the planters to clear more space. This time she drew a huge circle on the floor. Raba noticed how elegant and precise it was, the quality so fine it was as if the soft outward bulge of the circle kept the line stretched taut naturally. The girl tossed two cushions in the center. "Sit inside the circle," she instructed Raba, "facing west." She lit incense burners and candles at the cardinal points and then also stepped within.

Singing in a language Raba assumed was Welsh, Gwyneth walked slowly around the circle three times sunwise, bent over to trace the chalk perimeters with the knife. Still singing, she placed the knife in front of her cushion. She started to sit, then hesitated, almost breaking her rhythm. Reaching up, her hands burrowed through the sleek brown hair nestling against the nape of her neck, and unfastened the necklace. She knelt down to Raba, opened up the older woman's hands, and placed the necklace in them. Raba clasped her fingers around the jewelry. The silver was warm from Gwyneth's body, heavy and as fluid-feeling as mercury.

Gwyneth sat on her cushion back-to-back with Raba. The ridges of muscle bordering their vertebrae pressed and then softened against each other. Gwyneth's singing became smaller and smaller, subsiding into a hum that soaked through the stiffness of Raba's back to resonate within the cage of her ribs. The vibration sank, a low buzz, down to Raba's tailbone. She felt their spines aligning, knitting together like a zipper being drawn upwards. The boundaries between their two bodies dissolved. The song, no longer existing as sound, but as a pattern of submolecular movement, coursed upwards, slowly climbing the bone ladder. Power washed out from both of them to the edges of the chalk circle. From there, as the song climbed, it drew upwards, tighter and tighter, until it met at a point above their heads. Now they were encased in completeness.

As Raba merged into Gwyneth's body, she coursed along the girl's vertebrae as if they were a series of interlocked caverns; the intricacies of the bone like sensuous accruals of limestone deposits. A hum echoed through Gwyneth's backbone from the sheathed trunk of nerves the bones encased and guarded. The heat of the girl drifted through like warm air currents.

The only path Raba found here was an empty one, its sole function to be part of the structure Gwyneth existed in. Then Raba remembered how Gwyneth had reacted to the salve. Her journey had seemed to consist of vanishing inside herself.

Raba turned her attention to the bone itself. The beliefs of her people taught her that the last and hardiest of life lived within the bone, the most durable part of the fleshly shells they were given to live in. Even the lifeline of the Land itself survived, in this time of separation from the Dreamtime, within the rock, the barest bones of the earth.

Raba changed her direction, and diminished into the vertebrae. They became as cavernous as the previous spaces had been. Then smaller and smaller, she was pushed and crested along waves that were the rhythm of Gwyneth's breathing and the cadence of blood pushing through the girl's veins and arteries. Inwards, down and into the cellular structure: down into the chromosomes, glowing in dancing spirals that defined Gwyneth's body. At each step the space opened up to the black between the structures. Raba penetrated the molecular level.

Smaller and smaller, she was surrounded by more darkness at each level, until finally she shot through to a space that was blackness only. There was no longer anything physical to penetrate, just a sense of nothingness that reminded her of the tunnels in-between, but without the confines of those passages' walls. Raba coursed through a great vastness, speeding along a strong and particular trajectory. Time ceased to exist. She experienced a sense of infinite patience to match the seeming infinity of her journey.

After an unknowable duration, she saw a speck of light before her. It grew larger as she approached, until it overwhelmed the darkness, flattening out and resolving itself into a scene. At that point it maintained a set distance from Raba. Although she still sped along, she got no closer to it.

It was a view of a Land she'd never seen before; not in Australia, nor in photographs of other countries. She had no intuitive knowledge of it, as she did the rest of the world. Steep slopes were napped with unfamiliar trees. Sharp rocky angles framed a sky of a deep, sharp blueness not seen in Australia.

Raba scrambled within herself. Was she still speeding unawares through the darkness while this apparition held her hostage?

In the picture the hills led down to a lake far below. A sense of coldness permeated the landscape. Raba was startled. Until now, she'd ceased to notice any sense of temperature at all since launching into the final blackness.

Figures toiled up the incline. They stopped just inside her view and turned back towards the lake, laughing and pointing at it. The water flickered with silver. Raba guessed that a great school of fish sported there. The figures turned away from the lake, and she could see them more clearly. They began to talk animatedly, although Raba could hear no sounds. They were an odd assortment. There were pale-skinned people, white-fellas, wearing animal hides. And there were creatures that had to be animal spirits: beast-headed, perched erect on long hind legs. Raba had never seen spirits like this— so solid and fully within the world. She remembered as a child seeing the Rainbow Serpent, and the brief glimpse she'd had of its reality within its own dimension.

A woman in the group looked up towards a horned spirit, giving Raba a good view of her face: it was full, broad through the cheekbones. Her hair was a soft shade of brown, the color of a doe's pelt, and her eyes were the same bright, deep blue as the sky. She smiled, and Raba felt a ringing through her own heart. In spite of the physical differences, this woman was echoed in some part in Gwyneth, a song changed greatly through the generations, but still maintaining a bare wisp of the original melody in her friend.

This was it! This was Gwyneth's Dreamtime; a moment of its past still existing concurrent with the present. Raba hummed with excitement. If she could penetrate it, she would have blazed a trail that Gwyneth could follow. She pushed into it. Her heart sang: a return! A return for Gwyneth! No more of the sad displacement of life-long exile.

But as she pressed, there was no sense of contact, or of emerging into that reality. There was no sensation at all. Raba threw all her focus, everything she knew into her efforts. It was as if she was racing towards it, but it stayed always the same distance right in front of her, disconcertingly static.

Finally, she felt something give. She knew she would reach it. Then, abruptly, it ripped, and she plunged through a flashing illusion of tatters, speeding into darkness beyond. She turned to look as she sped by, carried on by her impetus. There was nothing left behind her, not even a glimmer of light. The image hadn't even had the substantiality of thin paper.

Raba had an infinity of time to think as she traveled onwards. She mourned as she went.

Eventually the darkness around her paled. She'd come full circle. She passed up and out through all the layers of Gwyneth's internal architecture. Distracted and tracking only by the ever-growing light, Raba almost went too far, leaving their joined bodies entirely. She found herself emerging past the barriers of the skin surfaces, and retreated back. The room was filling with morning sun.

Disengaging along the lengths of their spines, she regrouped inside her own body. Gwyneth seemed to be asleep. Her head had slipped and lay relaxed back over Raba's shoulder. Her hair, a brighter brown than that of that ancient fragment of her, cascaded silkily against Raba's cheek and neck.

Feeling Raba separate away from her, Gwyneth woke, gently and happily. She rolled around to face Raba. "Well?" she asked.

Raba kept her face guarded. "Did you feel anything?" she asked the girl.

"Just drawing the power up around us," Gwyneth said. "And interlocking with you. Then I got very drowsy, and fell asleep, I guess."

"Did you dream at all?" Raba asked.

"I remember dreaming, but not what I dreamed—just a wonderful sense of feeling rested and complete." She was eager, impatient. "Did you find anything? Did you find my Dreamtime? Did you find a way Home for me?"

Raba drew a deep breath. Gwyneth deserved total honesty. "Yes, I did find your Home. Or at least a fragment of it." The girl glowed. Raba described the scene of the hills and the lake. "But, Gwyneth, there's no way back to it."

Gwyneth was stunned. "How can you say that? You saw it. It exists."

Raba shook her head. "No. It's just a racial memory sunk deep in the core of your being. It doesn't exist as an actuality anymore. I tried to reach it, and it vanished. It was nothing more than an illusion."

"No!" Gwyneth protested. "That can't be true. You're wrong."

Raba could see she was still emerging from her shock, thinking desperately. "Look," the girl said, "you're from a different Dreamtime. That's why you couldn't enter it. But I could, because that's where I belong." She brightened at the thought, and talked faster. "I can get back. I know I can. You don't believe me—I can see that. It's all right. I can understand why you think that. But don't forget that all along I'm the one that's known. I knew about you, and I knew how to help you, and I knew you could find the way for me."

Raba said nothing. She'd been wrong before. Perhaps Gwyneth was right, and she would be able to find her way back. Raba wished that to be true. But in a quiet, still part of her, she knew that this time she wasn't wrong.

"Thank you for helping me," Gwyneth continued. "You'll see. I'll be fine. Would you mind going now? I need to rest, and then there's so much to do." She was frantic in her eagerness.

Raba sighed, remembering her own long retreat from the harshness of reality. There was nothing she could say, at least not now, that would convince Gwyneth that she was wrong. Gwyneth would have to find that out for herself.

But she hesitated, afraid to leave Gwyneth alone, afraid of

what the girl might do to herself in her deluded quest. She'd watch over Gwyneth, be there when the girl finally understood and accepted that there was no path Home. As Raba closed the door to the room shut behind her, Gwyneth was pulling books and objects from their shelves in an ecstatic frenzy.

The Derelicts

Raba feared for Gwyneth. There was a possibility of the girl sinking inside herself and not coming out again. In the singlemindedness of her quest she could become lost inside herself, or refuse to turn away from her goal and return, until her body finally died of neglect.

Raba monitored Gwyneth for days—keeping her distance, but never letting too many hours go by without some evidence that Gwyneth was up and conscious, or honestly asleep.

She watched for several weeks. Gwyneth lost weight and looked haggard, but eventually Raba realized she wasn't in immediate danger. Each time Gwyneth tried to follow the internal path that Raba had blazed, she came around full circle, up and out of herself, just as Raba had.

All Raba could do was wait for Gwyneth to accept how futile her efforts were.

Raba didn't spend all her time surreptitiously guarding Gwyneth. The Land called to her. *Sing songs to Me with your feet, Raba. Sing your path into Me to draw Me together whole again.* Walking became an obsession for her. She felt compelled to lay her feet down, to cover ground, for hours every day. Each time she traveled down a walkway or trail, she sensed that *she* led *it*, rather than the other way around; as if she defined each path's very existence, and its course.

Her academic work suffered. First her scholarly papers. They no longer held any importance for her, and she finally abandoned them. Then she began to neglect her actual schoolwork, compelled to wander instead. Raba found she couldn't think except when she was walking. But when she walked thoughts flowed with each flooding pulse of blood pumped from her heart through her body.

Everything that had happened to Gwyneth rang as harmonics with what was happening to her, Raba, and with what Raba now saw all around her. She tried to imagine herself as Gwyneth, deprived forever of the Dreamtime, and couldn't grasp the scope of that loss. Now, when she walked, the beautiful fantasy of the always-green lawns revealed themselves as a travesty; no more real than the landscape of Gwyneth's long-extinct Home. Everywhere Raba looked in the white-fella city she saw discontinuity and separation. It was a top-heavy phantasmagoria, toppling from its foundations of nothingness. Underneath the concrete she could feel the spirit of the Land sinking away, its cries for care and continuity unheard, its offered gifts unreceived.

She saw the white culture's disintegration as a terrible chain, stretching down the roads to the interior of the Land, and out to the ports. Across the oceans to other cities and other lands—it was a poisonous web with the life of the Land dying away beneath it.

Raba would return to her room horror-stricken. What had happened to Gwyneth's Dreamtime wasn't over. It had grown to encompass the world. Even now it eroded the Dreamtime of Raba's people. Only within herself could she feel her Dreamtime as a growing, vital force. Everywhere else in the waking life it progressively faded, sundering away.

Raba's wandering finally led her into an older district, a vestigial organ that the rest of the city had grown out and away from. It consisted mainly of bleak warehouses that had once presented a monolithic face to the world. Now only a few were intact. Far from the vital centers of commerce, they probably served as storage space for out-of-date and surplus stock. In between them, boarded-up stores formed blind gauntlets walling in the streets, their bleak united front punctuated by cavities of vacant lots littered with weeds, trash, and rubble from the buildings that had once occupied them. Although the Dry had not yet begun again, each breath of air smelled of broken concrete and dust.

Raba wasn't surprised she'd been drawn here. To her the seeming desolation was a transparent mirage, revealing behind it a great hope. Of all the places she'd traced her path, only here the white-fellas' influence thinned. Native weeds grew in the alleyways and empty spaces. They'd overtaken the railroad beds that once serviced the warehouses. They stubbornly grew up through the concrete, defeating it in infinitesimal increments. Untended, they grew, died, and grew again according to the seasons. Where buildings crumbled she felt the Land reemerging. And where the white man wasn't, the Land's voice could be heard more clearly.

A few dusty Aboriginal men napped in doorways, or, wrapped up, in the shade of broken walls; men as derelict as the buildings themselves. This was one of the few places in the city Raba could expect to find her people. Their process of dispossession was different from her own. Landless, jobless, surviving on government dole, they'd drifted naturally to these empty spaces. Alcohol and drugs anaesthetized the aching gap where once the Dreamtime had existed for them. Raba felt no fear of them—she could see them so clearly. She remembered with an almost bitter amusement her first days at the University, when she'd been so needlessly terrified of the other Aboriginal students. Isolated and blinded by her own self-anaesthetization, she'd deprived herself of their harmless company.

She walked for hours. Raba's senses had been registering movement behind her for a long time, not alerting her because there was no sense of hunting to it. But at some time Raba became consciously aware of being followed. She looked back. Desolate cityscape surrounded her. The only living things besides herself were a few of the Aboriginal swagmen squatting on the doorsteps, their eyes dimmed of all curiosity. One man leaned against a wall, fumbling in his coat pocket for something. He would be disappointed. Raba saw the neck of a small flask peering from the mouth of a different pocket.

Raba turned away, walked to the end of the block, rounded the corner, and waited. The footsteps that approached stopped, hesitated, then proceeded erratically. She found it hard to believe they could belong to her tracker.

The man who'd been standing and searching for his drink plodded around the corner. Head down, he didn't register Raba waiting motionless until he almost shambled into her. His eyes must have finally focused on her feet, for he reared his head with an audible "Hunh!" and stumbled backwards. Then he just stood, looking intensely bewildered.

Raba wrinkled her nose. A horribly rich patina of smells radiated from him like heat from the sun. He'd been following her downwind. But now, from where he'd dropped back to only five feet away, the stench he carried was like an overwhelming burden.

Back at the mission settlement people dressed as he did, in odd cast-off layers. With water scarce and precious, people also bathed infrequently. But there were other ways to keep clean, and their layered odors were usually of strong, healthy bodies. This man's scent was of weeks of alcoholic sweat rotting through unchanged and unwashed clothing. It chanted a long, sad tale of his body's dispiritedness and disintegration.

"What are you doing?" Raba asked, in English.

At first she wasn't sure if he understood. He looked around, as if her words were random sounds floating through the air. Then he gathered himself together.

"Follow you," he answered, in pidgin.

"What do you want?" she asked him.

"Follow you," he said again.

One of his hands strayed across his clothing, found the bottle in its hiding place, and stroked it, as if for comfort. It seemed to give him courage. He extracted the hand and extended one long, bony finger forward, hesitantly, as if to touch her. Raba was sure they both wore identical looks of confusion.

"But why?" she said.

"Must. Must follow," he insisted.

Raba wanted to talk to him in anything other than English, but the chance of them speaking similar dialects was remote. She tried a few gestures in "finger-talking." He looked at her blankly.

A thought came to her. It was so deeply a part of her past she couldn't believe it hadn't come to her as automatically as instinct. And at the same time it was so remote, something that hadn't concerned her for years. Should she even be talking to this man at all? For all she knew he might belong to a clan she was forbidden any contact with. Did spirits watch, angered that she spoke to him? She sensed only a vacantness that matched their urban surroundings. Perhaps within even this most tenuous of the white-fellas' domain the old taboos had no strength. But Raba didn't really believe that.

"What is your clan?" she asked him.

He blinked for a moment, surprised by her question. Some old pattern of self-recognition fell into place across his face, and he smiled.

"The great running birds, running longa their legs. That be my family," he nodded, happy, his identity firmly reestablished.

"Emu? Your clan is Emu?"

He nodded again.

Emotional shock rippled seismically through Raba. Once she'd carried Huroo's Emu spirit within her. Once she and Huroo had been as bonded and intertwined as a nut and its shell. No wonder this man was drawn to follow her. But the clan spirit in this derelict was ill-nourished, grown so faint as to be undetectable. That such a powerful spirit, which once threatened Huroo's life and later sustained him strongly, should be vanquished in this sad man, made Raba want to weep.

She remembered the fearsome old custom of "pointing the bone" to make a man wither away and slowly die. Did anything exist that was its opposite, that would "point life" back into one of her people? Once she'd sung Huroo's estranged Emu spirit into herself, trapping it temporarily in a looping path there. What could she do to bring forth this man's dormant totem? And with his alcohol-wrecked body, would that be wise? She looked at him. He wouldn't become any stronger if she waited.

"Follow you," the man repeated again, hopefully, as if on cue.

"I have a song for you," Raba said. "Will you take it?" He grasped her offered hands eagerly.

Raba took a deep breath, trying not to flinch from his smell, and began to sing.

> *Follow me*
> *Follow me*
> *Follow me*
> *Walk away*
> *Walk away*
> *Walk away*
> *Long bird running*
> *Long bird growing*
> *Long bird come again*

She sang the pattern of a path into him. It ticked in little pulses from the capillaries of her fingertips into his palms. He was beginning to look uncomfortable. He whined a little and shook his hands, as if he hoped to loosen her hold.

> *Long bird follow me walk away Home*
> *Long bird walkabout*
> *Long bird walkabout*

She felt toxins leaching out of him in slow, successive waves. Sweat dripped from his face, soaking his clothing. He tried to break free in earnest now, eyes rolling in panic at the violent realignment taking place within him. But Raba was rock. She was stillness that cannot be moved. Her fingernails cut deeply into his hands as he struggled. Even the slickness of the shallow blood that welled up there couldn't help him escape her grip.

> *Long bird walkabout free to the Dreamtime*
> *Long bird walkabout free to the Dreamtime*
> *Long bird walkabout free to the Dreamtime*

She chanted without pity or mercy through his weeping, through his pain. With broken words he begged her to let him go. She chanted until she felt something inside him emerge and begin to spread tentative new wings and stretch long, uncertain legs. She chanted until every cell of his body became a map his spirit could follow. Only then did she stop, and at last let him go. She was drained.

He stood there, sobbing, bewildered, trying to understand.

"Now you must leave, today," she commanded him.

"Follow you?" he asked shakily. His eyes told her he couldn't believe she'd desert him after what she'd just done.

"No. Follow *you*. You must follow yourself now. I've given you the way. Leave now while it's growing strong inside you. If you leave it will become even stronger. But if you stay, it will die again."

"Go where?"

"Go back to the bush."

"No family, no people left backa the bush. Not knowing

what to do." His thoughts were growing in clarity. "Mebbe come longa wrong tribe, break taboo."

She understood his very real fears. He would be a man alone, with no tribe or family. He'd forgotten or maybe never known the rituals. What if he broke taboos? What if he couldn't survive?

"There are many places where our people are no more," she told him. "The Land lies neglected there. It needs you, and will teach you how to sing the proper songs. If you stay away from drinking it will bring you proper dreams again. You'll remember the old ways. You'll set forth as our ancestors did, and a family will gather around you."

Hope lit in his eyes. "That be good. I just wait next check for money to go. Catch me big bus to faraway."

"No!" Raba said firmly. With that check he would buy another bottle, and forget. "You leave today. And walk. You must walk. The path is in your feet. They know the way. It will take you a few days to walk out of the city, but after that the Land isn't far."

Sliding the coat from his back, she pointed him eastward, away from his cronies on the last block. "It's time to go."

He started uncertainly, but each stride gained in purpose. While she watched him begin his journey, Raba wiped the blood from her hands and rummaged through the coat pockets until she found the bottle. After emptying it of what fluid remained in it, she dumped both it and the coat in a trash bin.

Perhaps she couldn't always be sure of her judgment. Perhaps there were things she was blind to. But now she knew that the Land was fully within her, and when it called she could heal without questioning. The swaggie's pain hadn't all seeped away yet. She ached from its residual dregs settling in her joints. But she was glad.

She returned home to her flat and stood in the shower until the hot water ran cold, feeling alcohol fumes peeling out and away from her, cleansing herself of the poisons she'd absorbed.

That night she went *badundjari* and found her *maban* where it lay, sunk in a deep pocket in the passages in-between. When she brought it forth and held it up to the sun the next morning, light shone through its pristineness to reveal her hand as darker crystal beneath it. She sang to the *maban*. The song it answered her with, from the depths of its facets, was her own.

On one of her night journeys, she emerged up through the floor of a brush shelter between two sleeping forms. One Raba recognized as her mother, Kultuwa. Her motionless body was older and heavier. Raba couldn't sense her father anywhere. Perhaps he was away, hunting or riding stock. Perhaps he'd died.

The other person was a young woman. But not so young that she could have been a daughter born after Raba's departure. Had Waku taken a second wife? Or if he was gone, her mother could be staying with another single woman. There was no sense of discord between the two. Their dreams rested peacefully one beside the other, so Raba neither worried nor grieved for things she could not know.

Something called to her from one edge of the tent. A small basket lay under a meager cache of supplies that was the most Aborigines might think of as possessions. Raba opened it. Inside, welcoming her, were tools and fetishes she'd carried with her when she'd left to embark on her career as a *Wuradilagu*. Kultuwa had saved them for her, hoping her daughter would return for them someday. The burden of guilt for being the cause of her parents' exile eased a little from Raba's heart. These objects had been kept with a sense of love for her. She felt no trace of resentment attached to them, but rather a stronger faith in her than she had felt for herself for many years.

As Raba left she saw a smile cross her mother's sleeping face, and knew Kultuwa would not be surprised to find the basket gone in the morning.

Several days later Raba sat carving on her first retrieval, the small knot of wood. She'd pulled up a chair by her door and waited, excited and apprehensive. There was a strain in the air like the tension before a storm. Gwyneth was approaching. Raba hadn't seen the girl in days, but she'd sensed her growing frustration, and knew Gwyneth at last confronted the impossibility of a return to Annwn. Now she was returning to Raba, in an electric knot of emotions too complex for Raba to analyze. Raba felt anxious. She had a gift for Gwyneth, a hope, but she didn't know if her friend would be able to hear and accept what she had to say. The atmosphere vibrated tautly. With their talents, both of them knew that one was coming and the other one waited.

Gwyneth's knock rang with stiff politeness when it came. Raba opened the door with a similar sense of anachronistic formality.

Raba had once heard an anecdote that in the past, upper class European women ate traces of arsenic to give themselves ethereally translucent complexions. Gwyneth looked like that now. Her face burned with a sheer glow that set off fine tracings of veins pulsing beneath the surface. Before she'd been naturally slender—narrow rather than thin. Now she was gaunt, her bone structure rubbing tight against skin like a starved dog's ribs.

She walked in without a greeting and sat down in Raba's overstuffed armchair.

"You were right. I was wrong," she said without preface. "It's gone and there's nothing I can do." Raba pulled the chair she'd been sitting in around to face the girl. She was frightened by Gwyneth's control.

"I've thought and tried to figure it out, much good that does me," Gwyneth's flat monotone continued. "Once my people loved and worshipped nature. Then Christianity spread like a plague. People were murdered in its name, their gods declared demons, and the old ways destroyed, sacrificed to the new religion. That was when we lost everything." Her voice flared to anger, then subsided back into dullness.

Raba laid her whittling knife and the wood down on the nightstand. "I've been thinking a lot about it, too," she said, proceeding cautiously. "And I think that, yes, Christianity may have dealt the last blows."

What she was going to say next would be hard for Gwyneth to hear. In the course of her walking Raba had seen a way out for the girl. She'd had the vision of an incredible undertaking. For it to succeed Gwyneth needed to understand fully what had happened in the past.

She picked up the piece of wood again and rubbed it back and forth in her hands nervously. "But the separation *started* thousands of years earlier. It started when your people stopped living *with* the Land as a part of it. Instead of listening to it, they told *it* what to do. Instead of receiving what it gave them freely, they settled down and began to grow crops. They grew what they wanted wherever they wanted to. They drew apart from the Land, making it first their servant and then their slave, until its spirit died away from them. You know that salve you use for your trances? It's made from various plants and should be used with respect for them and solely for their needs. But you've been taught to use it whenever you want to, for only your own benefit, with no thought for the plants at all.

"Christianity didn't help matters, but the connection with your Dreamtime was long since broken."

Gwyneth's face knotted in trying to assimilate Raba's words. Raba watched her struggle to accept what Raba was saying. It was a terrible burden. It meant acknowledging the guilt and misjudgment of her people, and giving up the comfort of scapegoat Christianity as the sole culprit for her loss. But Raba was right about the impossibility of returning to Annwn, and she was right again now. Gwyneth's face twisted with grief.

Still, she accepted it better than Raba had hoped for. Raba had expected an angry rejection, and a greater break between the two of them.

"Gwyneth, this is very important for you to grasp, because I think I've found a possible hope. But for you to move on, it will be vital not to repeat those mistakes in a new Dreamtime."

Like a miracle Gwyneth's face smoothed of its anguished contortions. "I knew it!" she whooped. "I've had the same idea, the same hope!" She flung herself onto Raba in a big hug. Laughter and speech tumbled in and out, making her nearly incomprehensible. "It was so dark for me, so awful. I almost gave up. I *did* give up. I had to, because there was nothing. Then all of a sudden there it was, the completely different way. I thought I'd have to ask you, but I should have known— known you'd see it, too, probably way before me. I knew you'd help me."

Raba was thrown off guard by Gwyneth's wild enthusiasm. Then she relaxed and hugged her friend back. Why should she be so surprised? Considering both of their abilities, and their relationship, it was natural they'd be led to the same conclusion.

She began to laugh, too. "I don't know why I'm laughing. It'll be hard, incredibly hard. I'm not even sure it's possible. It's just a hope."

"Oh no," protested Gwyneth. "Much more than a hope. You'd make it on your own anyway. With the two of us, getting there is a certainty."

Raba froze. Gwyneth's words seemed completely disconnected from Raba's idea: Gwyneth as the focal point for the beginnings of a new Dreamtime for the white-fellas.

"What do you mean, the two of us together?" she asked.

"When you leave for the Dreamtime, and take me with you. You know—going together, at the same time," the girl said.

"Gwyneth, what are you talking about?"

"I surprised you, didn't I?" the girl said. "You probably thought when I was so off-base about Annwn that I'd lost my abilities entirely. But I knew even then you'd be breaking through to your Dreamtime soon. That's why I was so desperate to find Annwn; before you went back and left me here alone. I couldn't have borne that. But I should have known you wouldn't leave me."

Raba sat in shock. Protests rose on her tongue—that she wasn't returning to the Dreamtime, that Gwyneth was crazy. But the words stayed unspoken. What stunned Raba was not the outrageousness of Gwyneth's statement, but that Gwyneth was right. Caught up in the process of transformation, Raba hadn't seen the Land's final goal in changing her: she was inexorably being drawn to the Dreamtime. Gwyneth's words freed her to see this. The clarity of the vision washed through Raba, filling and overwhelming her.

But just as her nearsightedness had kept her from perceiving her destiny, so Gwyneth had not seen her own.

"Gwyneth, that wasn't it. That wasn't what I saw for you." Raba picked her words with care. She wanted to give Gwyneth the dream she had for her as a special gift, not for it to crush her friend. "The vision I saw for you was something much greater than that. It was something entirely yours. Let me explain.

"You know our cycle of stories about how things were created in our Dreamtime?"

Gwyneth nodded. She looked wary, her enthusiasm dampened.

"You know how empty and desolate everything was then? Our ancestors traveled across the Land within that emptiness. Everything they did—the simplest things, was an event that helped form the Land."

"What does that have to do with me?" the girl interrupted. Raba felt a stubbornness accreting in Gwyneth, like an oyster forming a pearl around the irritation of a grain of sand. She felt power growing in the younger woman.

She hadn't looked at Gwyneth this way before. What she saw reminded her of something. It reminded her of the ancestor spirits that lived within the small sacred stones. Gwyneth wasn't quite human. Her body was merely a container. This perception made Raba surer than ever that her dream for Gwyneth was correct. But it would make it that much harder for her friend to accept. Paradoxically she could use her power to resist self-knowledge.

"Bear with me a bit longer. The separation from your Home and your Dreamtime has been spreading through the rest of the world. Soon everything will be depleted and empty, just as empty as this Land once was. Then it all can begin again. It can reseed itself around you. You will be one of the new ancestors for your world. Your actions will build it anew."

The flesh of Gwyneth's face hung slack on its spare skull in disbelief. Tears began to fill her eyes. "This is what it's come to," she whispered. "Now that you can return to your Dreamtime, you just want to get rid of me before you go. I've been all alone my whole life. For all that I've helped you, you'd still desert me?"

"Don't you remember what you said to me when I told you Annwn didn't exist?" asked Raba. "You said I couldn't get all the way there because it wasn't my Dreamtime. For the same reason I can't bring you with me to mine."

"But I was *wrong!*" Gwyneth's voice was shaking. "I couldn't get into Annwn either. I never even saw the image of it like you did. So maybe I *could* go with you. Let me try."

Raba shook her head, knowing as she did that she was admitting her return to the Dreamtime to both herself and Gwyneth. A fear ticked deep within her. What if somehow Gwyneth could penetrate into the Dreamtime? Raba sensed that her strong spirit, out of place and out of time, would distort into something truly terrifying. Raba shuddered inside.

Gwyneth still looked at her, silently pleading. When the girl saw Raba's resolve unmoved, she turned away to hide her crumpling features. For a few moments Raba heard only the heartbroken gasps of someone straining not to cry. Then there were no sounds, for a long while.

When Gwyneth finally turned back, her face was a rigid mask of rage. "Do you think I believe that?" she snarled. "I found you. I changed you. You have to take me with you."

Raba shook her head again.

Gwyneth's pale features froze into a frigid whiteness. "Just you try to leave without me," her voice soft and very, very low. "Just you try." She stalked to the door. Her face split into a rictus of a smile. "I'll enjoy watching you try."

"Gwyneth, come back." Raba's voice blew through the empty, open doorway.

Raba wanted things to be right for Gwyneth. But she couldn't speak if Gwyneth wouldn't hear. Gwyneth would never understand she'd been drawn to be the catalyst for Raba's changes. It was true that Raba owed her a debt, but there was only one way it could be discharged.

Raba picked up the knot of wood and began carving on it again. It wanted to be let free to sing its song. So she was whittling it into a bullroarer, the first made by a woman since the men stole the magic. She wanted to help whittle Gwyneth, too, into her true form. But Gwyneth couldn't hear her own song the way the wood could.

Hard Lessons in Witchcraft

At first Raba continued her life and the process of changing much as before. She'd waited for Gwyneth to come around once. She would wait again, for as long as the Dreamtime allowed her.

The next week, one afternoon after classes, she went back to the warehouse district. The thought that her derelict might not have left, or had returned, nagged at her. Her search turned up no trace of him, although she knew he could be hidden in any of the rabbit warren mazes formed by the broken buildings. But when she tried to sense him, she found only a glad absence.

She thought about asking some of the other men about him, but was afraid to, for this time they didn't huddle in the doorways as separate, nearly unconscious entities. Clustered together they watched her, talking among themselves. Did they miss their compatriot? Did they suspect she was responsible for his disappearance?

One of them shambled towards her. Raba held her ground, although inside she flinched away from him. A much older man than her first swaggie, he smelled equally bad, his hair and beard a matted, curling mass of gray turning white. He stood even shorter than Raba, so as he approached, his eyes seemed to lower in threat from beneath his shelved brow. When he reached her he dropped to his knees, making Raba jump. He looked up at her to draw her attention, then with one finger began drawing in the thin dust layering the concrete. Raba craned her neck to watch him.

The mark he made formed into the symbol of a long-neck Turtle. Then he pointed to himself. Raba understood. He was one of the old ones who had not forgotten the Law. She shook her head, stepped back a few paces to a respectful distance away from him, and drew her own totem, the Wallaby, in the dust. They were from contra-indicated clans.

His mouth split into a broken-toothed grin of approval. He gestured one of the other men over. "Brother-in-law Kingfisher, please tell my little sister here that we are glad she has come visiting us." Luckily he spoke a dialect close to Raba's own, for the other man didn't. She never would have understood the second man's gibberishlike speech, further slurred as it was by alcohol.

The old man drew crusty shirtsleeves up, exposing his scrawny, malnourished arms. Raba drew a deep breath. They were covered with sores—infected insect bites.

"Ask our little sister if she can help me."

Raba nodded, wishing she had her *maban* and healing kit. She'd bring them with her the next time she came. She almost laughed. She'd at last truly become a *Wuradilagu*, but in a way and in a place she never imagined.

One day she came back to her flat to find traces of Gwyneth's energy still glimmering in the keyhole. Although everything looked tidy, Raba sensed things had been moved about and then reset in their places. The half-carved whorl of wood had been picked up with an unsatisfied curiosity, then replaced. Small pinched samples of herbs were gone. Raba was glad she'd been with her indigents instead of at the University. She had all her healing objects with her.

Raba tensed herself to keep anger shut out. Gwyneth knew she didn't like her privacy invaded, so this was as much a way of harrying Raba as spying on her.

Gathering up her tools, Raba cached them one by one into easily reached niches in the passages-between. The last thing to be hidden was the *maban*. Raba looked at it, remembering where the elders had stored theirs. Pulling at her blouse, she untucked its ends from her slacks. She pressed the *maban* flat against her bare midriff. She felt the sensation of heat, and at first a slight grinding, like steel against stone. Then her skin melted painlessly, realigning its structure so that it matched the *maban's*, and the crystal blade soaked within her. Raba felt it as a clear, sharp heaviness, deep inside, reflecting all of her along its glassine planes, mirroring and magnifying her in the maze of its facets. This small, internal hall of mirrors echoed with the heart of the Dreamtime like a luminescent kaleidoscopic landscape. She shivered at its beauty. Raba knew if she wanted to she could sink within and lose herself forever exploring that infinite terrain.

Raba pulled herself away; not yet, not like this. She couldn't be a path just for herself. She couldn't abandon the rest of her world.

Several days later Gwyneth broke in again. Raba came home to a mauled apartment. Her upended mattress slid half on and half off the bed. Books lay scattered and torn on the floor. Embedded in the rug were angry shards of glassware and plates. Not finding anything, Gwyneth had childishly served notice of her frustration.

After that one outburst the vandalism stopped, but Gwyneth still checked in on Raba regularly. It became a game of absent/present that intrigued Raba. When she was gone Gwyneth would come; perhaps to see if there was something new she could find, or to remind Raba that she was still there, in the wings, or maybe just to maintain some sort of contact with Raba. Then the game would reverse itself with Raba returning to find the spoor of Gwyneth's visit.

One night Raba dreamed: *Walking and rewalking through red-gold sands, her steps strengthened the passage, tied all its threads weblike to a center.*

Something kept distracting her. Some small part of her

didn't help in the task. It was hidden in some other place altogether. In infinitesimal bits she eroded away, like a cliff nibbled by the sea. Embedding herself in the microscopic fragments, she found that in the waking-life she floated along smooth, cool currents of water. The sensation felt so pleasant and soothing she hadn't noticed her diminishment.

Once she understood this, she fought like a spawning fish against the river's pull, backtracking to the source. She coursed over muddy river beds so close to the sea she could taste their impending salinity. Upwards the trail led, over stone-lined streams to the thinness of a creek, and then to its heart, a spring not far from the University. There, wedged in the rocks just where the water, bloodlike, pumped from the Land, was a small figurine fashioned out of good, red, Australian earth. Although its features were already worn smooth by the water, Raba recognized it as an image of herself. Pilfered bits of her had been kneaded into it—hair combings, and threads of her clothing.

For a moment sadness engulfed Raba, that things had come to such a pass that Gwyneth would want to leach her into weakness like this. But then she had to laugh, for herself. It was such a good test, something she could play with. Raba allowed herself to be washed away, throwing herself into those particles. She swept down to the sea, out among the sands of the continental shelf. There she sank to the ocean floor, and let the small grains drift in a motion parallel to the shore with each wave that caressed her. Thus she initiated a process that would, ever so slowly, stretch her as the thinnest of membranes, to someday envelop and encompass the circumference of her beloved Land.

Raba fled to her rooms one afternoon after work, tired of breathing the thin, unnourishing atmosphere of the white-fellas' history. She was shedding more and more of her academic responsibilities. Graduate students now corrected most of the papers. Raba just lectured, but even that left her increasingly irritable. When would the Land finally call her? Guilt nagged at her. The University life may have numbed her, but it had kept her sane and alive all these years. Even while she prayed for the Land to take her, she also prayed for it to leave her time to finish off the semester here and discharge her obligations. And what of her swaggies? She wasn't ready to leave them yet.

Raba lay down on her bed, eager to release from the cares of the waking-life and enter the truer life of her dreamings. But she couldn't get comfortable. There was no sense of actual wrongness. She didn't feel right in a simply physical way. The bed felt lumpy. Raba pulled aside the covers, finding nothing. She hauled the mattress off the bed's wooden frame. Lying there was an object she'd never seen before. It was a homemade rope. During its twining black hen feathers had been woven through its three strands. A knot fixed each feather in place. Raba couldn't hear the actual words, but she felt the curse repeated three times into the tying of each knot—the feathers flew the angry curses at her like buzzing bees.

Angered, Raba threw it on the floor. Gwyneth was still trying to derail her with white-fella magic. She hadn't thought the girl so stupid. This lacked even the small impact of the clay figurine. At least that had been fashioned from the Land and bits of Raba herself.

When she sensed Gwyneth away at classes, Raba went over to the younger woman's apartment building, rode up the elevator, and wound the fetish around Gwyneth's doorknob as a sign of her contempt.

Two days later she felt mildly ill. Raba searched her bedding and found another rope, this one fashioned of Aboriginal hair-string braided together. Bower-bird feathers poked out through its interstices. The curses were the same.

Bower-birds didn't live in the confines of the city. The chance of Gwyneth finding a local Aborigine owning hair-string twine, let alone giving it to her, were virtually nonexistent. Gwyneth had gone back to the museum, raiding its native exhibits this time.

More exasperated than frightened, Raba chanted the curses back into themselves. She picked up the weapon gingerly, and again left it at Gwyneth's door.

That happened on a Friday. Raba spent the weekend among her people in the urban ruins. The beginning of the Dry was impending. In spite of the growing heat, she joined them in their version of a Corroboree around a campfire in a vacant lot.

She returned to find Gwyneth had left an even more strident declaration of war. Shattered shards of Gwyneth's favorite witch ball lay strewn across the floor of her flat. What

had the girl said about them? "They sort of suck in any evil
influences." That evil had been released. The once beautiful,
subtly intertwined colors of the ball looked ugly and muddy
now. All of Gwyneth's anger and loneliness, soaked up over
who knew how many years, wafted through Raba's room in
angry, smoky vapors. Raba wept. Gwyneth was slipping
further away.

It got worse.

Every night Raba dreamed herself away to the Outback.
Her strides were an embroidery stitching together the severed
borders of the Dreamtime and her people's waking-life. When
she was done they could return. Every time she slept she
walked her way closer to Home.

*She was walking, traversing the desert. Up and over the
sand ridges. Spearthrower, spears, a firestick, were all held
tightly in one arm. A fat lizard, ready for cooking, hung from
her belt. Walkabout was almost starting. Walkabout was
almost over. She ran down a dune, swinging her bullroarer.
The dunes funneled the sound back to her, "Raba coming,
Raba coming." If she could only run a little faster, she might
make it before nightfall, before she had to return to that other,
empty place. But the blackness rose up behind her, too soon,
threatening to overtake her. She had to leave her journey as
she felt the dark looming over her, its shadow coming between
her and the light, blotting out her way.*

Raba woke in terror to hear the door to her rooms begin to
open, then slam shut. Familiar footsteps ran away down the
hall. Raba lay with her eyes clenched shut, sweating and
gasping. It had been so close. So close to the Dreamtime. And
so close to losing everything. Her body, left in part in the
waking-life when she went *badundjari,* was too vulnerable.
Before Gwyneth had only menaced her surroundings, when
she was absent. Now Raba knew she had to take Gwyneth's
threats seriously.

She was at the library's door before it opened. She
ferreted through its archives with a fervor surpassing her
graduate days. Published research on European witchcraft was
off-hand, hard to find, usually included only as side references
and anecdotes in more scholarly tomes. Raba delved in her
memory for clues from past conversations with Gwyneth. This
led her to old herbals and esoteric volumes on folklore. Bit by

bit Raba built up a picture of Gwyneth's background, and the information she needed to hold her former friend at bay.

She discovered that the clay figurine was called a *corp creach*. The rope underneath her bed was a "witche's ladder." Raba's flat became as embellished as Gwyneth's. She bought strands of bright blue glass beads, and hung them as densely as curtains down her window panes. She scattered seeds with natural orbs of their own everywhere to outstare the "evil eye." Special warding knots bound any structural cracks in the flat. At every entrance Raba drew three white circles in chalk, and kept their dusty outlines well maintained. For extra measure she bought throwbolts at a hardware store and installed them herself.

No longer able to enter Raba's flat, Gwyneth's next attack was a gesture of impotence. Outside the door, she broke another of her witch balls, this one as beautifully crystalline as Raba herself.

Raba was protected. But now Gwyneth knew that Raba was afraid of her.

Whenever she lay down to dream, Raba thought she sensed Gwyneth prowling nearby, looking for a way to get in. Although she thought she'd fought the girl to a standstill, she couldn't be sure. That paralyzed her into inaction. As she saw it now, her whole history with Gwyneth formed an interlocking series of misdirected episodes. She'd consistently underestimated the younger woman. The more she recognized Gwyneth as an unknown, unpredictable adversary, the more Raba felt hobbled by indecision.

Her fear allowed her only the shallowest of sleep. When she tried to go *badundjari*, her body would retrieve her, alarmed at the faintest sound. Raba lay in her bed, muscles locked in tension till they cramped, crying for sleep. The next day she'd hobble to her classes exhausted and numb.

Meanwhile, the Land accelerated its demands on her. If Raba wouldn't come to it at night in the wholeness of dreaming, it would come to her. During the day the Dream-time percolated up through her daily life, saturating it so thoroughly that she began to lose the balance she'd been able to maintain earlier between the two existences. It was as if she was reliving that nightmare time before the Emu ceremony, when maddened spirits swarmed unleashed through the mission settlement.

She began to go to the warehouse district for reasons other than healing and helping return men to the bush. The first time she went, Warguna Bates, the old man, sensed there was a difference.

"Now little sister not feeling well," he greeted her through one of his proxies. "Ask her if we can share a healing for her."

"Tell my brother it is not illness I feel, but confusion from lack of rest. I am always having to be watching, so I get no sleep. If I stay here could you guard me?"

The old man studiously rolled a cigarette. He wouldn't look at her directly, but Raba saw a ripple cross his thatch of beard. A small smile must be playing along his mouth underneath.

"Tell my little sister that this sounds like *Wadjura* trouble."

"Something very like that," Raba admitted.

"Tell my little sister I have not had the pleasure of chasing off a *Wadjura* for many years. Tell her I am grateful to her for such an enjoyable opportunity." Warguna's eyes were sparkling, though his "translator" looked more than a little uneasy. "Tell her that if we cannot heal her, we be happy to protect her so she can heal herself."

In an empty lot they built up a large campfire. Several of the men dragged over an abandoned mattress reeking with mildew and layered with dirt. Numb with exhaustion, Raba collapsed onto it. The men formed a circle around her and the fire as the sun set. They faced outward, forming a physical barrier between her and her fears. Raba went to sleep listening to them talking and laughing quietly together, passing their bottles among themselves. Even here, sharing was second nature to them. Later, half-unconscious from drinking, they would jerk awake when they found themselves nodding off. Sensitized by Raba's presence, they were aware of something that watched and waited out in the darkness beyond the firelight, keeping its distance. They revived themselves with stories and songs.

Early the next morning Raba slipped, grimy and disheveled, back to her flat. Refreshed, showered, and changed, she could cope with the day.

The next time she returned to them, Warguna had one of his assistants pull her aside while she was applying an herb poultice to the bruises of a man who had fallen while rummaging through one of the deserted storefronts.

"Ask little sister if she wants to stay again with us tonight."

"Tell my older brother that I would be pleased if he would let me."

Warguna nodded before the "translation" was finished. "Tell little sister that many more men have returned to the bush."

Raba watched him carefully. Was he angry about this?

"Tell her that the day will come when she must go, too. When that happens, she must leave, and not come here anymore. She must not worry about us and stay. Tell her we will be well. We will find a way to follow her."

Raba bowed her head. If Warguna had been left on the Land, he would have made a great and gentle elder, a true Clever Man. She looked at him again. He reeked of alcohol and aged, unwashed clothing as much as the rest of them. But the other men gathered about him. She felt his protection drawn around them like a brush shelter in the Outback. Raba was ashamed of her presumptiveness. Warguna was a great elder.

Staying with the men proved to be only a partially effective method. On days that lacked that relief, Raba found it hard to walk through the University halls and maintain her grasp on their fragile reality. Through the gauzelike structure of the plastered walls and ceilings, Raba kept seeing sand, shimmering and bright. There were times when she knew that if she'd only allow herself, she would sink through and feel the hot, sugary texture of the sand on the bottoms of her feet.

She caught herself, over and over, on the verge of going *badundjari* in the very middle of waking-life. The Land made it clear that it was time for her to return to her homeland for the beginning of her journey. It was more than time.

Raba still felt torn by her responsibilities to the school. Warguna had pointedly relieved her of any obligations to the community of swaggies, and she'd given up on Gwyneth. But she couldn't ignore the debt she owed Dorothy and the University for all the years of nurturing and protection. Meaningless as she knew the work to be now, it was important to the other teachers and the students. She prayed to last just the few remaining weeks of the semester. Then she could leave safely, feeling uncompromised.

The pressure of the Land and Gwyneth proved too much. What good would it do to stay if one day she went *badundjari* in the middle of a class? The thought terrified Raba. She didn't want to think what the consequences would be. Her vulnerable husk would be left behind. What kind of taboos might that break, metamorphizing before a group of white-fellas? What would happen to her?

So one day Raba packed everything she needed into a small bag. She left a folder in the office addressed to George Collins with lesson plans and instructions for having one of the graduate students finish up the last few weeks of her course. Stopping at her bank she withdrew enough for her trip and food on the way.

She caught a tram heading for the main station, where one of the big interterritorial cruising buses would take her on the first leg of her journey.

Now that she was leaving, Raba's surroundings settled for one last time into a solidity around her, regaining their density, weight and depth. Raba felt a joy at the respite from the multilayered confusion, to be given this last experience of the white-fellas' life as a reality and not an illusion. Raba noticed everything; the cracking in the vinyl edging the seat in front of her, the way the tram smelled like rubber and sweating metal.

Raba expanded her senses to touch everything on the bus; floating among people, seeing how separated and apart they were from each other, how different they were from her own people, as if they were unconscious living statues. Unconscious, that is, until Raba came upon a hard knot that radiated hatred and want, and knew her. Raba jerked around in her seat, tumbling her bag into the aisle.

In the very back of the tram was Gwyneth. She sat by a window, gazing out at the passing city, as if this, too, were the last time *she* would see it. She wasn't even looking at Raba. She didn't need to. Raba began to shake. There'd been no sense of the girl tracking her. She guessed that the only reason she'd detected her now was that Gwyneth had chosen to let her. The girl's message was clear—*I could have followed you all the way Home without your knowing, so you might as well accept me, because you can't leave without me*. Raba guessed that as soon as she'd made her decision to leave, Gwyneth knew of her intent. If Gwyneth was this shrewd and powerful, Raba couldn't take the risk of continuing her journey right now. Perhaps the girl *could* follow her all the way into the Dreamtime.

Raba got off at the next stop, with a large group of passengers, miles short of the tram station. Gwyneth disembarked, too. Raba allowed herself a glimpse of her spare figure standing a little apart from the crowd, duffel bag slung over one shoulder. Even with that brief glance she could see the look of bitter disappointment on Gwyneth's face.

Feeling collapsed, Raba crossed the street to a stop for the reverse direction. Gwyneth followed at a stranger's casual distance. A tram arrived to return them to the University area. When Raba placed her foot on the bottom step she staggered, grabbing the handhold just in time not to fall, as waves of Dreaming streamed up her legs like water. The tram steps were blotted out. Raba could no longer feel their slotted tread. She hoisted herself up, hand over hand, the driver looking at her with the mixture of pity and repugnance reserved for drunks. Raba barely saw the change in her coin purse. Fumbling frantically, she trembled with palsy.

When she got off at the University, near the History department, Gwyneth didn't follow. Raba retrieved the papers left for George before he came in and found them.

She didn't accept defeat. She couldn't, and survive. Now that she knew how it would be with Gwyneth, she would plan more carefully.

Raba made a call to Dorothy Landell. "I'm taking you up on your offer," she told her old mentor. "Prefinals week is coming up, so I thought I'd catch a train and come see you . . . finally go on that shopping trip."

"But, dear, does that make sense? The semester is almost over, and then there's just grading. You'd be able to get away for some real vacation time, not just a few days."

Was it just Raba's imagination, or did Dorothy's voice sound more than merely practical? Did it sound anxious? Raba began to sweat. The seepage from the Dreamtime was greasing loose her precarious hold on this life. Was it betraying her? Was she acting strangely in ways she couldn't monitor, making Dorothy suspicious? She couldn't tell. Gritting her teeth, she tried to reconnect to a reality that seemed ever more distant.

"Well, you're quite right," she made herself say. "But I'm feeling so overloaded *now* that I'd just like to get away for a few days. Otherwise exams and grading will hit, and I'll truly be run into the ground by the end of it all." A thought inspired her. "I guess it's just that I came down so sick in January that I'm worried about overdoing it and getting the flu again. But maybe you're right. I'm being overly concerned. I'll visit during the holidays after all." She held her breath tensely and waited.

"No! No, don't do that! By all means come up now," Dorothy said.

Raba let her breath out in soundless relief. There was no mistaking Dorothy's genuine concern. Raba felt more confident of her grasp of the situation, but she made her next words sound doubting. "Well, if you're sure." A small guilt nagged at her. Her life in the white-fella's world, as a teacher, was ending. It meant little to her now. But it would continue to be everything to Dorothy. "Will it be all right, really? Your semester is winding down, too, and you'll be busy. I don't want to be in your way."

Dorothy answered with a merry laugh that made Raba's heart ache. This woman had loved and cared for Raba as much in her own way as Djilbara had. Raba knew that when she crossed over to the Dreamtime, in some way her memories of Dorothy would not be left behind.

"Of course you won't be a bother," Dorothy said. "I've been teaching the same courses for years. I could grade the tests in my sleep."

When Raba hung up, a part of her was almost grateful to Gwyneth. Perhaps this was how it was meant to be. Before, she'd felt so compelled by the Land that she would have just left. Now she'd been forced into a situation where she would see Dorothy one last time.

Let Gwyneth follow her to Broome if she could. In a strange town Gwyneth would have a harder time keeping track of Raba. She wouldn't have a base, and the territory would be unfamiliar. When it came time for Raba to leave from there for the Outback, it would be easier to shake her.

This time when Raba left her flat she took a mazelike route to the railway station; catching one tram, hopping off, backtracking, catching another. Each time she scanned the other passengers as she boarded to see if Gwyneth waited for her. She sat near the back exits, ready to slip out at any stop if Gwyneth got on. Her senses were extended like radar. Raba

arrived safely at the railway station and again checked. She
didn't see the girl anywhere.

Passing a postbox, Raba hesitated. The folder for George
was in her purse: enveloped, addressed, and stamped. She
could mail it from here. She shook her head, knowing she
couldn't risk it. Gwyneth might still show up. Raba needed to
maintain a retreat route. Once the letter was mailed she
couldn't retrieve it. The department would know within a few
days that she'd fled. Better to wait till she was safely at
Dorothy's.

Raba got in a queue for her ticket, looking around every
few seconds to see if Gwyneth had joined the line. The man
behind the counter looked like a character actor, a cinema
archetype. Elderly, balding, skin a scalded-pink, rimless
glasses, a transparent green visor was strapped around his
skull, casting his forehead with an eerily colored band.

"I'd like a one-way ticket to Broome," Raba told him, as
she reached into her purse for the money.

The man was busy sorting through some papers behind
the counter, out of her line of sight. He glanced up at her
briefly, then looked down again. "Next," he said.

"I *am* next," said Raba. "I'd like a ticket to Broome,
please."

"Move on," he said. "Next."

"I told you, I *am* next."

This time he looked up to fix her with a glare. "I've
already helped you," he said, with undisguised hostility. "And
I told *you* to move on." People behind her in line shifted
restlessly.

Raba was baffled. Then she felt a flush scorching upwards
from her throat to her cheeks, and stepped back out of line.
Even the most bigoted racists were rarely so blatant, but it did
happen occasionally. She forced herself to discard her feelings
of anger and humiliation. She couldn't afford them right now.
Soon enough, men like this wouldn't even be a memory to her.

There were several other ticket stations. She watched one
being manned by a portly young woman. An Aboriginal couple
was near the head of her line. They received tickets and passed
through to the train gate. Raba joined the end of that queue.

But when she got to the counter and asked for a ticket, the
woman looked at her blankly.

"I said, I'd like a ticket," Raba repeated.

The woman said nothing. Abruptly Raba realized that she didn't even see Raba, couldn't hear her. Raba fought rising panic. She fidgeted, waved her hands in the woman's face, trying to get her attention. Something in her said *Move, move. If you move she'll see you. It's the opposite of hunting. You want to be seen*. The woman was like a stone. The other people in line had no trouble seeing her. They stared with disturbed curiosity.

It all reminded Raba of something, but in reverse. *I'm not invisible*, she thought. *I'm moving, so she should see me. It's not stillness, like at the museum—the room with the pictures—the room becoming a picture. The museum* . . . Raba became very quiet, and turned around slowly. Leaning against the wall behind her was Gwyneth. The girl's face was a white mask stretched taut over nothingness, her eyes two blue, hungry holes. Raba felt an incredible sadness for Gwyneth. *Is this what has always been there, what you really are? A Wadjura? A starving, malevolent spirit?* She knew she had been right. Gwyneth must not ever be allowed into the Dreamtime.

Gwyneth waited, still hoping to go. Again her eyes spoke plainly. *You are in my domain. If you don't take me with you, I'll make sure you never go at all.*

Raba looked at her and spoke one word, the final word. "No."

Gwyneth's face transformed. It twisted for a moment in a terrible anger tinged with despair. Then it set in lines of determination and revenge. It was no longer the face of a young girl.

Raba turned to go. Gwyneth edged up. "Want some company on the way back?" she said softly, an enraged smile cutting a curved line in her tight face. Raba ignored her.

On the ride back to her flat, Raba thought. Gwyneth sat several seats behind her, like a sheepdog herding a wayward jumpbuck. Before, Gwyneth had been willing to let Raba leave, confident of her own ability to follow. Each time, however, she'd exposed herself to Raba. Why hadn't she stayed undetected? Then she could have been assured of following Raba. She must have reassessed Raba's power and found it strong enough to leave her behind. Her cat-and-mouse games were meant to frighten Raba into acquiescing and willingly taking Gwyneth along. It hadn't worked. Gwyneth could neither defeat nor control Raba, simply magic to magic, so she'd found another way to use her abilities. In the context of the white-fellas' world she was the stronger. She'd chosen to restrain Raba by controlling her surroundings. Gwyneth possessed the strength to manipulate her own people and box Raba in.

Walkabout

Raba called Dorothy. "I'm sorry to do this to you again, but I won't be able to make it after all," she said.

"Are you all right?" came Dorothy's anxious voice.

"I'm not coming down with anything. Professor Noddy has decided to call some last-minute meetings during cram week. Something about reorganizing our section of the department, so I'd better stay."

A long silence from the other end of the line greeted her excuse. *She knows I'm lying*, Raba thought.

"When I asked if you were all right, dear, I wasn't asking if you were sick with anything, like the flu. I've been quite worried about you." Dorothy's sigh carried over the miles. "I think I should tell you. I've gotten several phone calls recently from a young woman. Her name was Diana, I believe. She said she studied with you, was working on some projects with you."

Raba remembered sitting in the sand at the foot of the rhododendrons with Gwyneth like two children, Gwyneth drawing circles with her spoon. The girl lifting her face to explain, as the sun gilded her face a pale gold. Diana— Gwyneth's other name. She'd told Dorothy her name was Diana. Raba began to feel a heavy, hollow sensation in her gut.

"She said she was a friend of yours," Dorothy said. "Frankly, that surprised me, knowing how you keep to yourself. But she knew so much about you; things I never thought you'd be able to talk about. She sounded quite sincere. She said she was concerned about you."

Raba's mind skittered like a covey of frightened lizards. What had Gwyneth told Dorothy? How much had she figured out of Raba's past?

"She said you've been acting very . . . uh . . . erratic," Dorothy continued, her voice fearful and doubting.

What were the actual words Gwyneth had used?

"She asked if it was like . . . before, you know. I couldn't believe she knew about that, that you'd told her. So I knew you must really trust her, and that what she said must be . . ." Dorothy's voice crawled with pain.

Raba bit back hard from finishing the dangling sentence, ". . . must be true." How had Gwyneth found out? Several of those times when Gwyneth hadn't seemed to be lurking, had she actually been gone, delving in old records, perhaps phoning the sanatorium? Raba wanted to slam down the phone and sit alone in her room and scream. How long ago had this been? If she'd only known, she could have escaped during Gwyneth's absences. Raba recalled again that day the two of them sat on the small scrap of lawn, drawing in the edge of sand. What had Gwyneth said? Something about not letting Raba be trapped again. Raba felt very, very cold. That *was* what Gwyneth had meant. She'd known about the sanatorium that long ago.

"What is happening, dear? Please tell me what's really happening."

"I'm in trouble, Dorothy. It's not the department or anything. I lied about that. I just need to get away to you. But it's not like before. Not at all. Please believe me. It's something else altogether." She hoped her old friend heard the truth more than the desperation in her voice.

"Then come here, dear. You know I'll take care of you. Don't worry about the University or the job or anything. Just come."

Raba wanted to weep. "I will," she said. "Soon."

She went back to her room and gathered together all the research she'd collected on witchcraft. She began to braid her own witch's ladder. It grated on her to do it, to have to resort to Gwyneth's tactics. If she could just wreak enough mischief to weaken the girl, she could leave without harming her. She planned more escape routes. Perhaps Dorothy could be persuaded to come down and get her. The phone calls from Gwyneth that Dorothy had described sounded as if the girl had only tried to manipulate her old teacher emotionally. Were her powers limited by distance? Would she be able to control

Dorothy the way she'd controlled the ticket sellers at the station? Raba couldn't be sure. She decided to use that plan only if all else failed.

All through cram week Raba held herself in rigid calm. The Dreamtime crawled over her continuously; she shed it like a range calf twitching off clouds of bot flies. She survived the first day of finals; handing out tests, waiting, collecting them at the end of each class like a robot. The arsenal she'd been building for Gwyneth was almost ready.

As she approached the History building on Tuesday morning, she saw George Collins sitting on the steps. He seemed lost in thought, so she passed him quietly without a greeting. She had her hand on the door handle when he spoke. He faced away from her, so she almost didn't hear him.

"Landell? I don't mean to be an earbasher, but can I have a word with you? It'll just take a moment."

Raba sat down next to him on the steps.

George looked out into space for a few moments before speaking. When he started, he still didn't look at her. "I thought you should know that people have been talking about you. They're saying you're pretty ill, and should be taken off somewhere to get help. I thought you might want to watch out for yourself."

"Who's talking, George? What are they saying?"

"A couple of folks."

"You mean Noddy? And Joan Petrini?"

George shook his head. "Just a few more than that, I'm afraid."

Dear god! Raba thought. *He means the whole bloody History department!*

"You've been sliding a lot lately."

She nodded. "I know I have been."

"Well, people notice. Anyway, they're all in for it now. But the one that first dobbed you in was that student that's always hanging about you, the skinny little sheila. That's why they listened. She's been saying you're almost over the edge. And other things; like you're a boozer, that you go down and drink with the swaggies and the vagrants." He looked intensely uncomfortable. "One or two of the others—real bot-types, don't like blacks, you know—say that's typical. That it's in the blood and you're just going bush."

If Raba weren't so terrified, she'd laugh. At least in that they were close to the truth.

"Why are you telling me this?"

George finally looked at her, his watery eyes squinted thin from the sun's brightness. "I didn't think they were giving you a fair go. I've always thought you were all right, a real battler." He looked away again. "I once had some hard times. Fell apart and didn't know it." He laughed dryly. "I was that much a silly galah, because even Blind Freddy could have seen it. Thing is, I wish even one lousy bastard had told me. Things mightn't have gotten as bad as they did."

He got up. "So I'm telling you now. On the other hand, maybe by speaking up I'm doing you more harm than good."

"George, thank you. You're a good mate," Raba said.

George nodded as he entered the building.

Raba stood there rigid with terror. Gwyneth had finally understood and believed her at the train station. She at last knew that Raba would never take her to the Dreamtime. Gwyneth had nothing to lose. So now she was laying the groundwork to have Raba recommitted. If she couldn't go to the Dreamtime, she would make sure Raba never did either.

Raba saw a weakness in this. If Gwyneth were really as powerful as she wished Raba to think, she would be able to follow Raba no matter what Raba might do. She would be eager to let Raba go. Gwyneth didn't know enough to stop her after all.

Raba's jaw locked in a humorless grin. Every route of escape that relied on others in this white-fella city was suspect. Gwyneth's control there was too great. But she couldn't control Raba herself. Raba remembered her first, nameless indigent. She'd ordered him to leave by walking out. She would walk out, too.

Raba plotted as she made her way to her lecture class. With the suspicions she'd planted so far, Gwyneth could call forces out after Raba. It took a long time to walk out of the heart of the city by foot; ample time to convince the History department, the police, or even Dorothy, that Raba needed to be retrieved for her own good. Raba realized she'd still have to go through with her original plan of weakening Gwyneth first.

Her class was in the auditorium, one of the overcrowded prerequisite courses. Students entered through a door on the ground floor to one side of the podium. From there they streamed up to their cantilevered seats, picking up the day's test on the way. Raba perched on a stool behind the lectern, grading the morning's tests. With some of the teaching assistants helping, she'd been grading them as fast as they came in, keeping up with each day's output.

Someone slid in through the big swinging door. *Another latecomer,* Raba thought. *Well, they've only half a class now to finish up in.* As she reached for a blank test sheet to hand over, she glanced up. Gwyneth stood just inside the entrance, holding a pile of papers.

Seeing that she'd caught Raba's attention, she smiled almost shyly, and held the first piece of paper up.

It was a photograph of a building, or what was left of a building. Smashed flat, it looked as if it had been crushed by a massive fist. Standing in front was a dazed-looking man with loosely hanging arms, while in the background other people searched through the rubble. Picture followed picture in a testament to stunning destruction. Raba clutched the sides of the lectern. The pictures were of Darwin. The photographs changed. Gwyneth drew one forth that was of an Emu, running over a claypan under a clear sky. The next was of a hunt. A different Emu was being speared by two men in a scene familiar to Raba from her childhood. Subsequent scenes showed graphic details of the Emu being gutted, butchered, and dressed. Tears streamed down Raba's face. All she could think of was Huroo. There were still more pictures to come in Gwyneth's pile.

"No more, no more," she sobbed. Her tight, finely balanced control shattered and the Dreamtime swept through the gap in her defenses. The sea of student faces before her thinned. She felt herself begin to dissolve away from them. Her legs sank past the floor and her arms looked as if they were vanishing into the lectern. Her extremities melted to some-place dark, warm, real. *Not now,* she thought for a bare instant, *not here.* The Land called to her through the pores of her missing limbs.

Raba, leave. Come through. We've been waiting so long. It's time to come Home.

Gwyneth's face was a twisted, shocked rictus. *She over-played her hand,* Raba thought. The girl had hoped to push her into appearing insane. Instead, she was forcing Raba to leave directly into the Dreamtime. It must be her worst nightmare come to life.

Raba looked down at what was left of her legs. The shell of her body buckled in piled layers on the floor, like discarded snake skins. *So be it. If this part of me has to stay behind and die, let it*.

But the Dreamtime, oblivious to matters on this side of reality, tugged at the peelings, trying to draw them in, too. *All of you. All of you must come*. The skin pinched at the edges, caught, and began to rip. It wasn't working. Excruciating pain shot through Raba. Frantic, she yanked at the lectern, trying to pull her arms back out. It swayed with her weight and then toppled in on her, knocking over the stool as it went. As Raba fell her limbs jerked free. Face pinned to the floor under the lectern, she saw Gwyneth sidle out of the auditorium.

Students swarmed down the tiers of seats. Raba was aware of them as a babble of anonymous voices.

"What happened?"

"I don't know. All of a sudden the stand fell over."

"Is she all right?"

"She had some kind of fit."

Raba felt the lectern being rolled off her.

"Bloody hell. Can you see if anything's broken?"

"Put something in her mouth so she doesn't swallow her tongue."

A pencil was wedged between Raba's teeth.

"Not that, you silly bugger. It'll splinter."

Other hands pried her jaws open and the pencil was replaced with a long wedge of something plastic.

"Has anyone called a doctor?"

At the infirmary a nurse sprayed abrasions on her arms and legs with an antiseptic and taped them up while the doctor wrote out a prescription. When the nurse had finished and left, he sat behind his desk, tapping his pen against his teeth.

"Your department head, Professor Noddy, called me. He seems to think you've been going through some kind of nervous breakdown."

Raba winced.

The doctor noticed, and smiled. "After looking you over, I doubt that. However, I think it might be something just as frightening, if not more so. I'd like to run some tests on you right now, for epilepsy."

Raba suppressed a feeling of contempt. It wasn't epilepsy.

She tried to look appropriately upset. This could buy her time. She nodded her assent to the tests, wondering how long they would take to get through the lab. "Did you tell Professor Noddy about this?" she asked the doctor.

"Yes, of course," he said.

Then by now word would have spread. Until the lab tests came back, suspicion might slack off a little.

After the tests, a nurse drove her home.

Raba packed her dilly bag. She wouldn't wait to try to beat Gwyneth at her own game, to weaken her with her own arsenal. In spite of the doctor's diagnosis, Gwyneth might twist and influence the others' thoughts into disregarding him. Night had fallen. Raba wanted to take advantage of its cover and the margin of time she might have won. She was leaving now.

The phone rang down the hall. A few moments later a neighbor padded down to tell her the call was for her. It was Dorothy.

She sounded almost hysterical. "I just heard that you'd collapsed today and were in the University hospital. I called there and the switchboard said they'd let you go home."

"I'm all right," Raba told her. "The doctor said he thinks all the problems I've been having may be a form of epilepsy. He did a bunch of tests and said I'd probably be all right for now."

"Are you sure it was a seizure?"

"Yes. That's what the doctor said. That's why he ran the tests." Raba began to feel suspicious. "What else would it be? How did you know I had a seizure?"

"Oh dear God," Dorothy sounded panic-stricken. "You have to get out of there, immediately. That girl called me. She said you'd had a breakdown, not a seizure. She said you might . . . harm yourself, and had to be reinstitutionalized right away. She wanted me to sign papers, and was going to set it up so I could talk to someone on the phone and arrange telegram verification in the meantime. I refused. I don't know what's wrong, but I was there during that year and a half you were in the sanatorium, and I know it isn't like that. I won't let them drug you again like that. Come up here and be safe with me."

"I don't think I can get away in time."

"Then I'll come down there and fetch you."

Raba felt a rush of love for her old teacher. It might work, with Dorothy to vouch for her. And then she could escape safely with her.

But would it work? At close quarters would Gwyneth be able to manipulate Dorothy as she had the others? Raba didn't think so, but she couldn't be sure. And if Gwyneth had her put away before Dorothy could get there, what then? Once she was institutionalized, Raba guessed that Gwyneth could contrive to keep her drugged and lost forever. Raba knew she couldn't risk it. She had to leave by herself, tonight.

A thought occurred to her. "What did you say to . . ." What had Gwyneth called herself? ". . . Diana, when you told her you wouldn't sign the papers?"

"That I'd have to find out more. That I needed to talk to you first," Dorothy said.

Raba's skin prickled. Gwyneth knew by now that Raba had been warned. How quickly could she mobilize the right people against Raba?

"Dorothy, thank you for wanting to help. If it comes to that, you might have to rescue me. But I've got to try to get out of this myself." Raba heard a commotion. The stairwell acted as a funnel, amplifying noise. There was a clamor as a number of people entered the front of the building. "Dorothy, I hear someone coming. I've got to go."

Raba ran to her room and snatched up her dilly bag. As she raced to the rear stairs, the fire exit, she heard people treading up both flights of stairs. She cursed.

Ducking back into her room Raba eased the door shut behind her, locked it, and threw the extra bolts as noiselessly as possible. She almost made the mistake of flipping the light switches off. She thought just in time and slid over to the edge of her window, peering down through the strings of blue beads. Outside two uniformed men lounged against an ambulance. If she turned out the lights they might notice, and know for a certainty that she was in.

People were gathering at the door. Someone knocked. Raba didn't answer. "Miss Landell, are you in?" came a male voice.

"Of course she's in." It was Gwyneth. "I tell you, I know her. She may have done something drastic. Break the door down. You've got to get to her."

"We can't just go around breaking things like that. She might not even be there. Hey, mate," he called down the hallway. "Be a good bloke and rouse the supe. Get him to bring his keys up."

Once the building superintendent brought the keys they'd discover the resistance of the extra locks. As quietly as she could, Raba jammed a chair at an angle under the edge of the doorknob. The group outside was arguing loudly. She doubted that they heard her.

Raba stood in one corner, away from the windows. She'd bought herself only a few minutes. The room was too small and spare to hide her. Should she lock herself in the bathroom? It would only take them seconds to get her out of there. Raba whirled around, panicking, looking for a nonexistent escape.

There was the sound of keys in the lock. The tumblers clicked open, and someone yanked at the doorknob. "It's still locked," said the man. "She's got some kind of bolts on the inside."

"That proves she's in there. You've got to get to her," came Gwyneth's excited voice.

"I've brought my tool kit." It was the building super. "Let's go for the hinges next."

"Break the door down. Just break the damn door down. She's probably taken pills. She might be dying." Gwyneth was becoming hysterical.

"And if we break the door down she could be lying right there on the other side, unconscious, and we'd crush her. Stop being a silly galah. We'll get in fast enough. We'll smash the door in only if we have to."

Almost hysterical herself, Raba verged on weeping. If they reached her she'd be lost. Before she'd fled into the merciful nothingness of the sanatorium and the drugs. She knew now it was almost a miracle she'd ever emerged from that. This time, if she went back, it would be the end. She'd never escape from being lost within herself, the drugs trapping her, isolating her from the Land and the Dreamtime, laying claim to her forever. It would be numbness and whiteness again, until the day she died. She would never dream, never hear the Land again. She would be lost. Her people would be lost.

Even as she panicked she cherished each physical sensation of that panic. It might be the last she'd ever feel of anything. Blood jumped through her veins and arteries, bounding like water plunging through rapids. Raba started crying. Here inside herself was her path, the path she should leave by, and she couldn't reach it.

That thought stilled Raba. If she was meant to be the way for her people to return to their Home, why couldn't she follow that path herself? She just needed to release it, let it free so that it *could* be followed. She knew how she could escape.

With that thought came peace—and strength. Raba heard the chaos and commotion outside her door, Gwyneth's hysteria, and knew that she was stronger than that, in all ways. If she wished to, she could just open the door, and face them. "I was showering," she could say. "What is this all about?" Let Gwyneth try to control them. Raba's power and calmness, at last, would win. The Dreamtime coursed through her as a strong, fluid current, no longer at odds with her. If she wanted or needed to stay, it would work together with her, and she could choose her own time to leave.

Raba considered that for a moment. Should she linger and unknot the tangle of her life in the white-fella world? Why? What would be the point? Who would benefit? Not Raba, and certainly not the white-fellas. Raba chose. This was her time to leave.

Her hand moved involuntarily to her midriff and the *maban* emerged to lie flat in her hand. Grasping the handle, Raba turned it so she could see the fineness of its edge. She drew that narrowness across the soft, fleshy padding of one fingertip. Blood welled up and dripped to the floor. Raba knelt and saw a tiny glimpse of desert sand through it.

She ripped the bandages from her arm and drew the *maban* across her palm and down her arm in a series of quick slashes. She didn't cut deeply, not into the spouting arteries, but just through the veins. The blood there traversed the whole of her body, encompassing her like a map, and was returning to her heart to begin the journey anew. Freed now, its direction expanded into the room. Raba shook herself and blood splattered the apartment. Wherever it landed, it etched holes through the thinness of the white-fellas' existence; an existence thinner than paper, no more substantial than the illusion of Gwyneth's cherished Annwn. Raba saw more and more fragments of the Outback behind it.

At her back, hinges dropped with a sound like tinny bells.

Someone tested the door again. It still caught on the bolts and the jammed chair.

"Damn bloody, bloody hell. We're going to have to crash it in after all."

"Wait just a minute. Let me see first." That was the super, anxious about the property.

Blood covered the *maban*, except where Raba clutched its hilt. She sliced into the air in front of her. The fabric of this reality tore, paperlike, into tatters, flapping open as a bright, hot wind blew through from the other side. Before her was the solidity of bright blue sky and endless vistas of brilliant sand.

Bodies hurtled themselves against the door, making it creak and splinter, jarring the chair.

Gwyneth must have sensed the change taking place within the room. She started screaming. "No! No! Don't go! Please don't leave me! Don't leave me here all alone! I don't want to be alone again!" Stripped of vengeful power, her cries were simply the heart-rending wails of a child being abandoned. Raba hesitated. Gwyneth's broken voice rang with the same loss and hopelessness that she had felt when Djilbara and Huroo died. Would Gwyneth, too, vanish inside herself in despair, as Raba had done? Raba had come out of it: tough enough, Gwyneth might, too.

Raba shook her head. There was nothing further she could do for Gwyneth. She'd shown the girl a way. Raba's own people, and the Land, were waiting for her, and she'd almost tarried too long. Raba stepped through to place her feet on the hot, welcoming desert floor: All of her this time—not going *badundjari*, not leaving a vulnerable shell behind. What would the white-fellas see when they broke into her room? Blood soaking the rug, trailing down the walls? Raba thought about the night in the museum and smiled. Or would they, for just an instant, see what looked to be blood, changing into patches of red-gold sand, stirred by a wind that wasn't there? The shredded opening to the white-fellas' world snapped shut behind her, and Raba stood in the brightness of the Outback.

She knew where her Walkabout led. Across the desert, her feet remembering all the Ancestors' Great Wanderings, till she came to a cave in Arnhem Land. This time when she walked through the portrait of herself she'd meet no resistance. The paths in-between would be just a space to step over on her way Home. She would walk, laying down a trail her people could follow. With each stride she'd stitch together the sundered fabric of their existence and the Dreamtime.

And there, in the Dreamtime, beside the deep, restful pool that was what once had been Huroo, a Rainbow Serpent waited. Years ago, in her childhood, she had made the *Wanambi* a promise. Now she knew exactly what song she would bring it. She pulled the bullroarer from her dilly bag. Spinning it until it hummed, they sang that song together. Raba took a step, and began her Walkabout.

Epilog

Decades Later

Halley boarded the plane in Djakarta walking with slow steps through the sticky, heavy heat. She hated stewardessing this flight, the last leg of the Paris/Sydney run. It had become oppressive. The air in the Qantas jet would be dense with preoccupied fears: the droughts back home, the viral epidemics sweeping the world, all the bitter little wars like angry, pus-filled pockets.

She noticed the two Aborigines when she wheeled the snack cart down the aisle. Their happy, relaxed expressions and warm, brown skin tones stood out among the strained white faces surrounding them.

The man was middle-aged. White peppered his whorley black hair. Although his features were broadly primitive, he wore a fine European suit. When Halley brought around the midflight suppers, he thanked her in a soft, cultured voice. The whisper of French boulevards, not the Australian bush, colored his accent.

The woman appeared to be much younger and spoke with the twang of her native land. She dressed in style, but not as expensively or conservatively as the man.

"What do you think?" Halley asked Joan, her flightmate.

One of their favorite modes of staving off flight boredom was conjecturing about the passengers.

Joan looked over one crisply tailored shoulder down the aisles. "Could be just traveling coworkers. You know, a business jaunt. Or lovers."

"Or relatives," Halley loaded trays into a serving cart. "Maybe a father and daughter on the outs. She flew to Europe to make up and bring him back."

"No," Joan said. "They're both too Euro for that. Maybe they didn't know each other at all before this. Two displaced Abos who met each other on an earlier leg of the flight."

Halley shook her head. "They must be mad then, to come back. Don't they know what's happening to their people?"

Joan nodded. "Disappearing like bloody lemmings, all of them, running off into the bush and vanishing. Just one more daft thing in this awful world. They'd look quite upper-crust, even if they weren't Abos. Must be they don't think it has anything to do with them."

As the hours wore on Halley's feet began to swell and ache from the incessant march up and down the aisles. The other passengers' petulant demands wore down her spirit. She began to resent her Aborigines. Who were they to look so happy and content? Did they think themselves immune from all the cares surrounding them? Just wait till they had to deal with their own problems at home.

But as the plane began its long coast downwards to the airport, she softened and began to pity them. They seemed so innocent. They must have heard about the troubles in Australia—the drought, and the cities and wilds emptying mysteriously of their people. Maybe, urbanized and well educated, they thought they wouldn't be affected.

"Going home, are you?" she asked when she checked to make sure their belts were fastened. The young woman nodded. She beamed at the man as if Halley's words were a good omen.

Perhaps they had been, for the plane landed smoothly for once, missing the small potholes that diminishing work crews couldn't keep patched. It taxied to within a long walk's distance of the gate. The old connecting tubes were accordianed shut to the sides of the terminal like useless, vestigial appendages. Repair parts were expensive and hard to find. Halley sighed. She supposed the planes themselves would be next.

She promised herself for the hundredth time that on this layover she'd start looking for another job.

As the passengers emptied out into a heat that felt dry and glaring after the swelter of Indonesia, Halley straightened seats and put away pillows.

She looked out the wing windows when her Aborigines stepped off the plane steps, the last ones to disembark.

They took just a few steps before the young woman stopped. Leaning down, she took off her expensive pumps and stood in stockinged feet on the hot tarmac. Halley flinched, imagining the searing sensation on the soles of her own tired feet. But the Aboriginal woman just looked up at the man, smiled, and said something to him. He put an arm around her shoulders and laughed. She tapped his chest with one finger, also laughing, but apparently driving home some point. He nodded, took off his expensive wristwatch, and threw it over his shoulder, somewhere out of Halley's line of sight. They walked on, leaving the shoes forlornly alone on the baking pavement.

Halley gasped and started to extricate herself from the seats to rush out of the plane, retrieve the shoes, and run after the two.

Something held her to the windows. She thought she saw some blades of green grass forcing themselves through the parched runway. She blinked. It was an illusion. Nothing grew there. The couple kept walking, for a long time, far longer than it would have taken them to reach the airport gate. They never reached it. They just kept walking towards it, getting smaller and smaller in the distance, diminishing, until they disappeared.

Glossary

Badundjari—the practice of dream-walking; also, a dream spirit.

Barramundi—a large fish, a major food source for some Aboriginal tribes.

Billabong—a backwater or lagoon.

Corroboree—a big celebration, usually involving ceremonies of some type, music, dancing, and feasting.

Didjeridu—a stopless, end-blown wood or bamboo drone pipe; one of the Aborigines' main musical instruments.

Djibija place—a soul's origin place.

Djilbidi—Aboriginal law. See also *Julubidi*.

Djinagarbil—featherfeet killers. Tribal assassins who punish those who break Aboriginal law, so called because they affix feathers to the bottoms of their feet to avoid leaving footprints.

Garhain—batlike monsters from Arnhem Land.

Gum trees—eucalyptus trees.

Inapatua—characters from an Aboriginal Dreamtime legend; embryonic rocklike creatures that eventually became men and women.

Julubidi—the Law, the heritage from the Dreamtime.

Kookaburra—a bird with a loud, laughing cry.

Maban—a magical object with both curative and destructive powers, often made of quartz crystal, usually kept within a native "doctor's" body. Sometimes these men are also called *maban*.

Mimi spirits—tall, thin, manlike spirits, supposed to be excellent hunters.

Moon Man, Sun-Woman—in many Aboriginal myths, the sun

is a woman and the moon is a man, counter to most Western culture myths.

Mulga—a tree, member of the acacia family.

Nardoo—seed damper, a ground seed gruel.

Raba—kangaroo ears; also, the smallest of the thread crosses used in religious ceremonies.

Sugarbag—honey.

Wadjura—demons.

Wanambis—legendary Rainbow Serpents, enormous water-dwelling serpents, often maned or bearded. Rainbows are supposed to end at the waterholes they live in.

Wandjina spirits—spirit people of the creation period; they invented Aboriginal Law. Also, they are responsible for the gift of rain.

Wuradilagu—the title for an Aboriginal healing woman; she is also an expert in women's magic.

Bibliography

Bakker, Robert T. *The Dinosaur Heresies*. New York: William Morrow, 1986.

Cavendish, Richard, ed. *An Illustrated Encyclopedia of Mythology*. New York: Crescent Books, 1980.

Eliade, Mircea. *Australian Religions*. Ithaca, NY: Cornell University Press, 1973.

Harney, Bill. *Tales from the Aborigines*. Adelaide, Aust.: Rigby Limited, 1963.

Isaacs, Jennifer, ed. *Australian Dreaming: 40,000 Years of Aboriginal History*. Sydney: Landsdowne Press, 1980.

O'Grady, John. *Aussie English*. Sydney: Ure Smith, 1965.

Scollay, Clive. "Arnhem Land Aboriginals Cling to Dreamtime," *National Geographic*, Vol. 158, no. 5 (Nov. 1980).

Tonkinson, Robert. *The Jigalong Mob: Aboriginal Victors of the Desert Crusade*, Menlo Park, CA: Cummings Publishing, 1974.

Valiente, Doreen. *An ABC of Witchcraft Past and Present*. Washington D.C., Phoenix Publishing, 1973.

ABOUT THE AUTHOR

MICHAELA ROESSNER was born in San Francisco and raised in New York City, Pennsylvania, Virginia, Oregon, and Thailand. Returning to California for college, she eventually matriculated with a Master of Fine Arts in painting.

She's held a wide variety of jobs, including maskmaker, janitor, audio-visual technician, toy person for a children's store, free-lance office worker for arts and somatics organizations, and a year's stint as assistant editor for *Locus* magazine.

She attended the Clarion Writers' Workshop at Michigan State University in 1980.

Her other interests besides art and writing include martial arts, Feldenkrais work, cats, and good food.

She is married to fellow artist Richard C. Herman.